WHAT IF...

Civilization rested   nd
                on the fate of a single, shaky bridge...

The French had *not* sold the Louisiana Territory—and
                intended to defend it...

Time travelers attempted to thwart history's greatest
wars—and then came up against someone equally
                determined to stop them...

The Allied invasion of Normandy failed—at just the
beginning of a long streak of bad luck...

Hannibal went up against the Romans—and escaped
                to fight again...

The world looks very different in the universe next door!

DON'T MISS THESE OTHER FINE SCIENCE FICTION TITLES, AVAILABLE WHEREVER BANTAM SPECTRA BOOKS ARE SOLD:

What Might Have Been?

VOLUME 3: ALTERNATE WARS

Edited by Gregory Benford and Martin H. Greenberg

SPECTRA™

BANTAM BOOKS
NEW YORK · TORONTO · LONDON · SYDNEY · AUCKLAND

ALTERNATE WARS

A Bantam Spectra Book / December 1991

"If Lee Had Not Won the Battle of Gettysburg" reprinted from
If It Had Happened Otherwise, ed. by J. C. Squire, © 1931
by Longman's Green, London, and reprinted with permission from
the Longman Group, Ltd., London, England. All Rights Reserved.

ISBN 0-553-29008-8

Published simultaneously in the United States and Canada

Bantam Books are published by Bantam Books, a division of
Bantam Doubleday Dell Publishing Group, Inc. Its trademark,
consisting of the words "Bantam Books" and the portrayal of a
rooster, is Registered in U.S. Patent and Trademark Office and
in other countries. Marca Registrada. Bantam Books, 666 Fifth
Avenue, New York, New York 10103.

PRINTED IN THE UNITED STATES OF AMERICA

RAD   0 9 8 7 6 5 4 3 2 1

Contents

INTRODUCTION   vi

AND WILD FOR TO HOLD
Nancy Kress   1

TUNDRA MOSS
F. M. Busby   53

WHEN FREE MEN SHALL STAND
Poul Anderson   81

ARMS AND THE WOMAN
James Morrow   113

READY FOR THE FATHERLAND
Harry Turtledove   135

THE TOMB
Jack McDevitt   155

TURPENTINE
Barry N. Malzberg   175

GODDARD'S PEOPLE
Allen Steele   191

MANASSAS, AGAIN
Gregory Benford   219

THE NUMBER OF THE SAND
George Zebrowski   237

IF LEE HAD NOT WON THE BATTLE
  OF GETTYSBURG
**The Right Honourable Winston S.
  Churchill, M.P.**   251

OVER THERE
Mike Resnick   271

Introduction

No matter how good a story might be, no one will continue reading it if a fistfight breaks out in the same room.

Conflict focuses the mind wonderfully. When we consider the possible variations of history, war looms as the obvious mechanism for decisive change.

I personally feel that inventions and scientific progress are the most effective ways of changing the world, and the most lasting, but they are usually not very dramatic. And one can usually argue that if Watt, say, had not invented the steam engine, somebody else would have done so rather soon after. (An interesting countercase is paper, invented once by a Chinese monk and never independently reinvented. The secret was eventually stolen by Arabs, who tortured the secret out of a Chinese papermaker.) Wars, on the other hand, often yield unique, quirky results. The fate of an entire society can hinge on a single line of infantry. Those who proclaim that wars never settle anything should ask the inhabitants of Carthage for their opinion, or perhaps the adherents of Nazi Germany.

To be sure, many conflicts do not prove truly decisive. The problem of Germany's role in modern Europe was settled by the Second World War, not by the First; or arguably, by the Cold War that followed. But World War I did disrupt the deep foundations of European society, beginning its erosion of influence—which may prove to be the deeper issue, historically.

Wars do often afford us a clear look at interesting questions. Poul Anderson's classic short story "Delenda Est" shows us a world where Carthage defeated Rome; often his Time Patrol has to patch up conflicts gone (from our point of view) awry. In science fiction, alternative outcomes for World War II and the American Civil War top the list of most-studied events. (We earlier collected the notable Axis-triumph short stories in *Hitler Victorious*.) Like most science fiction, this view of history expresses an American outlook.

Probably the best novel that treats alternative wars is Ward Moore's *Bring the Jubilee*, which recalls life in the twenty-six states after Lee won at Gettysburg. It portrays a defeated, backwater North and a rigid South. Things have generally gone badly abroad, for the world missed the revolutionary impact of the United States. This allowed Moore to use a utopian-didactic mode, commenting indirectly on the crucial role of the War of Secession in our country, and of the United States in the world. To my taste it is immensely satisfying, packed with detail, precise in its ideas and plotting, rich in feeling for its era. The best World War II alternative novel is probably Brad Linaweaver's *Moon of Ice*, in which the Nazis do get the atomic bomb.

In assembling this collection of original studies of alternative wars, we have tried to span a wide range of outcomes. World War II gets the expected attention in "Tundra Moss," "Goddard's People," and "Ready for the Fatherland," which differ markedly in viewpoint and ambience. "Arms and the Woman" and "The Number of the Sand" consider ancient conflicts, each with an interesting, fresh spin.

Each author takes a different tack. Indeed, "The Number of the Sand" explicitly shows us the infinite possibilities implied by the Everett model of quantum mechanics, in which every physical event yields a spectrum of outcomes— with an entire alternative universe to suit.

Nancy Kress reflects on just what war means to us, and what the power to "correct" the past would mean, in a strong story, "And Wild for to Hold." It forms an interesting counterpoint with the fevered remembrance (for he was there) of Barry N. Malzberg for the greatest year of domestic violence in our time: 1968. An American propensity for foreign engagements, and their often unanticipated effect on us, appear as well in "Over There." Some alternatives, no matter how gaudy, may not add up to much.

I could scarcely neglect what my grandmother called the War of Northern Aggression. My own story here uses a vastly different context for a civil war that might have resulted from a Roman Empire that survived well through the 1200s. I argue that in many ways we would have advanced farther technologically, and it would have been a better world—though not one without uncomfortable resonances with our own. The Civil War was a breakdown of our greatest skill: compromise. We will need it again.

"The Tomb" considers the outcome if events in the closing acts of Roman history had gone differently—and makes a poignant point about the fate of historians as well. The breakup of empires and the fall of great nations are not always bad news, however. Poul Anderson portrays in evocative prose how the fresh, young United States would have fared if it had been faced with a far more powerful France, one that did not sell off the Louisiana Territory for quick cash and thereafter leave the distant revolutionaries alone. He reflects an opinion many have of the United States—that we have been not so much wily, savvy, and brave but instead, just plain lucky.

Bring the Jubilee was not the first study of an alternative American Civil War. For the most intriguing precursor to it, I have reached far back into 1931, when a politician many considered permanently finished as a major figure was struggling along, ignored in Parliament, making ends meet with his pen. He wrote histories, current commentary, and just about any odd free-lance piece he could. The diligent J. C. Squire commissioned a short essay from this back-bench figure for *If It Had Happened Otherwise: Lapses into Imaginary History.* (A curious word choice; I find historical speculations do not make anything "lapse" but rather illuminate.) The rest, as they say, is history.

Squire produced a remarkable book of rather scholarly essays by such noted literary figures as Belloc, Chesterton, and Harold Nicholson. It remains the classic essay collection of its kind. My favorite of them all is the piece that concludes this volume. World War I dominated the minds of many in 1931, and this vision of a Southern victory at Gettysburg performs the unusual feat of projecting a better world than our real one. I personally do not find the argument quite compelling, but it is fun, well done, and worth considering. It expresses a wish that a decade later animated history itself, at the hands of its author.

That is the purpose of such fiction, whether couched in overt drama or in the pseudofactual essay style. War is inevitably a calamity for some. Pondering its true impact is the obligation of all.

Gregory Benford

AND WILD FOR

TO HOLD

NANCY KRESS

The demon came to her first in the long gallery at Hever Castle. She had gone there to watch Henry ride away, magnificent on his huge charger, the horse's legs barely visible through the summer dust raised by the king's entourage. But Henry himself was visible. He rose in his stirrups to half-turn his gaze back to the manor house, searching its sun-glazed windows to see if she watched. The spurned lover, riding off, watching over his shoulder the effect he himself made. She knew just how his eyes would look, small blue eyes under the curling red-gold hair. Mournful. Shrewd. Undeterred.

Anne Boleyn was not moved. Let him ride. She had not wanted him at Hever in the first place.

As she turned from the gallery window, a glint of light in the far corner caught her eye, and there for the first time was the demon.

It was made all of light, which did not surprise her. Was not Satan himself called Lucifer? The light was square, a perfectly square box such as no light had ever been before. Anne crossed herself and stepped forward. The box of light brightened, then winked out.

Anne stood perfectly still. She was not afraid; very little made her afraid. But nonetheless she crossed herself again and uttered a prayer. It would be unfortunate if a demon took up residence at Hever. Demons could be dangerous.

Like kings.

Lambert half-turned from her console toward Culhane, working across the room. "Culhane—they said she was a witch."

3

"Yes? So?" Culhane said. "In the 1500s they said any powerful woman was a witch."

"No, it was more. They said it *before* she became powerful." Culhane didn't answer. After a moment Lambert said quietly, "The Rahvoli equations keep flagging her."

Culhane grew very still. Finally he said, "Let me see."

He crossed the bare, small room to Lambert's console. She steadied the picture on the central square. At the moment the console appeared in this location as a series of interlocking squares mounting from floor to ceiling. Some of the squares were solid real-time alloys; some were holo simulations; some were not there at all, neither in space nor time, although they appeared to be. The project focus square, which *was* there, said:

TIME RESCUE PROJECT
UNITED FEDERATION OF UPPER SLIB, EARTH
FOCUS: ANNE BOLEYN
       HEVER CASTLE, KENT, ENGLAND, EUROPE
       1525: 645:89:3
CHURCH OF THE HOLY HOSTAGE TEMPORARY
PERMIT #4592

In the time-jump square was framed a young girl, dark hair just visible below her coif, her hand arrested at her long, slender neck in the act of signing the cross.

Lambert said, as if to herself, "She considered herself a good Catholic."

Culhane stared at the image. His head had been freshly shaved, in honor of his promotion to project head. He wore, Lambert thought, his new importance as if it were a fragile implant, liable to be rejected. She found that touching.

Lambert said, "The Rahvoli probability is .798. She's a definite key."

Culhane sucked in his cheeks. The dye on them had barely dried. He said, "So is the other. I think we should talk to Brill."

* * *

The serving women had finally left. The priests had left, the doctors, the courtiers, the nurses, taking with them the baby. Even Henry had left, gone . . . where? To play cards with Harry Norris? To his latest mistress? Never mind—they had all at last left her alone.

A girl.

Anne rolled over in her bed and pounded her fists on the pillow. A girl. Not a prince, not the son that England needed, that *she* needed . . . a girl. And Henry growing colder every day, she could feel it, he no longer desired her, no longer loved her. He would bed with her—oh, that, most certainly, if it would get him his boy, but her power was going. Was gone. The power she had hated, despised, but had used nonetheless because it was there and Henry should feel it, as he had made her feel his power over and over again . . . her power was going. She was queen of England, but her power was slipping away like the Thames at ebb tide, and she just as helpless to stop it as to stop the tide itself. The only thing that could have preserved her power was a son. And she had borne a girl. Strong, lusty, with Henry's own red, curling hair . . . but a girl.

Anne rolled over on her back, painfully. Elizabeth was already a month old, but everything in Anne hurt. She had contracted white-leg, so much less dreaded than childbed fever but still weakening, and for the whole month had not left her bedchamber. Servants and ladies and musicians came and went, while Anne lay feverish, trying to plan. . . . Henry had as yet made no move. He had even seemed to take the baby's sex well: "She seems a lusty wench. I pray God will send her a brother in the same good shape." But Anne knew. She always knew. She had known when Henry's eye first fell upon her. Had known to a shade the exact intensity of his longing during the nine years she had kept him waiting: nine years of celibacy, of denial. She had known the exact moment when that hard mind behind the small blue eyes had decided: *It is worth it. I will divorce Katherine and make her queen.* Anne had known before he did when he decided it had all been a mistake. The price for making her queen had been too high. She was not worth it. Unless she gave him a son.

And if she did not . . .

In the darkness Anne squeezed her eyes shut. This was but an attack of childbed vapors; it signified nothing. She was never afraid, not she. This was only a night terror, and when she opened her eyes it would pass, because it must. She must go on fighting, must get herself heavy with a son, must safeguard her crown. And her daughter. There was no one else to do it for her, and there was no way out.

When she opened her eyes a demon, shaped like a square of light, glowed in the corner of the curtained bedchamber.

Lambert dipped her head respectfully as the high priest passed.

She was tall and wore no external augments. Eyes, arms, ears, shaved head, legs under the gray-green ceremonial robe—all were her own, as required by the charter of the Church of the Holy Hostage. Lambert had heard a rumor that before her election to high priest she had had brilliant, violet-augmented eyes and gamma-strength arms, but on her election had had both removed and the originals restored. The free representative of all the hostages in the solar system could not walk around enjoying high-maintenance augments. Hostages could, of course, but the person in charge of their spiritual and material welfare must appear human to any hostage she chose to visit. A four-handed spacer held in a free-fall chamber on Mars must find the high priest as human as did a genetically altered flier of Ipsu being held hostage by the New Trien Republic. The only way to do that was to forego external augments.

Internals, of course, were a different thing.

Beside the high priest walked the director of the Time Research Institute, Toshio Brill. No ban on externals for *him:* Brill wore gold-plated sensors in his shaved black head, a display Lambert found slightly ostentatious. Also puzzling: Brill was not ordinarily a flamboyant man. Perhaps he was differentiating himself from Her Holiness. Behind Brill his project heads, including Culhane, stood silent, not speaking unless spoken to. Culhane looked nervous: He was ambitious, Lambert knew. She sometimes wondered why she was not.

"So far I am impressed," the high priest said. "Impeccable hostage conditions on the material side."

Brill murmured, "Of course, the spiritual is difficult. The three hostages are so different from each other, and even for culture specialists and historians . . . the hostages arrive here very upset."

"As would you or I," the high priest said, not smiling, "in similar circumstances."

"Yes, Your Holiness."

"And now you wish to add a fourth hostage, from a fourth time stream."

"Yes."

The high priest looked slowly around at the main console; Lambert noticed that she looked right past the time-jump square itself. Not trained in peripheral vision techniques. But she looked a long time at the stasis square. They all did; outsiders were unduly fascinated by the idea that the whole building existed between time streams. Or maybe Her Holiness merely objected to the fact that the Time Research Institute, like some larger but hardly richer institutions, was exempt from the all-world taxation that supported the Church. Real-estate outside time was also outside taxation.

The high priest said, "I cannot give permission for such a political disruption without understanding fully every possible detail. Tell me again."

Lambert hid a grin. The high priest did not need to hear it again. She knew the whole argument, had pored over it for days, most likely, with her advisers. And she would agree; why wouldn't she? It could only add to her power. Brill knew that. He was being asked to explain only to show that the high priest could force him to do it, again and again, until she—not he—decided the explanation was sufficient and the Church of the Holy Hostage issued a permanent hostage permit to hold one Anne Boleyn, of England Time Delta, for the altruistic purpose of preventing a demonstrable, Class One war.

Brill showed no outward recognition that he was being humbled. "Your Holiness, this woman is a fulcrum. The Rahvoli equations, developed in the last century by—"

"I know the Rahvoli equations," the high priest said. And smiled sweetly.

"Then Your Holiness knows that any person identified by the equations as a fulcrum is directly responsible for the course of history. Even if he or she seems powerless in local time. Mistress Boleyn was the second wife of Henry the Eighth of England. In order to marry her, he divorced his first wife, Katharine of Aragon, and in order to do that, he took all of England out of the Catholic Church. Protestantism was—"

"And what again was that?" Her Holiness said, and even Culhane glanced sideways at Lambert, appalled. The high priest was playing. With a *research director*. Lambert hid her smile. Did Culhane know that high seriousness opened one to the charge of pomposity? Probably not.

"Protestantism was another branch of 'Christianity,'" the director said patiently. So far, by refusing to be provoked, he was winning. "It was warlike, as was Catholicism. In 1642 various branches of Protestantism were contending for political power within England, as was a Catholic faction. King Charles was Catholic, in fact. Contention led to civil war. Thousands of people died fighting, starved to death, were hung as traitors, were tortured as betrayers . . ."

Lambert saw Her Holiness wince. She must hear this all the time, Lambert thought. What else was her office for? Yet the wince looked genuine.

Brill pressed his point. "Children were reduced to eating rats to survive. In Cornwall, rebels' hands and feet were cut off, gibbets were erected in market squares and men hung on them alive, and—"

"Enough," the high priest said. "This is why the Church exists. To promote the holy hostages that prevent war."

"And that is what we wish to do," Brill said swiftly, "in other time streams, now that our own has been brought to peace. In Stream Delta, which has only reached the sixteenth century—Your Holiness knows that each stream progresses at a different relative rate—"

The high priest made a gesture of impatience.

"—the woman Anne Boleyn is the fulcrum. If she can be taken hostage after the birth of her daughter Elizabeth, who will act throughout a very long reign to preserve peace, and before Henry declares the Act of Supremacy that opens the door to religious divisiveness in England, we can prevent great loss of life. The Rahvoli equations show a 79.8% probability that history will be changed in the direction of greater peace, right up through the following two centuries. Religious wars often—"

"There are other, bloodier religious wars to prevent than the English civil war."

"True, Your Holiness," the director said humbly. At least it looked like humility to Lambert. "But ours is a young science. Identifying other time streams, focusing on one, identifying historical fulcra—it is such a new science. We do what we can, in the name of peace."

Everyone in the room looked pious. Lambert hid a smile. In the name of peace—and of prestigious scientific research, attended by rich financial support and richer academic reputations.

"And it is peace we seek," Brill pressed, "as much as the Church itself does. With a permanent permit to take Anne Boleyn hostage, we can save countless lives in this other time stream, just as the Church preserves peace in our own."

The high priest played with the sleeve of her robe. Lambert could not see her face. But when she looked up, she was smiling.

"I'll recommend to the All-World Forum that your hostage permit be granted, Director. I will return in two months to make an official check on the holy hostage."

Brill, Lambert saw, didn't quite stop himself in time from frowning. "Two months? But with the entire solar system of hostages to supervise—"

"Two months, Director," Her Holiness said. "The week before the All-World Forum convenes to vote on revenue and taxation."

"I—"

"Now I would like to inspect the three holy hostages you already hold for the altruistic prevention of war."

Later, Culhane said to Lambert, "He did not explain it very well. It could have been made so much more urgent . . . it *is* urgent. Those bodies rotting in Cornwall . . ." He shuddered.

Lambert looked at him. "You care. You genuinely do."

He looked back at her in astonishment. "And you don't? You must, to work on this project!"

"I care," Lambert said. "But not like that."

"Like what?"

She tried to clarify it for him, for herself. "The bodies rotting . . . I see them. But it's not our own history—"

"What does that matter? They're still human!"

He was so earnest. Intensity burned on him like skin tinglers. Did Culhane even use skin tinglers? Lambert wondered. Fellow researchers spoke of him as an ascetic, giving all his energy, all his time to the project. A woman in his domicile had told Lambert he even lived chaste, doing a voluntary celibacy mission for the entire length of his research grant. Lambert had never met anyone who actually did that. It was intriguing.

She said, "Are you thinking of the priesthood once the project is over, Culhane?"

He flushed. Color mounted from the dyed cheeks, light blue since he had been promoted to project head, to pink on the fine skin of his shaved temples.

"I'm thinking of it."

"And doing a celibacy mission now?"

"Yes. Why?" His tone was belligerent: A celibacy mission was slightly old-fashioned. Lambert studied his body: tall, well-made, strong. Augments? Muscular, maybe. He had beautiful muscles.

"No reason," she said, bending back to her console until she heard him walk away.

The demon advanced. Anne, lying feeble on her curtained bed, tried to call out. But her voice would not come, and who would hear her anyway? The bedclothes were thick, muffling sound; her ladies would all have retired for the night, alone or otherwise; the guards would be drinking the ale Henry had provided all of London to celebrate Elizabeth's christening. And Henry . . . he was not beside her. She had failed him of his son.

"Be gone," she said weakly to the demon. It moved closer.

They had called her a witch. Because of her little sixth finger, because of the dog named Urian, because she had kept Henry under her spell so long without bedding him. But if I were really a witch, she thought, I could send this demon away. More: I could hold Henry, could keep him from watching that whey-faced Jane Seymour, could keep him in my bed. . . . She was not a witch.

Therefore, it followed that there was nothing she could do about this demon. If it was come for her, it was come. If Satan, Master of Lies, was decided to have her, to punish her for taking the husband of another woman, and for . . . How much could demons know?

"This was all none of my wishing," she said aloud to the demon. "I wanted to marry someone else." The demon continued to advance.

Very well, then, let it take her. She would not scream. She never had—she prided herself on it. Not when they had told her she could not marry Harry Percy. Not when she had been sent home from the court, peremptorily and without explanation. Not when she had discovered the explanation: Henry wished to have her out of London so he could bed his latest mistress away from Katharine's eyes. She had not screamed when a crowd of whores had burst into the palace where she was supping, demanding

Nan Bullen, who they said was one of them. She had escaped across the Thames in a barge, and not a cry had escaped her lips. They had admired her for her courage: Wyatt, Norris, Weston, Henry himself. She would not scream now.

The box of light grew larger as it approached. She had just time to say to it, "I have been God's faithful and true servant, and my husband, the king's," before it was upon her.

"The place where a war starts," Lambert said to the faces assembled below her in the Hall of Time, "is long before the first missile, or the first bullet, or the first spear."

She looked down at the faces. It was part of her responsibility as an intern researcher to teach a class of young, some of whom would become historians. The class was always taught in the Hall of Time. The expense was enormous: keeping the hall in stasis for nearly an hour, bringing the students in through the force field, activating all the squares at once. Her lecture would be replayed for them later, when they could pay attention to it. Lambert did not blame them for barely glancing at her now. Why should they? The walls of the circular room, which were only there in a virtual sense, were lined with squares that were not really there at all. The squares showed actual, local-time scenes from wars that had been there, were there now, somewhere, in someone's reality.

Men died writhing in the mud, arrows through intestines and neck and groin, at Agincourt.

Women lay flung across the bloody bodies of their children at Cawnpore.

In the hot sun the flies crawled thick upon the split faces of the heroes of Marathon.

Figures staggered, their faces burned off, away from Hiroshima.

Breathing bodies, their perfect faces untouched and their brains turned to mush by spekaline, sat in orderly rows under the ripped dome on Io-One.

Only one face turned toward Lambert, jerked as if on a string, a boy with wide violet eyes brimming with anguish. Lambert obligingly started again.

"The place where a war starts is long before the first missile, or the first bullet, or the first spear. There are always many forces causing a war: economic, political, religious, cultural. Nonetheless, it is the great historical discovery of our time that if you trace each of these back—through the records, through the eyewitness accounts, through the entire burden of data only Rahvoli equations can handle—you come to a fulcrum. A single event or act or person. It is like a decision tree with a thousand thousand generations of decisions: Somewhere there was one first yes/no. The place where the war started and where it could have been prevented.

"The great surprise of time rescue work has been how often that place was female.

"Men fought wars, when there were wars. Men controlled the gold and the weapons and the tariffs and sea rights and religions that have caused wars, and the men controlled the bodies of other men who did the actual fighting. But men are men. They acted at the fulcrum of history, but often what tipped their actions one way or another was what they loved. A woman. A child. She became the passive, powerless weight he chose to lift, and the balance tipped. She, not he, is the branching place, where the decision tree splits and the war begins."

The boy with the violet eyes was still watching her. Lambert stayed silent until he turned to watch the squares—which was the reason he had been brought here. Then she watched him. Anguished, passionate, able to feel what war meant—he might be a good candidate for the time rescue team when his preliminary studies were done. He reminded her a little of Culhane.

Who right now, as project head, was interviewing the new hostage, not lecturing to children.

Lambert stifled her jealousy. It was unworthy. And shortsighted: She remembered what this glimpse of human misery had meant to her three years ago, when she was an historian candidate. She had had nightmares for weeks. She had thought the event was pivotal to her life, a dividing point past which she would never be the same person again. How could she? She had been shown the depths to which humanity, without the Church of the Holy Hostage and the All-World Concordance, could descend. Burning eye sockets, mutilated genitals, a general who stood on a hill and said, "How I love to see the arms and legs fly!" It had been shattering. She had been shattered, as the orientation intended she should be.

The boy with the violet eyes was crying. Lambert wanted to step down from the platform and go to him. She wanted to put her arms around him and hold his head against her shoulder. . . but was that because of compassion, or was that because of his violet eyes?

She said silently to him, without leaving the podium, *you will be all right. Human beings are not as mutable as you think. When this is over, nothing permanent about you will have changed at all.*

Anne opened her eyes. Satan leaned over her.

His head was shaved, and he wore strange garb of an ugly blue-green. His cheeks were stained with dye. In one ear metal glittered and swung. Anne crossed herself.

"Hello," Satan said, and the voice was not human.

She struggled to sit up; if this be damnation, she would not lie prone for it. Her heart hammered in her throat. But the act of sitting brought the Prince of Darkness into focus, and her eyes widened. He looked like a man. Painted, made ugly, hung around with metal boxes that could be tools of evil—but a man.

"My name is Culhane."

A man. And she had faced men. Bishops, nobles, Chancellor Wolsey. She had outfaced Henry, Prince of England and France, Defender of the Faith.

"Don't be frightened, Mistress Boleyn. I will explain to you where you are and how you came to be here."

She saw now that the voice came not from his mouth, although his mouth moved, but from the box hung around his neck. How could that be? Was there then a demon in the box? But then she realized something else, something real to hold on to.

"Do not call me Mistress Boleyn. Address me as Your Grace. I am the queen."

The something that moved behind his eyes convinced her, finally, that he was a mortal man. She was used to reading men's eyes. But why should this one look at her like that? With pity? With admiration?

She struggled to stand, rising off the low pallet. It was carved of good English oak. The room was paneled in dark wood and hung with tapestries of embroidered wool. Small-paned windows shed brilliant light over carved chairs, table, chest. On the table rested a writing desk and a lute. Reassured, Anne pushed down the heavy cloth of her nightshift and rose.

The man, seated on a low stool, rose, too. He was taller than Henry—she had never seen a man taller than Henry—and superbly muscled. A soldier? Fright fluttered again, and she put her hand to her throat. This man, watching her—watching her *throat*. Was he then an executioner? Was she under arrest, drugged and brought by some secret method into the Tower of London? Had someone brought evidence against her? Or was Henry that disappointed that she had not borne a son that he was eager to supplant her already?

As steadily as she could, Anne walked to the window.

The Tower Bridge did not lie beyond in the sunshine. Nor the river, nor the gabled roofs of Greenwich Palace. Instead there was a sort of yard, with huge beasts of metal growling softly. On the grass naked young men and women jumped up and down, waving their arms, running in place and smiling and sweating as if they did not know either that they were uncovered or crazed.

Anne took firm hold of the windowsill. It was slippery in her hands, and she saw that it was not wood at all but some material made to resemble wood. She closed her eyes, then opened them. She was a queen. She had fought hard to become a queen, defending a virtue nobody believed she still had, against a man who claimed that to destroy that virtue was love. She had won, making the crown the price of her virtue. She had conquered a king, brought down a chancellor of England, outfaced a pope. She would not show fear to this executioner in this place of the damned, whatever it was.

She turned from the window, her head high. "Please begin your explanation, Master..."

"Culhane."

"Master Culhane. We are eager to hear what you have to say. And we do not like waiting."

She swept aside her long nightdress as if it were court dress and seated herself in the not-wooden chair carved like a throne.

"I am a hostage," Anne repeated. "In a time that has not yet happened."

From beside the window, Lambert watched. She was fascinated. Anne Boleyn had, according to Culhane's report, listened in silence to the entire explanation of the time rescue, that explanation so carefully crafted and revised a dozen times to fit what the sixteenth-century mind could understand of the twenty-second. Queen Anne had not become hysterical. She had not cried, nor fainted, nor professed disbelief. She had asked no questions. When Culhane had finished, she had requested, calmly and with staggering dignity, to see the ruler of this place, with his ministers. Toshio Brill, watching on monitor because the wisdom was that at first new hostages would find it easier to deal with one consistent researcher, had hastily summoned Lambert and two others. They had all dressed in the floor-length robes used for grand academic ceremonies and never else. And they had marched solemnly into the ersatz sixteenth-century room, bowing their heads.

Only their heads. No curtsies. Anne Boleyn was going to learn that no one curtsied anymore.

Covertly Lambert studied her, their fourth time hostage, so different from the other three. She had not risen from her chair, but even seated she was astonishingly tiny. Thin, delicate bones, great dark eyes, masses of silky black hair loose on her white nightdress. She was not pretty by the standards of this century; she had not even been counted pretty by the standards of her own. But she was compelling. Lambert had to give her that.

"And I am prisoner here," Anne Boleyn said. Lambert turned up her translator; the words were just familiar, but the accent so strange she could not catch them without electronic help.

"Not prisoner," the director said. "Hostage."

"Lord Brill, if I cannot leave, then I am a prisoner. Let us not mince words. I cannot leave this castle?"

"You cannot."

"Please address me as 'Your Grace.' Is there to be a ransom?"

"No, Your Grace. But because of your presence here thousands of men will live who would have otherwise died."

With a shock, Lambert saw Anne shrug; the deaths of thousands of men evidently did not interest her. It was true, then. They really were moral barbarians, even the women. The students should see this. That small shrug said more than all the battles viewed in squares. Lambert felt her sympathy for the abducted woman lessen, a physical sensation like the emptying of a bladder, and was relieved to feel it. It meant she, Lambert, still had her own moral sense.

"How long must I stay here?"

"For life, Your Grace," Brill said bluntly.

Anne made no reaction; her control was aweing.

"And how long will that be, Lord Brill?"

"No person knows the length of his or her life, Your Grace."

"But if you can read the future, as you claim, you must know what the length of mine would have been."

Lambert thought: We must not underestimate her. This hostage is not like the last one.

Brill said, with the same bluntness that honored Anne's comprehension—did she realize that?—"If we had not brought you here, you would have died May nineteenth, 1536."

"How?"

"It does not matter. You are no longer part of that future, and so now events there will—"

"*How?*"

Brill didn't answer.

Anne Boleyn rose and walked to the window, absurdly small, Lambert thought, in the trailing nightdress. Over her shoulder she said, "Is this castle in England?"

"No," Brill said. Lambert saw him exchange glances with Culhane.

"In France?"

"It is not in any place on Earth," Brill said, "although it can be entered from three places on Earth. It is outside of time."

She could not possibly have understood, but she said nothing, only went on staring out the window. Over her shoulder Lambert saw the exercise court, empty now, and the antimatter power generators. Two technicians crawled over them with a robot monitor. What did Anne Boleyn make of them?

"God alone knows if I had merited death," Anne said. Lambert saw Culhane start.

Brill stepped forward. "Your Grace—"

"Leave me now," she said without turning.

They did. Of course she would be monitored constantly—everything from brain scans to the output of her bowels. Although she would never know this. But if suicide was in that life-defying mind, it would not be possible. If Her Holiness ever learned of the suicide of a time hostage . . . Lambert's last glimpse before the door closed was of Anne Boleyn's back, still by the window, straight as a spear as she gazed out at antimatter power generators in a building in permanent stasis.

"Culhane, meeting in ten minutes," Brill said. Lambert guessed the time lapse was to let the director change into working clothes. Toshio Brill had come away from the interview with Anne Boleyn somehow diminished. He even looked shorter, although shouldn't her small stature have instead augmented his?

Culhane stood still in the corridor outside Anne's locked room (would she try the door?). His face was turned away from Lambert's. She said, "Culhane . . . You jumped a moment in there. When she said God alone knew if she had merited death."

"It was what she said at her trial," Culhane said. "When the verdict was announced. Almost the exact words."

He still had not moved so much as a muscle of that magnificent body. Lambert said, probing, "You found her impressive, then. Despite her scrawniness, and beyond the undeniable pathos of her situation."

He looked at her then, his eyes blazing: Culhane, the research engine. "I found her magnificent."

She never smiled. That was one of the things she knew they remarked upon among themselves: She had overheard them in the walled garden. *Anne Boleyn never smiles*. Alone, they did not call her Queen Anne, or Her Grace, or even the Marquis of Rochford, the title Henry had conferred upon her, the only female peeress in her own right in all of England. No, they called her Anne Boleyn, as if the marriage to Henry had never happened, as if she had never borne Elizabeth. And they said she never smiled.

What cause was there to smile, in this place that was neither life nor death?

Anne stitched deftly at a piece of amber velvet. She was not badly treated. They had given her a servant, cloth to make dresses—she had always been clever with a needle, and the skill had not deserted her when she could afford to order any dresses she chose. They had given her books, the writing Latin but the pictures curiously flat, with no raised ink or painting. They let her go into any unlocked room in the castle, out to the gardens, into the yards. She was a holy hostage.

When the amber velvet gown was finished, she put it on. They let her have a mirror. A lute. Writing paper and quills. Whatever she asked for, as generous as Henry had been in the early days of his passion, when he had divided her from her love Harry Percy and had kept her loving hostage to his own fancy.

Cages came in many sizes. Many shapes. And, if what Master Culhane and the Lady Mary Lambert said was true, in many times.

"I am not a lady," Lady Lambert had protested. She needn't have bothered. Of course she was not a lady—she was a commoner, like the others, and so perverted was this place that the woman sounded insulted to be called a lady. Lambert did not like her, Anne knew, although she had not yet found out why. The woman was unsexed, like all of them, working on her books and machines all day, exercising naked with men who thus no more looked at their bodies than they would those of fellow soldiers in the roughest camp. So it pleased Anne to call Lambert a lady when she did not want to be one, as Anne was now so many things she had never wanted to be. "Anne Boleyn." Who never smiled.

"I will create you a Lady," she said to Lambert. "I confer on you the rank of baroness. Who will gainsay me? I am the queen, and in this place there is no king."

And Mary Lambert had stared at her with the unsexed bad manners of a common drab.

Anne knotted her thread and cut it with silver scissors. The gown was finished. She slipped it over her head and struggled with the buttons in the back, rather than call the stupid girl who was her servant. The girl could not even dress hair. Anne smoothed her hair herself, then looked critically at her reflection in the fine mirror they had brought her.

For a woman a month and a half from childbed, she looked strong. They had put medicines in her food, they said. Her complexion, that creamy dark skin that seldom varied in color, was well set off by the amber velvet. She had often worn amber, or tawny. Her hair, loose since she had no headdress and did not know how to make one, streamed over her shoulders. Her hands, long and slim despite the tiny extra finger, carried a rose brought to her by Master Culhane. She toyed with the rose to show off the beautiful hands, and lifted her head high.

She was going to have an audience with Her Holiness, a female pope. And she had a request to make.

"She will ask, Your Holiness, to be told the future. Her future, the one Anne Boleyn experienced in her own time stream, after the point we took her hostage to ours. And the future of England." Brill's face had darkened; Lambert could see that he hated this. To forewarn his political rival that a hostage would complain about her treatment. A *hostage*, that person turned sacred object through the sacrifice of personal freedom to global peace. When Tullio Amaden Koyushi had been hostage from Mars Three to the Republic of China, he had told the Church official in charge of his case that he was not being allowed sufficient exercise. The resulting intersystem furor had lost the Republic of China two trade contracts, both important. There was no other way to maintain the necessary reverence for the hostage political system. The Church of the Holy Hostage was powerful because it must be, if the solar system was to stay at peace. Brill knew that.

So did Her Holiness.

She wore full state robes today, gorgeous with hundreds of tiny mirrors sent to her by the grateful across all worlds. Her head was newly shaved. Perfect, synthetic jewels glittered in her ears. Listening to Brill's apology-in-advance, Her Holiness smiled. Lambert saw the smile, and even across the room she felt Brill's polite, concealed frustration.

"Then if this is so," Her Holiness said, "why cannot Lady Anne Boleyn be told her future? Hers and England's?"

Lambert knew that the high priest already knew the answer. She wanted to make Brill say it.

Brill said, "It is not thought wise, Your Holiness. If you remember, we did that once before."

"Ah, yes, your last hostage. I will see her, too, of course, on this visit. Has Queen Helen's condition improved?"

"No," Brill said shortly.

"And no therapeutic brain drugs or electronic treatments have helped? She still is insane from the shock of finding herself with us?"

"Nothing has helped."

"You understand how reluctant I was to let you proceed with another time rescue at all," Her Holiness said, and even Lambert stifled a gasp. The high priest did not make those determinations; only the All-World Forum could authorize or disallow a hostage-taking—across space *or* time. The Church of the Holy Hostage was responsible only for the inspection and continuation of permits granted by the Forum. For the high priest to claim political power she did not possess . . .

The director's eyes gleamed angrily. But before he could reply, the door opened and Culhane escorted in Anne Boleyn.

Lambert pressed her lips together tightly. The woman had sewn herself a gown, a sweeping, ridiculous confection of amber velvet so tight at the breasts and waist she must hardly be able to breathe. How had women conducted their lives in such trappings? The dress narrowed her waist to nearly nothing; above the square neckline her collarbones were delicate as a bird's. Culhane hovered beside her, huge and protective. Anne walked straight to the high priest, knelt, and raised her face.

She was looking for a ring to kiss.

Lambert didn't bother to hide her smile. A high priest wore no jewelry except earrings, ever. The pompous little hostage had made a social error, no doubt significant in her own time.

Anne smiled up at Her Holiness, the first time anyone had seen her smile at all. It changed her face, lighting it with mischief, lending luster to the great dark eyes. A phrase came to Lambert, penned by the poet Thomas Wyatt to describe his cousin Anne: *And wild for to hold, though I seem tame*.

Anne said, in that sprightly yet aloof manner that Lambert was coming to associate with her, "It seems, Your Holiness, that we have reached for what is not there. But the lack is ours, not yours, and we hope it will not be repeated in the request we come to make of you."

Direct. Graceful, even through the translator and despite the ludicrous imperial plural. Lambert glanced at Culhane, who was gazing down at Anne as at a rare and fragile flower. How could he? That skinny body, without muscle tone let alone augments, that plain face, the mole on her neck. . . . This was not the sixteenth century. Culhane was a fool.

As Thomas Wyatt had been. And Sir Harry Percy. And Henry, king of England. All caught not by beauty but by that strange elusive charm.

Her Holiness laughed. "Stand up, Your Grace. We don't kneel to officials here." *Your Grace*. The high priest always addressed hostages by the honorifics of their own state, but in this case it could only impede Anne's adjustment.

And what do I care about her adjustment? Lambert jeered at herself. Nothing. What I care about is Culhane's infatuation, and only because he rejected me first. Rejection, it seemed, was a great whetter of appetite—in any century.

Anne rose. Her Holiness said, "I'm going to ask you some questions, Your Grace. You are free to answer any way you wish. My function is to ensure that you are well treated and that the noble science of the prevention of war, which has made you a holy hostage, is also well served. Do you understand?"

"We do."

"Have you received everything you need for your material comfort?"

"Yes," Anne said.

"Have you received everything you've requested for your mental comfort? Books, objects of any description, company?"

"No," Anne said. Lambert saw Brill stiffen.

Her Holiness said, "No?"

"It is necessary for the comfort of our mind—and for our material comfort as well—to understand our situation as fully as possible. Any rational creature requires such understanding to reach ease of mind."

Brill said, "You have been told everything related to

your situation. What you ask is to know about situations that now, because you are here, will never happen."

"Situations that *have* happened, Lord Brill, else no one could know of them. You could not."

"In *your* time stream they will not happen," Brill said. Lambert could hear the suppressed anger in his voice and wondered if the high priest could. Anne Boleyn couldn't know how serious it was to be charged by Her Holiness with a breach of hostage treatment. If Brill was ambitious—and why wouldn't he be?—such charges could hurt his future.

Anne said swiftly, "Our time is now your time. *You* have made it so. The situation was none of our choosing. And if your time is now ours, then surely we are entitled to the knowledge that accompanies our time." She looked at the high priest. "For the comfort of our mind."

Brill said, "Your Holiness—"

"No, Queen Anne is correct. Her argument is valid. You will designate a qualified researcher to answer any questions she has—any at all—about the life she might have had, or the course of events England took when the queen did not become a sacred hostage."

Brill nodded stiffly.

"Good-bye, Your Grace," Her Holiness said. "I shall return in two weeks to inspect your situation again."

Two weeks? The high priest was not due for another inspection for six months. Lambert glanced at Culhane to see his reaction to this blatant political fault-hunting, but he was gazing at the floor, to which Anne Boleyn had sunk in another of her embarrassing curtsies, the amber velvet of her skirts spread around her like gold.

They sent a commoner to explain her life to her, and the life she had lost. A commoner. And he had as well the nerve to be besotted with her. Anne always knew. She tolerated such fellows, like that upstart musician Smeaton, when they were useful to her. If this Master Culhane dared to make any sort of declaration, he would receive the same sort of snub Smeaton once had. Inferior persons should not look to be spoken to as noblemen.

He sat on a straight-backed chair in her tower room, looking humble enough, while Anne sat in the great carved chair with her hands tightly folded to keep them from shaking.

"Tell me how I came to die in 1536." God's blood! Had ever before there been such a sentence uttered?

Culhane said, "You were beheaded. Found guilty of treason." He stopped and flushed.

She knew, then. In a queen, there was one cause for a charge of treason. "He charged me with adultery. To remove me, so he could marry again."

"Yes."

"To Jane Seymour."

"Yes."

"Had I first given him a son?"

"No," Culhane said.

"Did Jane Seymour give him a son?"

"Yes. Edward the Sixth. But he died at sixteen, a few years after Henry."

There was vindication in that, but not enough to stem the sick feeling in her gut. Treason. And no son. . . . There must have been more than desire for the Seymour bitch. Henry must have hated her. Adultery. . .

"With whom?"

Again the oaf flushed. "With five men, Your Grace. Everyone knew the charges were false, created merely to excuse his own cuckoldry—even your enemies admitted such."

"Who were they?"

"Sir Henry Norris. Sir Francis Weston. William Brereton. Mark Smeaton. And . . . and your brother George."

For a moment she thought she would be sick. Each name fell like a blow, the last like the ax itself. George. Her beloved brother, so talented at music, so high-spirited and witty. . . Harry Norris, the king's friend. Weston and Brereton, young and lighthearted but always, to her, respectful and careful . . . and Mark Smeaton, the oaf made courtier because he could play the virginals.

The long, beautiful hands clutched the sides of the chair. But the moment passed, and she could say with dignity, "They denied the charges?"

"Smeaton confessed, but he was tortured into it. The others denied the charges completely. Harry Norris offered to defend your honor in single combat."

Yes, that was like Harry: so old-fashioned, so principled. She said, "They all died." It was not a question: If she had died for treason, they would have, too. And not alone; no one died alone. "Who else?"

Culhane said, "Maybe we should wait for the rest of this, Your—"

"Who else? My father?"

"No. Sir Thomas More, John Fisher—"

"More? For my. . ." She could not say *adultery*.

"Because he would not swear to the Oath of Supremacy, which made the king and not the pope head of the church in England. That act opened the door to religious dissension in England."

"It did not. The heretics were already strong in England. History cannot fault that to me!"

"Not as strong as they would become," Culhane said almost apologetically. "Queen Mary was known as Bloody Mary for burning heretics who used the Act of Supremacy to break from Rome— Your Grace! Are you all right . . . Anne?"

"Do not touch me," she said. Queen Mary. Then her own daughter Elizabeth had been disinherited, or killed. . . . Had Henry become so warped that he would kill a child? His own child? Unless he had come to believe . . .

She whispered, "Elizabeth?"

Comprehension flooded his eye. "Oh. No, Anne! No! Mary ruled first, as the elder, but when she died heirless, Elizabeth was only twenty-five. Elizabeth became the greatest ruler England had ever known! She ruled for forty-four years, and under her England became a great power."

The greatest ruler. Her baby Elizabeth. Anne could feel her hands unknotting on the ugly artificial chair. Henry had not repudiated Elizabeth, nor had her killed.

She had become the greatest ruler England had ever known.

Culhane said, "This is why we thought it best not to tell you all this."

She said coldly, "I will be the judge of that."

"I'm sorry." He sat stiffly, hands dangling awkwardly between his knees. He looked like a plowman, like that oaf Smeaton. . . . She remembered what Henry had done, and rage returned.

"I stood accused. With five men . . . with George. And the charges were false." Something in his face changed. Anne faced him steadily. "Unless . . . were they false, Master Culhane? You who know so much of history. Does history say . . ." She could not finish. To beg for history's judgment from a man like this . . . no humiliation had ever been greater. Not even the Spanish ambassador, referring to her as "the concubine," had ever humiliated her so.

Culhane said carefully, "History is silent on the subject, Your Grace. What your conduct was . . . would have been . . . is known only to you."

"As it should be. It was . . . would have been . . . mine," she said viciously, mocking his tones perfectly. He looked at her like a wounded puppy, like that lout Smeaton when she had snubbed him. "Tell me this, Master Culhane. You have changed history as it would have been, you tell me. Will my daughter Elizabeth still become the greatest ruler England has ever seen—in *my* 'time stream'? Or will that be altered, too, by your quest for peace at any cost?"

"We don't know. I explained to you . . . We can only watch your time stream now as it unfolds. It had only reached October 1533, which is why after analyzing our own history we—"

"You have explained all that. It will be sixty years from now before you know if my daughter will still be great. Or if you have changed that as well by abducting me and ruining my life."

"Abducting! You were going to be killed! Accused, beheaded—"

"And you have prevented that." She rose, in a greater fury than ever she had been with Henry, with Wolsey, with anyone. "You have also robbed me of my remaining three years as surely as Henry would have robbed me of my old age. And you have mayhap robbed my daughter as well, as Henry sought to do with his Seymour-get prince. So what is the difference between you, Master Culhane, that you are a saint and Henry a villain? He held me in the Tower until my soul could be commended to God; you hold me here in this castle you say I can never leave where time does not exist, and mayhap God neither. Who has done me the worse injury? Henry gave me the crown. You—all you and my Lord Brill have given me is a living death, and then given my daughter's crown a danger and uncertainty that without you she would not have known! Who has done to Elizabeth and me the worse turn? And in the name of preventing war! You have made war upon *me*! Get out, get out!"

"Your—"

"Get out! I never want to see you again! If I am in hell, let there be one less demon!"

Lambert slipped from her monitor to run down the corridor. Culhane flew from the room; behind him the sound of something heavy struck the door. Culhane slumped against it, his face pasty around his cheek dye. Lambert could almost find it in herself to pity him. Almost.

She said softly, "I told you so."

"She's like a wild thing."

"You knew she could be. It's documented enough, Culhane. I've put a suicide watch on her."

"Yes. Good. I . . . she was like a wild thing."

Lambert peered at him. "You still want her! After that!"

That sobered him; he straightened and looked at her coldly. "She is a holy hostage, Lambert."

"I remember that. Do you?"

"Don't insult me, intern."

He moved angrily away; she caught his sleeve. "Culhane—don't be angry. I only meant that the sixteenth century was so different from our own, but—"

"Do you think I don't know that? I was doing historical research while you were learning to read, Lambert. Don't instruct me."

He stalked off. Lambert bit down hard on her own fury and stared at Anne Boleyn's closed door. No sound came from behind it. To the soundless door she finished her sentence: "—but some traps don't change."

The door didn't answer. Lambert shrugged. It had nothing to do with her. She didn't care what happened to Anne Boleyn, in this century or that other one. Or to Culhane, either. Why should she? There were other men. She was no Henry VIII, to bring down her world for passion. What was the good of being a time researcher if you could not even learn from times past?

She leaned thoughtfully against the door, trying to remember the name of the beautiful boy in her orientation lecture, the one with the violet eyes.

She was still there, thinking, when Toshio Brill called a staff meeting to announce, his voice stiff with anger, that Her Holiness of the Church of the Holy Hostage had filed a motion with the All-World Forum that the Time Research Institute, because of the essentially reverent nature of the time rescue program, be removed from administration by the Forum and placed instead under the direct control of the Church.

She had to think. It was important to think, as she had thought through her denial of Henry's ardor, and her actions when that ardor waned. Thought was all.

She could not return to her London, to Elizabeth. They had told her that. But did she know beyond doubt that it was true?

Anne left her apartments. At the top of the stairs she usually took to the garden, she instead turned and opened another door. It opened easily. She walked along a different corridor. Apparently even now no one was going to stop her.

And if they did, what could they do to her? They did not use the scaffold or the rack; she had determined this from talking to that oaf Culhane and that huge ungainly woman, Lady Mary Lambert. They did not believe in violence, in punishment, in death. (How could you not believe in death? Even they must one day die.) The most they could do to her was shut her up in her rooms, and there the female pope would come to see she was well treated.

Essentially they were powerless.

The corridor was lined with doors, most set with small windows. She peered in: rooms with desks and machines, rooms without desks and machines, rooms with people seated around a table talking, kitchens, still rooms. No one stopped her. At the end of the corridor she came to a room without a window and tried the door. It was locked, but as she stood there, her hand still on the knob, the door opened from within.

"Lady Anne! Oh!"

Could no one in this accursed place get her name right? The woman who stood there was clearly a servant, although she wore the same ugly gray-green tunic as everyone else. Perhaps, like Lady Mary, she was really an apprentice. She was of no interest, but behind her was the last thing Anne expected to see in this place: a child.

She pushed past the servant and entered the room. It was a little boy, his dress strange but clearly a uniform of some sort. He had dark eyes, curling dark hair, a bright smile. How old? Perhaps four. There was an air about him that was unmistakable; she would have wagered her life this child was royal.

"Who are you, little one?"

He answered her with an outpouring of a language she did not know. The servant scrambled to some device on the wall; in a moment Culhane stood before her.

"You said you didn't want to see me, Your Grace. But I was closest to answer Kiti's summons . . ."

Anne looked at him. It seemed to her that she looked clear through him, to all that he was: Desire, and pride of his pitiful strange learning, and smugness of his holy mission that had brought her life to wreck. Hers, and perhaps Elizabeth's as well. She saw Culhane's conviction,

shared by Lord Director Brill and even by such as Lady
Mary, that what they did was right because they did it.
She knew that look well: It had been Cardinal Wolsey's,
Henry's right-hand man and chancellor of England, the
man who had advised Henry to separate Anne from Harry
Percy. And advised Henry against marrying her. Until she,
Anne Boleyn, upstart Tom Boleyn's powerless daughter,
had turned Henry against Wolsey and had the cardinal
brought to trial. She.

In that minute she made her decision.

"I was wrong, Master Culhane. I spoke in anger.
Forgive me." She smiled and held out her hand, and she
had the satisfaction of watching Culhane turn color.

How old was he? Not in his first youth. But neither
had Henry.

He said, "Of course, Your Grace. Kiti said you talked
to the Tsarevitch."

She made a face, still smiling at him. She had often
mocked Henry thus. Even Harry Percy, so long ago, a
lifetime ago . . . No. Two lifetimes ago. "The what?"

"The Tsarevitch." He indicated the child.

Was the dye on his face permanent, or would it wash
off?

She said, not asking, "He is another time hostage.
He, too, in his small person, prevents a war."

Culhane nodded, clearly unsure of her mood. Anne
looked wonderingly at the child, then winningly at Culhane.
"I would have you tell me about him. What language does
he speak? Who is he?"

"Russian. He is—was—the future emperor. He suffers
from a terrible disease: You called it the bleeding sickness.
Because his mother, the empress, was so driven with worry
over him, she fell under the influence of a holy man
who led her to make some disastrous decisions while she was
acting for her husband, the emperor, who was away at war."

Anne said, "And the bad decisions brought about another war."

"They made more bloody than necessary a major
rebellion."

"You prevent rebellions as well as wars? Rebellions against a monarchy?"

"Yes, it—history did not go in the direction of monarchies."

That made little sense. How could history go other than in the direction of those who were divinely anointed, those who held the power? Royalty won. In the end, they always won.

But there could be many casualties before the end.

She said, with that combination of liquid dark gaze and aloof body that had so intrigued Henry—and Norris, and Wyatt, and even presumptuous Smeaton, God damn his soul—"I find I wish to know more about this child and his country's history. Will you tell me?"

"Yes," Culhane said. She caught the nature of his smile: relieved, still uncertain how far he had been forgiven, eager to find out. Familiar, all so familiar.

She was careful not to let her body touch his as they passed through the doorway. But she went first, so he could catch the smell of her hair.

"Master Culhane—you are listed on the demon machine as 'M. Culhane.'"

"The . . . oh, the computer. I didn't know you ever looked at one."

"I did. Through a window."

"It's not a demon, Your Grace."

She let the words pass; what did she care what it was? But his tone told her something. He liked reassuring her. In this world where women did the same work as men and where female bodies were to be seen uncovered in the exercise yard so often that even turning your head to look must become a bore, this oaf nonetheless liked reassuring her.

She said, "What does the 'M' mean?"

He smiled. "Michael. Why?"

As the door closed, the captive royal child began to wail.

Anne smiled, too. "An idle fancy. I wondered if it stood for Mark."

•   •   •

"What argument has the church filed with the All-World Forum?" a senior researcher asked.

Brill said irritably, as it were an answer, "Where is Mahjoub?"

Lambert spoke up promptly. "He is with Helen of Troy, Director, and the doctor. The queen had another seizure last night." Enzio Mahjoub was the unfortunate project head for their last time rescue.

Brill ran his hand over the back of his neck. His skull needed shaving, and his cheek dye was sloppily applied. He said, "Then we will begin without Mahjoub. The argument of Her Holiness is that the primary function of this institute is no longer pure time research but practical application, and that the primary practical application is time rescue. As such, we exist to take hostages, and thus should come under the direct control of the Church of the Holy Hostage. Her secondary argument is that the time hostages are not receiving treatment up to intersystem standards as specified by the All-World Accord of 2154."

Lambert's eyes darted around the room. Cassia Kohambu, project head for the institute's greatest success, sat up straight, looking outraged. "Our hostages are—on what are these charges allegedly based?"

Brill said, "No formal charges as yet. Instead, she has requested an investigation. She claims we have hundreds of potential hostages pinpointed by the Rahvoli equations, and the ones we have chosen do not meet standards for either internal psychic stability or benefit accrued to the hostages themselves, as specified in the All-World Accord. We have chosen to please ourselves, with flagrant disregard for the welfare of the hostages."

"Flagrant disregard!" It was Culhane, already on his feet. Beneath the face dye his cheeks flamed. Lambert eyed him carefully. "How can Her Holiness charge flagrant disregard when without us the Tsarevitch Alexis would have been in constant pain from hemophiliac episodes, Queen Helen would have been abducted and raped, Herr Hitler blown up in an underground bunker, and Queen Anne Boleyn beheaded!"

Brill said bluntly, "Because the Tsarevitch cries constantly for his mother, the Lady Helen is mad, and Mistress Boleyn tells the church she has been made war upon!"

Well, Lambert thought, that still left Herr Hitler. She was just as appalled as anyone at Her Holiness's charges, but Culhane had clearly violated both good manners and good sense. Brill never appreciated being upstaged.

Brill continued, "An investigative committee from the All-World Forum will arrive here next month. It will be small: Delegates Soshiru, Vlakhav, and Tullio. In three days the institute staff will meet again at oh-seven hundred, and by that time I want each project group to have prepared an argument in favor of the hostage you hold. Use the prepermit justifications, including all the mathematical models, but go far beyond that in documenting benefits to the hostages themselves since they arrived here. Are there any questions?"

Only one, Lambert thought. She stood. "Director— were the three delegates who will investigate us chosen by the All-World Forum or requested by Her Holiness? To whom do they already owe their allegiance?"

Brill looked annoyed. He said austerely, "I think we can rely upon the All-World delegates to file a fair report, Intern Lambert," and Lambert lowered her eyes. Evidently she still had much to learn. The question should not have been asked aloud.

Would Mistress Boleyn have known that?

Anne took the hand of the little boy. "Come, Alexis," she said. "We walk now."

The prince looked up at her. How handsome he was, with his thick, curling hair and beautiful eyes almost as dark as her own. If she had given Henry such a child . . . She pushed the thought away. She spoke to Alexis in her rudimentary Russian, without using the translator box hung like a peculiarly ugly pendant around her neck. He answered with a stream of words she couldn't follow, and she waited for the box to translate.

"Why should we walk? I like it here in the garden."

"The garden is very beautiful," Anne agreed. "But I have something interesting to show you."

Alexis trotted beside her obediently then. It had not been hard to win his trust—had no one here ever passed time with children? Wash off the scary cheek paint, play for him songs on the lute—an instrument he could understand, not like the terrifying sounds coming without musicians from yet another box—learn a few phrases of his language. She had always been good at languages.

Anne led the child through the far gate of the walled garden, into the yard. Machinery hummed; naked men and women "exercised" together on the grass. Alexis watched them curiously, but Anne ignored them. Servants. Her long, full skirts, tawny silk, trailed on the ground.

At the far end of the yard she started down the short path to that other gate, the one that ended at nothing.

Queen Isabella of Spain, Henry had told Anne once, had sent an expedition of sailors to circumnavigate the globe. They were supposed to find a faster way to India. They had not done so, but neither had they fallen off the edge of the world, which many had prophesied for them. Anne had not shown much interest in the story, because Isabella hàd, after all, been Katharine's mother. The edge of the world.

The gate ended with a wall of nothing. Nothing to see, or smell, or taste—Anne had tried. To the touch the wall was solid enough, and faintly tingly. A "force field," Culhane said. Out of time as we experience it; out of space. The gate, one of three, led to a place called Upper Slib, in what had once been Egypt.

Anne lifted Alexis. He was heavier than even a month ago; since she had been attending him every day he had begun to eat better, play more, cease crying for his mother. Except at night. "Look, Alexis, a gate. Touch it."

The little boy did, then drew back his hand at the tingling. Anne laughed, and after a moment Alexis laughed, too.

The alarms sounded.

• • •

"Why, Your Grace?" Culhane said. "Why again?"

"I wished to see if the gate was unlocked," Anne said coolly. "We both wished to see." This was a lie. She knew it. Did he? Not yet perhaps.

"I told you, Your Grace, it is not a gate that can be left locked or unlocked, as you understand the terms. It must be activated by the stasis square."

"Then do so; the prince and I wish for an outing."

Culhane's eyes darkened; each time he was in more anguish. And each time, he came running. However much he might wish to avoid her, commanding his henchmen to talk to her most of the time, he must come when there was an emergency because he was her gaoler, appointed by Lord Brill. So much had Anne discovered in a month of careful trials. He said now, "I told you, Your Grace, you can't move past the force field, no more than I could move into your palace at Greenwich. In the time stream beyond that gate—*my* time stream—you don't exist. The second you crossed the force field you'd disintegrate into nothingness."

Nothingness again. To Alexis she said sadly in Russian, "He will never let us out. Never, never."

The child began to cry. Anne held him closer, looking reproachfully at Culhane, who was shifting toward anger. She caught him just before the shift was complete, befuddling him with unlooked-for wistfulness: "It is just that there is so little we can do here, in this time we do not belong. You can understand that, can you not, Master Culhane? Would it not be the same for you, in my court of England?"

Emotions warred on his face. Anne put her free hand gently on his arm. He looked down: the long, slim fingers with their delicate tendons, the tawny silk against his drab uniform. He choked out, "Anything in my power, anything within the rules, Your Grace . . ."

She had not yet gotten him to blurt out "Anne," as he had the day she'd thrown a candlestick after him at the door.

She removed her hand, shifted the sobbing child against her neck, spoke so softly he could not hear her.

He leaned forward, toward her. "What did you say, Your Grace?"

"Would you come again tonight to accompany my lute on your guitar? For Alexis and me?"

Culhane stepped back. His eyes looked trapped.

"Please, Master Culhane?"

Culhane nodded.

Lambert stared at the monitor. It showed the hospital suite, barred windows and low white pallets, where Helen of Troy was housed. The queen sat quiescent on the floor, as she usually did, except for the brief and terrifying periods when she erupted, shrieking and tearing at her incredible hair. There had never been a single coherent word in the eruptions, not since the first moment they had told Helen where she was, and why. Or maybe that fragile mind, already quivering under the strain of her affair with Paris, had snapped too completely even to hear them. Helen, Lambert thought, was no Anne Boleyn.

Anne sat close to the mad Greek queen, her silk skirts overlapping Helen's white tunic, her slender body leaning so far forward that her hair, too, mingled with Helen's, straight black waterfall with masses of springing black curls. Before she could stop herself, Lambert had run her hand over her own shaved head.

What was Mistress Anne trying to say to Helen? The words were too low for the microphones to pick up, and the double curtain of hair hid Anne's lips. Yet Lambert was as certain as death that Anne was talking. And Helen, quiescent—was she nonetheless hearing? What could it matter if she were, words in a tongue that from her point of view would not exist for another two millennia?

Yet the Boleyn woman visited her every day, right after she left the Tsarevitch. How good was Anne, from a time almost as barbaric as Helen's own, at nonverbal coercion of the crazed?

Culhane entered, glanced at the monitor, and winced. Lambert said levelly, "You're a fool, Culhane."

He didn't answer.

"You go whenever she summons. You—"

He suddenly strode across the room, two strides at a time. Grabbing Lambert, he pulled her from her chair and yanked her to her feet. For an astonished moment she thought he was actually going to hit her—researchers *hitting* each other. She tensed to slug him back. But abruptly he dropped her, giving a little shove so that she tumbled gracelessly back into her chair.

"You feel like a fat stone."

Lambert stared at him. Indifferently he activated his own console and began work. Something rose in her, so cold the vertebrae of her back felt fused in ice. Stiffly she rose from the chair, left the room, and walked along the corridor.

A fat stone. Heavy, stolid yet doughy, the flesh yielding like a slug or a maggot. Bulky, without grace, without beauty, almost without individuality, as stones were all alike. A fat stone.

Anne Boleyn was just leaving Helen's chamber. In the corridor, back to the monitor, Lambert faced her. Her voice was low, like a subterranean growl. "Leave him alone."

Anne looked at her coolly. She did not ask whom Lambert meant.

"Don't you know you are watched every minute? That you can't so much as use your chamberpot without being taped? How do you ever expect to get him to your bed? Or to do anything with poor Helen?"

Anne's eyes widened. She said loudly, "Even when I use the chamberpot? Watched? Have I not even the privacy of the beasts in the field?"

Lambert clenched her fists. Anne was acting. Someone had already told her, or she had guessed, about the surveillance. Lambert could see that she was acting—but not *why*. A part of her mind noted coolly that she had never wanted to kill anyone before. So this, finally, was what it felt like, all those emotions she had researched throughout time: fury and jealousy and the desire to destroy. The emotions that started wars.

Anne cried, even more loudly, "I had been better had you never told me!" and rushed toward her own apartments.

Lambert walked slowly back to her work area, a fat stone.

Anne lay on the grass between the two massive power generators. It was a poor excuse for grass; although green enough, it had no smell. No dew formed on it, not even at night. Culhane had explained that it was bred to withstand disease, and that no dew formed because the air had little moisture. He explained, too, that the night was as man-bred as the grass; there was no natural night here. Henry would have been highly interested in such things; she was not. But she had listened carefully, as she listened to everything Michael said.

She lay completely still, waiting. Eventually the head of a researcher thrust around the corner of the towering machinery: a purposeful thrust. "Your Grace? What are you doing?"

Anne did not answer. Getting to her feet, she walked back toward the castle. The place between the generators was no good: The woman had already known where Anne was.

The three delegates from the All-World Forum arrived at the Time Research Institute looking apprehensive. Lambert could understand this; for those who had never left their own time-space continuum, it probably seemed significant to step through a force field to a place that did not exist in any accepted sense of the word. The delegates looked at the ground, and inspected the facilities, and asked the same kinds of questions visitors always asked, before they settled down actually to investigate anything.

They were given an hour's overview of the time rescue program, presented by the director himself. Lambert, who had not helped write this, listened to the careful sentiments about the prevention of war, the nobility of hostages, the deep understanding the Time Research Institute held of the All-World Accord of 2154, the altruistic extension of the Holy Mission of Peace into other time streams. Brill then moved on to discuss the four time hostages, dwelling heavily on the first. In the four years since Herr Hitler had become a hostage, the National Socialist Party had all but collapsed in Germany. President Paul von Hindenburg had died on schedule, and the new moderate chancellors were slowly bringing order to Germany. The economy was still very bad and unrest was widespread, but no one was arresting Jews or Gypsies or homosexuals or Jehovah's Witnesses or . . . Lambert stopped listening. The delegates knew all this. The entire solar system knew all this. Hitler had been a tremendous popular success as a hostage, the reason the Institute had obtained permits for the next three. Herr Hitler was kept in his locked suite, where he spent his time reading power-fantasy novels whose authors had not been born when the bunker under Berlin was detonated.

"Very impressive, Director," Goro Soshiru said. He was small, thin, elongated, a typical free-fall spacer, with a sharp mind and a reputation for incorruptibility. "May we now talk to the hostages, one at a time?"

"Without any monitors. That is our instruction," said Anna Vlakhav. She was the senior member of the investigative team, a sleek, gray-haired Chinese who refused all augments. Her left hand, Lambert noticed, trembled constantly. She belonged to the All-World Forum's Inner Council and had once been a hostage herself for three years.

"Please," Soren Tullio said with a smile. He was young, handsome, very wealthy. Disposable, added by the Forum to fill out the committee, with few recorded views of his own. Insomuch as they existed, however, they were not tinged with any bias toward the Church. Her Holiness had not succeeded in naming the members of the investigative committee—if indeed she had tried.

"Certainly," Brill said. "We've set aside the private conference room for your use. As specified by the Church, it is a sanctuary: There are no monitors of any kind. I would recommend, however, that you allow the body-guard to remain with Herr Hitler, although, of course, you will make up your own minds."

Delegate Vlakhav said, "The bodyguard may stay. Herr Hitler is not our concern here."

Surprise, Lambert thought. Guess who is?

The delegates kept Hitler only ten minutes, the catatonic Helen only three. They said the queen did not speak. They talked to the little Tsarevitch a half hour. They kept Anne Boleyn in the sanctuary/conference room four hours and twenty-three minutes.

She came out calm, blank-faced, and proceeded to her own apartments. Behind her the three delegates were tight-lipped and silent. Anna Vlakhav, the former hostage, said to Toshio Brill, "We have no comment at this time. You will be informed."

Brill's eyes narrowed. He said nothing.

The next day, Director Toshio Brill was subpoenaed to appear before the All-World Forum on the gravest of all charges: mistreating holy hostages detained to keep peace. The tribunal would consist of the full Inner Council of the All-World Forum. Since Director Brill had the right to confront those who accused him, the investigation would be held at the Time Research Institute.

How? Lambert wondered. They would not take her unsupported word. How had the woman done it?

She said to Culhane, "The delegates evidently make no distinction between political hostages on our own world and time hostages snatched from shadowy parallel ones."

"Why should they?" coldly said Culhane. The idealist. And where had it brought him?

Lambert was assigned that night to monitor the tsarevitch, who was asleep in his crib. She sat in her office, her screen turned to Anne Boleyn's chambers, watching her play on the lute and sing softly to herself the songs written for her by Henry VIII when his passion was new and fresh six hundred years before.

• • •

Anne sat embroidering a sleeve cover of cinnamon velvet. In strands of black silk she worked intertwined H and A: Henry and Anne. Let their spying machines make of that what they would.

The door opened and, without permission, Culhane entered. He stood by her chair and looked down into her face. "Why, Anne? Why?"

She laughed. He had finally called her by her Christian name. Now, when it could not possibly matter.

When he saw that she would not answer, his manner grew formal. "A lawyer has been assigned to you. He arrives tomorrow."

A lawyer. Thomas Cromwell had been a lawyer, and Sir Thomas More. Dead, both of them, at Henry's hand. So had Master Culhane told her, and yet he still believed that protection was afforded by the law.

"The lawyer will review all the monitor records. What you did, what you said, every minute."

She smiled at him mockingly. "Why tell me this now?"

"It is your right to know."

"And you are concerned with rights. Almost as much as with death." She knotted the end of her thread and cut it. "How is it that you command so many machines and yet do not command the knowledge that every man must die?"

"We know that," Culhane said evenly. His desire for her had at last been killed; she could feel its absence, like an empty well. The use of her name had been but the last drop of living water. "But we try to prevent death when we can."

"Ah, but you can't. 'Prevent death'—as if it were a fever. You can only postpone it, Master Culhane, and you never even ask if that is worth doing."

"I only came to tell you about the lawyer," Culhane said stiffly. "Good night, Mistress Boleyn."

"Good night, Michael," she said, and started to laugh. She was still laughing when the door closed behind him.

The Hall of Time, designed to hold three hundred, was packed.

Lambert remembered the day she had given the orientation lecture to the history candidates, among them what's-his-name of the violet eyes. Twenty young people huddled together against horror in the middle of squares, virtual and simulated but not really present. Today the squares were absent and the middle of the floor was empty, while all four sides were lined ten-deep with All-World Inner Council members on high polished benches, archbishops and lamas and shamans of the Church of the Holy Hostage, and reporters from every major newsgrid in the solar system. Her Holiness the high priest sat among her followers, pretending she wanted to be inconspicuous. Toshio Brill sat in a chair alone, facing the current premier of the All-World Council, Dagar Krenya of Mars.

Anne Boleyn was led to a seat. She walked with her head high, her long black skirts sweeping the floor.

Lambert remembered that she had worn black to her trial for treason, in 1536.

"This investigation will begin," Premier Krenya said. He wore his hair to his shoulders; fashions must have changed again on Mars. Lambert looked at the shaved heads of her colleagues, at the long, loose black hair of Anne Boleyn. To Culhane, seated beside her, she whispered, "We'll be growing our hair again soon." He looked at her as if she were crazy.

It *was* a kind of crazy, to live everything twice: once in research, once in the flesh. Did it seem so to Anne Boleyn? Lambert knew her frivolity was misplaced, and she thought of the frivolity of Anne in the Tower, awaiting execution: "They will have no trouble finding a name for me. I shall be Queen Anne Lackhead." At the memory, Lambert's hatred burst out fresh. She had the memory, and now Anne never would. But in bequeathing it forward in time to Lambert, the memory had become secondhand. That was Anne Boleyn's real crime, for which she would never be tried: She had made this whole proceeding, so important to Lambert and Brill and Culhane, a mere reenactment. Prescripted. Secondhand. She had robbed them of their own, unused time.

Krenya said, "The charges are as follows: That the

Time Research Institute has mistreated the holy hostage Anne Boleyn, held hostage against war. Three counts of mistreatment are under consideration this day: First, that researchers willfully increased a hostage's mental anguish by dwelling on the pain of those left behind by the hostage's confinement, and on those aspects of confinement that cause emotional unease. Second, that researchers failed to choose a hostage who would truly prevent war. Third, that researchers willfully used a hostage for sexual gratification."

Lambert felt herself go very still. Beside her, Culhane rose to his feet, then sat down again slowly, his face rigid. Was it possible he had . . . No. He had been infatuated, but not to the extent of throwing away his career. He was not Henry, any more than Lambert had been over him.

The spectators buzzed, an uneven sound like malfunctioning equipment. Krenya rapped for order. "Director Brill: How do you answer these charges?"

"False, Premier. Every one."

"Then let us hear the evidence against the Institute."

Anne Boleyn was called. She took the chair in which Brill had been sitting. *"She made an entry as though she were going to a great triumph and sat down with elegance"* . . . But that was the other time, the first time. Lambert groped for Culhane's hand. It felt limp.

"Mistress Boleyn," Krenya said—he had evidently not been told that she insisted on being addressed as a queen, and the omission gave Lambert a mean pleasure—"in what ways was your anguish willfully increased by researchers at this Institute?"

Anne held out her hand. To Lambert's astonishment, her lawyer put into it a lute. At an official All-World Forum investigation—a *lute*. Anne began to play, the tune high and plaintive. Her unbound black hair fell forward; her slight body made a poignant contrast to the torment in the words:

> Defiled is my name, full sore,
> Through cruel spite and false report,
> That I may say forever more,

Farewell to joy, *adieu* comfort.

Oh, death, rock me asleep,
Bring on my quiet rest,
Let pass my very guiltless ghost
Out of my careful breast.

Ring out the doleful knell,
Let its sound my death tell,
For I must die,
There is no remedy,
For now I die!

The last notes faded. Anne looked directly at Krenya. "I wrote that, my Lords, in my other life. Master Culhane of this place played it for me, along with death songs written by my... my brother..."

"Mistress Boleyn..."

"No, I recover myself. George's death tune was hard for me to hear, my Lords. Accused and condemned because of me, who always loved him well."

Krenya said to the lawyer whose staff had spent a month reviewing every moment of monitor records, "Culhane made her listen to these?"

"Yes," the lawyer said. Beside Lambert, Culhane sat unmoving.

"Go on," Krenya said to Anne.

"He told me that I was made to suffer watching the men accused with me die. How I was led to a window overlooking the block, how my brother George kneeled, putting his head on the block, how the ax was raised..." She stopped, shuddering. A murmur ran over the room. It sounded like cruelty, Lambert thought. But whose?

"Worst of all, my Lords," Anne said, "was that I was told I had bastardized my own child. I chose to sign a paper declaring no valid marriage had ever existed because I had been precontracted to Sir Henry Percy, so my daughter Elizabeth was illegitimate and thus barred from her throne. I was taunted with the fact that I had done this, ruining the prospects of my own child. He said it over and over, Master Culhane did..."

Krenya said to the lawyer, "Is this in the visuals?"

"Yes."

Krenya turned back to Anne. "But Mistress Boleyn—these are things that because of your time rescue did *not* happen. Will not happen in your time stream. How can they thus increase your anguish for relatives left behind?"

Anne stood. She took one step forward, then stopped. Her voice was low and passionate. "My good Lord—do you not understand? It is because you took me here that these things did not happen. Left to my own time, I *would have been responsible for them all*. For my brother's death, for the other four brave men, for my daughter's bastardization, for the torment in my own music . . . I have escaped them only because of *you*. To tell me them in such detail, not the mere provision of facts that I myself requested but agonizing detail of mind and heart—is to tell me that I alone, in my own character, am evil, giving pain to those I love most. And that in this time stream you have brought me to, I *did* these things, felt them, feel them still. You have made me guilty of them. My Lord Premier, have you ever been a hostage yourself? Do you know, or can you imagine, the torment that comes from imagining the grief of those who love you? And to know you have caused this grief, not merely loss but death, blood, the pain of disinheritance—that you have caused it, and are now being told of the anguish you cause? Told over and over? In words, in song even—can you imagine what that feels like to one such as I, who cannot return at will and comfort those hurt by my actions?"

The room was silent. Who, Lambert wondered, had told Anne Boleyn that Premier Krenya had once served as a holy hostage?

"Forgive me, my Lords," Anne said dully, "I forget myself."

"Your testimony may take whatever form you choose," Krenya said, and it seemed to Lambert that there were shades and depths in his voice.

The questioning continued. A researcher, said Anne, had taunted her with being spied on even at her chamberpot—Lambert leaned slowly forward—which had made

Anne cry out, "It had been better had you never told me!" Since then, modesty had made her reluctant even to answer nature, "so that there is every hour a most wretched twisting and churning in my bowels."

Asked why she thought the Institute had chosen the wrong hostage, Anne said she had been told so by my Lord Brill. The room exploded into sound, and Krenya rapped for quiet. "That visual now, please." On a square created in the center of the room, the visuals replayed on three sides:

"*My Lord Brill . . . was there no other person you could take but I to prevent this war you say is a hundred years off? This civil war in England?*"

"*The mathematics identified you as the best hostage, Your Grace.*"

"*The best? Best for what, my Lord? If you had taken Henry himself, then he could not have issued the Act of Supremacy. His supposed death would have served the purpose as well as mine.*"

"*Yes. But for Henry the Eighth to disappear from history while his heir is but a month old . . . we did not know if that might not have started a civil war in itself. Between the factions supporting Elizabeth and those for Queen Katharine, who was still alive.*"

"*What did your mathematical learning tell you?*"

"*That it probably would not,*" Brill said.

"*And yet choosing me instead of Henry left him free to behead yet another wife, as you yourself have told me, my cousin Catherine Howard!*"

Brill shifted on his chair. "*That is true, Your Grace.*"

"*Then why not Henry instead of me?*"

"*I'm afraid Your Grace does not have sufficient grasp of the science of probabilities for me to explain, Your Grace.*"

Anne was silent. Finally she said, "*I think that the probability is that you would find it easier to deal with a deposed woman than with Henry of England, whom no man can withstand in either a passion or a temper.*"

Brill did not answer. The visual rolled—ten seconds, fifteen—and he did not answer.

"Mr. Premier," Brill said in a choked voice, "Mr. Premier—"

"You will have time to address these issues soon, Mr. Director," Krenya said. "Mistress Boleyn, this third charge—sexual abuse..."

The term had not existed in the sixteenth century, thought Lambert. Yet Anne understood it. She said, "I was frightened, my Lord, by the strangeness of this place. I was afraid for my life. I didn't know then that a woman may refuse those in power, may—"

"That is why sexual contact with hostages is universally forbidden," Krenya said. "Tell us what you think happened."

Not what *did* happen—what you *think* happened. Lambert took heart.

Anne said, "Master Culhane bade me meet him at a place... it is a small alcove beside a short flight of stairs near the kitchens.... He bade me meet him there at night. Frightened, I went."

"Visuals," Krenya said in a tight voice.

The virtual square reappeared. Anne, in the same white nightdress in which she had been taken hostage, crept from her chamber, along the corridor, her body heat registering in infrared. Down the stairs, around to the kitchens, into the cubbyhole formed by the flight of steps, themselves oddly angled as if they had been added, or altered, after the main structure was built, after the monitoring system installed.... Anne dropped to her knees and crept forward beside the isolated stairs. And disappeared.

Lambert gasped. A time hostage was under constant surveillance. That was a basic condition of their permit; there was no way the Boleyn bitch could escape constant monitoring. But she had.

"Master Culhane was already there," Anne said in a dull voice. "He... he used me ill there."

The room was awash with sound. Krenya said over it, "Mistress Boleyn—there is no visual evidence that Master Culhane was there. He has sworn he was not. Can you offer any proof that he met you there? Anything at all?"

"Yes. Two arguments, my Lord. First: How would I

know there were not spying devices in but this one hidden alcove? I did not design this castle; it is not mine."

Krenya's face showed nothing. "And the other argument?"

"I am pregnant with Master Culhane's child."

Pandemonium. Krenya rapped for order. When it was finally restored, he said to Brill, "Did you know of this?"

"No, I . . . it was a hostage's right by the Accord to refuse intrusive medical treatment. . . . She has been healthy. . . ."

"Mistress Boleyn, you will be examined by a doctor immediately."

She nodded assent. Watching her, Lambert knew it was true. Anne Boleyn was pregnant, and had defeated herself thereby. But she did not know it yet.

Lambert fingered the knowledge, seeing it as a tangible thing, cold as steel.

"How do we know," Krenya said, "that you were not pregnant before you were taken hostage?"

"It was but a month after my daughter Elizabeth's birth, and I had the white-leg. Ask one of your experts if a woman would bed a man then. Ask a woman expert in the women of my time. Ask Lady Mary Lambert."

Heads in the room turned. Ask whom? Krenya said, "Ask whom?" An aide leaned toward him and whispered something. He said, "We will have her put on the witness list."

Anne said, "I carry Michael Culhane's child. I, who could not carry a prince for the king."

Krenya said, almost powerlessly, "That last has nothing to do with this investigation, Mistress Boleyn."

She only looked at him.

They called Brill to testify, and he threw up clouds of probability equations that did nothing to clarify the choice of Anne over Henry as holy hostage. Was the woman right? Had there been a staff meeting to choose between the candidates identified by the Rahvoli applications, and had someone said of two very close candidates, "We should think about the effect on the Institute as well as on history. . . "? Had someone been developing a master theory based on a percentage of women influencing history?

Had someone had an infatuation with the period, and chosen by that what should be altered? Lambert would never know. She was an intern.

Had been an intern.

Culhane was called. He denied seducing Anne Boleyn. The songs on the lute, the descriptions of her brother's death, the bastardization of Elizabeth—all done to convince her that what she had been saved from was worse than where she had been saved to. Culhane felt so much that he made a poor witness, stumbling over his words, protesting too much.

Lambert was called. As neutrally as possible she said, "Yes, Mr. Premier, historical accounts show that Queen Anne was taken with white-leg after Elizabeth's birth. It is a childbed illness. The legs swell up and ache painfully. It can last from a few weeks to months. We don't know how long it lasted—would have lasted—for Mistress Boleyn."

"And would a woman with this disease be inclined to sexual activity?"

"'Inclined'—no."

"Thank you, Researcher Lambert."

Lambert returned to her seat. The committee next looked at visuals, hours of visuals—Culhane, flushed and tender, making a fool of himself with Anne. Anne with the little tsarevitch, an exile trying to comfort a child torn from his mother. Helen of Troy, mad and pathetic. Brill, telling newsgrids around the solar system that the time rescue program, savior of countless lives, was run strictly in conformance with the All-World Accord of 2154. And all the time, through all the visuals, Lambert waited for what was known to everyone in that room except Anne Boleyn: She could not pull off in this century what she might have in Henry's. The paternity of a child could be genotyped in the womb.

Who? Mark Smeaton, after all? Another miscarriage from Henry, precipitately gotten and unrecorded by history? Thomas Wyatt, her most faithful cousin and cavalier?

After the committee had satisfied itself that it had heard enough, everyone but Forum delegates was dismissed.

Anne, Lambert saw, was led away by a doctor. Lambert smiled to herself. It was already over. The Boleyn bitch was defeated.

The All-World Forum investigative committee deliberated for less than a day. Then it issued a statement: The child carried by holy hostage Anne Boleyn had not been sired by Researcher Michael Culhane. Its genotypes matched no one's at the Institute for Time Research. The Institute, however, was guilty of two counts of hostage mistreatment. The Institute's charter as an independent, tax-exempt organization was revoked. Toshio Brill was released from his position, as were Project Head Michael Culhane and intern Mary Lambert. The Institute stewardship was reassigned to the Church of the Holy Hostage under the direct care of Her Holiness the high priest.

Lambert slipped through the outside door to the walled garden. It was dusk. On a seat at the far end a figure sat, skirts spread wide, a darker shape against the dark wall. As Lambert approached, Anne looked up without surprise.

"Culhane's gone. I leave tomorrow. Neither of us will ever work in time research again."

Anne went on gazing upward. Those great dark eyes, that slim neck, so vulnerable. . . . Lambert clasped her hands together hard.

"*Why?*" Lambert said. "Why do it all again? Last time use a king to bring down the power of the church, this time use a church to—before, at least you gained a crown. Why do it here, when you gain nothing?"

"You could have taken Henry. He deserved it; I did not."

"But we didn't take Henry!" Lambert shouted. "So why?"

Anne did not answer. She put out one hand to point behind her. Her sleeve fell away, and Lambert saw clearly the small sixth finger that had marked her as a witch. A tech came running across the half-lit garden. "Researcher Lambert—"

"What is it?"

"They want you inside. Everybody. The queen—the other one, Helen—she's killed herself."

The garden blurred, straightened. "How?"

"Stabbed with a silver sewing scissors hidden in her tunic. It was so quick, the researchers saw it on the monitor but couldn't get there in time."

"Tell them I'm coming."

Lambert looked at Anne Boleyn. "You did this."

Anne laughed. *This lady*, wrote the Tower constable, *hath much joy in death*. Anne said, "Lady Mary—every birth is a sentence of death. Your age has forgotten that."

"Helen didn't need to die yet. And the Time Research Institute didn't need to be dismantled—it *will* be dismantled. Completely. But somewhere, sometime, you will be punished for this. I'll see to that!"

"Punished, Lady Mary? And mayhap beheaded?"

Lambert looked at Anne: the magnificent black eyes, the sixth finger, the slim neck. Lambert said slowly, "You want your own death. As you had it before."

"What else did you leave me?" Anne Boleyn said. "Except the power to live the life that is mine?"

"You will never get it. We don't kill here!"

Anne smiled. "Then how will you 'punish' me—'sometime, somehow'?"

Lambert didn't answer. She walked back across the walled garden, toward the looming walls gray in the dusk, toward the chamber where lay the other dead queen.

TUNDRA MOSS

F. M. BUSBY

Until the Alaska Communication System sent him here to live in a Quonset hut on Amchitka Island, PFC Buster Morgan hadn't known weather that was all sideways. Nor slogged through mud over his ankles while gusting wind dried the surface and blew dust in his eyes.

Tonight it was blowing sixty, maybe sixty-five. Over seventy made it hard to walk; you had to lean into it. And it could shift in no time, slap you flat in the mud.

When God made the Aleutians he couldn't have been sober.

Squinting against cold, slashing rain, Buster kept his dim light on one edge of the boardwalk. Losing track of that edge could put you in deep mud. He had the walks' layout down pat; just by flashlight, he couldn't have told where he was.

The boardwalks, connecting huts throughout the area, were planks laid crosswise over paired phone poles. Long as you didn't get blown off, you could get anywhere you wanted.

Where Buster wanted was the messhall, for a snack before graveyard shift and a sandwich to take along. The cooks were good about leaving stuff out special for the hootowl crew.

He'd had a good day's sleep. At shift's end that morning, after breakfast the sun showed. So he and Scooter in crypto and Silent Yokum the shift chief and teletype operator Chmielevski—Shemmy, who missed women even more than most—hiked down the moss-cushioned ravine to the Bering shore. Under the bluff lay no real beach; jagged rocks cluttered the narrow strip of sand.

This stretch was so bad that the cable ship had landed the Adak and Attu teletype cables at the next cove west, below a bowl-shaped valley. Buster had been there with Sergeant Thorne, to open the steel-covered cable hut and unseal the terminal boxes for the quarterly landline tests. Learning that chore was why Buster was brought along. And to carry some of the bulkier gear.

Today the four walked only to the creek mouth at the near cove. Shemmy said he hoped there'd be a sea otter again, floating with food laid out on its chest, eating each piece from its front paws. Then rolling over and over, fast, to wash off.

Or the time one spooked a seabird bobbing offshore. It shot up from the water, missing by maybe a foot as the bird fled, then lay and rolled. Just for fun, the otter did that.

No such fun this day. Scooter pointed to a whale spout, but nothing else was happening. Buster turned to the dirt bluff. With the wind strong behind him he ran straight at it, then on *up*, sixty degrees or better, the wind holding him.

Almost at the top he remembered *you can't trust the wind!* He doubled forward, grabbed tundra grass and clambered, hands and feet both. He'd barely topped the bluff when it went dead calm.

"It all depends, George," the president said. "If Stalin allows us the refueling bases, we can go ahead with the northern prong of the offensive. If he doesn't . . ." Roosevelt shrugged.

"Yes, sir." General Marshall knew the problem. Doolittle's one-way raid, striking four cities although Tokyo got all the news play, had been worth it in morale. But for a real campaign, men and planes were too valuable to be used only once. And from the Aleutians, bombers couldn't reach Japan and return. Without the use of Siberian bases, no northern offensive could succeed.

FDR hadn't chosen to run the war this way. Along with Churchill, he had wanted a Europe First policy. But a mild stroke kept him from delivering his "day of infamy" speech in person. Public and congressional pressure, then, insisted that the country's major effort go toward avenging Pearl Harbor.

It wasn't only Stalin, Marshall thought, who kept the president worried. MacArthur's obsession with the Philippines made him hard to manage. The man was a strategic genius; his concept of island-hopping, bypassing strongpoints, left major southern Pacific Jap forces dying on the vine. But he *would* keep pushing for a premature Philippine assault. Damn it.

Roosevelt sighed; the general looked at him more closely. Always tired these days; perhaps that was why he catered too much, in the general's opinion, to "Uncle Joe."

Marshall didn't trust the Old Bolshevik. But for an effective Aleutian thrust, Stalin's cooperation was vital.

From the headland, the hootowl shift quartet trudged back up toward the ACS area, staying clear of the central sag in the ravine's deep moss cover. Thin spots weren't always obvious; you could fall through. Up nearer the ridge, Scooter led the way with bouncing steps off springy humps of moss. "Beautyrest..."

Coming slantwise against the wind, the Navy PBY was over them before they heard it. Barely a hundred feet up, the big flying boat was drifting sideways more than not. Eerie.

Wind or no wind, the four reached the messhall in time to have lunch, then went to their Quonset—filled with ten men's clutter, and like every hut in the area, smelling of stove oil. Graveyard did take it out of you; Buster folded early and didn't get up for dinner. What woke him, not long before time to relieve Thorne on duty, was somebody screeching on the radio.

It was the Late Mystery. Buster remembered one about an armed maniac stalking the island with a killer wolf. Late at night Weevil Hawkins had *believed* it, holed up in the messhall with his carbine, and damn near shot Buster Morgan at the door.

Tonight's sounded good, but Buster had to go. He pulled up his parka hood, went through the little storm porch and stepped outside. To struggle a hundred yards through sideways rain.

On the messhall porch he stomped mud off his feet. Here on The Rock all windows were covered; there'd been no Jap planes over for several months, but still you kept blackout. So until he opened the inner door, Buster couldn't know who was inside.

Nobody was. Weevil had been rotated Stateside, anyway.

If you want to stay out of drafts, stay out of Russia.

Sure thing, thought M/Sgt. Hardeman, but that's where they sent me. The embassy building in Moskva was old; heating wasn't its strong point. Especially in this anteroom, where he sat with half a pot of chilling coffee, waiting for word from Ambassador Harriman and wishing he'd never heard of the U.S. Diplomatic Corps.

The trouble was, they heard of him first. So here he sat, he and his crypto clearance, in Moskva. Drinking vodka off-duty instead of bourbon, and each day sweating against a Dear John letter from Eloise, whom he hadn't married for her patience.

The coffee wasn't fit to drink. Hardeman propped his chin on one hand and closed his eyes. The ambassador's secretary didn't catch him asleep, though; the man's shoes squeaked.

"Here." The paper Hardeman was handed carried several lines of number groups. "Send this to CINCCOM, for the president, via SHAEF for Eisenhower's records. On each leg, return copy will be required for validation. Repeat transmission until good copy is confirmed; sender will then authorize further relay."

"Yes, sir." The sheet was marked Operational Priority and Send In Clear. Looking at the string of six-digit numbers, Hardeman grinned. Book code: each number group denoted a page, line, and word within the line. Since no one but originator and recipient knew *which* book, anyone else would play bloody hell trying to decode the apparently simple cipher. Including Ike.

Well, that was Franklin Roosevelt for you.

Hardeman took the message down to Comcenter. This time of night the radioteletype to Britain was fairly solid. But it still took one rerun to confirm correct copy.

Being alone in the messhall always felt strange. Buster fast-fried a slice of meat and made a couple of potato patties; while they sizzled he fixed a sandwich for later. After eating and washing up, he filled his canteen. This building, with a shower and washroom on the far end, had the only running water in the ACS area. It came from a tundra lake; one washing turned white cloth khaki. And to keep the big water bugs out of your mouth, you drank from the canteen with your teeth closed.

Time to go.

Lieutenant Akaji disliked having to reprove subordinates; he wished, heartily, that his small raiding force did not include Private Miyake.

In the matter of obeying orders, Miyake simply did not try. Back from reconnaissance with Corporal Yamagiwa and Privates Suyama and Arimura, Akaji found the impromptu shelter warm, its driftwood fire banked. Perhaps two hours, it had burned.

Which meant that Miyake had lit fire as soon as he was left alone. Even though, in these latitudes at this time of year, for hours enough twilight lingered to show smoke against sky. Let alone the smell of it, should Americans walk nearby, above.

The man had no excuse. Here at the bottom of the ravine, roofed by decades' growth of tundra moss, no wind came; padded clothing gave warmth enough. But Miyake was an obdurate man.

He had almost cost their lives, let alone the mission, even before they reached Amchitka's shore. Perhaps halfway between the submarine and the looming headland, the inflated raft pitching in harsh swells, Miyake inexplicably stood. In saving him from immersion they came close to capsizing.

And as all had been told, life expectancy in Arctic waters was less than twenty minutes, padding or no.

Akaji felt his spirit sink. A sacrifice mission should be a glorious venture. If only this man were assigned elsewhere! Or, Akaji's demon whispered, he *had* fallen into the sea...

Miyake was of some use; now he heated rations and sake. As they ate, Akaji reviewed matters. It was their second night ashore. During the first they collapsed and hid the liferaft, then sought shelter. Tundra moss bridges clefts and smooths contours; it was Corporal Yamagiwa who espied, where the headland's bluff met the ravine's mouth, an overhang of moss which could be undercut to provide entrance.

Through the underlying tangle of dead moss and roots, with much effort the five made a tunnel up along the ravine's bottom, nearly forty yards to a place where the banks widened. Here they chopped and pushed and flattened vegetable debris to open a cave: barely five feet wide and four high, but nearly eight lengthwise. And with good, fresh water running down the center.

Overhead lay several feet of solid, untouched growth. Except for the one ragged hole, not wholly clear but thinned enough to allow the escape of smoke.

They lay less than a half mile from the nearest American huts. But if caution were adhered to—if Miyake would heed restraint—the enemy might as well seek them on Paramushiru!

And tonight's reconnaissance had found for Akaji the Americans' communication lifeline. He did not know why it must be interrupted at this time, only that he had been ordered to do so.

How to disable it was the question. Bullets had not worked. The exposed part of the steel box, roughly the size of a small trunk, was possibly the lesser portion; pushing and prying could not budge it. And when, deeming it safe, Akaji directed Yamagiwa to fire at the box's padlock, the rifle bullets ricocheted without effect.

In the area between box and shoreline, where water cut a gash down the bank, it was young, eager Suyama who discovered several feet of exposed cable. Handlamp taped to emit only a slim pencil of light, Lieutenant Akaji inspected the find.

A large, heavy cable: its outer sheath, under tattered wrappings of tarred jute, consisted of almost a dozen spiraled steel finger-thick wires. Like the padlock, it withstood rifle fire. The final attempt splattered lead against Arimura's helmet; an inch lower would have taken his eye.

Sipping the last of his cooling sake, Akaji sighed. Next and soon he would lead two of his men to the rolling tundra above and reconnoiter the nearby American unit. To find targets for ingenious sabotage, the more effective if unsuspected as such.

He would take Suyama and Arimura, leaving Corporal Yamagiwa to ensure Miyake's behavior.

From the messhall it was maybe eighty yards to Operations. Two huts sat side by side, dug into the hillside at the rear. Entering the longer one Buster went past the locked crypto room and the desks—captain's, chief op's, and unit clerk's—to the teletype shop, where he hung up his parka.

The shorter Quonset alongside was all Operations; at its rear a covered hallway connected the two.

The hallway leaked some.

Entering Ops from the back, Buster saw the Adak and Attu cable gear to his right, across from the teletype machines for Post HQ, Navy, Air Command and Navy Weather, all idle this time of night. In between sat the cable amplifiers and power bays, the trick chief's desk, and the oil stove. The Quonset's walls, brown fiberboard, showed drab under a single row of fluorescents.

Buster glowered at the stove. It sat where you couldn't run an oil line; fuel had to be carried by hand. And Smitty, the chief op, had laid it on his maintenance crew to keep it filled.

It was a chore Buster didn't appreciate: running oil from a stand-mounted barrel into the can, wind blowing much of it onto his pants. One night he'd stood, looking across to the blinking red lights of Baker Strip, the bomber runway, and caught himself thinking it was a *town* over there. Really crazy . . .

He found Thorne feeding reversals into the Adak cable apex and adjusting the artificial line's external resistor boxes to reduce the imbalance kicks, drawn in ink on moving paper ribbon.

Two-way cable circuits used a double Wheatstone bridge; each end sent into an apex and received *across* it, balancing the cable against a heat-stabilized artificial line. To read the tiny incoming pips through the much greater sent signal, that balance was crucial. The slightest change of sea temperature, or a chip of oxidation growing in a soldered splice, could throw it off.

This part, Buster knew. The rest, signal shaping and all, building the received twitches into enough of a square wave to fool a teletype machine: those things left him stumped.

Luckily for him, once the shaping was set up it stayed put.

The Aleutian cable ran eight such legs end to end: Whittier–Kodiak–Cold Bay–Dutch Harbor–Umnak–Atka–Adak–Amchitka–Attu. Then a simpler rig on to Shemya. Whittier connected to Alaska Command near Anchorage via Alaska Railroad lines and ACS local loops.

There was no way *anyone* could tap submarine cable.

With Adak down, perforated tape from Attu was piling up; tape *to* Attu, it looked like, had all gone out. Nothing clacked but the Attu reperf and monitor printer; Silent Yokum and Frank Chmielevski, tonight's operators, sat with coffee, nodded hello, and looked bored. Scooter must be in the crypto room, working. Or maybe taking a nap. Morgan grinned; security had its uses.

He walked over to Thorne, who had been to cable school and knew his business; the man looked around, saying, "I've got most of it; you should have it up to traffic pretty soon."

"Sure. Have yourself some sack time." Thorne left. Buster checked the resistor dial readings against the last log entry. Thorne had changed the head-end balance appreciably and was working down the cable. Careful not to throw a big surge and maybe break the thin glass siphon pen, Buster fiddled.

Thorne was right; in a few minutes Buster flattened the two remaining peaks to mere wiggles. He ran the reversals up to signal speed. No bad spots, so he patched the circuit back to normal and sent QUICK BROWN FOX tape. From Adak, Buster's old drinking buddy Slim Barger responded with his own test tape. Solid both ways; they put the circuit back to message traffic.

Looking at his useless info copy of Harriman's latest to Marshall, Dwight Eisenhower frowned. Book code again. Maybe what Moscow said to Washington *was* none of his business—and compared to Marshall and MacArthur, certainly tainly he was the new boy in school. Still, when Averill talked over his head to George so obviously, he felt slighted.

Eisenhower shrugged. Sooner or later, Mac would take the Japs' measure. Then the European Theater of Operations would get the attention it merited. And he with it.

With Adak restored, Buster went across to the shop. He was adjusting relays when Silent Yokum the trick chief came to tell him the oil had run out. Always on graveyard! Buster shucked on his parka, picked up the five-gallon can and went outside.

The wind was beating seventy; Morgan walked crouched. Up the slope to the oil dump and over to the rack. He held the can to the tap and pushed the handle, but no oil came.

The damn barrel was empty!

He rolled it off and went for a full one. But by himself he couldn't get one free without bringing down the whole stack.

He went back inside. Silent Yokum being a sergeant and all, Buster braced Chmielevski. "Shemmy? I need some help."

Shemmy wasn't Frank's pet nickname, but it beat some he'd had. You take what comes. He got his parka and followed Morgan.

It seemed to him he was running in bad luck. Like going to shower with the shampoo his folks sent him and pouring almost half before he smelled it for bourbon. Which ran fifty bucks a fifth off the merchant marine, a month's pay for a buck private.

Or the day he put gas in the stove instead of oil, and lucky somebody smelled the difference before he lit it. That's when Smitty put the job onto Maintenance.

Isolated duty wasn't good for Frank. Except for the nurses and Red Cross girls you saw sitting in the officers' section at Post Theater, there weren't any *women*. Not any. None.

He wasn't a gash hound like the guys said. He *liked* girls, and they could tell he did; that's why he'd always scored so steady. He really missed it; the Rock was driving him bughouse.

One of these days, though, he'd get lucky. . . .

After he helped get the barrel loose, he waited while Morgan ran oil. Then they went back in and got the stove filled.

Lying in mud under a truck, Lieutenant Akaji watched the Americans wrestle an oil drum onto a rack, fill a container, and return to their pair of hemicylindrical huts.

Leading the way, Akaji had brought Suyama and Arimura up to this area of scattered huts. Most would be sleeping quarters. One leaked smells of food; at its farther end a pipe led down to a fairsized tundra lake. Wading out to plug the pipe's open end with moss, Arimura returned giggling. No great act of sabotage—yet in their peril here, good for the men's morale.

So vulnerable, these Americans! Given a platoon, automatic weapons, and explosives other than mere grenades, Akaji could destroy this unit, matériel *and* personnel, and be quickly safe to ground. But with only four enlisted men, it could not be.

Reconnaissance photos marked this area as the communications unit Akaji must cripple. But how? Run from hut to hut, hurling grenades and leaving havoc? The comm center itself, almost certainly the paired huts the soldiers had reentered? But known damage was the most easily countered, and soonest repaired.

No. The submarine cable, the circuit that could not be intercepted, was the vital link. It must be broken. And in a fashion as near to untraceable as could be managed.

So that the Americans would not know where to begin.

When the code clerk Denison brought Ambassador Harriman's message, George Marshall sighed with relief. Roosevelt waved for him to do the decoding. "Tell me the gist."

"Yes, sir." It didn't take long. "Averill reports that our use of Siberian bases for refueling is approved, effective now."

FDR's palm smote the desk. "Good work! Denison, code my order of this date to Alaska Command: General Buckner at Fort Richardson. Via the secure submarine cable circuit from Anchorage, he is to alert our bomber groups on Amchitka and Shemya to commence Operation Downdraft in—let me see—ten days."

Alarmed, Marshall cleared his throat. "That's awfully short notice, sir, for the necessary coordination with Mac."

But Roosevelt had the bit in his teeth. "They can do it. And so can we. By Jove, we'll have to."

Crossing the rocky stretch below the cable hut, Lobo Tex Riggins felt goosebumps. Daylight was only a promise, but in the wet muck, below the wash gully where several feet of cable lay uncovered, he spotted tracks. And not of familiar design.

Well, this was the kind of thing he was paid to do, and two years in the Alaska Scouts had made him good at it. They called him Lobo for the way he made time over rough terrain, and how he worked when he got there. Like those hideout Japs on Attu.

The sky was lightening; on the cable armor wires he saw shiny marks. "Bullets. Softnose." U.S. troops didn't carry softnose much. And the shoe tracks—he looked some more—still weren't quite right.

None of this said it *couldn't* be some dogface with wore-out shoes and a grudge. But didn't say it was, either.

Lobo went up to the cable hut. Not your usual shed, like the big one at Attu with the stove in it. Here, some fruitcake put a grenade to one of those, so the Signal Corps set up a steel box—torchwelded together on the spot—half-buried, with rocks in the bottom to hold it down. And except for the washout he'd just been looking at, cables and landlines were buried, too.

He peered closer. On the hut's padlock, more lead smears. He frowned. Could be some dumb GI kid, shooting things up just 'cause they were handy; there's always a lot of that.

If it wasn't . . . Lobo shrugged. Heading east, the tracked mud petered out among the rocks. So follow the shoreline around to the docks at Constantine Harbor. Either he'd catch up to somebody or he wouldn't.

He'd report this, do a stakeout. If there was real trouble, another Scout or two could help. Malemute Red was tied up on Norton Sound, but Afognak Pete was savvy. If Pete was out of the stockade yet. For now, Lobo had four-five miles to go before he got back to HQ, for his first hot breakfast in over a week.

Major Spencer had his ass in a sling. CINCCOM's message, off the Ketchikan cable, was the hottest item to hit Fort Rich since the go-ahead to take Attu. But General Simon Bolivar Buckner was up at Fairbanks on a "morale inspection." And the Alaska RR lines were out: a landslide near McKinley Park.

These orders detailed coordination with MacArthur's CINPAC; if they didn't arrive on time, the whole operation was cold soup. The general was needed here at Anchorage sooner than now—and there was no secure way to tell him so.

Spencer considered forwarding the message in Buckner's name. But if he guessed wrong, he'd always be a major. Or maybe less.

Pooped, Buster was glad when his relief showed up. He signed off the log and was on his way out when Captain Rodgers, the Officer-in-Charge, sent him to pick up a message from Post HQ. Couldn't wait a half hour for the circuit to open. . . .

Outside in unexpected sunshine he took a shortcut around and up the hillside, above the lake where ACS got its brown water. At HQ he ran into a lot of routine GI crap he wasn't used to. Working around the clock, ACS didn't have time for that stuff.

Back to Ops he dropped the sealed envelope into the slot alongside the crypto room door. Too tired to bother with breakfast, he went straight to his hut—watching an approaching storm wall cut visibility off solid, while to his other side, forty miles away gleamed the snowy peaks of Semisopochnoi.

If you don't like the weather, wait a minute.

He ate half a Snickers bar, went to bed, and was halfway to sleep when Scooter came in. "Hey, you know the rumor, there's an Alaska Scout on duty here, patrolling the beaches? That message you brought was the post commander asking for two more."

With coded stuff, Scooter was sometimes like a little kid.

General Buckner returned to Fort Richardson a day early; Major Spencer met him in a jeep. Thirty minutes later Buckner's directive was on its encrypted way. To ACS and to Whittier, then through Arctic depths to Aleutian HQ at Adak.

As the teletype clattered, Buckner stood over its operator. "I like that cable. The one circuit they can't intercept."

Sadly, Akaji considered the exquisite silver penknife, a parting gift from his wife Mayu. Of items available, only its blade was both thin and sturdy enough for the job at hand.

In dim slit of light from his handlamp, Akaji set the tip between two thick steel wires. With Arimura's handaxe he tapped until the blade penetrated. In fear it might miss the central conductor, Akaji held breath.

But his next blow brought a thin blue flash; jolting shock threw him headlong in the mud. Slowly he rose, unable to keep his voice steady as he said, "I believe that is far enough."

Now he struck sidewise; the impaling blade snapped. Akaji hammered its broken end farther, drawing momentary sparks as he drove it flush. Finding his ruined penknife was not easy; for long moments he held it, thinking of Mayu who had given it. Then abruptly, swallowing regret, he threw it high and far, to make a tiny splash in Arctic seas.

"Come, Arimura. It is time we foxes scurried to cover."

With the detachment's field phones all on one big party line, the one over Shemmy's bunk rang so much that Buster was used to it. Not until Scooter leaned over and shook him did he come awake. "Adak's gone *all* to hell. Thorne says grab a bite and get your ass in gear."

Sitting up, fumbling his clothes together, Buster got out of the sack. Thorne wasn't a man to panic; if he said jump he had a reason. "Okay, Scoot; tell him I'm on the way."

Outside, rain came in spurts, like somebody throwing it a bucket at a time. The wind was having itself a clambake. Up the path, the outhouse had tipped over again, half its guy wires torn loose. So far it hadn't ever got away completely.

Right now he'd use the Officers'. It was closer, anyway.

Lobo Tex meant to get on stakeout earlier, but he loved poker and purely hated to leave a winning streak. Close on midnight, he neared the cable landing. Wind was gusting loud, but he quiet-walked anyway because he was in the habit.

Off toward the beach he heard something, a hammering noise, so he took out his handpiece and moved quicker. Nobody there, though; he wiped the gun dry as he could and reholstered it.

Also he had, shoulder-slung, a cased Springfield ought-three. But that one was for daylight and distance.

At the steel hut and where the cable lay unburied, he found no kind of trail to chase. Last time he'd been here, though, tracks had headed east. Lobo followed the shoreline that way.

In the messhall Buster fried and ate some eggs, filled his canteen, and fixed two sandwiches to go. Then, outside and heading for Operations, again he bucked the hellacious wind.

Coming into Ops he found Captain Rodgers chewing on Thorne. "That garbled radio message is clear on one point: we're to expect an Urgent by cable. An *Urgent*. And you say the Adak cable's out. Nothing more. Sergeant, what the hell is wrong?"

When Thorne's dark skin went pale he looked almost greenish. He said, "I don't know yet, sir. I need some time to find out."

Shaking his head, the OIC stalked off toward the other hut. Buster came up. "Thorne? What's it doing?"

"Balance went to hell; trying to check it I broke the pen."

Buster hadn't ever seen Thorne this way. He said, "Go

eat something, lemme take a look." Giving the sarge orders? Well, maybe it needed doing, just now. . . .

Thorne parka'd up and went out. Buster took a deep breath. The captain hadn't given Thorne any chance to think. He didn't believe PFCs *could* think, so likely he'd leave Buster alone.

To break a pen, either Thorne screwed up or the cable itself was shot. Thorne didn't screw up much. Buster rigged the test set. Conductor Resistance, normally about twelve hundred, was down around forty. Pretty much like the quarterly test, with the landline shorted at the cable hut.

This one he couldn't blame on Adak.

"What d'you mean, the message isn't going out?" Standing over Slim Barger, Major Poulsen glowered. "The tape's moving, isn't it? And the meters—" he gestured toward the cable amplifier cabinet "—they're all wiggling the way they always do. So how do you know. . . ?"

The trouble with Adak duty in the ACS was having the Area Commander on your back. Slim stayed patient. "Sir, you see that needle *there*?" Signal input, sitting solid on zero. "Amchitka isn't giving us any signal. None at all, sir."

"That doesn't prove they're not reading ours! It could be any simple trouble. Just because—"

"One of two things, sir. Power failure there, or the cable's out. Either way, they're not receiving. And power— it shouldn't take this long to come up on emergency."

"But if it's the cable . . ." Poulsen looked worried.

"Our balance is good; any trouble, it's their end."

The major's evident relief didn't last long. "But we've *got* to get that message through. The general said, expressly . . ."

Breaking off, Poulsen scowled. "How's the radioteletype?"

"Running test both ways, sir. Garbling badly here. That on-off RTTY signal isn't much good when the aurora kicks up."

"Can't use it for an Urgent, anyway." The major cracked his knuckles. "What else could we try?"

Major Knowitall was *asking*? Barger thought. Adak and Amchitka both had frequency-shift RTTY to Seattle. "If you had authorization, sir . . ." And Slim told him the rest of it.

Poulsen nodded. "I'll tell the general. And if *he* suggests it . . ." Then, "Stay on that cable problem. And keep me advised."

He stalked out, leaving Barger to face a dead receive meter. The test set told him that the only voltage on the cable was earth currents, and that the Amchitka end had to be shorted.

Back to sending test tape. Into an unmistakably dead end.

Captain Rodgers glared. "You're sure the line's shorted?"

Buster Morgan nodded. "Yes, Captain. The reading's solid."

Hands clenched behind his back, Rodgers took two paces away, pivoted, and returned. "Where's Thorne?"

"The messhall, sir. Shall I go get him?"

"No. Start putting gear together. Anything you can use to repair a damaged cable."

"I'm not a splicer, sir." And neither was Thorne. The nearest one Buster knew of was Absher, if he was still on Adak.

"You can cut and patch, rig something to get the signal through. Make sure you have—" he spread his arms "—hell, you know what you need. Get to it."

Starting to walk away, he turned again. "When Thorne gets back, I'll run you two down in the jeep."

"Down?" Down that steep tundra valley? "I don't think—"

"*I'll* do the thinking. And I'll set you down there in one piece. Though God knows how we'll get the jeep back up."

"The message reached Adak, Mr. President," said George Marshall. "Buckner confirms that much. But no farther."

"Does he know what the difficulty is?"

"The secure circuit. Adak has no contact with Amchitka."

Roosevelt grimaced. "And Mac's primed to move on schedule. Fully depending on the Aleutian thrust to split enemy response."

Marshall never said I told you so; now was no time to begin. "General MacArthur's risks are not much worsened, sir. It is our plan of surprise, our one-two punch, that I hate to lose."

"For want of a nail..."

"Or likely a tenpenny fuse on a Godforsaken wind-blown rock."

But Roosevelt was off on a new scent. "What of Eisenhower's proposal to expand daylight bombing? In particular, certain installations on the Baltic coast, almost due north of Berlin."

Marshall racked his brain. "That would be Peenemünde." Silver leaves to four stars, in as many years, was quite a rise. Sometimes, Marshall thought, Ike got too big for his breeches.

Rounding the headland, Lobo Tex scanned the creek-mouth area. Not much to see, but it felt wrong. The kind of tingle he'd had once when a rattler didn't rattle but he heard it anyway.

The creek was easy wading, but past it he lost the feeling. Something behind, he should have stopped to look at.

The creek, yeah. Lobo dipped fingers into icy water, brought them up to smell. He couldn't put a name to it, but something wasn't what you'd expect. And the way the terrain lay, no GI area drained into here.

It took him a time longer to find the hole in the bank.

Buster hadn't pegged the captain for a cowboy driver, but once the jeep turned downhill, Katy bar the door. The topheavy vehicle slithered, speeding up no matter what Rodgers did. The slitted-down headlights showed only moss that all looked alike.

Flat and grating, Rodgers cursed. Brakes sent the jeep skidding wild; the man had to gun hard to straighten out.

Buster hung on with all four paws; beside him, Thorne had better be doing the same. At this rate they'd all wind up in the drink! But Rodgers swung the jeep at an angle, then the other way, half-broadside to get more resistance, like skiers in the newsreels. Tricky as hell; jeeps tip over too easy. If this thing rolled, the homemade cab would crunch like an egg crate.

Now the captain yelled: a highpitched ki-yippy like a rodeo hand. Why, the crazy bastard was *enjoying* this!

A trick of the lights showed the final dropoff all too near. Rodgers cramped the wheel and slammed brakes; the jeep spun end for end and Rodgers floored it. In four-wheel drive the cleated tires threw moss like a cat in a sandbox.

Less than five yards from the edge, they stopped.

"All right, men. Hand me some of that gear. Let's get out there and fix the sonofabitch."

Great—if they had any idea where the trouble was. . . .

The cable hut sat unharmed except for bullet smears; the fault had to be down at the beach. Glad that the dark hid how scared he felt, Buster picked his way down the bank.

Akaji brooded. The Americans' secure circuit was disabled, yes, but repairable. If within three days he could render it useless, he could signal the submarine for rendezvous.

Such thoughts led nowhere; he had not the means. He and the others must remain here, inflicting such damage as might be devised, so long as their lives endured.

They would move westward, to unpopulated, less perilous terrain. And there create a more secure shelter from which to mount further incursions.

They would, at times, need to raid the Americans' food supplies. That need would serve as continued tactical training.

Preparing for sleep, Akaji was pleased; he had achieved greater serenity than his predicament could possibly warrant.

Lobo Tex paused. The mouth of the hole showed some spade marks but didn't tell him whose. Last time out he'd noticed a moonshine still was gone from East Cape; could've moved to here. So Lobo Tex had in mind, this didn't *have* to be Japs.

Most likely was, though; he didn't smell any mash. So did he feel like crawling up that hole all by himself?

Not right away. Anybody in there, be most apt to come out at night. At the cable landing he'd heard noises, but not since; if they'd holed up again, his best bet was wait here and watch.

He checked inside, a few feet; didn't find any traps or alarms, and backed out again. To set up one of his own. Nothing fancy, just a half dozen rocks placed where somebody coming out would knock a few off to hit the boulder straight below.

Loud enough to wake him up. Locating himself for a good clear shot at somebody outlined against nothing but sky, Lobo Tex crawled into his fartsack to catch some sleep.

Thorne spotted the uncovered stretch of cable, but it was the captain who found the little shard of metal wedged between two armor wires. "Somebody spiked this thing, men. Now then—how do we fix it?" As rain came in bursts.

Thorne had worked with a splicer, rigging the new cable hut. Now the sergeant said, "We'll have to cut some armor wires—four at least. Pull that thing out, melt rubber to seal the Anhydrex insulation. If the conductor's damaged..."

He took a deep, shuddering breath. "We should make a full splice, but even if I knew how, there isn't time." He spread his hands. "Over the Anhydrex is steel tape. All right, I cut so it overlaps when I lay it back, and lash on extra armor. But—"

"You'll do fine," said Rodgers. "How do we cut the armor?"

The hacksaw blade wore out fast; they had only one spare. Rodgers sent Morgan for some more, and for a head start ran the jeep as far as it would go, up the least steep part of the slope.

When it stalled, Buster jumped out. "Thanks!" He saw the jeep was making it back down okay, so he leaned into the spraying wind and began to climb. Once up on the level he just kept trudging, until finally he reached the Detachment area.

He was hungry again, but that would have to wait.

Chmielevski always knew he'd get lucky sometime, and his night off, tonight, sure looked like it. Red Cross girls *never* had to do with anyone but officers. Yet after the movie he'd been trudging back up from Post Theater to the Detachment area, and this redhead girl Clarice Dawson, driving a jeep all alone, gave him a lift. And then a drink of whiskey. Back home it would have been pretty bad whiskey, but here on The Rock there wasn't any such thing.

They'd stopped near the edge of the ACS area, off the road but not out of sight. With the engine on idle: low battery.

They got to talking, like old times back home. Shemmy just had to try and kiss her, he couldn't help it, and now here they went hand in hand down the tundra slope. Him carrying her sleeping bag. Well, he knew he had to get lucky *some*time. . . .

Silent Yokum and Scooter were in Ops. Buster said, "Somebody spiked the cable; I need saw blades and some stuff."

In the shop he found the blades, and wire to lash across the armor break. To avoid more talk, he went straight out the front.

His shortest route lay across the area, out the headland. He was past the Motor Pool when off the road a little he saw a jeep, motor idling. Then down the ravine he heard rifle fire.

Somebody yelled, ". . . *shot* me, dammit!"

And a woman screamed.

Awake in seconds, Lobo Tex got himself out of the bag and set to placing those sounds. Upslope, and not all that far. But part came from the *hole;* somebody in there was shooting out.

Which way to do this? Whoever was being shot at was topside, so going up the tunnel might surprise somebody.

Lobo uncased both guns and slung the rifle so he could get at it. Moving his alarm rocks aside he slid into the hole.

Scratchy, compacted moss roots dug him from both sides. Jap tunnel, all right. GIs, they'd make it bigger.

The confined blast of gunfire jarred Akaji awake, dazed. Fumbling brought his light to hand; it showed Miyake crouched awkwardly, aiming his rifle up the smokehole "Hold!" But Miyake, deliberately ignoring him, fired again.

Akaji repeated the command; Miyake did not lower his weapon. Dimly Akaji discerned the other three, frozen in lack of purpose.

The mission—! For *any* chance of success—Akaji drew his pistol. With little regret, he shot Miyake through the head.

"Gather your equipment," he said. "We must leave here."

Amid sudden silence, he heard rustlings from the tunnel.

• • •

Buster found himself in the jeep, heading down to where the noise was. This wasn't steep like the next valley, but squinting at patches of dim light he felt the jeep teeter and knew he was too near the treacherous center; he pulled to the right a little.

Ahead he saw a man on the ground and a woman trying to pull him up. Double-clutching the jeep down to compound, Buster got it stopped. Another shot sounded; he jumped and hit the dirt.

The man yelled, "They're down the hole! I stepped in it and fell; sonofabitch shot me from below." Buster knew the voice: Shemmy's. But who was the woman?

And what to *do*? Wait a minute—the gas can, flat against the jeep's side. He tore at its web belting; the can came free. He scrambled past the two and slid to rest alongside the hole.

"What—?" No time to answer. Buster took the cap off and tipped the can flat; gas poured out, down the hole. Then with a convulsive shove he sent the can after its contents.

He was reaching for a matchbook to light and throw down, when the explosion pelted him with moss.

Akaji smelled the gasoline; when he felt it spatter on him, he realized the source. "Leave everything! We must escape!"

To one side he glimpsed movement; Yamagiwa's rifle lifted.

But he was the *dependable* one! "No!"

Too late. Yamagiwa fired. The flash created inferno.

A few yards into the tunnel, Lobo Tex had no warning; the *Whoom!*, the heat and impact, stunned and half-strangled him. All he could do—fighting not to pass out *or* breathe more of the searing fumes—was wriggle backward to open air.

Even before he could quit coughing he had his Springfield ready. Any half-fried Jap did come out, wouldn't get far.

From the hole, flame popped and whistled.

"Godamighty!" Shemmy rose to one knee. "Clarice honey, I never would've thought..." Then, "Hey Buster! Wha'd you do?"

The woman's voice came calmer than she had any right to. "You have to help me. His leg—"

Buster took Shemmy's other arm, which held some bulky object. "Come on; maybe I can get the jeep up out of here."

Once they were in, Buster turned uphill and gunned ahead. When the engine began to lug he slacked off, letting the slope eat momentum. And reached the edge of the road. Barely.

"*Left* now." Her tone made it an order, but Buster stopped. Voice higher, she said, "The hospital, for heaven's sake!"

"Hospital?" Shemmy sounded plaintive. "What's the rush?"

Buster asked, "How much you bleeding?"

"Not a lot. Hey, I can even walk."

Buster nodded. "All right. Ma'am, it's only about fifty yards to Ops. Call Post Hospital; they'll send a wagon."

Bringing the woman along, Shemmy climbed down. She didn't like it. "Are you both insane? This man's been *shot*."

What Shemmy had under his arm was a sleeping bag. He said, "Can't it wait?" Maybe it could, maybe not, but Buster couldn't.

"I have things they need at the cable hut. *Now*. Okay?"

In a hurry to get there, he didn't wait for an answer.

If Rodgers could move a jeep down and not wreck it, Buster figured he could too. He was more than halfway when he saw he was wrong. The jeep broke loose; he could barely keep it aimed downhill, let alone slow it. As dim-lit patches of moss flashed by, he wished he'd unmasked his lights and the hell with orders.

Skidding, he saw the ACS jeep square in his path. *Hellfire!* He swung the wheel and hit brakes, but slammed into it broadside.

Grazing the cable hut, the captain's jeep went off the drop.

Breathing hard, Buster picked up what he'd brought, climbed out, and walked over to the edge. "Thorne? Captain Rodgers?"

The captain's voice had an edge to it. "Jesus Christ, Morgan! What took you so long?"

"Yes, Mr. President; *very* satisfactory." The Aleutian raids were beginning to help tip the balance. In Marshall's opinion, the Pacific War was now embarked on its final phase.

If MacArthur could be kept in check. Toward that end, the general had a thought. "Sir? About Mac; a suggestion?"

The cigarette holder waved. "Yes, of course."

"Well sir, supposing that *if* he stays strictly in line, he will be given full command of the eventual occupation of Japan?"

The famous Roosevelt chuckle. "Capital. Oh, capital!"

Tired or not, George Marshall never went to bed without checking his briefing room digest. Tonight's was not designed to help him get a good night's rest.

Eisenhower reported that fighter pilots escorting daylight bombers had observed, emanating from a ship lying well north of Peenemünde in the Baltic Sea, a phenomenal explosion. It had thrown a blinding glare across more miles than Marshall cared to believe, and a glowing toroidal cloud into the stratosphere.

Marshall called Oak Ridge. "How soon can you test?" The answer made him set the phone down harder than he intended. Hitler was at least a year ahead of the Manhattan Project.

Evaluation time. With the Aleutian offensive in support of MacArthur's southern push, Japan was a matter of months.

But Europe was going to be a bitch.

Author's Note

The specific depictions of Franklin D. Roosevelt, George C. Marshall, Dwight D. Eisenhower, and Simon Bolivar Buckner, plus attribution of various offstage activities to Douglas MacArthur, Malemute Red, and Averill Harriman, are fictitious. As are the other characters in this story.

The ACS Aleutian cable, however, did move a great lot of secure message traffic.

When Free Men Shall Stand

POUL ANDERSON

Clouds hid that dawn, prolonging night toward endlessness. A wind arose. At first it went sultry as the air had lain, then slowly cooled, strengthened, loudened. River smells mingled with those of town, of smoke, kitchens, warehouses, wastes, horses and their droppings, men and their sweat. A few early, heavy raindrops fell down the wind; thunder grumbled afar.

Blind where they waited, troopers shifted in their saddles, muttered among each other, passed forbidden flasks from hand to hand. Hoofs stamped on pavement, bits jingled, leather creaked. Here and there a cigar or a pipe made a flickery red star. They should have had real stars above them, to pale before an honest morning. Instead, rue de Bourgogne hemmed them in darkness, which a few gleams from shuttered windows only seemed to deepen, and doors were barred against them.

They were bold men in the Appomattox Horse, Indian fighters, their oldest bearing scars and memories of the First French War; they had been at the forefront of the assault that cleared the way into New Orleans; but James Payne could well-nigh feel the morale draining from them. He sensed it in himself. So did his mount. It became a mute contest to hold the both of them steady.

"Sir," he heard at his elbow, "ain't they never goin'a start? Must be past six by now."

"Shut up, Sergeant," Payne snapped.

"Yes, sir. Sorry, sir." Hollis was a dependable man. That he had spoken at all was a bad sign.

"First light sooner by canal," said Hog Eye on the lieutenant's left. Fewer walls to shut it out, a shimmer on the water, maybe the coal glow of enemy campfires.

Payne's mind flew homeward—sunrise silvering the

woods along the Blue Ridge; Harpers Ferry, where the rivers meet and the rapids run white, Mary Elizabeth Dodge and words spoken in a rose garden . . .

Guns crashed him back. Did he hear bugles and shouts? Suddenly the wind was full of brimstone. "Jesus Christ!" Hollis yelled. "They're goin'!" The whole platoon cried aloud.

"Hold tight," Payne ordered.

How had daybreak so sneaked and pounced? All at once he picked shadows from the murk, gleam off carbines and drawn sabers, then shapes, ornate grilles edging balconies, then colors, blue tunics and caps, sky still dark and formless but ever more mercury glints of rain. His pulse thuttered, his head felt curiously light. When he spoke, he heard the voice as a stranger's. "Have y'all forgotten? We move when Lee has the Frenchies' full attention. Remind our boys. Pass the word along."

Those in earshot nodded and obeyed. A shiver went through the ranks, as far down the street as they filled it. Firmness followed. Good men, thought the remote calm part of Payne's awareness. Not yet blooded to this kind of warfare, where gallantry isn't enough; but ready to learn it.

Have I learned it? Me, twenty-five years old, no, young? Awful young to die. Lord Jesus, into Thy hands I give myself. Forgive me my trespasses. Don't let me be afraid. Watch over Mother and everybody. Please. Amen.

Flame lifted above roofs and exploded on high. A rocket. The signal. "We're off, Sergeant," Payne said.

He touched spurs to his horse. Traveler nickered and broke into a ringing trot, left on rue d'Orléans, on toward the rampart. The gate there swung wide. As he went between its blockhouses, he glimpsed a cannoneer, who waved. The Stars and Stripes flapped wildly from a staff. Thunder rolled more and more often, louder now than the racket of combat.

The new defenses beyond were all too near, hastily thrown together when the fresh enemy troops appeared, barely sufficient to repel three assaults. Payne rode among fascines and gabions—trenches were no good in this swampland—into the open.

Glancing battleward, he saw only smoke and confusion through the hardening rain. If everything went as it ought to, Captain Lee's sortie had drawn the Imperials toward it, for he led the main squadron, and this might well be the start of an effort to break out. It wasn't, of course. The besiegers were too many, too well armed and well established. The maneuver was simply a massive feint, which was to end in withdrawal back into town—cover for the real mission, which belonged to Payne's enlarged platoon.

Or so the plan read. The lieutenant felt a grimace in his mouth. He wasn't a West Point man, but his officers in the reserve corps at William and Mary had been, and high among their maxims stood: "The first casualty of any battle will probably be your battle plan."

No matter. His duty was plain. The troop was deploying as it emerged, forming a blunt wedge for him to lead, to drive.

"Yonder," said he whom they called Hog Eye, and pointed. Payne's gaze followed the buckskin-clad arm over two miles or more. At the end of blurred vision he made out a house half wrecked, and a vague bulk that might be his target.

Must be. Hog Eye would know. The Cherokee had led the scouts who first warned that the foe were dragging a monster gun into position. ("Barged across the river, upstream of here," General Houston had concluded. "They can't bombard from that side; the town's shore batteries command it. But landward they'll have the range of us, and knock our works down in two–three days, I reckon. Less'n we can discourage 'em. Y'all game?")

"Bugler, sound the advance. Trot."

"Sir." The notes soared.

Water splatted dirty, hock-high. You couldn't make better speed through this mud, not unless you wanted to wear your horses out. Crécy, Agincourt. Save their strength for the final charge. But how nightmare-slowly you rocked forward. A row of cypress, bearded and gloomy; ruts alongside a rail fence; the house growing clearer ahead, its forlorn chimney, the cannon on a carriage that could have borne stones for a pyramid, its mule train, men in formation, rifles, muskets, whatever they had, flash, flash, flash, an Imperial standard sodden above them, nearly as mired as they. . . .

"Full charge." Payne drew his revolver.

Spurs, muscles astrain between thighs, thud and splash, *crack-crack* and *bee*-buzz, somewhere a scream, Hollis's saddle vacant, but now in at them, onto them, ride them down!

A man fired at Payne, missed, raised his bayonet, and braced himself. His face gaped through the rain, a boy's face, the barest dark fuzz on its olive skin, Spanish, most of the Imperial force hereabouts was actually Spanish, not French or Creole, don't plunge against that point. The revolver bucked in Payne's grip. The boy's face erupted, dissolved, splashed. He fell, and Payne felt hoofs break ribs.

The Americans were among them, firearms emptied, sabers free. Some of the enemy drew wicked broad knives and tried to hamstring the beasts that ramped above. Payne spied Hog Eye in action. The Indian didn't whoop or anything; he worked, silent, wielding his blade as methodically as though it were a scythe. Otherwise the melee was a whirling fever-dream.

Which broke.

Payne stared around him. Surviving hostiles were in panic flight, every direction. Wind hooted, rain hissed, like silence's voice. The thunder seemed far away, too. Louder were moans and screams off the ground, from men who maybe knew why they had been torn and horses that did not. The horses threshed horribly. Whenever lightning leaped, puddles sheened muddy red.

Payne realized he had been an engine, a harvester. He changed it into another kind of machine, a chess automaton such as he'd read about. Hollis was down, but Martin rode in that place. "Sergeant, put this artillery out of commission," Payne directed.

"Sir!" Teeth gleamed in glee. Martin brought his gasping mount around and barked orders. His gang already knew what to do. A spike was insufficient; besides, this turned out to be one of the new percussion-fired pieces. Cram the damned thing full of its own powder from breech to muzzle, cut the carriage till the mouth was in the earth, lay a fuse, touch a match, and skedaddle.

Payne rode about, seeing to the care of his wounded, the recovery of his dead. Losses weren't as bad as they might have been. Where was Hog Eye? Off on his own, no doubt. No matter what unit you attached them to, Houston's redskins gave strict heed to none but the Raven. How did the diversionary skirmish go? No telling. There was only the remote coughing of it, overridden whenever the thunder sounded.

Abruptly, freakishly, the rain paused. From the saddle Payne saw over miles of grass and marsh, from the Mississippi and the steeples of New Orleans clustered behind its walls, to the glimmer on Lake Pontchartrain. He saw soldiers, toys at their distance, quick-step by hundreds from the misty edge of sight. Cavalry covered their flanks, and fieldpieces trundled after. A little nearer, Lee's squadron was disengaging to retreat.

The Imperials had reinforcements to call on, closer than we knew about, Payne understood. More than we guessed they might. Newly ferried down from St. Louis or wherever? They've got the whole rest of this continent for a hinterland. Fingers closed around his heart.

The rain returned, heavier.

Hog Eye appeared through it, reined in, and sketched a salute. "We cut off," he stated impassively. "Never make it back inside before they in our way."

"They'd surround us," Payne's tongue added. "We've got to head north, fast."

"No supplies."

"We'll requisition what we can, and otherwise cinch our belts tight." Why did he explain? To make it clear to himself, so he could make it clear to his noncoms? Or because this scout would eventually, if they lived, report directly to Houston? "First we'll complete our task, demolish the gun. Then—reinforcements of our own ought to be bound here, you know. We got a message off before the

Impies cut our telegraph. But looks like they'll meet still more strength than we reckoned when we called for help. They need a warnin'."

Maps unrolled in his mind: the narrow approaches to New Orleans between sea, lakes, and river; the military railhead at Natchez, doubtless enemy-occupied but tracks reaching east from it, a strand of the web that Andrew Jackson had decreed be spun across the States; yes, surely any relief expedition would come along it. Your job, son, is to pull what's left of your command out of this hole and take it thataways.

Payne straightened. Weariness dragged at his shoulders. It was a luxury neither he nor his men could afford. Martin was busy, but Corporal Bradford sat close at hand. Payne issued his orders.

For a moment lightning whitened the Cathedral of St. Louis against a heaven where every raindrop speared incandescent. The sight blinked away amid monstrous thunder, and again candle-flame reflections curtained off most of the world beyond the glass. Though a grandfather clock declared that the sun had risen, the room continued to need its chandelier.

The chandelier was crystal, suited to a chamber as gracious as everything else within the Cabildo. Government house, church, Presbytère, and several mansions nearby had seemed very European to Houston. They looked across rue de Chartres to the Place d'Armes and barracks, then onward to the markets, the waterfront, and the great brown river, like aristocrats, yet not without a part in the common life. Besides, here were the living links to Paris, Madrid, Rome, London. New Orleans wasn't really a frontier settlement. Much of the land beyond might still be thinly peopled or wild, north to the Arctic Ocean or west to the Pacific; but white men had dwelt here for more than a hundred years, and in Mexico, Havana, Rio, Buenos Aires, Lima for some three hundred; and all of them acknowledged the same Emperor.

That was a thought to daunt an American. He must not let it.

"Difficult, waiting, no?" said Gaston Lamoureux at his back.

Samuel Houston, major general, Army of the United States, turned from the window. "It is that," he sighed. "A lot easier leadin' boys out than sendin' them. Leastways, if you've got any kind of spirit or, or conscience."

"Unsuitable for you, 'owever."

"Too old, you mean? Shucks, I'm only—what is it? —fifty-six." Houston forced a smile. "Don't need spectacles except to read and write, nor a cane or anything else."

"I t'ink not of age," Lamoureux replied. His English, while accented, was fluent; he had been long in Dublin before they transferred him to the New World, where he regularly dealt with Americans. It was one reason Houston was glad to have him on hand. Houston's French lessons had been few and in the far past, and until now he'd had scant practice. Service in the last big war hadn't counted. He'd just fought then. Cherokee had remained his useful foreign language.

"Se time 'as gone w'en 'igh commanders rode in se van," Lamoureux went on. "You should put be'ind you all sose years of yours among se Indians."

"I know!" Houston strode from the window. This place was a cage, carpet, portraits, bookshelf with bust of Napoleon I enlaureled, delicate chairs, mahogany table, escritoire at which Lamoureux perched, all hemming him in.

But it was a refuge as well. He must needs stay in the building he had made his headquarters, at least till word came about the foray. Finally he could endure the staff room no longer, silences punctuated by banalities, sense of putting on a show for an audience who expected it but had other things on their minds, same as he did. He'd given his officers an excuse and sought here, where he allowed Lamoureux to continue the historical researches that beguiled his retirement. As usual, the puckered little man was awake betimes, happy to shove codices and documents aside for some talk.

Houston stopped at the table, fumbled in his breast

pocket, drew out a cigar, reached for the silver box of matches. He shouldn't smoke so early in the day, on an empty belly. He should go open the door and tell the orderly who waited outside to bring coffee. And maybe beignets; the siege hadn't yet closed all bakeries and patisseries. No, damn it, he wanted what fire he could get, between his jaws if not his hands.

He glowered at Lamoureux. "I'm not ignorant, whatever you think," he said.

The Frenchman looked straight back at him, countenance creasing multitudinously as he smiled without many teeth behind the lips. Light glistened on bald, liver-spotted head and gold-framed lenses. "Certainly not. I meant simply sat time never flows upstream. You will understand. You are in fact a man of se most complex, my general, farmer, explorer, schoolmaster, Indian friend and agent, politician, soldier; and I 'ave 'eard you cite ce *Iliad* in as natural a fashion as a man might quote from yesterday's newspaper. If you are no Pericles, you are at least a Lysander."

"Uh, thanks," said Houston, pleased despite himself. "Though I'm not quite that ruthless, I hope. And I reckon I wouldn't have burned Athens, either." He grinned. "Time hasn't diminished *you* any, sir, not where it comes to long-windedness." A jape felt good.

Lamoureux chuckled like parchment rustling. "It is se proper function of a diplomat."

I suppose, Houston thought. Did you welcome your assignment to New Orleans? Small use any more for diplomacy in Europe, after the Concord of Vienna, was there? But here, well, all right, Louisiana's gone back from Spanish to direct French rule, the king of Mexico's as much a puppet as the king of Spain or the queen of England, and so on and so forth—but here you've had us to deal with.

A match scratted in Houston's fingers. He brought it to the tobacco and drew deep. Harshness eased his heart. "Diplomat," he said slowly. In conversation, too, was relief. "The art of gettin' along with people."

Lamoureux shrugged. "As a means to an end. Alsough one does not admit sat in public."

Lightning glared anew, thunder boomed. Houston found a chair and sat down, mostly because it seemed impolite to keep looming over the other and he didn't want to give offense. He wanted company, somebody to save him from fretting about the action that the storm veiled from him. "You've sure been pleasant to me."

"You treat me kindly."

"I've no cause not to, sir. But how do you really feel? We are at war, your country and mine."

Lamoureux's tone gentled, as if in compassion. "I 'ave no personal animosity. Wars 'appen. Naturally, patriotism requires I pray for your speedy defeat, but you, my general, are a chivalrous opponent. Yes, I may call you 'umane."

"Not much bloodshed when we took this town, no. But not much resistance."

Lamoureux's calm cracked in a scowl. "You 'ave our Governor Antonio López de Santa Ana to sank for sat, I believe." He rolled the name out with sarcastic sonorousness.

Houston couldn't forbear to laugh. "Sure, we knew about him. His leadership was part of our strategy. Too bad he escaped, hey?"

"Indeed too bad. I pity sem in Mexico, and selfishly wish we do not get 'im back. But *hélas*, 'e 'as—you say?—connections."

"We'll spare you that."

Lamoureux donned the mask of scholarly detachment. "Of course, you want to keep New Orleans and control se mout' of se Mississippi. Se Emperor cannot permit you."

Houston turned serious. "Why not, really? We'd pay well. We'd make concessions. It'd be a good peace; ought to last."

Again, quite briefly, Lamoureux frowned. "It is painful to say, but you should know permanent peace between our nations is impossible. We can only 'ope to stay friends person by person, as 'uman beings."

"Why's it impossible? I've heard Frenchmen call us the heirs of the English, and I don't believe a word of it. We threw them off us way back in '76. Besides, you've settled with them yourselves. Why keep old grudges?"

"We fought sem for 'alf a t'ousand years. We would be fools to let you take seir place. It is not a matter of 'atred, I swear. Many of us like you Americans, yes, we admire you for your courage and energy."

Houston inclined his head. "And I remember reading how Tom Jefferson said every civilized man has two mother countries, his own and France."

"You are gracious, my general. But I speak about policy, necessity. Se *pervenche*—se, se periwinkle?—it 'as lovely flowers. But a prudent gardener will not let it grow freely. Else it soon overruns se 'ole garden."

"Well, sure, our population's growin' pretty fast, but if that's all you mean—"

"A single part of my intention. Sere are many sings to make sis conflict ineluctable. May I speak frankly?"

Houston rolled smoke over his tongue and streamed it forth. "Go ahead. I don't care for pussyfootin'."

"W'y did you not accept your defeat gracefully after se last war and abide by se quite generous terms we granted? A spirit of revenge? 'Ope to gain back w'at you lost, and more? I sink only in part. I sink you fear, far down inside your souls, sat if you do not eat se Empire, it will piece by piece eat you. And so you 'ave acted to become se predator before you become se prey."

"Come *on,* now! This war has perfectly plain causes."

"Oh, your President Polk, 'e was shrewd. I admire 'is timing. A debated succession in Paris w'ile se sepoys mutiny in India and rebellion erupts in Sout' America— yes, a well-chosen year to increase se provocations beyond w'at we could tolerate."

Houston flushed. "I ought to resent that," he snapped.

"Please do not be angry. You said I could express my honest opinion. My friend, se very presence of se United States subverts us. Our German colonists in Louisiana, our British in Canada, our Spanish and Portuguese every-w'ere else, sey see you independent and grow restless Se Russians in seir Nort'western possession, sey, too, remember because of you 'ow once seir Tsar was not anosser lackey but lord of 'is own empire. And your illegals in our fur trade, sey were also inevitable. But you deliberately send agents out, stirring up revolt. You wink at piracy. Your forcing se wild Sauk and Winnebago tribes across our border, sat was only w'at you call se last straw."

"Well, if your government had been more willin' to negotiate—"

"Let us not deal in excuses. I am not angry, me. Sis is all in se nature of nations." Lamoureux paused. "And we Europeans, we are accustomed to taking se long view. We can let you wait for our full attention. Meanw'ile, pardon me, but it seems you cannot 'old New Orleans. I beg you surrender it before sere is more useless killing. I can speak for you to my colleagues. Santa Ana is fled. Se French aut'orities 'o are left, sey still listen a little to an old man's words. I sink we could arrange you march out wit' full honors, if you do it soon."

Houston stiffened. "I'm not a sailor," he snapped, "but I'll quote John Paul Jones anyway: 'I have just begun to fight.'" A loud rap sounded on the door. "Come in!"

An ensign stepped through and saluted. He was young, white-cheeked, shaken. "Sir," he blurted, "they need you back in the staff room. The Virginians are returnin'. They, they report new hostile troops, a swarm of 'em—"

Houston was already out the door.

The enemy did not give pursuit. Maybe no one saw Payne's retreat through the driving rain. Maybe no one thought it worth the trouble and risk, when the noose was being drawn tighter around the city and it was unsure what American forces might be where to the north. Payne didn't know or much care. He was content to offer thanks, and ride.

The next days were nevertheless hellish. He didn't head straight east for U.S. territory; yon bridge was surely well guarded, with French at both ends of it. Instead he took his band northeast cross-country, fording the Bogue Chitto, till he came on the road along the Pearl River and followed that north. It was broad, graveled, well graded, a military highway in both the Empire and the Republic. The stream provided water. But there was no food for men, and mainly snatched grass for horses. Once beyond the marshlands, territory higher and drier, they passed plenty of farms and villages. However, crops weren't ripe, and they dared not stop to forage. The best they could grab was an occasional pig or some chickens, which didn't go far whenever they took a few hours' rest. Otherwise they must struggle on, while inhabitants stared after them in sullen resentment.

Struggle it was, ever more, as hunger and exhaustion whittled on them. Three of the wounded developed fever and died, to be buried in shallow graves with a hasty prayer. Soon half a dozen others could go no longer. Payne left them in the churches nearest to where they gave out, hoping the priests would keep the people from lynching them. Because this took time, and he must do it for each, talking to that man, taking whispered messages for folks at home, it hurt still worse than it had hurt to leave the wholly incapacitated behind on the battlefield alongside the dead. Officers might expect good treatment and eventual parole; enlisted prisoners' chances of surviving malnourishment and sickness in the stockades were poor.

The platoon must keep moving, though. It was God's mercy that they weren't attacked. To be sure, when Houston came down through here, he captured and burned every outpost on his way, widely to right and left. Maybe the garrisons hadn't yet been replaced. Maybe the Imperials figured it was smarter for the time being just to keep patrols about, on the watch for any new invasion—for the Americans had cut their telegraph lines, and when they got their first reinforcements, they cut those the Americans had strung. Be that as it may, if a detachment spied Payne's starvelings and sent after assistance, that would be that.

The border was ghostly. When word came that war had been declared, the French struck at once out of New Orleans, unexpectedly hard. They reduced Fort Burr to ruin before they withdrew. Now their Fort Lafitte was likewise charred timbers, ashes, and bones among broken things.

Few Americans had ventured to settle hereabouts, when the exact line between the Grand Duchy of Louisiana and the state of Mississippi remained in dispute and was, in fact, one occasion of this war. Greenwood brooded on either side of the road, heavy with shadows and earth odors. A squirrel ran up a tree, a cardinal winged by in vivid scarlet, a mockingbird trilled—somehow they sharpened desolation. Payne's troop stumbled onward.

Then on the fourth evening of their journey—or the fifth? He could not immediately remember—Hog Eye glided out of some brush. The scout alone had seemed immune to misery and, sparing his mount, ranged around afoot, Indian-style. He drew nigh the lieutenant's stirrup and said, impassivity yielding to a broad grin, "Hurry now. Your soldiers. Short ride."

A cheer of sorts muttered along the lines as the news passed back. The animals themselves seemed to smell relief. Their heads lifted, and when the forest stopped, they broke into a trot. Hoofs thumped, metal jingled. By God, Payne thought, we'll meet them like Virginians.

Road and river wound on through a plantation. Sunbeams from the west reached long across pastures where livestock grazed, fields of sprouting corn and cotton, shade trees around the big house. At this hour the slaves must be done hoeing and back in their cabins. Southbound with Houston, Payne had wondered whether so big a property so near the frontier wasn't tempting Fate. Well, he'd decided, the owner of such a spread could afford enough armed guards to put up a resistance till help came from Pearl Bridge Station.

That had been Payne's goal, the Army post where the military railroad crossed this river on its way to the Mississippi. Natchez was likely in French hands, but he felt sure the enemy hadn't made it much farther east. He'd report in and stand by for whatever orders came over the wire. Probably they'd be to feed his men up and wait till the reinforcements arrived, then join them.

But yonder the regiments were! So they'd already

reached Pearl Bridge, made it the place where they got off the trains, and started toward New Orleans. For a hysterically funny moment Payne speculated on how Massa felt about his rescuers, bivouacked in choice meadows that would be trampled clay tomorrow morning.

Never mind. "Bugler," Payne croaked, "I want 'dress lines' and a smart advance. Scout"—to Hog Eye—"back in your saddle and ride on my left." He didn't quite know why he said that, unless it was because the Cherokee, not in uniform but in leather and oddments, was neater and cleaner than anybody else, and was Sam Houston's man.

Fires smoked, tents stood taut, sentries paced across acres. Horses seemed a lot fewer than mules, field guns about as many as supply wagons. Mostly infantry and artillery, passed through Payne's mind. Cavalry was auxiliary and minor. Crossing a ridge, from the crest he caught an overview of the camp. It was laid out as a grid, with mathematical precision. Vague memories stirred, Latin classes, Roman *castra*. Were the cannon on the perimeter placed equally exactly? He was too tired and hungry to be certain.

A squad of riders galloped to meet him. Their uniforms were a darker blue than his. The corporal in charge saluted crisply. "Where are you from, please, sir?" he asked. His accent twanged flat.

Payne identified himself, his command, and their point of departure. The corporal whistled. "Quite a ways, sir. Uh, we're the Fifth and Seventh Illinois, the Third Michigan, and the Wisconsin Rangers."

Wonder drove fatigue from Payne's attention. "Michigan, Wisconsin? Shouldn't you be holdin' the Canada line?"

"No need, sir. Not that we hear much in the ranks, but I do know the Yankees have got Maine back and are moving in on Quebec. Maybe they've taken it by now, maybe Montreal, too. The Canucks got enough to keep 'em busy." The corporal broke off. "Beg pardon, sir. Not for me to talk about." He was quite young. "If the lieutenant please, let's proceed. Our officers will get you quartered fast, I bet."

Maine is ours! Gladness jumped in Payne. The next

peace treaty, by God, we won't cede it again. And we'll kick all the goddamn Pierres out, too.

Exhilaration sank as he rode into a section where the tents sheltered Negroes. Negroes, armed, a few bearing stripes on their sleeves—he'd been aware of such units but never expected to see any in these parts. Better keep his mouth shut, though. He must admit they were as clean and orderly as the whites. In truth, the entire camp, thousands of men, hummed and clicked quietly. Also around their fires, they sat alert, and sprang up to salute when they saw the bars on his shoulders. It was more like a military academy than any army in the field.

A Southern army, that is, he realized.

Heartiness waited at the end of his ride, in the person of a large blond captain named Bergmann, who bade him welcome and bawled orders in a German accent. Payne was quickly seated on a folding stool, a tin cup of coffee in one hand and a sandwich in the other. His platoon was dispersed among surrounding groups—"Ve vill assemble dem in de morning, *Leutnant*"—except for Hog Eye. "Johansen, you take de Inchun ofer to de niggers and tell Sergeant Grant to zee to him." Payne paid slight heed. How good to shed responsibility for a while and rest, rest, rest. Warmth crept into the corners of him. He nodded. . . .

Bergmann shook him awake. "Kvick! De general vants you should report. Aftervard vill be a cot and zix nice hours sleep for you. First ve clean you a liddle, ha?"

Payne blinked. "Wouldn't the general understand how come I'm dirty?"

"Yah, yah, but you vant to be like a pig? Ve are zoldiers here, boy. Got hot vater, zoap, sponch, and den clean clothes vot fit maybe not too bad. Ve vash and repair your own outfit later."

Scrubbing himself, Payne regained some life. Nor did it hurt that the uniform lent him was Ranger. Everybody knew what those boys had done in the Indian wars.

Bergmann guided him to the commander's tent, chatting at drumfire rate. He was among the Germans who'd emigrated after King Joseph hanged the signers of the Heidelberg Manifesto and put down the uprising that resulted. Soon he was altogether devoted to his adopted country. It had given him a farm, presently a family and a vote. The stiff service requirements of Illinois—cadet corps; three full years after leaving school; then three months' active duty annually, till the war made it full-time again— were to him less a task than a joy, a second occupation more interesting than his cows and corn. "Europeans, bah! Ve vip dem back to deir kennels and teach dem respect for men, by damn!"

"You've got tough opposition ahead," Payne warned. "I think, from what I've seen, you'll be pretty heavily outnumbered."

Bergmann spat. "Numbers? Dey don't know how to fight no more dan packs of dogs. Ve seen action against dem already in Minnesota. I don't t'ink does greaser troops here giff us any more trouble dan de frogs did."

"M-m, I hope you haven't left the North unguarded."

"No, no. We is just vat de high command can spare."

Payne mustered nerve. "Is that how come you got niggers along?"

Bergman blinked. "Vot you got against darkies? Dey do serfice same like us. Ve don't haff slafes in de Nort'."

"I know. But, well, sir, not meanin' any offense or anything, but I don't believe it's wise bringin' them south. The sight could give ours ideas. I'd hate havin' to make examples, the way they had to in 'Bama a few years ago."

"You got dem kviet, dough, did you not?" It was hard to tell by the yellow sunset glow whether Bergmann's face reddened. His tone chilled. "You should not talk, boy. I saw dat Inchum vit' you. I hear you Sudderners got whole corps of Inchuns. *Dat* is de great mistake. Vere I come from, ve know does murdering saffages too vell."

Payne swallowed. "Sorry, sir. I told you I didn't mean any offense." Let the newcomers argue with Sam Houston, if they dared.

Bergmann eased. "All right, all right. Not to vorry much, so long as vite men keep strongest, ha? Maybe better first ve vorry about all dose Jews coming in."

"Well, true, we are gettin' quite a few of them in our seaboard cities. Not like among the Yankees, not yet..."

But then they had reached the big tent. Lanterns inside filled it with dull light, unrestful shadows, and oil smells.

Major General Stephen Watts Kearny sat behind a table, maps spread before him, taking notes. From time to time he lifted a briar pipe from a bowl and took a puff. Nonetheless his appearance, his manner, the whole iron-gray being of him made Payne, bathed or no, feel like a boy caught in truancy. Lieutenant and captain snapped salutes. Kearny returned the gesture and indicated two campstools. "At ease," he said. "Be seated, gentlemen." Despite long service elsewhere, a trace of the Northeast lingered in his voice.

Payne and Bergmann made haste to obey. "I gather you've quite a story to tell us," the general continued. "We're happy for all the information we can get. Well done, Lieutenant."

He's human, Payne thought. He don't act easy like old Sam, but he's no martinet; and you better not bungle with Houston, either. "Thank you, sir."

"Speak. Proceed chronologically if you can."

Payne commenced. Kearny interrupted after a minute: "It isn't clear to me how that first lot of fresh Imperials arrived right after you took New Orleans, and bottled you up. No proper account came through."

"No, sir, I reckon not. I hear tell our dispatcher was still sendin' when they showed, and barely got away."

"Do you happen to know?"

"We officers of the Appomattox Horse were told, sir. You see, we were to make a sortie against a siege gun the enemy was bringin' to bear. General Houston reckoned somethin' like this might happen, some of us be forced north. Not that he knew more troops were on their way, but it could've happened somehow. In that case, we might as well try carryin' the news. I don't s'pose any of his couriers made it to Pearl Bridge?"

"Evidently not. You were lucky, you men. Of course, mine wouldn't have heard anything while they were crammed in the troop trains, but when we arrived, no further word was waiting for me."

A vision passed before Payne, wires and rails spread across a fourth of the continent, electrical halloos racing north and east—surely to end in the head of the supreme commander, old Winfield Scott—and then the decision, the orders, and locomotives fired up a thousand miles away, men and animals embarking, guns and munitions and stores loaded—how fast it had gone, after all. They were sharp enough in the South, but you would not have seen that kind of machine efficiency there. And the lonesome whistles through the night, the prairie miles falling behind—yes, his countrymen had built strongly on the foundations that President Jackson laid.

"Well, what did go wrong?" Kearny demanded.

"The way I was told, sir, while our main army made straight for New Orleans, a couple of regiments swung down into West Florida and ripped out the rail lines, figurin' then the Imperials couldn't get troops from there to Louisiana till we were settled in too firmly for them."

Kearny nodded. "That's obvious. Westward, the Empire hasn't got much this side of the Rio Grande, and the Comanches and Mexican guerrillas keep it occupied. Go on."

"Well, sir, what I heard—it was learned from prisoners, I reckon—was that the French had a lot of ships at Cuba that we didn't know about. Navy, fixin' to move against ours. And there's a cable between Havana and St. Augustine. So the steamers that they had amongst them went to Florida, took on the Spanish units, and carried them across the Gulf to Lake Borgne. Caught us by surprise, they did, and drove us back into the city."

Kearny tugged his neat beard. "I thought that was how it might have been."

"And now, sir, they've fetched still more. I don't know where from. Northwards, I'd guess. But anyhow, I saw 'em comin', just when my platoon was out there disablin' that cannon. They'll have numbers now to bar those narrow strips of land around Lake Pontchartrain—"

Kearny chopped the words off. "Leave strategy and tactics to your superiors, Lieutenant. What I want you to do is think back, think hard, ransack your memory."

His questions flew like musket balls, probing into the chaos that had been action, striking after facts, estimates, possibilities. When at length he said, "Enough," Payne barely checked himself from collapsing off his stool.

"You've been helpful," Kearny finished. "I daresay I can get more out of you after you've rested, and in any event you can point out things on our line of march. Captain, I want Lieutenant Payne reporting to me again in the morning, right after breakfast. Make all necessary arrangements for him and his men. Dismissed." His glance went back to the maps.

The two rose, saluted, left.

Dusk was thickening into night. Stars glimmered through warm air and a haze of smoke. Lanterns glowered on poles, bobbed in hands. Banked fires smoldered ruddy. Some distance off, in a space left vacant, one still burned high. Payne couldn't see it clearly, for men surrounded it—several hundred, maybe, and more in the lanes between tents. Amid and above them, upheld on a pole, a steel cross gave back the flickery light. A hymn began, deep voices, a swinging, tramping chant that sent ghost fingers up and down his backbone.

In the blood the Lord did shed for us we take our cleansing bath,
That His holy spirit lead us on the straight and thorny path
Till the nations of unrighteousness have felt His mighty wrath.
We march to victory.
   Glory, glory, hallelujah,
   Glory, glory, hallelujah,
   Glory, glory, hallelujah,
   We march to victory!

Day squatted surly on the world. Clouds seemed only to cast more heat downward. Air lay waterlogged into silence, except for the whine of innumerable mosquitoes. Houston felt sorry when his inspection along the shore side was over. He breathed a little easier there and saw a huge river vista instead of walls everywhere around him.

Of course, he'd also judged it necessary, or at least smart, to make the tour once again. Thus far the batteries, booms, and torpedoes he'd captured were interdicting enemy vessels. He had a growing notion, though, that a fleet was bound over the gulf to force a passage. It would account for the low level of French activity since they lost their big gun. Ordinarily a siege was not a matter of sitting still. Fights raged around the whole neighborhood, till they got into the city and then might well go on street by street, day after day. But if aid from the sea was expected, why not wait for it and meanwhile let hunger and eventually sickness do their sappers' work?

Or did the Imperials simply mean to starve the Americans out? That ought to spare much destruction and shouldn't take awfully long. Since this was a keystone place, he had found both civil and military storehouses full. However, when their stock must be doled out to the population as well as the army, it went fast, no matter how meagerly. Houston had been tempted to expel the inhabitants. But that would be barbarous—and, he admitted, lose him their hostage value.

Besides, he didn't think the French enjoyed keeping so many troops staked here. They were needed elsewhere, to defend Florida and the upstream marches, in due course to join a counteroffensive. Yet they didn't appear to be preparing to storm New Orleans. Therefore, he figured, they probably expected their navy units would be along soon.

As he left the inner emplacement on the west side, several of his bodyguard went down the stairs first. The others came right behind him and promptly fanned out. They were a wild sight, those Shawnees, Cherokees, and Chickasaws, like a tomahawk thrown into a crystal bowl. He could have put them in uniform—most of their kind wore civilized clothes at home—but in skins, feathers, and paint they overawed the city and kept things peaceful. He didn't want snipers potting at him, nor want to shoot people who got out of hand. You couldn't really blame such folks, could you?

He strode on along the wharf. A few men lounged on the decks of four idled ships. The rest must be ashore passing the time in sailor wise—no dearth of loose women, nor rum very scarce. Sentries faced to and fro, sunlight reflected harsh off bayonets. Fishing boats and oar-powered trawlers were out under the protection of the cannon, taking what they could to sell at fancy prices. Well, it helped. Otherwise the scene was almost deserted, eerily quiet.

No, wait. A familiar small figure stood by an unused cleat, stoop-shouldered, hands behind back, staring across the water. Impulsively, Houston moved toward him and halted. "Howdy, sir," he greeted. His Indians formed a semicircle and poised alert.

The Frenchman blinked at him and said an automatic *"Bon jour"* before adding, with a parched laugh, "Pardon, please. I forgot w'ere I am. I was 'alf a century and an ocean away."

"Left your books for a while, eh?" Why not a few minutes' conversation before the return to grimness?

Lamoureux shrugged. "One feels need for some sky now and sen. Even old men do. Or per'aps especially old men. We 'ave not much time for it any more." His look strayed again to the great slow current. "Also, 'ere is se sense of 'istory I search for and do not find in most philosophers."

"History? Isn't all this country kind of new and rough?"

"It is of Europe—as are you, my friend, w'esser you like it or not." Lamoureux's voice dropped so low that he became hard to make out. "But w'at I have in mind is more old and deep san sat—older san se Pyramids, and it will remain long after sey are crumbled to dust. Se flowing, se onwardness. Fate, if you wish to use sat word. Causality, se serene working out of nature's law among us as among se planets—sat is w'at se river teaches."

"I see."

"Sere is comfort in knowing we are in se stream of

time, a tiny part, nossing sat makes any difference, but still a part of se Oneness."

"You've said as much before." Houston shook his head. "And I don't buy it. We've got free will. We can and we do help decide how things will go. Why, blind accident does; and we can cope with it, too."

Lamoureux smiled. "Se 'istory of your nation predisposes you to believe sat, but—"

"Sure. Shouldn't it? King George thought he could keep our fathers under his heel. The whole world did. But they learned different, because free men chose to take arms."

"I sink we French 'ad somesing to do wis se outcome. And as I was about to say, you must agree sat once se Empire was victorious in Europe, se changes in your own society sat followed were inevitable."

"Well, required, some of them."

"And se rest, sey were logical corollaries."

"No, not really. When President Jackson called for a second Constitutional Convention, most of us delegates just meant to strengthen the government so we could defend ourselves better—"

"But 'e made pressure and forced you to adopt more radical provisions."

"He had his reasons, whether or not men like me were happy with them." The talk had gone down a trail Houston didn't care for. He tried a diversion. "Besides, look, I spoke of sheer accident playin' a role. If Jackson hadn't died in office in his fourth term, his Uniform Military Service amendment would've passed, sure. But he did and it didn't."

"It will, or somesing similar, unless se Empire reduces you to se status of Britain."

"Ah, ha! You say 'unless.' You mean it's not fated."

"In 'indsight, 'istorians will see sat w'atever does 'appen was certain to 'appen, just as I see today sat we stand 'ere, you and I, because se French and Spanish fleets broke se British off Cape Trafalgar."

Houston had often heard that battle called one of the decisive ones—without mastery of the seas, England was doomed, long though it took to wear her down—but he was vague on details. Anyhow, he naturally felt that what happened on land was always more important. "They couldn't have done it if they hadn't spent years first, building up their naval strength," he argued. "Somebody had to make that decision."

"True," Lamoureux conceded. "Matters are less simple san I pretend. Many factors work togesser, and it is seldom clear to us 'ow sey do. My sense of inevitability is more intuitive san scientific, I grant you. Neverseless, 'ere on se bank of sis mighty river, I *feel* se current of time."

Still he looked outward. "In fact, before you came, my soughts, sey 'ad wandered up sat stream, 'alf a century. For, do you see, I was reminded of *la Manche*—se English Channel, agleam on a winter day outside Boulogne."

"Not much like, I'd say."

Lamoureux shivered. His tone had gone remote; it was if he spoke to himself, foreign language or no. "Yes, it was a cold light. 'Ow cold. Our ships in se 'arbor, sey were many, many, masts and spars a leafless forest. We men, we sat or stood or paced in an upstairs room of ce *hôtel de ville*, a warm room wis fire and candles, drapes and carpet, clear glass for us to see t'rough from 'igh above, as if we were gods. Yet I 'ave never felt a sight was more forbidding san sose steely waters under sat leaden sky. I rejoiced in my 'eart w'en I learned we would not cross sem. And I was young sen, wis flame in me." He sighed. "We were all young. Se Emperor 'imself, 'e was only—'e was not quite t'irty years of age. Se 'ole world was young, for us."

"The Emperor?" asked Houston, startled. "The first Napoleon? You met him?"

Lamoureux returned to heat and silence and tarry smells. "Oh, 'e was not Emperor sen. We 'ad still our name of a republic, and Bonaparte, 'e was not even First Consul so far. 'E 'ad se title of General of se Army of England, for an attack across se Channel was being prepared. But in se reality, after 'is victories, 'e was as powerful in France as any osser man. I stood in 'is awe—in awe of 'im. Everybody did."

"What were you doin' there, if I may ask?"

"I was merely a clerk, a . . . a secretary on se staff of se foreign minister, Prince Talleyrand-Périgord. 'E 'ad many assistants more important by far. But because I was no-body, and 'ad shown I could keep confidences, and sis matter must be discussed in deepest secrecy, it was me 'e chose to take to Boulogne to record for 'im. And so I was sere w'en 'e, and General Berthier, and Napoleon's brosser Lucien, and Napoleon 'imself weighed se grand decision."

"And figured they'd better not try to invade England," Houston knew.

"Correct. Se fleet was not yet strong enough; se risk was too large. But if sis plan was canceled, somesing else must be done. Else sey would seem weak, and soon lose control."

Houston nodded. "Ridin' a wild stallion, they were, hm?"

"A tiger, Prince Talleyrand said. I sink, besides, 'e argued against attacking England because 'e 'ad friends sere, and interests. 'E was utterly corrupt—but intelligent—yes, I know well w'y at last se Emperor sent 'im to end 'is days on St. 'Elena. Sere in Boulogne, 'e 'ad proposed striking into Egypt, to cut se British off from India. And Napoleon, 'e took fire at sat idea. Audacious as Alexander marching east, fame immortal, oh, sis Sout'land sun does not so blaze so bright as sat little dark man in sose winter days! I could not stand before 'im; se splendor of se vision swept me away into itself. But of course I did not matter. I was less san se lowliest *moustache* in 'is army.

"Lucien, 'owever, Lucien could resist 's is brosser 'o 'e 'ad tumbled wis in sat poor 'ouse in Corsica. And Berthier 'ad talked Lucien over. 'E was a brave man, too, Berthier, none more valiant, but 'e 'ad a different idea, not so magical but more . . . systematic? 'E persuaded Lucien to 'elp 'im persuade Talleyrand and Napoleon.

"To go to Egypt, sey said, would be to court disaster. If se English 'o were scouring se Mediterranean, if sey found our ships, we could lose everysing we sent on sat expedi-tion. Let us for now stay in Europe. *Les allemands*—se Germans might be well subdued; but Italy was only newly conquered and restless. We should secure it beyond any possibility of revolt, Berthier said. And sen we should go into Spain and Portugal—Talleyrand could easily invent reasons—and over se straits to Tangier. So would we shut se Mediterranean to se English, reduce seir fleet sere in detail, and build more ships for ourselves at our leisure. . . . But you know sis, for it is w'at 'appened.

"Me, I remember hours of dispute in sat room in Boulogne. Se short winter day drew to a close. Servants brought food sat se men barely bit at. And I, I 'ung in a corner, my writing board on my knees, t'rowing down quill after quill as I wore sem out, never seeing w'at sey scrawled, so lost was I in se spectacle—'ow 'e 'o stood colossal at Campo Formio and decreed, 'e now stormed and shouted and, yes, sulked—sen suddenly se first fire went out, but ce new fire caught 'old, and *'Oui,'* 'e said, oh, 'ow softly, *'comme Charlemagne'*—but sis time we do not wisdraw across Roncesvalles!"

Lamoureux stopped short, gulped for air, hugged himself, old blood turned cold within the Louisiana heat. Someday, Houston thought, will I be like that, harkin' back to when my Indians called me their Raven? Please, God, no.

He started to lay a hand on the other man's shoulder, though he wasn't sure what to say. A sudden thud of gunfire afar saved him.

Ahead, eastward, shone Lake Pontchartrain and the highest spires of New Orleans. On the left, Lake Maurepas snuggled close to the vast sheet of water; on the right ran the Mississippi. Between them reached some ten miles of mostly open ground, flat, boggy, intensely green with grasses, reeds, stands of cypress and gum, cottonwoods bordering the highway along the river. Aside from hunters, humans had made little use of it until, here and in the narrow strip between the lakes, the Imperials set their defenses against assault from outside.

Payne shifted in the saddle, restless as his mount. "Sir, if you'll just let me and my boys lead your horse . . ." It wasn't that he was stupid-eager, it was that he had come to feel he must show these stolid Northerners what Virginians were worth.

"How fast d'you expect to charge over this mud?" Kearny snapped.

"We'd come on the road and those drained shoulders, sir, hit their left and roll them up."

Kearny shook his head. "A Southern thing to do. The last of the Celtic war bands, your state militias. No."

"Sir—"

"Shut up." Kearny lifted telescope to eye.

Without a hill beneath him he could see little, and most of it already lost in smoke. Artillery dueled, flash and roar down the opposing lines, blunt earth-quivers where round shot struck, fountains where canister burst to spray horseflesh and manflesh. Americans had stood off attack after attack while Kearny's crews worked their guns into position. Now the infantry simply stood.

A shell exploded nearby. Three men became red remnants. Others dragged wounded comrades and their own hurts back to the rear. A mule stayed behind, threshing in a tangle of guts. Its screams were hideously womanish.

Kearny lowered the telescope. His face showed nothing beneath the weathered and grimed skin, but Payne thought the lips within the beard had whitened the least bit. "Poor lads," he said low. "Well, ours can take this better than those spigs can."

I don't see how any human beings can much longer, Payne thought.

Not Hog Eye, for one. "I find my chief," the Indian had said, appearing out of dawn-dusk to pluck the lieutenant's sleeve; and with the same suddenness, he was gone. But it wasn't fair to call him a coward. This just wasn't his style of fighting. He'd make his secret way to the city and Houston.

Anyhow, he'd taken enough foul words on the march south, whenever he came forth among whites; and he couldn't have felt at home among the blacks, either. Some of his people kept slaves, too.

For his part, Payne had mostly ridden near Kearny,

and learned he'd damn well better have an instant and accurate answer to every question flung at him. This general didn't tiptoe forward. His men double-timed the whole distance. Water, gumbo, skirmishers on their flanks hardly slowed them at all. And still they arrived ready for combat. Payne liked to believe his scraps of information had helped, ever so little.

A new din grabbed at him. Incredibly, his mind had wandered. He stood in his stirrups to peer north. A moment's breeze scattered sulfury smoke clouds and he saw, yes, a blue swarm—ants at their distance, but myrmidons, sparks where metal threw back sunlight, and—did he only imagine?—a gnat's-wing dance of colors, American colors.

He whooped. "They did it, sir! By God, they did it!"

"I expected they would," Kearny answered.

—expected that the fourth of his forces that he detached, foot alone, rifles and naked steel, would storm the earthworks and cannon and troops between the lakes, overwhelm them in an hour's slaughter, pass through without heavy loss, and take the rest of the enemy from behind.

Confusion crawled over the green and the wet yonder. The Imperials had seen what was bound for them and were trying wildly to regroup and meet it. Kearny spoke to the officer on his right, who saluted and cantered off. More came, received their orders, and departed.

"Sir—" Payne begged.

"Not yet," the general denied him. "Wait a while. I don't hold with sending men to useless death." A brief grin. "It's worse than a crime, it's a blunder."

Bugles rang. Drums rolled. In rank upon rank, the Americans who had been waiting advanced.

Fire darted among them. They fell and they fell. Each time, the one behind stepped up to take that place, and the jog trot never slackened. On horseback though he was, Payne felt the mass of them beat through the ground into his bones. When at last they had passed, the litter bearers followed, coolly gathering those wounded who lived. Payne's mind flew ahead, into a soldier he never knew, a young fellow, a boy maybe, French, Spanish, Creole, Cajun, mestizo, whatever, who crouched against some turfs and watched the blue host move in on him. Roses by moonlight, a snatch of song, or his mother's hands tucking him into his crib once. . . .

The tide reached the barriers and burst over them. An Imperial standard toppled, white and gold down into the muck underfoot.

Payne shuddered with horror and glory. "Sir, that, that's magnificent!"

"It's proper training, discipline, supply, and leadership," Kearny said. Almost wearily: "Very well, a cavalry charge may serve some useful purpose at this stage. Major Cleland's been urging it himself. Report to him."

"Sir!" Payne was off.

Of the hour that came after, he kept no clear memories. They whirled, they hewed, they bled, sometimes they shrieked. During that span he was cool enough, aware and in control, too busy for fear or fury. Men dropped, right, left, behind, shot as they rode or pitched from the saddle when their horses crumpled and toppled. There was no exact moment when they penetrated the foe, just more and more alien uniforms, saberwork, pressing at a crowd that split and then enclosed him, poor Traveler finally sinking with scarlet a-spurt from three different cuts, but Payne found his feet and lashed about, but the blade had gone so heavy, moved so slowly—and then, and then the new uproar, blue trampling gray aside, and somehow he was in Hog Eye's arms. . . .

Recollection began making sense again about sundown. Cleland had taken charge of their survivors. An orderly found Payne at an offside spot, slumped on the ground, resting, emptily staring into empty air. His wounds, miraculously minor, were bandaged and didn't hurt too much. Exhaustion deadened that sort of thing some.

The orderly said that General Houston would like to see him if the lieutenant felt up to it.

Certainly the lieutenant did! A measure of excitement in him, Payne limped after the man.

The western sky turned the waters as luminous a gold

as itself. The soldiers had herded prisoners together under guard, fixed hospital tents for their badly hurt, made bivouac. They'd begun collecting the dead of both sides. That job wouldn't be finished today, though. Payne wondered about burial. It wasn't very good practice in these parts. But how can you build tombs for so many before they rot?

Nor was this a pleasant ground to camp on; and with fuel low, fires were sparse, food cold. Tomorrow they'd have better quarters, in and about the city. Tonight must be endured. Nonetheless, Payne went between serried arrays and saw men cleaning their outfits as best they were able. He didn't suppose the camp of those who had come from New Orleans was anything like so neat.

A tent with a plank floor had been raised for Kearny. The floor extended a ways beyond it. He stood on this, under open heaven, with Houston. The light made gilt of the gray in their hair. Their cigars waxed and waned, small red demon stars. A hush had fallen, camp noises the merest undertone, so that Payne heard their voices clearly as he approached.

"Gallant youngster," Houston was saying. "I want to promote him on the spot, right this evenin'. It'll do his men good, too, after all they been through."

"Whatever's left of them," Kearny replied. "I'm sorry now I let them go. They did screen my horse, which did loosen up that flank of the enemy, but the results weren't worth the cost."

"You can't reckon such things just by countin'. A regiment lives by its battle honors. That's why we sallied to help you today, whatever your opinion of the move."

"And whatever the consequences when the French steam up the river." Kearny sighed. "Well, I guess we can cope with them regardless."

"And go on from here." Excitement throbbed in Houston's throat. "We can take all Texas, I swear."

Payne halted at the deck and stood unnoticed, diffident.

"Given sufficient and adequate troops," Kearny said.

Houston stiffened. "The South has plenty, suh."

Kearny turned to face him head on. "Sir, no offense. Your men are brave. Their leaders are often brilliant.

And . . . I do understand what it means, names on regimental flags, the names of fields where, win or lose, men fought well. Forgive me if I said the wrong thing. It's been a long day, hasn't it?"

Not altogether mollified, Houston replied quietly, "I'd still like to know just what you meant."

Kearny drew breath. "Why, simply this. We, the United States of America, have the Empire to cope with. The end of these hostilities, the next peace treaty, won't buy us more than time to make ready—time equally available to them. We can't go on relying on professional cadres, volunteers, and whatever higgledy-piggledy lot of service requirements the various states have enacted. The Jackson Constitution needs further work. The Northwestern militia are our best from the standpoint of organization and preparedness, but I admit they are not good enough either. We need a stricter code. Start boys drilling when they start school. Give men longer active duty hitches each year. Provide for the quick-mobilization not only of units but also of industry and the press. And we need these laws the same for all Americans."

"I don't know as how I like that," Houston said slowly.

Kearny's tone went low. "I can't say with all my heart that I do. But look at what happened today."

"Yes, I'll grant you that," Houston said. "Your regiments were . . . Cromwell's Ironsides reborn."

No, thought Payne, somewhere in his weariness and exaltation. His glance went beyond the tent, on into the ranked shelters and ordered guns bulking across this land. No, they weren't, they aren't any such thing. They are the future.

Arms and the Woman

JAMES MORROW

"What did you do in the war, Mommy?"

The last long shadow has slipped from the sundial's face hours ago, melting into the hot Egyptian night. My children should be asleep. Instead they're bouncing on their straw pallets, stalling for time.

"It's late," I reply. "Nine o'clock already."

"Please," the twins implore me in a single voice.

"You have school tomorrow."

"You haven't told us a story all week," insists Damon, the whiner.

"The war is such a *great* story," explains Daphne, the wheedler.

"Kaptah's mother tells *him* a story every night," whines Damon.

"Tell us about the war," wheedles Daphne, "and we'll clean the whole cottage tomorrow, top to bottom."

I realize I'm going to give in—not because I enjoy spoiling my children (though I do) or because the story itself will consume less time than further negotiations (though it will) but because I actually want the twins to hear this particular tale. It has a point. I've told it before, of course, a dozen times perhaps, but I'm still not sure they get it.

I snatch up the egg-timer and invert it on the night-stand, the tiny grains of sand spilling into the lower chamber like seeds from a farmer's palm. "Be ready for bed in three minutes," I warn my children, "or no story."

They scurry off, frantically brushing their teeth and slipping on their flaxen nightshirts. Silently I glide about the cottage, dusting the lamps and curtaining the moon, until only one candle lights the twins' room, like the campfire of some small, pathetic army, an army of mice or scarab beetles.

"So you want to know what I did in the war," I intone, singsong, as my children climb into their respective beds.

"Oh, yes," says Damon, pulling up his fleecy coverlet.

"You bet," says Daphne, fluffing her goose-feather pillow.

"Once upon a time," I begin, "I lived as both princess and prisoner in the great city of Troy." Even in this feeble light, I'm struck with how handsome Damon is, how beautiful Daphne. "Every evening, I would sit in my boudoir, looking into my polished bronze mirror..."

Helen of Troy, princess and prisoner, sits in her boudoir, looking into her polished bronze mirror and scanning her world-class face for symptoms of age—for wrinkles, wattles, pouches, crow's feet, and the crenelated corpses of hairs. She feels like crying, and not just because these past ten years in Ilium are starting to show. She's sick of the whole sordid arrangement, sick of being cooped up in this overheated acropolis like a pet cockatoo. Whispers haunt the citadel. The servants are gossiping, even her own handmaids. The whore of Hisarlik, they call her. The slut from Sparta. The Lakedaimon lay.

Then there's Paris. Sure, she's madly in love with him, sure, they have great sex, but can't they ever *talk*?

Sighing, Helen trolls her hairdo with her long, lean, exquisitely manicured fingers. A silver strand lies amid the folds like a predatory snake. Slowly she winds the offending filament around her index finger, then gives it a sudden tug. "Ouch," she cries, more from despair than pain. There are times when Helen feels like tearing all her lovely tresses out, every last lock, not simply these graying threads. If I have to spend one more pointless day in Hisarlik, she tells herself, I'll go mad.

Every morning, she and Paris enact the same depressing ritual. She escorts him to the Skaian Gate, hands him his spear and his lunch bucket, and with a quick tepid kiss sends him off to work. Paris's job is killing people. At sundown he arrives home grubby with blood and redolent of funeral pyres, his spear wrapped in bits of drying viscera. There's a war going on out there; Paris won't tell her anything more.

"Who are we fighting?" she asks each evening as they lie together in bed. "Don't you worry your pretty little head about it," he replies, slipping on a sheep-gut condom, the brand with the plumed and helmeted soldier on the box.

Until this year, Paris wanted her to walk Troy's high walls each morning, waving encouragement to the troops, blowing them kisses as they marched off to battle. "Your face inspires them," he would insist. "An airy kiss from you is worth a thousand nights of passion with a nymph." But in recent months Paris's priorities have changed. As soon as they say good-bye, Helen is supposed to retire to the citadel, speaking with no one, not even a brief coffee klatch with one of Paris's forty-nine sisters-in-law. She's expected to spend her whole day weaving rugs, carding flax, and being beautiful. It is not a life.

Can the gods help? Helen is skeptical, but anything is worth a try. Tomorrow, she resolves, she will go to the temple of Apollo and beg him to relieve her boredom, perhaps buttressing her appeal with an offering—a ram, a bull, whatever—though an offering strikes her as rather like a deal, and Helen is sick of deals. Her husband— pseudohusband, nonhusband—made a deal. She keeps thinking of the Apple of Discord, and what Aphrodite might have done with it after bribing Paris. Did she drop it in her fruit bowl . . . put it on her mantel . . . impale it on her crown? Why did she take the damn thing seriously? Why did any of them take it seriously? Hi, I'm the fairest goddess in the universe—see, it says so right here on my apple.

Damn—another gray hair, another weed in the garden of her pulchritude. She reaches toward the villain—and stops. Why bother? These hairs are like the hydra's heads, endless, cancerous, and besides, it's high time Paris realized there's a mind under that coiffure.

Whereupon Paris comes in, sweating and snorting. His helmet is awry; his spear is gory; his greaves are sticky with other men's flesh.

"Hard day, dear?"

"Don't ask." Her nonhusband unfastens his breastplate. "Pour us some wine. Looking in the speculum, were you? Good."

Helen sets the mirror down, uncorks the bottle, and fills two bejeweled goblets with Château Samothrace.

"Today I heard about some techniques you might try," says Paris. "Ways for a woman to retain her beauty."

"You mean—you *talk* on the battlefield?"

"During the lulls."

"I wish you'd talk to *me*."

"Wax," says Paris, lifting the goblet to his lips. "Wax is the thing." His heavy jowls undulate as he drinks. Their affair, Helen will admit, still gives her a kick. In the past ten years, her lover has moved beyond the surpassing prettiness of an Adonis into something equally appealing, an authoritative, no-frills sexuality suggestive of an aging matinee idol. "Take some melted wax and work it into the lines in your brow—presto, they're gone."

"I *like* my lines," Helen insists with a quick but audible snort.

"When mixed with ox blood, the dark silt from the River Minyeios is indelible, they say. You can dye your silver hairs back to auburn. A Grecian formula." Paris sips his wine. "As for these redundant ounces on your thighs, well, dear, we both know there's no cure like exercise."

"Look who's talking," Helen snaps. "*Your* skin is no bowl of cream. *Your* head is no garden of sargasso. As for your stomach, it's a safe bet that Paris of Troy can walk through the rain without getting his buckle wet."

The prince finishes his wine and sighs. "Where's the girl I married? You used to care about your looks."

"The girl you married," Helen replies pointedly, "is not your wife."

"Well, yes, of course not. Technically, you're still *his*."

"I want a wedding." Helen takes a gluttonous swallow of Samothrace and sets the goblet on the mirror. "You could go to my husband," she suggests. "You could present yourself to high-minded Menelaus and try to talk things out." Reflected in the mirror's wobbly face, the goblet grows weird, twisted, as if seen through a drunkard's eyes. "Hey, listen, I'll bet he's found another maid by now—he's something of a catch, after all. So maybe you actually did him a favor. Maybe he isn't even mad."

"He's mad," Paris insists. "The man is angry."

"How do you know?"

"I know."

Heedless of her royal station, Helen consumes the remainder of her wine with the crude insouciance of a galley slave. "I want a baby," she says.

"What?"

"You know: a baby. *Baby*: a highly young person. My goal, dear Paris, is to be pregnant."

"Fatherhood is for losers." Paris chucks his spear onto the bed. Striking the mattress, the oaken shaft disappears into the soft down. "Go easy on the *vino*, love. Alcohol is awfully fattening."

"Don't you understand? I'm losing my mind. A pregnancy would give me a sense of purpose."

"Any idiot can sire a child. It takes a hero to defend a citadel."

"Have you found someone else, Paris? Is that it? Someone younger and thinner?"

"Don't be foolish. Throughout the whole of time, in days gone by and eras yet to come, no man will love a woman as much as Paris loves Helen."

"I'll bet the plains of Ilium are crawling with camp followers. They must swoon over you."

"Don't you worry your pretty little head about it," says Paris, unwrapping a plumed-soldier condom.

If he ever says that to me again, Helen vows as they tumble drunkenly into bed, I'll scream so loud the walls of Troy will fall.

The slaughter is not going well, and Paris is depressed. By his best reckoning, he's dispatched only fifteen Achaians to the house of Hades this morning: strong-greaved Machaon, iron-muscled Euchenor, ax-wielding Deichos, a dozen more— fifteen noble warriors sent to the dark depths, fifteen breathless bodies left to nourish the dogs and ravens. It is not enough.

All along the front, Priam's army is giving ground without a fight. Their morale is low, their *esprit* spent.

They haven't seen Helen in a year, and they don't much feel like fighting anymore.

With a deep Aeolian sigh, the prince seats himself atop his pile of confiscated armor and begins his lunch break.

Does he have a choice? Must he continue keeping her in the shadows? Yes, by Poseidon's trident—yes. Exhibiting Helen as she looks now would just make matters worse. Once upon a time, her face launched a thousand ships. Today it couldn't get a Theban fishing schooner out of dry dock. Let the troops catch only a glimpse of her wrinkles, let them but glance at her aging hair, and they'll start deserting like rats leaving a foundering trireme.

He's polishing off a peach—since delivering his famous verdict and awarding Aphrodite her prize, Paris no longer cares for apples—when two of the finest horses in Hisarlik, Aithon and Xanthos, gallop up pulling his brother's war chariot. He expects to see Hector holding the reins, but no: the driver, he notes with a sharp pang of surprise, is Helen.

"Helen? What are *you* doing here?"

Brandishing a cowhide whip, his lover jumps down. "You won't tell me what this war is about," she gasps, panting inside her armor, "so I'm investigating on my own. I just came from the swift-flowing Menderes, where your enemies are preparing to launch a cavalry charge against the camp of Epistrophos."

"Go back to the citadel, Helen. Go back to Pergamos."

"Paris, this army you're battling—they're *Greeks.* Idomeneus, Diomedes, Sthenelos, Euryalos, Odysseus—I *know* these men. Know them? By Pan's flute, I've *dated* half of them. You'll never guess who's about to lead that cavalry charge."

Paris takes a stab. "Agamemnon?"

"Agamemnon!" Sweat leaks from beneath Helen's helmet like blood from a scalp wound. "My own brother-in-law! Next you'll be telling me Menelaus himself has taken the field against Troy!"

Paris coughs and says, "Menelaus himself has taken the field against Troy."

"He's here?" wails Helen, thumping her breastplate. "My husband is *here?*"

"Correct."

"What's going on, Paris? For what purpose have the men of horse-pasturing Argos come all the way to Ilium?"

The prince bounces his peach pit off Helen's breastplate. Angrily he fishes for epithets. Mule-minded Helen, he calls her beneath his breath. Leather-skinned Lakedaimon, runs his internal invective. He feels beaten and bettered, trapped and tethered. "Very well, sweetheart, very well..." Helen of the iron will, the hard ass, the bronze bottom. "They've come for *you*, love."

"What?"

"For you."

"Me? What are you talking about?"

"They want to steal you back." As Paris speaks, Helen's waning beauty seems to drop another notch. Her face darkens with some unfathomable mix of anger, hurt, and confusion. "They're pledged to it. King Tyndareus made your suitors swear they'd be loyal to whomever you selected as husband."

"*Me?*" Helen leaps into the chariot. "You're fighting an entire, stupid, disgusting war for *me?*"

"Well, not for you per se. For honor, for glory, for arete. Now hurry off to Pergamos—that's an order."

"I'm hurrying off, dear"—she raises her whip—"but not to Pergamos. On, Aithon!" She snaps the lash. "On, Xanthos!"

"Then where?"

Instead of answering, Paris's lover speeds away, leaving him to devour her dust.

Dizzy with outrage, trembling with remorse, Helen charges across the plains of Ilium. On all sides, an astonishing drama plays itself out, a spectacle of shattered senses and violated flesh: soldiers with eyes gouged out, tongues cut loose, limbs hacked off, bellies ripped open; soldiers, as it were, giving birth to their own bowels—all because of her. She weeps openly, profusely, the large gemlike tears running down her wrinkled cheeks and striking her breastplate. The agonies of Prometheus are a picnic compared to the weight of her guilt, the Pillars of Herakles are feathers when balanced against the crushing tonnage of her conscience.

Honor, glory, arete: I'm missing something, Helen realizes as she surveys the carnage. The essence eludes me.

She reaches the thick and stinking Lisgar Marsh and reins up before a foot soldier sitting in the mud, a young Myrmidon with what she assumes are a particularly honorable spear hole in his breastplate and a singularly glorious lack of a right hand.

"Can you tell me where I might find your king?" she asks.

"By Hera's eyes, you're easy to look at," gasps the soldier as, arete in full bloom, he binds his bleeding stump with linen.

"I need to find Menelaus."

"Try the harbor," he says, gesturing with his wound. The bandaged stump drips like a leaky faucet. "His ship is the *Arkadia*."

Helen thanks the soldier and aims her horses toward the wine-dark sea.

"Are you Helen's mother, by any chance?" he calls as she races off. "What a face you've got!"

Twenty minutes later, reeling with thirst and smelling of horse sweat, Helen pulls within view of the crashing waves. In the harbor beyond, a thousand strong-hulled ships lie at anchor, their masts jutting into the sky like a forest of denuded trees. All along the beach, Helen's countrymen are raising a stout wooden wall, evidently fearful that, if the line is ever pushed back this far, the Trojans will not hesitate to burn the fleet. The briny air rings with the Achaians' axes—with the thud and crunch of acacias being felled, palisades being whittled, stockade posts sharpened, breastworks shaped, a cacophony muffling the flutter of the sails and the growl of the surf.

Helen starts along the wharf, soon spotting the *Arkadia*, a stout pentekontor with half a hundred oars bristling from her sides like the quills of a hedgehog. No sooner has she crossed the gangplank when she comes upon her husband, older now, striated by wrinkles, but still unquestionably he. Plumed like a peacock, Menelaus stands atop the forecastle, speaking with a burly construction brigade, tutoring them in the proper placement of the impalement stakes. A handsome man, she decides, much like the warrior on the condom boxes. She can see why she picked him over Sthenelos, Euryalos, and her other beaus.

As the workers set off to plant their spiky groves, Helen saunters up behind Menelaus and taps him on the shoulder.

"Hi," she says.

He was always a wan fellow, but now his face loses whatever small quantity of blood it once possessed. "Helen?" he says, gasping and blinking like a man who's just been doused with a bucket of slop. "Is that *you?*"

"Right."

"You've, er . . . aged."

"You too, sweetheart."

He pulls off his plumed helmet, stomps his foot on the forecastle, and says, angrily, "You ran out on me."

"Yes. Quite so."

"Trollop."

"Perhaps." Helen adjusts her greaves. "I could claim I was bewitched by laughter-loving Aphrodite, but that would be a lie. The fact is, Paris knocked me silly. I'm crazy about him. Sorry." She runs her desiccated tongue along her parched lips. "Have you got anything to drink?"

Dipping a hollow gourd into his private cistern, Menelaus offers her a pint of fresh water. "So what brings you here?" he asks.

Helen receives the ladle. Setting her boots wide apart, she steadies herself against the roll of the incoming tide and takes a greedy gulp. At last she says, "I wish to give myself up."

"What?"

"I want to go home with you."

"You mean—you think our marriage deserves another chance?"

"No, I think all those infantrymen out there deserve to live. If this war is really being fought to retrieve me, then consider the job done." Tossing the ladle aside, Helen holds out her hands, palms turned upward as if she's testing for raindrops. "I'm yours, hubby. Manacle my wrists, chain my feet together, throw me in the brig."

Against all odds, defying all *logos*, Menelaus's face loses more blood. "I don't think that's a very good idea," he says.

"Huh? What do you mean?"

"This siege, Helen—there's more to it than you suppose."

"Don't jerk me around, lord of all Lakedaimon, asshole. It's time to call it quits."

The Spartan king stares straight at her chest, a habit she's always found annoying. "Put on a bit of weight, eh, darling?"

"Don't change the subject." She lunges toward Menelaus's scabbard as if to goose him, but instead draws out his sword. "I'm deadly serious: if Helen of Troy is not permitted to live with herself"—she pantomimes the act of self-slaughter—"then she will die with herself."

"Tell you what," says her husband, taking his weapon back. "Tomorrow morning, first thing, I'll go to my brother and ask him to arrange a truce with your father-in-law."

"He's not my father-in-law. There was never a wedding."

"Whatever. The point is, your offer has merit, but it must be discussed. We shall all meet face-to-face, Trojans and Achaians, and talk the matter over. As for now, you'd best return to your lover."

"I'm warning you—I shall abide no more blood on my hands, none but my own."

"Of course, dear. Now please go back to the citadel."

At least he listened, Helen muses as she crosses the weatherworn deck of the *Arkadia*. At least he didn't tell me not to worry my pretty little head about it.

"Here comes the dull part," says whiny-tongued Damon.

"The scene with all the talking," adds smart-mouthed Daphne.

"Can you cut it a bit?" my son asks.

"Hush," I say, smoothing out Damon's coverlet. "No interruptions," I insist. I slip Daphne's cornhusk doll under her arm. "When you have your own children, you can tell the tale however you like. As for now, listen carefully. You might learn something."

• • •

By the burbling, tumbling waters of the River Simois, beneath the glowing orange avatar of the moon goddess Artemis, ten aristocrats are gathered around a vast oaken table in the purple tent of Ilium's high command, all of them bursting with opinions on how best to deal with this Helen situation, this peace problem, this Trojan hostage crisis. White as a crane, a banner of truce flaps above the heads of the two kings, Priam from the high city, Agamemnon from the long ships. Each side has sent its best and/or brightest. For the Trojans: brainy Panthoos, mighty Paris, invincible Hector, and Hiketaon the scion of Ares. For the Achaian cause: Ajax the berserker; Nestor the mentor, Menelaus the cuckold, and wily, smiling Odysseus. Of all those invited, only quarrelsome Achilles, sulking in his tent, has declined to appear.

Panthoos rises, rubs his foam-white beard, and sets his scepter on the table. "Royal captains, gifted seers," the old Trojan begins, "I believe you will concur when I say that, since this siege was laid, we have not faced a challenge of such magnitude. Make no mistake: Helen means to take our war away from us, and she means to do so immediately."

Gusts of dismay waft through the tent like a wind from the underworld.

"We can't quit now," groans Hector, wincing fiercely.

"We're just getting up to speed," wails Hiketaon, grimacing greatly.

Agamemnon steps down from his throne, carrying his scepter like a spear. "I have a question for Prince Paris," he says. "What does your mistress's willingness to return to Argos say about the present state of your relationship?"

Paris strokes his great jowls and says, "As you might surmise, great King, my feelings for Helen are predicated on requitement."

"So you won't keep her in Pergamos by force?"

"If she doesn't want me, then I don't want her."

At which point slug-witted Ajax raises his hand. "Er, excuse me. I'm a bit confused. If Helen is ours for the asking, then why must we continue the war?"

A sirocco of astonishment arises among the heroes.

"Why?" gasps Panthoos. "*Why*? Because this is *Troy*, that's why. Because we're kicking off Western Civilization here, that's why. The longer we can keep this affair going, the longer we can sustain such an ambiguous enterprise, the more valuable and significant it becomes."

Slow-synapsed Ajax says, "Huh?"

Nestor has but to clear his throat and every eye is upon him. "What our adversary is saying—may I interpret, wise Panthoos?" He turns to his Trojan counterpart, bows deferentially, and, receiving a nod of assent, speaks to Ajax. "Panthoos means that, if this particular pretext for war—restoring a woman to her rightful owner—can be made to seem reasonable, then *any* pretext for war can be made to seem reasonable." The mentor shifts his fevered stare from Ajax to the entire assembly. "By rising to this rare and precious occasion, we shall pave the way for wars of religion, wars of manifest destiny—any equivocal cause you care to name." Once again his gaze alights on Ajax. "Understand, sir? This is the war to inaugurate war itself. This is the war to make the world safe for war!"

Ajax frowns so vigorously his visor falls down. "All I know is, we came for Helen and we got her. Mission accomplished." Turning to Agamemnon, the berserker lifts the visor from his eyes. "So if it's all the same to you, Majesty, I'd like to go home before I get killed."

"O, Ajax, Ajax, Ajax," moans Hector, pulling an arrow from his quiver and using it to scratch his back. "Where is your aesthetic sense? Have you no appreciation of war for war's sake? The plains of Ilium are roiling with glory, sir. You could cut the arete with a knife. Never have there been such valiant eviscerations, such venerable dismemberments, such—"

"I don't get it," says the berserker. "I just don't get it."

Whereupon Menelaus slams his wine goblet on the table with a resounding thunk. "We have not gathered in Priam's tent so that Ajax might learn politics," he says impatiently. "We have gathered so that we might best dispose of my wife."

"True, true," says Hector.

"So what are we going to do, gentlemen?" asks Menelaus. "Lock her up?"

"Good idea," says Hiketaon.

"Well, yes," says Agamemnon, slumping back onto his throne. "Except that, when the war finally ends, my troops will demand to see her. Might they not wonder why so much suffering and sacrifice was spent on a goddess gone to seed?" He turns to Paris and says, "Prince, you should not have let this happen."

"Let *what* happen?" asks Paris.

"I heard she has wrinkles," says Agamemnon.

"I heard she got fat," says Nestor.

"What have you been feeding her?" asks Menelaus. "Bonbons?"

"She's a *person*," protests Paris, "she's not a marble statue. You can hardly blame *me* . . ."

At which juncture King Priam raises his scepter and, as if to wound Gaea herself, rams it into the dirt.

"Noble lords, I hate to say this, but the threat is more immediate than you might suppose. In the early years of the siege, the sight of fair Helen walking the ramparts did wonders for my army's morale. Now that she's no longer fit for public display, well . . ."

"Yes?" says Agamemnon, steeling himself for the worst.

"Well, I simply don't know how much longer Troy can hold up its end of the war. If things don't improve, we may have to capitulate by next winter."

Gasps of horror blow across the table, rattling the tent flaps and ruffling the aristocrats' capes.

But now, for the first time, clever, canny Odysseus addresses the council, and the winds of discontent grow still. "Our course is obvious," he says. "Our destiny is clear," he asserts. "We must put Helen—the old Helen, the pristine Helen—back on the walls."

"The old Helen?" says Hiketaon. "The pristine Helen? Are you not talking fantasy, resourceful Odysseus? Are you not singing a myth?"

The lord of all Ithaca strolls the length of Priam's tent, massaging his silky beard. "It will require some wisdom from Pallas Athena, some technology from Hephaestus, but I believe the project is possible."

"Excuse me," says Paris. "*What* project is possible?"

"Refurbishing your little harlot," says Odysseus. "Making the dear, sweet strumpet shine like new."

Back and forth, to and fro, Helen moves through her boudoir, wearing a ragged path of *angst* into the carpet. An hour passes. Then two. Why are they taking so long?

What most gnaws at her, the thought that feasts on her entrails, is the possibility that, should the council not accept her surrender, she will have to raise the stakes. And how might she accomplish the deed? By what means might she book passage on Charon's one-way ferry? Something from her lover's arsenal, most likely—a sword, spear, dagger, or death-dripping arrow. O, please, my lord Apollo, she prays to the city's prime protector, don't let it come to that.

At sunset Paris enters the room, his pace leaden, his jowls dragging his mouth into a grimace. For the first time ever, Helen observes tears in her lover's eyes.

"It is finished," he moans, doffing his plumed helmet. "Peace has come. At dawn you must go to the long ships. Menelaus will bear you back to Sparta, where you will once again live as mother to his children, friend to his concubines, and emissary to his bed."

Relief pours out of Helen in a deep, orgasmic rush, but the pleasure is short-lived. She loves this man, flaws and all, flab and the rest. "I shall miss you, dearest Paris," she tells him. "Your bold abduction of me remains the peak experience of my life."

"I agreed to the treaty only because Menelaus believes you might otherwise kill yourself. You're a surprising woman, Helen. Sometimes I think I hardly know you."

"Hush, my darling," she says, gently laying her palm across his mouth. "No more words."

Slowly they unclothe each other, methodically unlocking the doors to bliss, the straps and sashes, the snaps and catches, and thus begins their final, epic night together.

"I'm sorry I've been so judgmental," says Paris.

"I accept your apology," says Helen.

"You are so beautiful," he tells her. "So impossibly beautiful . . ."

As dawn's rosy fingers stretch across the Trojan sky, Hector's faithful driver, Eniopeus the son of horse-loving Thebaios, steers his sturdy war chariot along the banks of the Menderes, bearing Helen to the Achaian stronghold. They reach the *Arkadia* just as the sun is cresting, so their arrival in the harbor becomes a flaming parade, a show of sparks and gold, as if they ride upon the burning wheels of Hyperion himself.

Helen starts along the dock, moving past the platoons of squawking gulls adrift on the early morning breeze. Menelaus comes forward to greet her, accompanied by a man for whom Helen has always harbored a vague dislike— broad-chested, black-bearded Teukros, illegitimate son of Telemon.

"The tide is ripe," says her husband. "You and Teukros must board forthwith. You will find him a lively traveling companion. He knows a hundred fables and plays the harp."

"Can't *you* take me home?"

Menelaus squeezes his wife's hand and, raising it to his lips, plants a gentle kiss. "I must see to the loading of my ships," he explains, "the disposition of my battalions—a full week's job, I'd guess."

"Surely you can leave that to Agamemnon."

"Give me seven days, Helen. In seven days I'll be home, and we can begin picking up the pieces."

"We're losing the tide," says Teukros, anxiously intertwining his fingers.

Do I trust my husband? wonders Helen as she strides up the *Arkadia*'s gangplank. Does he really mean to lift the siege?

All during their slow voyage out of the harbor, Helen is haunted. Nebulous fears, nagging doubts, and odd presentiments swarm through her brain like Harpies. She beseeches her beloved Apollo to speak with her, calm her, assure her all is well, but the only sounds reaching her ears are the creaking of the oars and the windy, watery voice of the Hellespont.

By the time the *Arkadia* finds the open sea, Helen has resolved to jump overboard and swim back to Troy.

"And then Teukros tried to kill you," says Daphne.

"He came at you with his sword," adds Damon.

This is the twins' favorite part, the moment of grue and gore. Eyes flashing, voice climbing to a melodramatic pitch, I tell them how, before I could put my escape plan into action, Teukros began chasing me around the *Arkadia*, slashing his Janus-faced blade. I tell them how I got the upper hand, tripping the bastard as he was about to run me through.

"You stabbed him with his own sword, didn't you, Mommy?" asks Damon.

"I had no choice. You understand that, don't you?"

"And then his guts spilled, huh?" asks Daphne.

"Agamemnon had ordered Teukros to kill me," I explain. "I was ruining everything."

"They spilled out all over the deck, right?" asks Damon.

"Yes, dear, they certainly did. I'm quite convinced Paris wasn't part of the plot, or Menelaus either. Your mother falls for fools, not homicidal maniacs."

"What color were they?" asks Damon.

"Color?"

"His guts."

"Red, mostly, with daubs of purple and black."

"Neat."

I tell the twins of my long, arduous swim through the strait.

I tell them how I crossed Ilium's war-torn fields, dodging arrows and eluding patrols.

I tell how I waited by the Skaian Gate until a farmer arrived with a cartload of provender for the besieged city . . . how I sneaked inside the walls, secluded amid stalks of wheat . . . how I went to Pergamos, hid myself in the temple of Apollo, and breathlessly waited for dawn.

• • •

Dawn comes up, binding the eastern clouds in crimson girdles. Helen leaves the citadel, tiptoes to the wall, and mounts the hundred granite steps to the battlements. She is not sure of her next move. She has some vague hope of addressing the infantrymen as they assemble at the gate. Her arguments have failed to impress the generals, but perhaps she can touch the heart of the common soldier.

It is at this ambiguous point in her fortunes that Helen runs into herself.

She blinks—once, twice. She swallows a sphere of air. Yes, it is she, herself, marching along the parapets. Herself? No, not exactly: an idealized rendition of herself, the Helen of ten years ago, svelte and smooth.

As the troops march through the portal and head toward the plain, the strange incarnation calls down to them.

"Onward, men!" it shouts, raising a creamy-white arm. "Fight for me!" Its movements are deliberate and jerky, as if sunbaked Troy has been magically transplanted to some frigid clime. "I'm worth it!"

The soldiers turn, look up. "We'll fight for you, Helen!" a bowman calls toward the parapets.

"We love you!" a sword-wielder shouts.

Awkwardly, the incarnation waves. Creakily, it blows an arid kiss. "Onward, men! Fight for me! I'm worth it!"

"You're beautiful, Helen!" a spear-thrower cries.

Helen strides up to her doppelgänger and, seizing the left shoulder, pivots the creature toward her.

"Onward, men!" it tells Helen. "Fight for me! I'm worth it!"

"You're beautiful," the spear-thrower continues, "and so is your mother!"

The eyes, Helen is not surprised to discover, are glass. The limbs are fashioned from wood, the head from marble, the teeth from ivory, the lips from wax, the tresses from the fleece of a darkling ram. Helen does not know for certain what forces power this creature, what magic moves its tongue, but she surmises that the genius of Athena is at work here, the witchery of ox-eyed Hera. Chop the creature open, she senses, and out will pour a thousand cogs and pistons from Hephaestus's fiery workshop

Helen wastes no time. She hugs the creature, lifts it off its feet. Heavy, but not so heavy as to dampen her resolve.

"Onward, men!" it screams as Helen throws it over her shoulder. "Fight for me! I'm worth it!"

And so it comes to pass that, on a hot, sweaty, Asia Minor morning, fair Helen turns the tables on history, gleefully abducting herself from the lofty stone city of Troy.

Paris is pulling a poisoned arrow from his quiver, intent on shooting a dollop of hemlock into the breast of an Achaian captain, when his brother's chariot charges by.

Paris nocks the arrow. He glances at the chariot.

He aims.

Glances again.

Fires. Misses.

Helen.

Helen? *Helen*, by Apollo's lyre, his Helen—no, two Helens, the true and the false, side by side, the true guiding the horses into the thick of the fight, her wooden twin staring dreamily into space. Paris is not sure which woman he is more astonished to see.

"Soldiers of Troy!" cries the fleshly Helen. "Heroes of Argos! Behold how your leaders seek to dupe you! You are fighting for a fraud, a swindle, a thing of gears and glass!"

A stillness envelops the battlefield. The men are stunned, not so much by the ravings of the charioteer as by the face of her companion, so pure and perfect despite the leather thong sealing her jaw shut. It is a face to sheathe a thousand swords, a face to lower a thousand spears, a face to unnock a thousand arrows.

Which is exactly what now happens. A thousand swords: sheathed. A thousand spears: lowered. A thousand arrows: unnocked.

The soldiers crowd around the chariot, pawing at the ersatz Helen. They touch the wooden arms, caress the marble brow, stroke the ivory teeth, pat the waxen lips, squeeze the woolly hair, rub the glass eyes.

"See what I mean?" cries the true Helen. "Your kings are diddling you . . ."

Paris can't help it: he's proud of her, by Hermes's wings. He's puffing up with admiration. This woman has nerve, this woman has arete, this woman has chutzpah.

This woman, Paris realizes as a fat, warm tear of nostalgia rolls down his cheek, is going to end the war.

"The end," I say.

"And then what happened?" Damon asks.

"Nothing. *Finis*. Go to sleep."

"You can't fool us," says Daphne. "All *sorts* of things happened after that. You went to live on the island of Lesbos."

"Not immediately," I note. "I wandered the world for seven years, having many fine and fabulous adventures. Good night."

"And then you went to Lesbos," Daphne insists.

"And then *we* came into the world," Damon asserts.

"True," I say. The twins are always interested in how they came into the world. They never tire of hearing about it.

"The women of Lesbos import over a thousand liters of frozen semen annually," Damon explains to Daphne.

"From Thrace," Daphne explains to Damon.

"In exchange for olives."

"A thriving trade."

"Right, honey," I say. "Bedtime."

"And so you got pregnant," says Daphne.

"And had us," says Damon.

"And brought us to Egypt." Daphne tugs at my sleeve as if operating a bell rope. "I came out first, didn't I?" she says. "I'm the *oldest*."

"Yes, dear."

"Is that why I'm smarter than Damon?"

"You're both equally smart. I'm going to blow out the candle now."

Daphne hugs her cornhusk doll and says, "Did you really end the war?"

"The treaty was signed the day after I fled from Troy. Of course, peace didn't bring the dead back to life, but at least Troy was never sacked and burned. Now go to sleep—both of you."

Damon says, "Not before we've . . ."

"What?"

"You know."

"All right," I say. "One look. One quick peek, and then you're off to the land of Morpheus."

I saunter over to the closet and, drawing back the linen curtain, reveal my stalwart twin standing upright amid Daphne's dresses and Damon's robes. She smiles through the gloom. She's a tireless smiler, this woman.

"Hi, Aunt Helen!" says Damon as I throw the bronze toggle protruding from the nape of my sister's neck.

She waves to my children and says, "Onward, men! Fight for me!"

"You bet, Aunt Helen!" says Daphne.

"I'm worth it!" says my sister.

"You sure are!" says Damon.

"Onward, men! Fight for me! I'm worth it!"

I switch her off and close the curtain. Tucking in the twins, I give each a big soupy kiss on the cheek. "Love you, Daphne. Love you, Damon."

I start to douse the candle—stop. As long as it's on my mind, I should get the chore done. Returning to the closet, I push the curtain aside, lift the penknife from my robe, and pry open the blade. And then, as the Egyptian night grows moist and thick, I carefully etch yet another wrinkle across my sister's brow, right beneath her salt-and-pepper bangs.

It's important, after all, to keep up appearances.

Ready for the Fatherland

HARRY TURTLEDOVE

Field Marshal Erich von Manstein looked up from the map table. Was that the distant rumble of Soviet artillery? No, he decided after a moment. The Russians were in Sinelnikovo today, yes, but Sinelnikovo was still fifty-five kilometers north of his headquarters. Of course, there were no German troops to speak of between there and here, but that would not matter—if he could make Hitler listen to him.

Hitler, however, was not listening. He was talking. He always talked more than he listened—if he'd listened just once, Manstein thought, the Sixth Army might have gotten out of Stalingrad, in which case the Russians would not be anywhere near Sinelnikovo. They'd come more than six hundred kilometers since November.

"No, not one more step back!" Hitler shouted. The Führer had shouted that when the Russians broke through around Stalingrad, too. Couldn't he remember from one month to the next what worked and what didn't? Behind him, Generals Jodl and Keitel nodded like the brainless puppets they were.

Manstein glanced over at Field Marshal von Kleist. Kleist was a real soldier; surely he would tell the Führer what had to be said. But Kleist just stood there. Against the Russians, he was fearless. Hitler, though, Hitler made him afraid.

On my shoulders, Manstein thought. Why, ever since Stalingrad, has everything—everything save gratitude— landed on my shoulders? Had it not been for him, the whole German southern front in Russia would have come crashing down. Without false modesty, he knew that.

Sometimes—not nearly often enough—Hitler glimpsed it, too.

One more try at talking sense into the Führer, then. Manstein bent over the map, pointed. "We need to let the Soviets advance, sir. Soon, soon they will overextend themselves. Then we strike."

"No, damn it, damn you! Move on Kharkov now, I tell you!"

S.S. Panzer Division Totenkopf, *the force with which he wanted Kharkov recaptured, was stuck in the mud outside Poltava, a hundred fifty kilometers away. Manstein said as much. He'd been saying it, over and over, for the past forty-eight hours. Calmly, rationally, he tried once more: "I am sorry, my Führer, but we simply lack the resources to carry out the attack as you desire. A little more patience, a little more caution, and we may yet achieve satisfactory results. Move too soon and we run the risk of—"*

"I did not fly to this godforsaken Russian excuse for a factory town to listen to the whining of your cowardly Jewish heart, Field Marshal." Hitler invested the proud title with withering scorn. "And from now on you will keep your gross, disgusting Jewish nose out of strategic planning and simply obey. Do you understand me?"

Manstein's right hand went to the organ Hitler had mentioned. It was indeed of impressive proportions and impressively hooked. But to bring it up, to insult it, in what should have been a serious council of war was— insane was the word Manstein found. As insane as most of the decisions Hitler had made, most of the orders he had given, ever since he'd taken all power into his own hands at the end of 1941, and especially since things began to go wrong at Stalingrad.

Insane . . . Of itself, Manstein's hand slid down from his nose to the holster that held his Walther P-38 pistol. Of itself, it unsnapped the holster flap. And of itself, it raised the pistol and fired three shots into Adolf Hitler's chest. Wearing a look of horrified disbelief, the Führer crumpled to the floor.

Generals Jodl and Keitel looked almost as appalled as

Hitler had. So did Field Marshal von Kleist, but he recovered faster. He snatched out his own pistol, covered Hitler's toadies.

Manstein still felt as if he were moving in a dream, but even in a dream he was a General Staff-taught officer, trained to deduce what needed doing. "Excellent, Paul," he said. "First we must dispose of the carrion there, then devise a story to account for it in suitably heroic style."

Kleist nodded. "Very good. And then—"

"And then . . ." Manstein cocked his head. Yes, by God, he did hear Russian artillery. "This campaign has been botched beyond belief. Given the present state of affairs, I see no reasonable hope of our winning the war against the Russians. Do you agree?"

Kleist nodded again.

"Very good," Manstein said. "In that case, let us make certain we do not lose it. . . ."

27 July 1979—Rijeka, Independent State of Croatia

The little fishing boat putt-putted its way toward the harbor. The man who called himself Giorgio Ferrero already wore a black wool fisherman's cap. He used his hand to shield his eyes further. Seen through the clear Adriatic air, the rugged Croatian coastline seemed almost unnaturally sharp, as if he were wearing a new pair of spectacles that were a little too strong.

"Pretty country," Ferrero said. He spoke Italian with the accent of Ancona.

So did Pietro Bevacqua, to whom he'd addressed the remark: "That it is." Bevacqua and Ferrero were both medium-sized, medium-dark men who would not have seemed out of place anywhere in the Mediterranean. Around a big pipe full of vile Italian tobacco, Bevacqua added, "No matter how pretty, though, me, I wish I were back home." He took both hands off the boat's wheel to show by gesture just how much he wished that.

Ferrero chuckled. He went up to the bow. Bevacqua guided the boat to a pier. Ferrero sprang up onto the dock, rope in hand. He tied the boat fast. Before he could finish, a pair of Croatian customs men were heading his way.

Their neatly creased khaki uniforms, high-crowned caps, gleaming jackboots, and businesslike assault rifles all bespoke their nation's German alliance. The faces under those caps, long, lined, dark, with the deep-set eyes of icons, were older than anything Germany dreamed of. "Show me your papers," one of them said.

"Here you are, sir." Ferrero's Croatian was halting, accented, but understandable. He dug the documents out of the back pocket of his baggy wool pants.

The customs man studied them, passed them to his comrade. "You are from the Social Republic, eh?" the second man said. He grinned nastily. "Not from Sicily?"

Ferrero crossed himself. "Mother of God, no!" he exclaimed in Italian. Sicily was a British puppet regime; admitting one came from there was as good as admitting one was a spy. One did not want to admit to spying, not in Croatia. The Ustashi had a reputation for savagery that even the Gestapo envied. Ferrero went on, in Croatian again, "From Ancona, like you see. Got a load of eels on ice to sell here, my partner and I."

"Ah." Both customs men looked interested. The one with the nasty grin said, "Maybe our wives will buy some for pies, if they get to market."

"Take some now," Ferrero urged. If he hadn't urged it, the eels would not have got to market. He knew that. The pair of fifty-dinar notes folded in with his papers had disappeared now, too. The Croatian fascists were only cheap imitations of their German prototypes, who would have cost much more to bribe.

Once they had the eels in a couple of sacks, the customs men gave only a cursory glance at Bevacqua's papers (though they did not fail to pocket his pair of fifty-dinar notes, either) and at the rest of the ship's cargo. They plied rubber stamps with vigor and then strode back down the dock, obviously well pleased with themselves.

The fishermen followed them. The fish market was, sensibly, close to the wharves. Another uniformed official demanded papers before he let Ferrero and Bevacqua by.

The sight of the customs men's stamps impressed him enough that he didn't even have to be paid off.

"Eels!" Ferrero shouted in his bad but loud Croatian. "Eels from Italian waters! Eels!" A crowd soon formed around him. Eels went one way, dinars another. While Ferrero cried the wares and took money, Bevacqua kept trotting back and forth between market and boat, always bringing more eels.

A beefy man pushed his way to the front of the crowd. He bought three hundred dinars' worth of eels, shoving a fat wad of bills into Ferrero's hand. "For my restaurant," he explained. "You wouldn't happen to have any squid, would you?"

Ferrero shook his head. "We sell those at home. Not many like them here."

"Too bad. I serve calamari when I can." The beefy man slung his sack of eels over his shoulder, elbowed himself away from Ferrero as rudely as he'd approached. Ferrero rubbed his chin, stuck the three hundred dinars in a pocket different from the one he used for the rest of the money he was making.

The eels went fast. Anything new for sale went fast in Rijeka; Croatia had never been a fortunate country. By the time all the fish were gone from the hold of the little boat, Ferrero and Bevacqua had made three times as much as they would have by selling them in Ancona.

"We'll have to make many more trips here," Bevacqua said enthusiastically, back in the fishing boat's cramped cabin. "We'll get rich."

"Sounds good to me," Ferrero said. He took out the wad of bills the fellow from the restaurant had given him. Stern and unsmiling, the face of Ante Pavelic, the first Croatian *Poglavnik*, glared at him from every twenty-dinar note he peeled off. Pavelic hadn't invented fascism, but he'd done even more unpleasant things with it than the Germans, and his successors weren't any nicer than he had been.

In the middle of the notes was a scrap of paper. On it was scrawled a note, in English: *The Church of Our Lady of Lourdes. Tomorrow 1700.* George Smith passed it to

Peter Drinkwater, who read it, nodded, and tore it into very small pieces.

Still speaking Italian, Drinkwater said, "We ought to give thanks to Our Lady for blessing us with such a fine catch. Maybe she will reward us with another one."

"She has a fine church here, I've heard," Smith answered in the same tongue. The odds the customs men had planted ears aboard the boat were small, but neither of them believed in taking chances. The Germans made the best and most compact ears in the world, and shared them freely with their allies.

"May Our Lady let us catch the fish we seek," Drinkwater said piously. He crossed himself. Smith automatically followed suit, as any real fisherman would have. If he ever wanted to see Sicily—or England—again, he had to *be* a real fisherman, not just act like one.

Of course, Smith thought, if he'd really wanted to work toward living to a ripe old age, he would have been a carpenter like his father instead of going into Military Intelligence. But even a carpenter's career would have been no guarantee of collecting a pension, not with fascist Germany, the Soviet Union, the U.S.A., and Britain all ready to throw sunbombs about like cricket balls. He sighed. No one was safe in today's world—his own danger was merely a little more obvious than most.

Not counting Serbian slave laborers (and one oughtn't to have counted them, as they seldom lasted long), Rijeka held about 150,000 people. The older part of the city was a mixture of medieval and Austro-Hungarian architecture; the city hall, a masterpiece of gingerbread, would not have looked out of place in old Vienna. The newer buildings, as was true from the Atlantic to the fascist half of the Ukraine, were in the style critics in free countries sneered at as Albert Speer Gothic: huge colonnades and great vertical masses, all intended to show the individual what an ant he was when set against the immense power of the state.

And in case the individual was too dense to note such symbolism, less subtle clues were available: an Ustashi roadblock, where the secret police hauled drivers out of their Volkswagens and Fiats to check their papers; three or four German Luftwaffe troops, probably from the antiaircraft missile base in the hills above town, strolling along as if they owned the pavement. By the way the Croats scrambled out of their path, the locals were not inclined to argue possession of it.

Smith watched the Luftwaffe men out of the corner of his eye till they rounded a corner and disappeared. "Doesn't seem fair, somehow," he murmured in Italian to Drinkwater. Out in the open like this, he could be reasonably sure no one was listening to him.

"What's that?" Drinkwater murmured back in the same language. Neither of them would risk the distinctive sound patterns of English, not here.

"If this poor, bloody world held any justice at all, the last war would have knocked out either the Nazis or the bloody Reds," Smith answered. "Dealing with one set of devils would be bad enough; dealing with both sets, the way we have the last thirty-odd years, and it's a miracle we haven't all gone up in flames."

"We still have the chance," Drinkwater reminded him. "Remember Tokyo and Vladivostok." A freighter from Russian-occupied Hokkaido had blown up in American-occupied Tokyo harbor in the early 1950s, and killed a couple of hundred thousand people. Three days later, courtesy of the U.S. Air Force, the Russian port also suddenly ceased to be.

"Funny how it was Manstein who mediated," Smith admitted. "Of course, Stalin's dying when he did helped a bit, too, eh?"

"Just a bit," Drinkwater said with a small chuckle. "Manstein would sooner have thrown bombs at the Russians himself, I expect, if he could have arranged for them not to throw any back."

Both Englishmen shut up as they entered the square in front of the cathedral of Our Lady. Like the Spanish fascists, the Croatians were ostentatiously pious, invoking God's dominion over their citizens as well as that of the equally holy state. Any of the men and women heading for the Gothic cathedral ahead might have belonged to the Ustashi; it approached mathematical certainty that some of them did.

The exterior of the church reminded Smith of a layer cake, with courses of red brick alternating with snowy marble. A frieze of angels and a statue of the Virgin surmounted the door to the upper church. As Smith climbed the ornate stairway toward that door, he took off his cap. Beside him, Drinkwater followed suit. Above the door, golden letters spelled out ZA DOM SPREMNI— Ready for the Fatherland—the slogan of fascist Croatia.

Though Our Lady of Lourdes was of course a Catholic church, the angels on the ceiling overhead were long and thin, as if they sprang from the imagination of a Serbian Orthodox icon-painter. Smith tried to wipe that thought from his mind as he walked down the long hall toward the altar: even thinking of Serbs was dangerous here. The Croats dominated Serbia these days as ruthlessly as the Germans held Poland.

The pews of dark, polished wood, the brilliant stained glass, and the statue of the Virgin behind the altar were familiarly Catholic, and helped Smith forget what he needed to forget and remember what he needed to remember: that he was nothing but a fisherman, thanking the Lord for his fine catch. He took out a cheap plastic rosary and began telling the beads.

The large church was far from crowded. A few pews away from Smith and Drinkwater, a couple of Croatian soldiers in khaki prayed. An old man knelt in front of them; off to one side, a Luftwaffe lieutenant, more interested in architecture than spirituality, photographed a column's acanthus capital. And an old woman with a broom and dustpan moved with arthritic slowness down each empty length of pew, sweeping up dust and scraps of paper.

The sweeper came up on Smith and Drinkwater. Obviously a creature of routine, she would have gone right through them had they not moved aside to let her by. "Thank you, thank you," she wheezed, not caring whether she broke the flow of their devotions. A few minutes later, she bothered the pair of soldiers.

Smith looked down to the floor. At first he thought the sweeper simply incompetent, to go right past a fair-sized piece of paper. Then he realized that piece hadn't been there before the old woman went by. He worked his beads harder, slid down into a genuflection. When he went back up into the pew, the paper was in his pocket.

He and Drinkwater prayed for another hour or so, then went back to their fishing boat. On the way, Drinkwater said, "Nothing's simple, is it?"

"Did you expect it to be? This is Croatia, after all," Smith answered. "The fellow who bought our eels likely hasn't the slightest idea where the real meeting will be. It's the God's truth he's better off not knowing, that's for certain."

"Too right there," Drinkwater agreed. "And besides, if we were under suspicion, the Ustashi likely would have come down on us in church. This way we run another set of risks for—" He broke off. Some names one did not say, not in Rijeka, not even if no one was close by to hear, not even in the middle of a sentence spoken in Italian.

Back at the boat, the two Englishmen went on volubly— and still in Italian—about how lovely the church of Our Lady of Lourdes had been; no telling who might be listening. As they talked, Smith pulled the paper from the church out of his pocket. The message was short and to the point: *Trsat Castle, the mausoleum, night after tomorrow, 2200.*

The mausoleum? Bloody melodrama, Smith thought. He passed the note to Drinkwater. His companion's eyebrows rose as he read it. Then he nodded and ripped the paper to bits.

Both men went out on deck. Trsat Castle, or what was left of it after long years of neglect, loomed over Rijeka from the hills outside of town. By its looks, it was likelier to shelter vampires than the Serbian agent they were supposed to meet there. It was also unpleasantly close to the Luftwaffe base whose missiles protected the local factory district.

But the Serb had made his way across Croatia—no easy trick, that, not in a country where *Show me your papers* was as common a greeting as *How are you today?* —to contact British military intelligence. "Wouldn't do to let the side down," Smith said softly.

"No, I suppose not," Drinkwater agreed, understanding him without difficulty. Then, of themselves, his eyes went back to Trsat Castle. His face was not one to show much of what he was feeling, but he seemed less than delighted at the turn the mission had taken. A moment later, his words confirmed that: "But this once, don't you wish we could?"

Smith contrived to look carefree as he and Drinkwater hauled a wicker basket through the streets of Rijeka. The necks of several bottles of wine protruded from the basket. When he came up to a checkpoint, Smith took out a bottle and thrust it in a policeman's face. "Here, you enjoy," he said in his Italian-flavored Croatian.

"I am working," the policeman answered, genuine regret in his voice. The men at the previous checkpoint hadn't let that stop them. But this fellow, like them, gave the fishermen's papers only a cursory glance and inspected their basket not at all. That was as well, for a Sten gun lurked in the straw under the bottles of wine.

Two more checkpoints and Smith and Drinkwater were up into the hills. The road became a dirt path. The Englishmen went off into a narrow meadow by the side of that path, took out a bottle, and passed it back and forth. Another bottle replaced it, and then a third. No distant watcher, assuming any such were about, could have noticed very little wine actually got drunk. After a while, the Englishmen lay down on the grass as if asleep.

Maybe Peter Drinkwater really did doze. Smith never asked him afterwards. He stayed awake the whole time himself. Through his eyelashes, he watched the meadow fade from green to gray to black. Day birds stopped singing. In a tree not far away, an owl hooted quietly, as if surprised to find itself awake. Smith would not have been surprised to hear the howl of a wolf—or, considering where he was, a werewolf.

Still moving as if asleep, Smith shifted to where he could see the glowing dial of his wristwatch: 2030, he saw. It was full dark. He sat up, dug in the basket, took out the tin tommy gun, and clicked in a magazine. "Time to get moving," he said, relishing the feel of English on his tongue.

"Right you are." Drinkwater also sat, then rose and stretched. "Well, let's be off." Up ahead—and the operative word was *up*—Trsat Castle loomed, a deeper blackness against the dark, moonless sky. It was less than two kilometers ahead, but two kilometers in rough country in the dark was nothing to sneeze at. Sweating and bruised and covered with brambles, Smith and Drinkwater got to the ruins just at the appointed hour.

Smith looked up and up at the gray stone towers. "In England, or any civilized country, come to that, a place like this would draw tourists by the bloody busload, you know?"

"But here it doesn't serve the state, so they didn't bother keeping it up," Drinkwater said, following his thought. He ran a sleeve over his forehead. "Well, no law to say we can't take advantage of their stupidity."

The way into the castle courtyard was open. Whatever gates had once let visitors in and out were gone, victims of some long-ago cannon. Inside . . . inside, George Smith stopped in his tracks and started laughing. Imagining the sort of mausoleum that would belong to a ruined Balkan castle, he had visualized something somber and Byzantine, with tiled domes and icons and the ghosts of monks.

What he found was very different: a neoclassical Doric temple, with marble columns and entablature gleaming whitely in the starlight. He climbed a few low, broad steps, stood, and waited. Drinkwater came up beside him. In the judicious tones of an amateur archaeologist, he said, "I am of the opinion that this is not part of the original architectural plan."

"Doesn't seem so, does it?" Smith agreed. "It—"

In the inky shadows behind the colonnade, something stirred. Smith raised the muzzle of the Sten gun. A thin laugh came from the darkness. A voice followed: "I have had a bead on you since you came inside. But you must be my Englishmen, both because you are here at the time I set and because you chatter over the building. To the Ustashi, this would never occur."

Smith jumped at the scratch of a match. The brief flare of light that followed showed him a heavy-set man of about fifty, with a deeply lined face, bushy eyebrows, and a pirate's mustache. "I am Bogdan," the man said in Croatian, though no doubt he thought of his tongue as Serbian. He took a deep drag on his cigarette; its red glow dimly showed his features once more. "I am the man you have come to see."

"If you are Bogdan, you will want to buy our eels," Drinkwater said in Italian.

"Eels make me sick to my stomach," Bogdan answered in the same language. He laughed that thin laugh again, the laugh of a man who found few things really funny. "Now that the passwords are out of the way, to business. I can use this tongue, or German, or Russian, or even my own. My English, I fear, is poor, for which I apologize. I have had little time for formal education."

That Smith believed. Like Poland, like the German Ukraine, Serbia remained a military occupation zone, with its people given hardly more consideration than cattle: perhaps less than cattle, for cattle were not hunted for the sport of it. Along with his Italian, Smith spoke fluent German and passable Russian, but he said, "This will do well enough. Tell us how it is with you, Bogdan."

The partisan leader drew on his cigarette again, making his face briefly reappear. Then he shifted the smoke to the side of his mouth and spat between two columns. "That is how it goes for me, Englishman. That is how it goes for all Serbia. How are we to keep up the fight for freedom if we have no weapons?"

"You are having trouble getting supplies from the Soviets?" Drinkwater asked, his voice bland. Like most of the Balkans' antifascists, Bogdan and his crew looked to Moscow for help before London or Washington. That he was here now—that the partisans had requested this meeting—was a measure of his distress.

He made a noise deep in his throat. "Moscow has betrayed us again. It is their habit; it has been their habit since '43."

"Stalin betrayed us then, too," Smith answered. "If the Russians hadn't made their separate peace with Germany that summer, the invasion of Italy wouldn't have been driven back into the sea, and Rommel wouldn't have had the men to crush the Anglo-American lodgment in France." Smith shook his head—so much treachery since then, on all sides. He went on, "Tell us how it is in Serbia these days."

"You have what I need?" Bogdan demanded.

"Back at the boat," Drinkwater said. "Grenades, cordite, blasting caps . . ."

Bogdan's deep voice took on a purring note it had not held before. "Then we shall give the Germans and the Croat pigs who are their lackeys something new to think on when next they seek to play their games with us in our valleys. Let one of their columns come onto a bridge—and then let the bridge come down! I do not believe in hell, but I shall watch them burn here on earth, and make myself content with that. Have you also rockets to shoot their autogiros out of the air?"

Smith spread his hands regretfully. "No. Now that we are in contact with you, though, we may be able to manage a shipment—"

"It would be to your advantage if you did," Bogdan said earnestly. "The Croats and Germans use Serbia as a live-fire training ground for their men, you know. They are better soldiers for having trained in actual combat. And that our people are slaughtered—who cares what happens to backwoods Balkan peasants, eh? Who speaks for us?"

"The democracies speak for you," Smith said.

"Yes—to themselves." Bogdan's scorn was plain to hear. "Oh, they mention it to Berlin and Zagreb, but what are words? Wind! And all the while they go on trading with the men who seek to murder my nation. Listen, Englishmen, and I shall tell you how it is . . ."

The partisan leader did not really care whether Smith and Drinkwater listened. He talked, letting out the poison that had for so long festered inside him. His picture of Serbia reminded Smith of a fox's-eye view of a hunt. The Englishman marveled that the guerrilla movement still lived, close to two generations after the Wehrmacht rolled down on what had been Yugoslavia. Only the rugged terrain of the interior and the indomitable ferocity of the people there kept resistance aflame.

"The Germans are better at war than the cursed Croats," Bogdan said. "They are hard to trap, hard to trick. Even their raw troops, the ones who learn against us, have that combination of discipline and initiative which makes Germans generally so dangerous."

Smith nodded. Even with Manstein's leadership, fighting the Russians to a standstill had been a colossal achievement. Skirmishes along the borders of fascist Europe— and in such hunting preserves as Serbia—had let the German army keep its edge since the big war ended.

Bogdan went on, "When they catch us, they kill us. When we catch them, we kill them. This is as it should be." He spoke with such matter-of-factness that Smith had no doubt he meant exactly what he said. He had lived with war for so long, it seemed the normal state of affairs to him.

Then the partisan's voice changed. "The Germans are wolves. The Croats, their army and the stinking Ustashi, are jackals. They rape, they torture, they burn our Orthodox priests' beards, they kill a man for having on his person anything written in the Cyrillic script, and in so doing they seek to turn us Serbs into their own foul kind." Religion and alphabet divided Croats and Serbs, who spoke what was in essence the same language.

"Not only that, they are cowards." By his tone, Bogdan could have spoken no harsher condemnation. "They come into a village only if they have a regiment at their backs, and either flee or massacre if anyone resists them. We could hurt them far worse than we do, but when they are truly stung, they run and hide behind the Germans' skirts."

"I gather you are coming to the point where that does not matter to you," Smith said.

"You gather rightly," Bogdan said. "Sometimes a man must hit back, come what may afterward. To strike a blow at the fascists, I am willing to ally with the West. I would ally with Satan, did he offer himself as my comrade." So much for his disbelief, Smith thought.

"Churchill once said that if Germans invaded hell, he would say a good word for the devil," Drinkwater observed.

"If the Germans invaded hell, Satan would need help because they are dangerous. If the Croats invaded hell, he would have trouble telling *them* from his demons."

Smith laughed dryly, then returned to business: "How shall we convey to you our various, ah, pyrotechnics?"

"The fellow who bought your eels will pay you a visit tomorrow. He has a Fiat, and has also a permit for travel to the edge of Serbia: One of his cousins owns an establishment in Belgrade. The cousin, that swine, is not one of us, but he gives our man the excuse he needs for taking his motorcar where we need it to go."

"Very good. You seem to have thought of everything." Smith turned away. "We shall await your man tomorrow."

"Don't go yet, my friends." Agile as a chamois, Bogdan clattered down the steep steps of the mausoleum. He carried a Soviet automatic rifle on his back and held a squat bottle in his hands. "I have here slivovitz. Let us drink to the death of fascists." He yanked the cork out of the bottle with a loud pop. "*Zhiveli!*"

The harsh plum brandy burned its way down Smith's throat like jellied gasoline. Coughing, he passed the bottle to Drinkwater, who took a cautious swig and gave it back to Bogdan. The partisan leader tilted it almost to the vertical. Smith marveled at the temper of his gullet, which had to be made of something like stainless steel to withstand the potent brew.

At last, Bogdan lowered the slivovitz bottle. "Ahh!" he said, wiping his mouth on his sleeve. "That is very fine. I—"

Without warning, a portable searchlight blazed into the courtyard from the open gateway into Trsat Castle. Smith froze, his eyes filling with tears at the sudden transformation from night to brighter than midday. An amplified voice roared, "Halt! Stand where you are! You are the prisoners of the Independent State of Croatia!"

Bogdan bellowed like a bull. "No fucking Croat will take me!" He grabbed for his rifle. Before the motion was well begun, a burst of fire cut him down. Smith and Drinkwater threw themselves flat, their hands over their heads.

Something hot and wet splashed Smith's cheek. He rubbed the palm of his hand over it. In the actinic glare of the searchlight, Bogdan's blood looked black. The partisan leader was still alive. Shrieks alternated with bubbling moans as he writhed on the ground, trying to hold his guts inside his belly.

Jackboots rattled in the courtyard as men from the Ustashi, including a medic with a Red Cross armband, dashed in from the darkness. The medic grabbed Bogdan, stuck a plasma line in his arm. Bogdan did his best to tear it out again. A couple of ordinary troopers kept him from succeeding. "We'll patch you up so you can sing for us," one of them growled. His voice changed to gloating anticipation: "Then we'll take you apart again, one centimeter at a time."

A rifle muzzle pressed against Smith's forehead. His eyes crossed as they looked down the barrel of the gun. "Up on your feet, spy," said the Ustashi man holding it. He had 7.92 millimeters of potent persuasion. Smith obeyed at once.

An Ustashi major strode into the brilliant hole the searchlight had cut in the darkness. He marched up to Smith and Drinkwater, who had also been ordered to his feet. Smith could have shaved on the creases in his uniform, and used his belt buckle as a mirror for the job. The perfect outfit served only to make him more acutely aware of how grubby he was himself.

The major studied him. The fellow had a face out of a fascist training film: hard, stern, handsome, ready to obey any order without question or even thought, not a gram of surplus fat anywhere. An interrogator with a face like his could make a prisoner afraid just by looking at him, and instilling fear was half an interrogator's battle.

"You are the Englishmen?" the major demanded. He spoke English himself, with a better public-school accent than Smith could boast. Smith glanced toward Drinkwater. Warily, they both nodded.

Like a robot's, the major's arm shot up and out in a perfect fascist salute. "The Fatherland thanks you for your help in capturing this enemy of the state and of the true faith," he declared.

On the ground, Bogdan's groans changed tone as he realized he had been betrayed. Smith shrugged. He had a fatherland, too—London told him what to do, and he did it. He said, "You'd best let us get out of the harbor before dawn, so none of Bogdan's people can be sure we had anything to do with this."

"It shall be as you say," the major agreed, though he sounded indifferent as to whether Smith and Drinkwater gave themselves away to Bogdan's organization. He probably *was* indifferent; Croatia and England loved each other no better than Croatia and the Communists. This time, it had suited them to work together. Next time, they might try to kill each other. They all knew it.

Smith sighed. "It's a rum world, and that's a fact."

The Ustashi major nodded. "So it is. Surely God did not intend us to cooperate with such degenerates as you. One day, though, we shall have a true reckoning. *Za dom Spremni!*"

Fucking looney, Smith thought. If the major read that in his eyes, too bad. Croatia could not afford an incident with England, not when her German overlords were dickering with London over North Sea petroleum rights.

The trip down to Rijeka from Trsat Castle was worse than the one up from the city. The Englishmen dared not show a light, not unless they wanted to attract secret policemen who knew nothing of their arrangement with the Ustashi major and who would start shooting before they got the chance to find out. Of course, they ran the same risk on (Smith devoutly hoped) a smaller scale traveling in the dark.

Traveling in the dark down a steep hillside also brought other risks. After Peter Drinkwater fell for the third time, he got up swearing: "God damn the Russians for mucking about in Turkey, and in Iraq, and in Persia. If they weren't trying to bugger the oil wells there, you and I wouldn't have to deal with the likes of the bloody Ustashi—and we'd not have to feel we needed a bath afterwards."

"No, we'd be dealing with the NKVD instead, selling out Ukrainian nationalists to Moscow," Smith answered. "Would you feel any cleaner after that?"

"Not bloody likely," Drinkwater answered at once. "It's a rum world, all right." He stumbled again, but caught himself. The path was nearly level now. Rijeka lay not far ahead.

The Tomb

JACK McDEVITT

The city lay bone white beneath the moon. Leaves rattled through courtyards and piled up against shattered walls. Solitary columns stood against the sky. The streets were narrow and filled with rubble.

The wind off the Atlantic carried the smell of the tide. It sucked at the forest, which had long since overwhelmed the city's defenses and crept into its forums and market-places. A surge of oak and pine in the north had washed over a hill and crashed into sacred environs anchored by a temple and a tomb.

The temple was a relatively modest structure, projecting from the side of the hill. It was, in fact, almost diminutive, but a perceptive visitor would have recognized both Roman piety and Greek genius in its pantheonic lines. The roof was gone, and the circular walls had disappeared within the tangle of trees and brambles.

The front of the building, save for a single collapsed pillar, remained intact. A marble colonnade, still noble in appearance, looked out across a broad plaza. Carved lions slumbered on pedestals, and stone figures with blank eyes and missing limbs kept watch over the city.

Twelve marble steps descended from the temple into the plaza. They were as wide as the building itself, precisely chiseled, rounded, almost sensual. The marble was heavily worn.

One would have needed several minutes to walk across the plaza. Public buildings, in varying states of disintegration, bordered the great square. They stood dark and cold through the long evenings, but when the light was right, it was possible to imagine them as they had been when the city was alive.

The eastern side, opposite the temple, opened onto a

fountain and a long pool. Both were dry and full of dust. Weary strollers, had there been any, would have found stone benches placed strategically for their use.

The tomb stood beyond the fountain on a direct line with the temple. It was an irregular octagon, constructed of tapered stone blocks, laid with military simplicity. The structure was gouged and scorched as high as a man on horseback might reach. If ever the tomb had borne a name, it lay now among the chunks of stone scattered at its base.

The tomb itself lay open. There was no evidence that a slab had ever sealed the gaping shaft. But it must have been so.

A device that resembled a sword had been cut into marble above the entrance. In keeping perhaps with the spirit of the architecture, it, too, was plain: The hilt, the blade, and the cross guard were all rectangular and square-edged.

The vault rose into a circular, open cupola. Two stone feet stood atop the structure, placed wide in what could only have been a heroic stance. One limb was broken off at the ankle, the other at the lower part of the shin.

On a tranquil night, one might easily apprehend the tread of divine sandals.

Three horsemen, not yet quite full-grown, descended from the low hills in the northwest. In the sullen wind, they could smell the age of the place.

They wore animal skins and carried iron weapons. Little more than boys, they had hard blue eyes and rode with an alertness that betrayed a sense of a hostile world. The tallest of the three drew back on his reins and stopped. The others fell in on either side. "What's wrong, Kam?" asked the rider on the left, his eyes darting nervously across the ruins.

"Nothing, Ronik . . ." Kam rose slightly off his mount's haunches and looked intently toward the city. His voice had an edge. "I thought I saw something moving."

The night carried the first bite of winter. Falon, on Kam's right, closed his vest against the chill, briefly fingering a talisman, a goat's horn once worn by his grandfather and blessed against demons. His mount snorted uncertainly. "I do not see anything," he said.

The three riders listened for sounds in the night.

"Where?" asked Ronik. He was broad-shouldered, given to quick passions. He was the only one of the three who had killed. "Where did you see it?"

"Near the temple." Kam pointed. They were still high enough to see over the city's fortifications.

"No one would go there," said Ronik.

The words hung on the night air. No *man*, thought Falon. But he said nothing.

"*We* are going there," said Kam. He was trying very hard to sound indifferent.

Falon stroked his horse's neck. Its name was Carik and his father had given it to him before riding off on a raid from which he had never returned. "It might have been best," he said, "if we had not bragged quite so loudly. Better first to have done the deed, stayed the night, and then spoken of it."

Kam delivered an elaborate shrug: "Why? You're not afraid, are you, Falon?"

Falon started forward again. "My father always believed this city to be Ziu's birthplace. And that"—he looked toward the temple—"his altar."

They were following an ancient roadway. It had once been paved but was little more than a track now, grassed over, occasional stones jutting from the bed. Ahead, it drove straight on to the front gate of the city.

"Maybe we should not do this," said Ronik.

Kam tried to laugh. It came out sounding strained.

Falon gazed across the ruins. It was hard to imagine laughter within those walls, or children being born. Or cavalry gathering. The place felt, somehow, as though it had *always* been like this. "I wonder," he said, "if the city was indeed built by gods?"

"If *you* are afraid," said Kam, "you may return home. Ronik and I will think no less of you." He made no effort to keep the mockery out of his voice.

Falon restrained his anger. "I fear no man," he said. "But it *is* impious to tread on the works of the gods."

They were advancing at a walking rate. Kam did not answer, but he showed no inclination to assume his customary position in the lead. "What use," he asked, after a moment, "would Ziu have for fortifications?"

This was not the only ruined city known to the Kortagenians: Kosh-on-the-Ridge, and Eskulis near Deep Forest, Kalikat and Agonda, the twin ports at Pirapet, and three more along the southern coast. They were called after the lands in which they were found; no one knew how their builders had named them. But there were tales about this one, which was always referred to simply as "The City." Some thought it had no name because, of all the ancient walled settlements, it was the oldest. Others thought it a concession to divine origin.

"If not the home of gods," said Ronik, "maybe *devils*."

There were stories: passersby attacked by phantoms, dragged within the walls, and seen no more. Black wings lifting on dark winds and children vanishing from nearby encampments. Demonic lights, it was said, sometimes reflected off low clouds, and wild cries echoed in the night. Makanda, most pious of the Kortagenians, refused to ride within sight of the city after dark, and would have been thunderstruck had he known their intentions.

They rode slowly forward, speaking in whispers. Past occasional mounds. Past solitary oaks. The wind stiffened and raced across the plain. And they came at last to the city gate.

The wall had collapsed completely at this point, and the entrance was enmeshed in a thick patch of forest. Trees and thickets crowded together, disrupting the road and blocking entry.

They paused under a clutch of pines. Kam advanced, drew his sword, and hacked at branches and brush.

"It does not want us," said Ronik.

Falon stayed back, well away from Kam's blade, which swung with purpose but not caution. When the way was clear and the city lay open, and Kam had sheathed his weapon, he advanced.

The streets were dark and still.

"If it would make either of you feel better," Kam said, "we need not sleep in the plaza."

The horses seemed uneasy.

"I don't think we should go in there at all," said Ronik, his eyes had narrowed, and his features, usually aggressive and energetic, were wary. Falon realized he was frightened. But less adept than his companions at concealment.

Kam's mount took a step forward, a step back. "What do *you* think, Falon?"

The road opened out into a broad avenue. It was covered with grass, lined by crumbling walls and broken courtyards. "We have said we will stay the night," said Falon, speaking softly to prevent the wind from taking his words into the city. "I do not see that we have a choice."

Inside, somewhere amid the dark streets, a dry branch broke. It was a sharp report, loud, hard, like the snapping of a bone. And as quickly gone.

"Something *is* in there," said Ronik, backing away.

Kam, who had started to dismount, froze with one leg clear of the horse's haunches. Without speaking, he lowered it again and tightened his grip on the reins.

"Ziu may be warning us," said Ronik.

Kam threw him a look that could have withered an arm.

Ronik returned the glare. Kam was oldest of the three, and the others usually acceded to his judgment, but Falon suspected that, if it came to a fight, Ronik would prove the more capable. And perhaps the less likely to flee.

"Probably a wolf," said Falon, not at all convinced that it was. Wolves, after all, did not snap branches.

"I am not going in." Ronik dropped his eyes. "It would be wrong to do so."

Kam came erect. "There's a *light*," he whispered.

Falon saw it. A red glow, flickering on the underside of the trees. In the plaza. "A fire," he said.

A shudder worked its way through his belly. He damned himself and fought it down.

"It's near the *tomb*." Kam turned his horse, started back through the trees. Ronik moved to follow, paused, and clasped Falon's shoulder to pull him along.

Falon tried to ignore his own rising panic. "Are we children to be frightened off because someone has built a fire on a cool night?"

"We don't know *what* it might be." Kam's tone had grown harsh. Angry. His customary arrogance had drained completely. "I suggest we wait until daylight. And then see who it is."

Falon could not resist: "Now who is afraid?"

"You know me better," said Kam. "But it is not prudent to fight at night." He turned his mount, and started out.

Ronik was tugging at Falon. "Let's go," he said. "We can retire to a safe distance, in the hills. Stay there tonight, and return to camp tomorrow. No one will ever know."

"We would have to lie," said Falon. "They will ask."

"Let them *ask*. If anyone says I am afraid—" Kam gripped his sword hilt fiercely—"I will kill him."

Falon shook free of Ronik's hand. Ronik sighed, began to back out through the copse, and encountered some difficulty getting his wide shoulders through the twisted branches. He kept his face toward the city, several times jerking his arm toward Falon in a frustrated effort to persuade him to follow.

The forest smelled of pine and dead leaves and old wood.

Kam's voice, impatient: "Hurry..." As if he saw something coming.

Falon was about to comply when Ronik—good, decent Ronik, who had been his friend all his life—spoke the words that pinned him within the city: "Come with us, Falon. It is no disgrace to fear the gods."

And someone else replied with Falon's voice: "No. Carik and I will stay."

"Ziu does not wish it. His will is clear."

"Ziu is a warrior. He is not vindictive. I do not believe he will harm me. I will stay the night. Come for me in the dawn."

"Damn you." Kam's mount, visible through the hole they had cut in the forest, moved first one way, then another. "Farewell, then. We will return in the morning. I hope you will still be here." And they wheeled their horses and fled, one swiftly, the other with reluctance, out along the paved road.

The wind moved through the trees.

Have no fear. I will not betray you.

The red glow of the fire faded and went out. Falon made no effort to track its source.

He rode deliberately into the city. Down the center of the avenue. Past rows of shattered walls and occasional open squares. Past enormous broken buildings. The hoofs were loud in the night.

He stopped in a wide intersection, gathered his courage, and dismounted.

The city lay silent and vast about him.

He spoke to Carik, rubbed his muzzle, and continued on foot, leading the horse. The temple came into view, standing serenely on a mild slope.

His heart hammered, and he debated whether it would not be prudent after all to join Kam and Ronik. And the answer to that was clearly *yes*. Yet he knew that if he ran now, fled beyond the gate, he would in the end have to come back.

Leaves swirled behind him, and Falon glanced fretfully over his shoulder.

Something about the temple stirred him. Some emotion to which he could not put a name fluttered deep in his soul. He walked to the next intersection and looked again. Ghostly illumination filled the building.

Carik moved closer to him.

It was *moonlight*. Nothing more: a trick of the night.

The temple looks complete, but the roof is off. The moon shines directly inside.

He decided against sleeping in the plaza. Better to camp out of the way. Just in case.

He found a running spring and a stout wall on the east side of the avenue. Anything coming toward him from the direction of the tomb would have to cross that broad space.

Falon removed Carik's saddle, loosened the bit, and hobbled the animal. He set out some grain, and sat down himself to a meal of nuts and dried beef. Afterward he rubbed Carik down and took a final look around. Satisfied that he was alone, he used saddle and animal skins to make a bed, placed his weapons at hand, and tried to sleep.

The moon sank behind the wall. Shamed by his own fears, Falon withdrew into the skins and listened for sounds in the city.

Afterward he was never sure whether he had actually slept. But suddenly, deep in the night, he was acutely, vividly awake: The smell of grass was strong, insects buzzed, the wind stirred. A few paces away, Carik shook himself.

There had been a sound out there that didn't belong: a footstep, perhaps. Or a falling rock. He glanced at the horse, which stood unconcerned. Good: It could see over the wall, and if something were approaching, Carik would sound a warning.

Beneath the skins, Falon pressed his hand against the goat's horn to assure himself it was still there. His fingers closed on his sword.

Somewhere, far off, he heard the clink of metal. Barely discernible, a whisper in the wind.

The horse heard it, too. Carik turned his head toward the temple.

Falon got to his feet and looked out across the ruins.

A deeper darkness had fallen over the thoroughfares and courtyards. The temple, no longer backlit by the moon, stood cold and silent.

The sound came again, this time different: a rock colliding with a hard surface. Bounding along.

He was thoroughly awake now, and a few gray streaks had appeared in the east. Dawn was yet far away, but he could retreat, leave the city and its secrets, and still claim truthfully to have stayed the night. And who could blame him?

A light flickered in the plaza.

He couldn't see it directly, but shadows moved across the face of the temple.

Falon shivered.

"Wait," he said to Carik, and slipped over the wall.

• • •

Rubble and cold starlight.

He crept through the dark streets, crossed an intersection, passed silently through a series of courtyards, and moved in behind a screen of trees that looked out over the square.

A lantern had been set on the ground before the tomb. In its yellow light, a robed figure crouched like an animal on hands and knees.

It seemed compounded of night and wind and a sense of things long dead.

Its face was hidden within the folds of a hood.

Falon froze. The creature was digging in the dirt with its fingers. Abruptly it stopped, grunted, looked at something in its hand. Held it near the lantern. Flipped the object into the dark. Falon listened to it crash out toward the middle of the plaza and recognized one of the sounds he'd heard.

He *saw* the source of the other: The area was thoroughly dug up. Piles of earth were heaped everywhere, and an iron spade leaned against a tree.

Falon surveyed the plaza, noted sparks from a banked campfire behind a wall to the north. The figure in the robe seemed to be alone.

It repeated the process, picking up a second object, a stone, turning it several different ways, holding it under the lantern. This time it murmured its satisfaction and got clumsily to its feet. Light penetrated the folds of the hood: It *was* human. A man.

A portion of ground had been cleared, and filled with individual rocks. The figure hunched over them, rearranged them, added the one he held. Lifted it again, placed it elsewhere. Said something Falon couldn't make out. But he understood the pleasure in the voice.

Falon wished he were close enough to see better. It appeared that the man was assembling pieces of statuary. One of the pieces looked like an arm.

With a sudden swirl of robes, the figure raised his lantern as if he knew he was not alone, straightened with an obvious effort, picked up a stick he had laid by, and started toward Falon. He went only a few steps, however, before he stopped, poked at the ground with the stick, and fell again to his knees.

He scrabbled in the tall grass, grumbling and muttering in a strange tongue, thrusting the light forward, and throwing rocks about in a frightful manner. The creature gasped and wheezed throughout this frenetic exercise.

Falon released the breath he had not realized he was holding, touched the goat's horn with the tips of his fingers, and stepped out of the shadows.

The hooded man should have seen him, since the young warrior stood directly in his line of vision. But he did not, and continued rather to poke and prod in the weeds.

Falon closed to within a sword's thrust. "Who are you?" he asked.

The man, startled, finally aware he had a visitor, looked up. "Hello." With considerable effort he got to his feet, wiped clay and dust from his robe, and raised his hand in greeting.

Falon did not return the gesture. "I am Falon the Kortagenian," he said, appraising threat potential and dismissing it. He saw neither arms nor skill.

"And I am Edward the Chronicler." Edward stood so that the light from the lantern played across his features. He looked simultaneously cheerful and wary. His eyes drifted across Falon's blade, which he had not bothered to draw.

"And what sort of chronicle do you compose," asked Falon, "that you dare the spirits of this place?"

Edward seemed to relax somewhat. "If you are really interested," he said, "it is indeed the spirits I pursue. For if they live anywhere on the earth, it is surely here." He swept up the lamp and held it so he could read Falon's face. "A boy," he said. "Are you alone, child?"

The man was short and quite stout. His head was immense, too large even for the corpulent body that supported it. He had a tiny nose, and his eyes were sunk deep in flesh. A series of chins hid his throat altogether from view. His voice suggested he was accustomed to receiving deference.

"I am no child," said Falon, "as you will discover to your sorrow should you fail to show due respect."

"Ah." Edward bowed. "Indeed I shall. Yes: You may rely on that, friend Falon."

"Edward that pursues spirits: What is your clan?"

The dark eyes fastened on him from within the mounds of flesh. "I am late of Lausanne. More recently of Brighton." He collapsed onto a bench, drew back his hood. The man would have been approximately the age of his father. But he was a different sort. This one had never ridden hard. "What," he continued with good humor, "brings you to this poor ruin in the dead of night, Falon?"

"I was passing and saw lights." Yes: That sounded fearless. Let the stranger know he was dealing with a man who took no stock in demons and devils.

"Well," offered Edward in the manner of one who was taking charge, "I am grateful for the company."

Falon nodded. "No doubt." He glanced surreptitiously at the tomb, at the open vault. The passageway into the interior was dark and quiet. "Your accent is strange."

"I am Briton by birth."

Falon had met others from the misty land. He found them gloomy, pretentious, overbearing. It seemed to him that they rarely spoke their minds. "Why are you here?"

Edward sighed. "I would put a name to one of the spirits. And answer a question." He picked up a leather bag. "Can I offer you something to eat?"

"No. I have no need." Falon looked past him, at the temple. "What is the question?"

Edward's eyes locked on him. There was something in them that was unsettling. Something ancient and weary that seemed kin with the city itself. "Falon, do you know who built this place?"

"No. Some of our elders think it has *always* been here."

"Not a very enlightening reply. It was constructed ages ago by a race whom we now remember only dimly. If at all." He turned a sharp eye on Falon.

Falon was too interested to take offense. "And who were they, this forgotten race?" The man spoke with authority, and Falon was accustomed to taking others at their word. Skepticism was not in his nature.

The Briton took a long breath. "They were called Romans," he said.

Falon ran the name across his lips. "I have never heard of them."

Edward nodded. Branches creaked, the flame in the lantern wobbled. "The world," he said, "is full of their temples and cities. The hand that carved *this* tomb created others very much like it across the Alps, in the valley of the Tigris, among the pyramids. They built an immense civilization, Falon. Bridges, temples, viaducts. Roads to tie it together. A system of laws. They gave peace and stability to much of the world." His dark eyes seemed to have fastened on the temple. "But today the Romans and their name are dust, blown across the forests and plains."

Too many words for Falon to follow. He thought of a confederacy of clans that was now attempting to impose its will on the Kortagenians. He supposed the chronicler had something similar in mind, although no one *he* knew had ever shown an inclination toward city-building. "What happened to them, Edward the Chronicler?"

"*That* is the question I have pursued all my days. To discover what force can initiate the decline and cause the collapse of such power."

"Only the gods," said Falon. "These Romans must have offended Woden grievously, that he would destroy even the memory of their accomplishments."

Edward's gaze seemed unsettled. It touched Falon, the tomb, a point somewhere among the stars. "They were forgotten," he said at length, "because they failed to create an institution, independent from the state, that could carry their memory forward."

Falon nodded, not understanding, but not wishing to betray his ignorance.

"A society of scholars, perhaps, might have done it. An academy. A foundation. Possibly even a religious group—"

Falon shrugged it all away, into the night. "What spirit," he asked, "would you name?"

Edward looked toward the stones with which he'd been working. "The occupant of the tomb."

A supernatural chill ran through Falon. He hesitated to reply, not sure of his voice. "Then you are indeed late," he said finally, pleased with his boldness.

The Briton was smiling. Falon saw that several pieces of a human figure had been assembled. The arm was almost complete. There was part of a leg, a shoulder, a trunk, a shield. The leg broke off at the shin.

The shield was emblazoned with the same sword device that marked the front of the vault.

"No," he said. "I think not."

Something moved in the trees.

"Then who is he?"

Edward joined his hands within his sleeves to warm them. "A matchless commander, the hero who might have prevented the general disaster. Dead now these fourteen hundred years, more or less; the chronicles are sometimes inexact." He straightened his robe, adjusted it across his shoulders. "Does the name Maxentius mean anything to you?"

"No," said Falon.

"He was a tyrant who controlled the Roman capital when this city was young. A vicious, licentious, incompetent coward." Edward's voice shook with indignation. "Under his sway, no man's dignity was safe, nor any woman's honor. Wives and daughters were dragged before him and abused. Those who protested were put to death. The people were enslaved. The soldiers were the only order of men whom he appeared to respect. He filled Rome and Italy with armed troops, connived at their assaults against the common people, encouraged them to plunder and massacre. He was, I suspect, a symbol of all that went wrong with the Empire."

Falon's hand fell to his weapon. "I would gladly have ridden against such a monster," he said.

The Briton nodded. "There was one who did. His name was Constantine, and I have no doubt he would have welcomed you to his cause."

Falon felt a surge of pride.

"Constantine appears to have recognized that the empire, which was fragmented in his time, was disintegrating. But he laid plans how it might be preserved. Or, if it were already too late, and collapse could not be prevented, he considered how the essence of its greatness might be passed on." Edward stood unmoving against the night. "Had he been able to seize power from Maxentius, things might have been different."

"He failed in the effort?"

"He was a reluctant crusader, Falon. And he marched against Maxentius only when the tyrant threatened to invade *his* domains."

"I cannot approve of such timidity," said Falon.

Edward smiled. "I would be disappointed if you did. But Constantine wished to conserve the peace and welfare of his realm."

"And where was his realm?"

"Britain," he said. "And here."

"But I do not understand." Falon grasped Edward's shoulder, turned him that he could look into his face. "If this Constantine was a commander of great ability, as you have said, how did it happen that he did not prevail?"

"Heroes do not win all engagements," Edward said slowly. "Maxentius sent army after army against him. Constantine swept them away. Most of the Italian cities between the Alps and the Po not only acknowledged his power but also embraced his cause. And at last he appeared before Rome itself. The seat of the tyrant." Edward paused. They were exposed out here, and the wind cut through Falon's thin vest. The Briton stopped his narrative and stared up at him. "Are you cold?" he asked.

"No. Please go on."

"Maxentius had by far the larger army. He also had armored cavalry, a type of opponent that *you*, Falon, will never see. Fortunately. But he chose not to rely on military force alone." Without another word and without explanation, he walked into the shadows. Moments later he returned with a woven garment and held it out to the young warrior.

Falon pulled it over his shoulders. "Thank you."

Edward resumed his seat. "There was, across the Tiber, a float bridge that connected the city with the plain. This was the Milvian Bridge. Maxentius directed his engineers to weaken it. Then he rode out of his capital to engage the invader.

"Constantine was waiting, and the armies fell quickly to battle. For much of the afternoon the conflict raged back and forth, and the issue was uncertain. It was one more of a series of calamitous events that sucked the lifeblood of the Empire. However that may be, Constantine's troops pressed forward, and gradually the tyrant gave way."

"Now," urged Falon, "strike the chief."

"Yes," said Edward. "One might almost think you were there. And he did: He rallied his personal guard and led them them against that part of the line in which he could see the tyrant's colors. The banners wavered at the onslaught, and the shock of the charge broke the Roman line. The defenders panicked. But Maxentius, with his picked men, retreated across the fateful bridge. Unmindful of caution, Constantine pursued, bleeding from a dozen wounds.

"And in that terrible moment, when his great enemy had reached the center of the bridge, the tyrant gave the signal, and the span was hurled into the Tiber."

"The coward," said Falon with a snarl. And then, philosophically, "Valor is not always sufficient to the day. Constantine need not be ashamed."

"No. Certainly not."

"And did there arise a hero to avenge him?"

"Yes. But that is another story, for the avenger lacked political wisdom, and soon after his success the empire's lights dimmed and went out. Then the world fell into a night that has had no dawn."

"But what connection has the tale with this vault? Is the tomb indeed empty?"

Edward arranged his robe, draped it over his knees. He held out the lantern to Falon. "Perhaps you would care to look?"

"No." He drew away. "It is quite all right."

The Briton rose. "You should assure yourself. Please. Follow me."

They entered the passageway, Edward leading with his lantern, stepping over mulch and earth and weeds. It was narrow, the ceiling was low, and the rock walls were cracked. Falon had to duck his head.

It sloped at a modest angle and ended in a small chamber. The chamber was bare, devoid of furniture or marking save for a marble shelf laid against the inner wall. "There were rumors," said Edward, "that Constantine survived. One account, of which I have a copy, maintained that he was taken half-drowned from the Tiber and returned to a friendly but unnamed city. The story holds that he lived in this city one year. Other sources say three. It's difficult to recover the details. All agree that he hoped to lead another army against Maxentius but that he never fully recovered. And when he died . . ." Edward shrugged. "I've looked for many years, seeking the truth of the event."

"And how would you know the truth?"

"Easily," he said. "Find his tomb." He kicked away dead leaves and dirt and pointed toward scratches on the stone floor. "Here is where his sarcophagus once stood. There, on the shelf, they placed his armor."

"Then this *is* his tomb?"

"Oh, yes, I am quite satisfied on that score. Yes: Unquestionably he was interred here. And a great deal more, I fear."

Falon wondered how he could possibly know such things.

"While he lived, he talked of building a second Rome, in the East." Edward's voice was filled with regret. "Something to survive."

The smoke thrown up by the lantern was already growing thick.

Edward lapsed into silence. He coughed, tried to wave away the noxious cloud.

Falon's eyes had begun to water. "Let's finish this outside," he said.

"What?"

"*Outside.*" He seized Edward's elbow and steered him back up into the starlight. The air was cold and tasted good. Falon took it gratefully into his lungs. "How do you *know*?" he asked. "How can you be sure it's *his* tomb? It is not marked."

"Oh, yes, it *is*. Look behind you." He pointed at the statue, which lay partly assembled. "Look on the shield."

A burst of wind pulled at his garment.

Edward held the lantern close. In its flickering light, Falon saw only the curious sword. It was identical to the blade on the vault.

"I do not know the sign," he said.

"It was *his* device."

Falon pressed his fingers against it. "Can you be so certain? There are many who use weapon devices."

"This is *not* a weapon," said Edward. "It was a symbol sometimes used by an obscure religious cult. For many centuries, in fact, a mark of shame. Said to have magic properties. It's called a cross."

Falon fingered his talisman. The sense of the horn's power was reassuring. "The mark is strange to me."

"Only Constantine ever used it."

"You said something else was buried in there with him."

Edward picked up his bag. "An old man's idle dream, perhaps. I wonder whether everything we might have been does not lie inside this vault."

Brilliant Sirius was framed within the cupola atop the tomb. "It's getting colder," he said after a moment. "I suggest we retire to my camp and restart the fire."

Turpentine

BARRY N. MALZBERG

The sociologist was defiant all the way to Kirk's office, but when he saw the scene, when he got what you could call a sociological perspective of the ordnance, his mood changed right quick. What is this? he said. What the fuck is this? Trust a sociologist to toss a *fuck* in when he is talking to the troops. That's what they teach them in the schools now, get down, get right, be *relevant*, talk out of that hip side of your mouth. Saying *fuck* puts everybody at his or her ease, like the sociologist and you, you are on the same side of the party, fighting the *e*stablishment. Except we don't really go along with that shit anymore, there is our side and there is the rest of them and the line is not to be crossed by sociologists, white sociologists from the University of Chicago with a Ph.D. in population, as the catalog we had researched put it. Give us the plans, Richard said, just give us the plans. We know you have them.

The sociologist stared, little guy, maybe five and a half feet, still gripping the satchel he had snatched when we grabbed him from his office. What are you talking about? he said. He took in the scene pretty good; we could see him making sociological calculations behind that forehead of his. I should have gotten out of here, he said. That was my mistake. When the going was good, I should have got. We had trashed Kirk's office pretty good by then, although nothing as to what the press was going to say later. I could figure out what the press would say. By the time the Rosenthals were through with us, they would have the dung piled feet deep; as they say would be talking about the jism on the carpets instead of into the Barnard girls, where it had been properly aimed. But there was no way to put off that kind of crap; as Richard said, you took your shot and you aimed it and the rest of it

177

was establishment blues, that was all. The plans, he said
again. The underground reactor, the tunnels, the way in.
We know you have them. They were planted in your office
a month ago when the stuff started getting serious. I want
them now.

The sociologist stared at Richard. You're crazy, he said.
You've got to be crazy. What are you talking about, nuclear
reactors, tunnels? That's for the Department of Physics,
not for me. I'm in the soft sciences.

You in soft sciences, mother, Richard said, going into
his deep Panther act. Maybe I should explain that we
were a mixed crowd—heavily mixed, as they say, boys and
girls, black and white—but Richard in shades and full
regalia had asked for the whole show and we had fallen
back against the walls. If there was one thing he knew,
Richard had said, it was how to put the screws to a white
sociologist. Watch me jive, he had said, lean back and
learn how we're going to deal with the rest of these
mothers from the point of revolution *on*. We had laughed
then but it didn't seem so funny now, Richard himself
being carried away a bit with the shades and the chain act.
But we were deep in by then and no arguing it. You *real*
soft, Richard said. Let me explain to you, he said, coming
up to the sociologist and giving him the finger in the gut,
one, two, three, the rhythm boys. Back when things
started moving around here about a month ago, foxy old
Administration whose very offices you will note we now
*occ*upy thought that it would be best to get the plans, the
secret plans for the underground tunnels out of the head
offices and to some place relatively innocent. *Inno-cent*
you get that, you understand the frame? We're just trying
to be helpful and refresh your memory.

I don't know what's going on here, the sociologist said.
Believe me, you have me at a loss. I am willing to help,
but I never heard of anything like this. You have me at a
loss, I told you, I want—

You see my friend Ronald X here? Richard said. Ronald
X is my security consultant, my comrade-in-arms, you
dig? He is a desperate man.

That is right, I said, I am a desperate man.

He comes from a greatly deprived background, Richard said. You know all about cultural deprivation, they give out Ph.D.'s in that subject. Your guy Alinsky in Chicago, he runs seminars on the streets about people like my friend Ronald X. There is *capital funding* from the government to study the deprivations in the head of this desperate man over here.

The sociologist stared at Richard as if he had never seen anyone like him before. Possibly this is true. It is possible that Richard was a new experience for the sociologist, just as he had been for me back in those times when we were sharing backgrounds down at the Union. You can see what a desperate man he is from the look in his eyes, Richard said. He is from CCNY, which makes him even more frantic because he does not have that fine education and potentially prestigious degree behind him. He is just your basic nigger, Ronald X, and he is very angry.

I want your help, I said, I want you to find me the plans. That is a simple request and then I will not be so desperate. I will leap over my cultural background and be as solid and reasonable as you. But right now I am strictly speaking not civilized.

The sociologist seemed tormented, or perhaps the word was abstract. These shades of meaning are more for Richard than me. Clear to us, though, *no* part of Chicago population studies seemed to have prepared him for this, or at least he had not taken the course. That had been an elective, dealing with mad up-against-the-wall niggers in the president's office at 2:00 A.M. with about twenty-five hundred police ringing the campus and the place going crazy. Maybe if he went back to school for some postpostgraduate work he would remember to take that course next time. But right now he was flat out of luck. That out-of-luck expression seemed to filter through all of his hard little features and then he said, I still don't know what the deal is. But I'll go back with you and look through desk drawers. I don't care.

That is a righteous cooperative attitude, Richard said, we can praise that motherfucking attitude. Richard always leaves the g on when he uses the big word. He says that it makes them more terrified, proper grammatical perspective in a brute scheme, something like a doctor explaining the logistics of testicular cords just before he cuts your balls off. Brings it all home. We'll just send you on your way then, Richard said, and soon you'll be back.

I stayed behind to help you, the sociologist said. I didn't want to run out of the buildings, I wanted to show solidarity.

Well, you showing it, Richard said. Ain't he showing it, Ronald? Let's go.

I take the sociologist by the arm in a deep Muslim squeeze and propel him through the door. Some of the brothers separate themselves from the wall and follow us, but this is our party and I know it. Richard has left it all up to me, this part, and I would say I were proud if I did not have so much else on my concentrated and busy mind.

They got reactors, Richard had said to me a few hours earlier, while we were working the plan, this just after we had crashed through into Kirk's office and sent them running. We're going to get hold of them. We're going to get the nukes.

It's a dumb plan, Jonathan said. Look at me. Listen to me. We can't get at reactors.

They got a motherfucking atomic pile under this place, Richard said. Everybody knows that. Had it for years. You can feel the little heat, the explosions bouncing through the grass when you cut across the quad. Once I was taking a leak in the physics building, I could feel *atomic heat* pass through my generous organ.

I didn't say they weren't there, Jonathan said. Everyone knows it, all right. But messing with nukes is high-caliber business. They get wild, we get hold of atomic shit.

Your trouble, Richard said, you a gentle-ass white guy from the suburbs of *Mahopac* or somewhere, you're interested in symbolic gestures, in *radicalization*, in heavy rioting in dress gear. Both me and Ronald, though, we got a different background, we got a somewhat different grasp of the situation. We're here, we're going to take it all the way.

This is not the answer, Jonathan said. He took out a handkerchief, shook it, removed his glasses, began to wipe them. We're doing just what we should. We got the buildings clear, we got the campus secure. The campus is ours tonight. They're afraid to come in, and we can get out anytime we want. Now we press the nonnegotiable demands.

You white boys amuse me, Richard said. He took the glasses from Richard's hand, gave them a few strokes with his fingers. You think this is display, you with your nonnegotiable demands, your symbolic gestures, your *liberating* the president's office. You're full of shit, that's what you are. You're playing and they're playing. But we're not, that's the whole difference. Ronald and I, we're in this for keeps. Wake up in the morning, you can go back to Mahopac. Wake up in the morning, Ronald and I are still black. He's humping for dollars at CCNY, I'm kissing ass down here in the department of stripes and ribbons, but they put the lights on and we're niggers. So we're serious. We got to be serious, that's our condition.

So what are you going to do? Jonathan said. You're going to hold up the university, that's it? You're going to go nuclear on them? That's heavy shit, heavy water down there, you fuck around with it, you'll blow all of us up.

I got techniques, Richard said, I got plans. Me and my ringleader, Ronald, we got big plans. We get access to the atomics, they're not going to be so quick to rush in.

Jonathan put the glasses back on his nose. He looked like what he was going to become, a professor of literature, the glasses flashing clean bright white light now. In that angle I could see Richard's point, finally, and the answer that went through me was as clean as the light. That's about it, I said, the man has just about put it right.

They're not coming in anyway, Jonathan said. They're ringing the buildings but they're not going anywhere. I tell you, it's a triumph, we got them paralyzed. We're getting our story out to the press and they're listening.

You white fool, Richard said, you think they're listening? They're just holding off, letting the little boys and girls play. Three days from now, they can't tear-gas us out, they'll come in with grenades and clean out the place. You're in a playpen, boy, you don't understand anything. But it's a lot more serious for us and that's the fucking truth. The confab is over. Split. We're going to get us a sociologist and some directions.

Jonathan looked at me. Can't you understand? he said. If we go for the reactor, that's a whole different gig. That changes the rules on them and they'll come in and kill us.

You never understood, did you? I said. I grabbed him by neat handfuls of his shirt, pulled him toward me. We not interested in symbolic gestures, I said, we not interested in little white boys' and girls' game, playing around in the toilets, making the nursery school mad. We are in this for *keeps* now and you just opened the door to that. You let us in, you wanted a collaboration, you wanted a multiracial movement, you wanted a national protest— well, that's what you got. And now it's time to stand aside and let the men work this out.

Jonathan looked at me and then away, stared at Richard. The stare was a good preparation for what we would see from the sociologist a little bit later. I can't believe it, he said, you *are* serious. You really think that this is going to work.

We don't care if it works, Richard said, it's just something we do, dig? We go all the way. You want multiracial, you got it. You want up against the wall, this is it. We not talking about humping in the president's chair, leaving Kirk a little white stuff on the walls. We talking about power, about possession. So that's it. You understand the situation?

He surely do, I said to Richard. He surely does. I do not think that it is necessary to discuss it with the stud anymore.

Oh one more thing, Richard said. You staying with us, you understand?

Of course I'm staying with you, Jonathan said. I wouldn't—

You think you sneak out of the building about 4:00 A.M., you turn to white in the morning sun and go back to Mahopac, you got it wrong. You in it all the way, just like us. We got fifteen bloods with carbines and serious intentions, you change your mind on that.

He's not changing his mind, I said. His mind is visibly unchanged.

Richard laughed. I did some laughing, too. Then we went back into the main room and announced that there would be a continuation of the plan, there being no need to tell the boys and girls in the outer echelon anything more at this point, and then we went hunting for a sociology professor. Jonathan had been very good at getting hold of the secret plans and administration fallback positions. We had to give him credit for that. Before our little disagreement, so thoroughly resolved, Jonathan had been a real worker for the cause. Of course, he had had a different name for it.

In the concrete it was just Richard and me, looking at the dials, watching the dials do their little dance, hearing the thunder of the machines, smelling all of those compressors and atom splitters and heavy isotopic remedies. The sociologist had come across like a hooker, and the plans had been airtight. Everything was exactly where it was supposed to be, us and the place together. Now, Richard said, adjusting his weapon and rubbing his hands, now we show them some *real* nonnegotiable demands. Nonnegotiable isn't a slip of paper and four little white girls screaming and shaking their tits. Nonnegotiable is here it is baby or we blow up Riverside Park and the West End tavern and the place where Kirk's asshole sits, too. How about that? He giggled, higher-pitched than I've ever heard him. Can a CCNY guy dig it? he said.

I can dig it, I said. I can dig a lot. It is heavy business.

I think we can do this, Richard said. I got five, six guys with heavy-tech brains and good mechanical aptitudes, I think they can really twist those dials and make this thing work. I thought it was a wild chance when we started, yes. Wild; I know it, he said, I thought Jonathan was crazy. But now it's not so wild. I think it can work.

What can work? I said. Anything?

Anything at all. We'll put a few demands, we'll test them out. For openers, Richard said, I want New York City.

What's that? I said.

Oh, not all of it, he said. They can keep Harlem. They can even keep Brownsville and Bed-Stuy, they so crazy for it. But they can hand me Park Avenue and Seventy-ninth and the stock exchange and we'll go on from here. He gave me a gleaming smile. That's what I think.

Looking at Richard, it occurred to me—and not for the first time—that the boy was really crazy, that he was as crazy as the sociologist and maybe Jonathan thought he was. But that didn't make him any less lovable, only a hell of a lot more dangerous, I thought. We better rejoin the troops, I said. The troops be getting anxious soon.

Oh, we rejoin, Richard said. We rejoin and then we reup. How would you like Arpels? Me, I'm going to take Tiffany's. We're going to shake things up a little in this city. You know why? he said.

Because we are desperate men, I said. Because we are the underclass, we are the natives right out of Congoland and we got nothing to lose.

That's right, Richard said. Oh, you is a righteous lad, all right.

The white boys and girls aren't going to take that too much to heart, I said.

No, they ain't, Richard said. But they let us in, didn't they? You invite the piper, you buy the meal.

The rumbling goes on and on as we draft our statement and then it is time to get back to the troops. But only for a while, I think. We have our battle plan now. We have our heads toward the situation. Soon enough, maybe, there will be no need for the troops. When they go through the stuff left in Kirk's office, maybe they don't necessarily find our names and pedigrees after all. It depends. It is, as they say, a fluid situation. It is closing in on the end of the sixties and everything is not as it was here in walrusland.

• • •

The first communiqué meets silence and the second communiqué gets only a beat from whoever is on the phone at the other end. The third communiqué, however, setting a midnight deadline, does get some response. We'll get back to you, they say. They do not believe it. Obviously they do not believe it. We have to begin reading off some coordinates and serial numbers on isotope containers before the tone of the responses changes.

I think they believe us now, Richard said. I do believe that they believe we got nukes here and we are ready like the boys in Vietnam to die. I think midnight will see some interesting responses.

We have asked them to withdraw all of their troops by midnight and also to issue a statement of capitulation. Otherwise the first reactor goes off. We have guarantees that this can be done although, of course, one can never be sure. The phone, dead for so long, is suddenly lively. They plead for more time, time to work things out. We read them a few more serial numbers. A senior physicist from the State Department, or that is what he says he is, gets on the line and we have to convince him, too. After a while he goes away.

The sociology professor is crashed out on the floor, a couple of ladies around him, rubbing his shoulders. We tell him that we will not necessarily identify him as the collaborator but he will have to stay with us for a while. We will, however, make it as easy and pleasant for him as possible. The white girls are cooperative, as is so often the case with white girls and white men, also black men now that you asked.

We sit and pass the time, Richard and I sharing some old stories. Our backgrounds may be different, me with my gentle middle-class thing and he on the harder rock, but they are also quite similar. We are both niggers, after all. They plead for another twelve hours' extension and Richard gets on the horn this time and tells them this is the commander and they can fuck themselves. Two hours, that is it; 2:00 A.M. and their troops and dogs are off the campus or the first reactor goes on-line. We will talk about Tiffany's later. They say they will get back to us.

Jonathan comes in from the back room, where we have stashed him. After three hours' sleep we would expect him to be more reasonable or at least less wired, but this is not the case. He is more frantic than ever.

I've been thinking this through, he said. Been talking to a few people.

That's good, Richard said. Talk is always good. High communication, that was your original demand, right?

We have to pull back, Jonathan said, this isn't going to work. It won't work with these odds.

It's working fine, Richard says. Don't you think so, Ronald? I shrug. Working okay by me, I say.

This guy, Jonathan said, this LBJ. He just pulled out, you understand? The war did him in, *he* did him in. All he wanted in the world was to be the king and they took it away from him and worst of all he had to sink the knife in himself, you dig that?

I dig that fine, Richard says, it is a satisfying source of pleasure. It is an inspiration. It sends us on our way.

So this guy lost everything, Jonathan says, Old LBJ, he doesn't care anymore, don't you see? The worst that can happen has happened. He won't be president.

Still got the Hump, Richard says. He giggled. The Hump will keep the chair mighty warm, also his mouth, don't you agree?

You don't get it at all, Jonathan says, you really don't get it. He grabs Richard's wrists. You are dealing with a guy who has already lost everything. He has nothing more to lose, not the hump, not anything. He doesn't care, you're pushing him over the edge. He is leaning over, half-trying to bring Richard up.

Let go of my wrists, white man, Richard says very quietly. Just release your grip.

Damn it, Jonathan says, I worked this out. I may be white but I'm not stupid. You're dealing with a guy who has already lost everything, you're putting him in a box now, don't you see?

See? Richard says. I see everything. I am far-ranging. You are still grasping my wrists. You let them go within the next ten seconds or you see who will lose everything and how.

He hates New York, Jonathan says, letting him go, crouching beside us. He thinks that everything that beat him came out of New York anyway. Now he's got the enemy at home, waving nukes. You know what that means?

I know what it means, I say. It means that we are finally making an impression.

We're making an impression, Jonathan says, we're making a *big* impression. He's going to hit us, that's what's going to happen. He'll send in the Strategic Air Command.

Oh, white boy, Richard says, you have a fertile mind and heart. The Strategic Air Command. He chuckles. You don't understand who has who by the balls here, he says. You don't understand the situation.

I understand the situation, Jonathan says, we are in heavy shit. We are in the heaviest shit. We are dealing with a crazy man by being crazy. You know what happens then?

I don't know, Richard says, help me.

He's just looking for an excuse, Jonathan says. You've given him all the excuse he needs. You've brought Vietnam home.

Time he got to Vietnam ,Richard says. Time for sure.

And he's got the provocation now. He'll use the bomb.

Richard says, Jonathan, you losing your cool. Nuke out a bunch of college kids with a reactor? Shit, what you talking about? We can't do *nothing* with that machine, that little bitty old separator. That's the word from the Chemistry Department. We can rattle the bones, Richard says, but we can't pull no action.

LBJ doesn't know that, Jonathan says. LBJ's no nuclear scientist.

Neither are we, Richard says. He's figured that out already. But he's got poor public relations.

You don't get it, Jonathan says. He doesn't know about bitty old separators and radioactivity. Doesn't *care*, either. For him, we've turned into Viet Cong. He thinks he's got the Viet Cong right here at home and he's going to trash us out, that's what I think.

Talk to the Chemistry Department, Richard says. Examine their *iso*topes, see what they got to say.

LBJ has freaked out, Jonathan says. He's over the line. he doesn't care what we can do, he's got the excuse. I'm telling you, we better back off.

Richard takes Jonathan by the wrist, hauls himself up, gives him a push. *You* back off, he says. You back off all your life, in the morning you're still white. It's a game for you and now the stakes are a little too high. But you can't get out. He points to the sociology professor, the professor hiding between four tits over on the carpet, the little coeds stroking his hair.

You and he are black as us tonight, he says. You going to stay through the end, see this through one time.

We'll see it through, Jonathan says. You fool, there's nowhere to hide. There's no place to go, you think it's any safer on Thirty-fifth Street or up in Inwood than it is right here? We can't get out anywhere, none of us. We're cooked to a circumference of four hundred and fifty miles. Because we're the enemy and now he's got the rationalization he needs.

It's throwdown time, Richard says. That honky, he's not going to throw it down, that's all.

You'll see, Jonathan says. He walks out the open door. It feels as if we have been shouting, but for all the notice our conversation takes, we might have been whispering. Or maybe all the troops, the sociology professor and his companions, they, too, are simply asleep. It is deep night, and in the extinguished spaces now I can barely see Richard.

White boy, Richard says. Establishment bitch. Just another one all the time.

What if he's right? I say.

What's that?

I said, What if he's right? What if LBJ doesn't give a shit anymore? What if he just hits us with everything he has? Jonathan's right, he's a dead man anyway. He's out of office. How long is he going to live?

You're as crazy as the rest of them, Richard says. Me,

I'm going to get a little sleep, be alert at 2:00 A.M. Need my beautify sleep for some serious negotiating.

He could be right, he says. You just know it.

You, too, Ronald? Richard says. His eyes are round, maybe amused, hard to tell in the dark. You going to go establishment on me, too?

I'm not going anywhere.

That's good. Because it's too late, Richard says, you get that? It's just too goddamned late and we're going to see it through now. We got the plan and the plan is going to work right through to the end and that's the end of the plan. He rambles off toward the couch. Crash me back in half an hour, he says. Stand the sentry. Play watch.

I get up, follow him partway across the room, then lean against the wall to brace myself, feeling unsteady. There is a sudden shift and uneasiness in the room. I can hear the sound of distant humming.

It would happen so fast, I say to Richard, we wouldn't even know it had happened.

He says nothing.

I have read about these things, I say. It is like a head-on automobile crash. If you know it's happened, it hasn't happened. It's so fast you are dead before you know it.

I am already asleep, Richard says, I am finding my righteous moments.

In the dark, I lean against the wall. The professor is muttering something. Maybe other things are going on outside; the lawn seems suddenly close against me and I can smell the stink of the occupiers.

And then there is an amazing light, the light of Calvary.

I see the light; I know it is happening.

Which means then according to Richard that if I see it going on it isn't going on, except it is.

It is and it *is*.

And the screaming, and the fire...

Goddard's People

ALLEN STEELE

A morning in wartime: May 24, 1944, 5:15 A.M. PST. Day is barely breaking over the California coastline; for the crew of the B-24 Liberator *Hollywood Babe*, it's the fifth hour of their mission. The bomber has been holding a stationary position since midnight over the ocean southeast of the Baja Peninsula, flying in narrow circles at twenty-five thousand feet. Their classified mission has been simple: Watch the skies. The vigil is about to end.

Gazing through the cockpit windows, the captain notices a thin white vapor trail zipping across the dark purple sky. Many miles above and due west of his plane's position, the streak is hopelessly out of *Hollywood Babe*'s range, even if the bomber was ordered to intercept the incoming object. Becoming alert, he glances over his shoulder at the civilian in the jump seat behind him.

"Sir, is that what you're looking for?" the captain asks.

The civilian, an agent of the Office of Strategic Services, quickly leans forward and stares at the streak. "Son of a bitch," he murmurs under his breath. For a moment he can't believe what he's seeing. Only yesterday he had been telling someone that MI-6 must be getting shell-shocked, because now they were sending science fiction yarns to the OSS. But, incredible or not, this was exactly what the OSS man had been told to watch for.

He turns to the radio man in the narrow compartment behind the cockpit. "Sergeant, alert White Sands now!" he yells over the throb of the B-24's engines. "It's on its way!"

Many miles away, warning Klaxons howl at a top-secret U.S. Army facility in the New Mexico desert. Around a spotlighted launch pad, technicians and engineers scurry away from the single-stage, seventy-five-foot winged silver rocket poised on the pad. Cold white oxygen fumes venting from the base of the rocket billow around the steel launch tower. The gantry is towed back along railroad tracks by a locomotive, and fuel trucks race away to a safe distance where the ground crew and several soldiers wait, their eyes fixed on the pad.

In a concrete blockhouse four hundred yards from the launch pad, more than a dozen men are monitoring the launch. Among them, nine civilian scientists are hunched over control panels, anxiously watching hundreds of dials and meters as they murmur instructions to each other. In the middle of the blockhouse a frail, scholarly man peers through a periscope at the launch pad as the countdown reaches the final sixty seconds.

For more than two years, these ten men have worked toward this moment; now, in the last minute, most of them are scared half to death. If the launch is unsuccessful, there will be no second chance. If the rocket blows up, as so many other rockets have before it, the Navy pilot inside the machine will die. But far worse than that, New York City, thousands of miles to the east, will suffer a devastating attack. An eighty-ton incendiary bomb will drop into the middle of Manhattan, and there will be nothing in heaven or on earth to stop it. If the launch is successful, it will be the crowning achievement of American technology; if it fails, it may be the beginning of the end for free society. The stakes are that high.

"Ten . . . nine . . . eight . . ." an Army officer recites tonelessly. Staring through the periscope, Robert Hutchings Goddard absently wipes his sweaty palms against the rubber grips and silently begins to pray. . . .

Forty-seven years ago, in the early morning hours of a summer day in World War II, a huge rocket called the A-9—the *Amerika Bomber*—hurtled down a horizontal track in Germany and climbed to the highest altitude ever achieved, 156 miles above the earth. Horst Reinhart, a young Luftwaffe lieutenant, became the first man in space. One hour and thirty-six minutes later, the rocket christened the *Lucky Linda* blasted off from New Mexico, and U.S.

Navy pilot Rudy "Skid" Sloman's triumphant howl was picked up by ham radio operators across the continent as the United States became the world's second spacefaring nation.

This much is well known; what has been largely lost to history, though, is the leading role played by a mild, stoop-shouldered physics professor from Worcester. Not because of neglect—Robert H. Goddard's place in the annals of spaceflight as the father of American rocketry has been assured—but because of enduring cold war suspicions. In the years since his death in 1945, facts about his private life, particularly during the Second World War, have remained hidden, mainly because of national security interests. Goddard was known to have had a vague "consultant" role in Project Blue Horizon, but little more has been discovered by Goddard's biographers. The official story is that Goddard spent the war teaching at Clark University in Worcester, Massachusetts. Not much else is in the public record.

Yet if that part of Robert Goddard's biography is opaque, even less is known about the top-secret research group that was once code-named Team 390. Each year, on the anniversary of *Lucky Linda*'s flight, the seven survivors of the American rocket team gather at a sportsman's lodge in New Hampshire, on the shore of Lake Monomonock. Once again, in the lodge's den, the secret tale is told. As the seven old men speak, more than a few times their eyes wander to the framed photo of Goddard that hangs above the mantel.

They are all that remain of Team 390, but they rarely call themselves by that name. Now as then, they are known among themselves simply as Goddard's people.

The affair began on the morning of January 19, 1942, when OSS agent William Casey (later to become the Director of Central Intelligence during the Reagan Administration) arrived in Washington, D.C., from London on a U.S. Army DC-3. An attaché case handcuffed to his wrist contained a top-secret Nazi document that British

MI-6 agents had discovered on the island of Peenemünde. By noon, the document—code-named Black Umbrella, unofficially known as the "Sanger Report"—was on the desk of President Franklin D. Roosevelt.

The United States had been directly involved in World War II for only six weeks when the Sanger report was unearthed. Isolationism had crumbled after the Japanese attack on Pearl Harbor, and fear was running high in the country that North America itself was the next target of the Axis powers; in Washington itself, antiaircraft guns and air-raid sirens were already being erected on city rooftops. Black Umbrella could not have arrived at a better time to have been taken seriously.

Peenemünde is on an island off the coast of Germany in the Baltic Sea. Once the site of a seldom-visited fishing village, during the war the island had become the location of secret Nazi rocket research for the German Army. Germans had been vigorously developing liquid-fuel rockets even before Adolf Hitler had become chancellor, and the Nazis had incorporated rocket research into their war plans, recruiting a team of civilian rocket scientists, with Wernher von Braun as its chief scientist. British Intelligence had known that Peenemünde was the site of secret rocket experiments; a large missile called the A-4 was alleged to be in the final phases of R&D. "Silver" and "Gold," two MI-6 agents working undercover in Peenemünde as janitors, had been monitoring the continuing development of the A-4 rocket, later to be known by the Allies as the V-2.

However, in recent months more puzzling things had been happening in Peenemünde. Something new was being developed in a warehouse that was kept locked and guarded at all times; rumors around the base had it that an even more ambitious weapon than the A-4 was being built by von Braun's rocket team. High Command officers such as Hermann Göring, Rudolf Hess, and Heinrich Himmler had been regularly visiting Peenemünde, spending long hours in the warehouse. Yet Silver and Gold had no idea of what was going on, except that it was even more top-secret than the A-4 project.

Finally, the two agents had a stroke of luck. For a few precious, unguarded moments, a four-hundred-page document stamped "State Secret" had been carelessly left out on von Braun's desk by his personal secretary. Without reading the report, Silver had used a miniature camera to photograph as many pages as possible. The team then managed to smuggle the microfilm out of Germany, not knowing what information it contained except that it was part of a report that should have been kept under lock and key. The microfilm made its way to Whitehall in London, where MI-6 intelligence analysts had translated the contents. Horrified by what was found in the report, they rushed the transcript to Washington.

Black Umbrella was a detailed proposal by Dr. Eugen Sänger, an Austrian rocket scientist employed at the Hermann Göring Institute, the Luftwaffe's research center. Sänger had proposed construction of a one-man, winged rocket plane, an "antipodal bomber" capable not only of orbital flight but also of flying around the world to attack the United States. The rocket plane—nicknamed the *Amerika Bomber* by Sänger—was to be almost a hundred feet long, weigh a hundred tons, and be propelled by a liquid-fuel rocket engine. Carrying an eighty-ton bomb load, it was to be launched on a rocket-propelled sled that would race down a two-mile track to a sharp incline. The rocket plane would disengage from the sled at the end of the track and, now accelerating at 1,640 feet per second, would climb under its own power to suborbital altitude.

Using the earth's rotation for a "slingshot" effect, the *Amerika Bomber* would make a series of dives and climbs along the top of the atmosphere, skipping like a rock on the surface of a pond as it orbited the earth. The skips would not only help preserve fuel but also keep the rocket plane far above the range of conventional aircraft. In this way the bomber could fly over Europe, Asia, and the Pacific Ocean to the United States. Two of its atmospheric skips could carry it across the continent and, after diving to an altitude of forty miles above the East Coast, the ship could drop an eighty-ton bomb on New York City. The *Amerika Bomber* then could fly across the Atlantic back to Germany, landing like an airplane on a conventional airstrip.

It would be obviously a tremendous effort by the Nazis to develop and successfully launch the Sänger bomber; New York was not a military target, either. But the sheer terror of the scheme—the vision of a Nazi rocket plane diving from space to drop an eighty-ton incendiary bomb on Times Square—would be worth its value in propaganda alone. And if a squadron of antipodal bombers were built, as Sänger suggested, Germany would be in control of the highest of high grounds: outer space.

There was little doubt in the White House that the Nazis could pull off Black Umbrella. According to British intelligence, German civilians had been actively engaged in sophisticated rocket research since the 1920s under the aegis of the Verin für Raumschiffarht, commonly referred to as the German Rocket Society. Almost immediately after Adolf Hitler became chancellor, the Gestapo had seized all journals and records of the German Rocket Society, and the German Army had scooped up almost all members of the VfR, including Hermann Oberth, von Braun's mentor. It was also known that the German Army was diverting enormous amounts of men and matériel to Peenemünde, although it was also suspected that the Nazis had another, more secret missile base somewhere else, deep within the German borders.

According to declassified White House minutes of the meeting, President Roosevelt turned to OSS director William "Wild Bill" Donovan after hearing the report on the Sanger project. "So, Bill, who's in charge of *our* rocket program?" he asked.

"We don't have a rocket program, Mr. President," Donovan replied.

"All right," Roosevelt said calmly, "then who is the leading rocket expert in America?"

"I don't know if there is one," Donovan said.

"Yes, there is," answered the president. "Somewhere out there, there's got to be someone who knows as much about these things as von Braun. Find him. He's now the most important man in the country."

• • • •

The man they found was Robert H. Goddard, and he didn't feel like the most important man in the country. He was only a brilliant scientist who had long since become fed up with being called a crackpot.

Goddard had been obsessed with rockets since reading H. G. Wells's *The War of the Worlds* as a youngster. Born in Worcester, Massachusetts, in 1882, Goddard had pursued his obsession throughout his life; he earned his bachelor's degree in engineering from Worcester Polytechnic Institute and shortly thereafter became a professor of physics at Clark University. Goddard's secret dream was to build a rocket capable of landing men on Mars. It was a wild idea that would drive the scientist throughout his life, and also earn him as much trouble as encountered by predecessors such as Galileo Galilei and Percival Lowell.

In January 1920 the Smithsonian Institution, one of Goddard's sources of funding for his early rocket research, published a sixty-nine-page monograph written by him. Titled "A Method of Reaching Extreme Altitudes," it mainly described how liquid-fuel rockets (themselves still only a theoretical possibility) could replace sounding balloons for exploring the upper atmosphere. The paper was mostly comprised of equations and tables and thus would have escaped the notice of the general public had it not been for brief speculation at its end of how such rockets, perhaps someday in the future, could be used to reach the moon. Goddard wrote that a rocket could crash-land on earth's satellite and explode a load of magnesium powder that would be visible to astronomers on Earth.

Compared to Goddard's real objectives of manned space exploration, this was a rather modest proposal, but the press didn't see it that way. Newspapers reported Goddard's speculation with little accuracy and less respect. He was either scoffed at from such pinnacles as *The New York Times* (which claimed that rocket propulsion was impossible in outer space because there was no air for rockets to push against) or treated as wild-eyed fantasy by papers such as the local *Worcester Telegram* (whose headlines speculated that passenger rockets carrying tourists into space would be possible within a decade). Few newspapers took Goddard seriously; for the most part he was regarded as a crazy college egghead.

Goddard, a shy and soft-spoken person, was appalled by the press attention and embarrassed by the ridicule. He henceforth took his research underground, particularly his experiments with rocket design and his efforts to launch a liquid-fuel rocket. Although he continued to devise means of sending rockets into space—including his own design for a rocket plane—he carefully hid his notebooks in his laboratory file cabinet, in a folder ironically marked "Gunpowder Experiments." There were no reporters present in the hilltop farm field in nearby Auburn, Massachusetts, on the cold morning of March 16, 1926, when Goddard successfully fired the world's first liquid-fuel rocket.

By 1942, though, Robert Goddard was no longer in Worcester. Following the explosion of one of his rockets, the Auburn town council outlawed all types of "fireworks" within city limits. Following a brief series of experiments at the U.S. Army's Camp Devens in nearby Ashby, Goddard went on a sabbatical from Clark University in 1931 and moved his residence and rockets to Roswell, New Mexico. There were a couple of contributing reasons for the move besides the unacceptability of rocketry in Massachusetts. Throughout his life, the professor had battled tuberculosis, which the damp New England climate scarcely helped, and the arid southwestern desert also was a better site for rocket tests. In this sense, rural New Mexico was a fair trade for urban Massachusetts. He broke the sound barrier with a rocket in 1936, and by 1942 Goddard rockets were reaching record altitudes and achieving greater sophistication. Although largely unpublicized, his rocket experiments were on a par with the A-series rockets being developed in Nazi Germany. Few people knew about the feats that Goddard rockets were performing over the New Mexico high desert.

Yet Goddard's fortunes had also suffered, largely because of the bad press he had already endured. Although he continued to receive grants from the Guggenheim Foundation and from one of his admirers, Charles A. Lindbergh, the Smithsonian Institution had stopped funding his research. And though he had already developed solid-fuel ordnance such as the bazooka for the U.S. Army, the war department had expressed no interest in his liquid-fuel rocket research. Obscurity had become a double-edged sword for Goddard: He had found the solitude he craved, yet he was struggling to finance his experiments.

All that changed on the morning of January 29, 1942, when two civilians from the OSS and an officer from the U.S. Army General Staff, Colonel Omar Bliss, found Robert Goddard in the assembly shed at Goddard's ranch with an assistant, working on another high-altitude rocket. The rocket scientist greeted his unexpected visitors with courteous surprise; he dismissed his assistant and sat down on a bench outside the shed to hear what they had to say.

Bliss, now living in retirement on Sanibel Island, Florida, remembers the meeting he had with Goddard. "He was completely shocked, horrified," Bliss says. "He told us that he had kept up with German research during the '30s and knew that they were making progress with their rockets, but he had no idea that their work had come this far. We asked if Sänger's plan was possible and he thought about it a minute, then told us that if they had the resources and a little luck, yes, they could make it work. He knew that von Braun and Oberth were working for the Nazis, and he had no doubts that they and others had the knowledge to develop the *Amerika Bomber*."

The men from Washington asked Goddard if he had any ideas how to prevent New York from being blitzed from space; Goddard indicated that he had a few notions. "Then we asked him if he would help us," Bliss recalls. "I was afraid that he would refuse. People had treated him so unfairly before, after all. But he at once nodded his head, yes, he would do whatever was necessary to stop the Nazis."

The space race had begun.

•   •   •

Robert Goddard's role in what would become known as Project Blue Horizon, however, was not played in New Mexico. For various reasons, the War Department returned the professor to his hometown. Although *Lucky Linda* would be launched from the White Sands Test Range less than a hundred miles from Goddard's ranch, Washington decided that the best place for Blue Horizon's brain trust was in Massachusetts.

The Department of War wanted to keep Goddard within arm's reach, and Massachusetts is closer to Washington, D.C., than New Mexico is. Yet it was also decided not to take unnecessary risks. Goddard was reputed to tinker with his rockets personally while they were on the launch pad. This fact was known by Dr. Vannevar Bush, President Roosevelt's science adviser, who gave orders for "the professor" to be kept away from the rockets themselves. In hindsight, this was good logic. Over the next two years of the crash program there were in White Sands many spectacular explosions, one of which claimed the lives of two technicians. It would have been disastrous if Goddard himself had been killed during one of these accidents.

There was some resistance by the war department to having Project Blue Horizon in Worcester, however. Another top-secret military R&D program was already under way in Massachusetts: the radar-defense project being developed in Cambridge at MIT's so-called "radiation laboratory." It was felt by many in the Pentagon that having two secret projects working so near to each other would be risky. Goddard was not eager to return to Worcester, either. It had become difficult for him to endure the New England climate, and he especially chafed at not being able to witness each rocket test. Bush argued, however, that neither Clark University nor MIT were high-profile enough (at the time) to attract Nazi spies; having Blue Horizon camouflaged by a college campus, like MIT's "Rad Lab," made perfect sense.

The White House won out over the Pentagon, and Goddard went along with his relocation orders, Esther Goddard, always protective of her husband's health, naturally returned to Worcester with Robert. They moved back into their former residence, where Goddard had been born, and readjusted to life in New England's second-largest city.

To build the security cover for Blue Horizon, the FBI coerced Clark University's directors into reinstating Goddard's status as an active faculty member. It was arranged that Goddard's only real academic work load was to teach a freshman class in introductory physics. In the university's academic calendar for the semesters in 1942 through 1943, though, there was a listing for an advanced-level class, "Physics 390," whose instructor was "to be announced." But even senior physics students at Clark found it impossible to enroll in the class; it was always filled at registration time.

Goddard's "graduate students" in Physics 390 were a group of nine young men enlisted from the American Rocket Society, unrepentant rocket buffs and farsighted engineers with whom Goddard had corresponded over the years. Goddard had quickly handpicked his group from memory; the war department and the FBI had contacted each person individually, requesting their volunteer help. None refused, though the Selective Service Administration had to issue draft deferrals for four members. The FBI moved them all to Worcester and managed to get them quietly isolated in a three-decker on Birch Street near the campus.

Team 390 (as they were code-named by the FBI) were strangers even among themselves. Almost all were from different parts of the country. Only two members, Lloyd Kapman and Harry Bell, both from St. Louis, had met before, and although Taylor Brickell and Henry Morse were known to each other from the letters page of *Astounding Science Fiction*, of which they were both devoted readers, they had never met face to face. The youngest, Roy Cahill, had just passed his eighteenth birthday; the oldest, Hamilton "Ham" Ballou, was in his midthirties and was forced to shave off his mustache to make him appear younger.

And there were other problems. J. Jackson Jackson

was the only black member of the team, which tended to make him stand out on the mostly white Clark University campus (his odd name earned him the nickname "Jack Cube"). Michael Ferris had briefly been a member of the American Communist Party during his undergraduate days, which meant that he had undergone intensive scrutiny by the FBI and nearly been refused on the grounds of his past political activity before he had agreed to sign a binding pledge of loyalty to the United States. And Gerard "Gerry" Mander had to be sprung from a county workhouse in Roanoke, Virginia: A rocket he had been developing had misfired, spun-out across two miles of tobacco field, and crashed into a Baptist preacher's house.

Once they were together, though, Blue Horizon's R&D task force immediately hit it off together. "We spoke the same language," recalls Gerry Mander, who now lives in Boston and who was then the team's "wildcat" engineer. "Rockets were our specialty, and putting something above the atmosphere was a dream we all shared. I mean, I was a young snot from backwoods Virginia, so sharing a room with a colored man like Jack Cube, at least at the time, seemed more unlikely than putting a guy in orbit. But Jack talked engineering, so we had that much in common, and in a couple of days I didn't even care."

"We were all a bunch of rocket buffs," says Mike Ferris, the team's chemistry expert, "and the War Department had given us *carte blanche* to put a man in space." He laughs. "Man, we were like little kids thrown the key to the toy store!"

Team 390 had little doubt about what was needed. The only device capable of intercepting the Sänger bomber was another spacecraft, and the only reliable navigation system was a human pilot. Since the 1920s, Robert Goddard had written, in his "gunpowder experiments" notebooks, rough designs for a rocket plane, along with notes for gyroscopic guidance systems and other plans that turned out to be useful for the team. Studies at the California Institute of Technology had also suggested that a single-stage rocket plane could be sent into space on a suborbital trajectory, with the ship gliding back through the atmosphere like a sailplane.

The team postulated that a spaceplane, launched by a liquid-fuel engine and ascending at a forty-five-degree angle, could function as a one-man space fighter capable of intercepting the *Amerika Bomber*. Upon studying the Sanger report, Team 390 further realized that the bomber would be most vulnerable during the ascent phases of its flight. At these points the ship was slowest and least maneuverable, a sitting duck for another spacecraft's ordnance. So if the U.S. ship was launched from New Mexico just as the German ship was flying over the Pacific coast, it could intercept the *Amerika Bomber* before it reached New York City and shoot it down with ordinary solid-fuel rockets.

"We came up with it in one night over beer and pretzels in the Bancroft Hotel bar," says Henry Morse, the team's electrical engineer who now lives in Winchester, New Hampshire. "Bob wasn't with us that night, but we had gone through his notebooks and read all that stuff he had thought up, so it was mainly a matter of putting it together. We knew we didn't need a very sophisticated ship, nothing like a space shuttle today. Of course, we didn't have time to make anything like a space shuttle. Just something quick and dirty."

"Quick and dirty" soon became buzzwords for Goddard's people. The team took the plan to Goddard the following morning, during their "class" in Goddard's lab at the university. By the end of the day, following many hours of arguing, scribbling notes on the chalkboard, and flooding the trash can with wadded-up notes, Team 390 and Goddard settled on the plan. The professor was amused that his "grad students" had come up with the scheme in a barroom. "If Mrs. Goddard will let me out of the house, I'd like to be in on the next session," he told Morse.

The FBI, though, was not amused when they discovered that Team 390 had been discussing rockets in a downtown Worcester bar. There was always the chance of Nazi spies.

The FBI was especially sensitive, given the proximity to the MIT Rad Lab only forty miles away. Team 390 was ordered to stay out of the Bancroft, and J. Edgar Hoover assigned special escorts for Goddard and his team. The team thought the FBI was overreacting.

"It was a pain, of course," Roy Cahill recalls. "We couldn't visit the men's room without having a G-man escorting us. They were almost parked all night outside Bob's house and our place on Birch Street. Esther couldn't stand it at first, but she changed her mind after the City Hall thing."

By early 1943, the V-2 missiles were perfected and the first rockets launched against targets in Great Britain. The Allies had been flying air raids upon V-2 launch sites in occupied northern France, and finally against Peenemünde itself. During one of the early reconnaissance missions over France, Ham Ballou—temporarily brought over to England to gather much-needed intelligence on the V-2 rockets—flew over the Normandy coastline in the backseat of a P-38J Lightning, snapping pictures as the pilot dodged antiaircraft flak. Ballou returned to Worcester with little that was immediately useful to Team 390, but for a while he was able to claim that he was the only person among Goddard's people who had come under enemy fire—until Goddard himself almost caught a bullet.

Following a devastating Allied air raid on Peenemünde, the German High Command covertly transferred the principal R&D of the *Amerika Bomber* 250 miles inland, to Nordhausen, where the base of a mountain had been hollowed out into vast caverns by prisoners from the nearby Dora concentration camp. This was the secret Nazi rocket facility that MI-6 had been unable to locate. Many of the same European Jews who built the Nordhausen site were later sacrificed, over the objections of von Braun and Oberth, in grotesque experiments that tested human endurance to high-altitude conditions.

Little of this mattered to SS commandant Heinrich Himmler. Now that the Luftwaffe had now taken over the A-9 project from the German Army, he was more concerned with the fact, surmised through briefings with von

Braun, that the German rocket team's work had been largely inspired by Goddard's research; he suspected that the United States might be embarked on a secret rocket program of its own. Although Gestapo agents in America had not found any evidence of a U.S. space initiative, Himmler decided not to take chances. In March 1943 he ordered the assassination of the only known American rocketry expert: Robert Hutchings Goddard.

For all his brilliance, Goddard was also absent-minded about the mundane tasks of life; he could forget to fold his umbrella when he walked in from the rain. On March 30, 1943, the Worcester city clerk's office sent the professor a letter informing him that he had not paid his city taxes. Goddard received the letter while working in his lab. Both irritated and alarmed, he put on his coat and immediately bustled out to catch the Main South trolley downtown. He left so quickly that his FBI escort, who was relieving himself in the men's room, missed the professor's departure.

But the Nazi Gestapo agent who had been watching Goddard for a week and waiting for such a break, didn't miss the opportunity. Following Goddard from his post on the Clark campus, the assassin also took the downtown trolley, getting off at the same stop in front of City Hall. As Goddard marched into the building, the Nazi slipped his silenced Luger Parabellum from his trench-coat pocket and followed the scientist inside.

At the same moment, Worcester police officer Clay Reilly was walking downstairs from the second floor of City Hall when he spotted a trench-coated man, carrying a gun, closing in on another man, who was walking toward the tax assessor's office. The second man was unaware that he was being pursued, but Reilly immediately sized up the situation.

"I didn't think twice," Reilly, now retired from the force, says in retrospect. "I pulled my pistol and shouted for the guy to freeze. He decided to mess with me instead."

Reilly was a crack shot on the WPD firing range; his skill didn't fail him then. The Gestapo agent turned and aimed at Reilly, but the officer nailed the assassin with one shot to the heart before the Nazi could squeeze his trigger. Goddard himself fled from City Hall, where he was spirited away by his FBI escort, who had just arrived in his car.

No identification was found on the body of the man Patrolman Reilly had shot. The *Worcester Telegram* reported the story the next day under the front-page headline "Mystery Killer Shot in City Hall." No one knew that he had been trying to kill Goddard; Reilly didn't recognize the scientist, and Goddard had not remained at the scene. Clay Reilly was promoted to sergeant for his quick thinking, but it wasn't until long after the war that the policeman was informed of the identity of the man he had shot or the person whose life he had saved, nor the fact that J. Edgar Hoover himself had insisted on his promotion.

"Everything changed for us after that," says Henry Morse. "I guess we were sort of looking at Blue Horizon like it was a kid's adventure. Y'know, the Rocket Boys go to the Moon. But Bob's close call sobered us up."

The incident also sobered up the White House. On the insistence of Vannevar Bush, the FBI hastily sought a new base of operations in New England for Team 390. Within a week of the attempted assassination, a new locale for Project Blue Horizon was found: the Monomonock Gun & Rod Club, which had been closed since the beginning of the war. The lodge was in the tiny farm community of Rindge, due north of Worcester just across the New Hampshire state line, close enough to Worcester to allow the rocket team to relocate there quickly. Because the club was accessible by a single, unmarked dirt road only, it had the isolation the FBI believed was necessary to keep Team 390 hidden from the world.

The FBI purchased the property, and in the dead of night on April 6, 1943, all the rocket team's files and models were loaded into a truck. As far as Clark University's collegiate community was concerned, Dr. Goddard had taken an abrupt leave of absence due to health reasons, and nobody on campus seemed to notice the sudden departure of the small, insular group of grad students from Physics 390.

The Monomonock Gun & Rod Club was set in seven acres of New Hampshire forest on the northwestern side of Lake Monomonock. The club consisted mainly of a two-story whitewashed lodge that dated back to the turn of the century; it had a handsome front porch that overlooked the serene main channel of the lake, a couple of Spartan rooms on the upper floor that contained a dozen old-style iron beds, and a single outhouse beyond the back door. Mail from relatives was still sent to Worcester and forwarded once a week to New Hampshire; except for Esther Goddard, none of the families of the rocket team was made aware of the fact that their sons and husbands were now in New Hampshire.

The former sportsmen's club was a far cry from the comforts of Clark University; most of the rocket team were unused to roughing it in the woods. Mice had taken up occupancy in the kitchen next to the long dining room, and the only sources of heat were a fireplace in the den and a potbellied stove on the second floor. One of the first orders of business was to knock down the hornet nests in upper bedrooms and under the porch eaves. "The first week we were there, we almost went on strike," says Gerry Mander with a laugh. "If we hadn't been in a race against time, we might have told Bush and Hoover and all the rest to stick it until they found us some decent accommodations. As it was, though, we knew we had little choice."

Yet there was another major problem in the relocation. In New Mexico, the engineering team at White Sands was building unmanned prototype rockets based on the plans sent by Goddard's team, firing the rockets as soon as they could be made. The major hurdle was in producing a reliable engine for the spaceplane, now dubbed the "X-1." It had to be able to lift 65,500 pounds to orbit, yet most of the prototypes exploded, sometimes on the launch pad. For each small success, there were dozens of setbacks. There had been several pad explosions already, and in the latest failure a couple of technicians had been killed when the liquid-hydrogen tank ruptured during pressurization.

"Part of the problem was that the team wasn't in New Mexico to oversee the final stages of each test," Morse says. "We were expected to build rockets without getting our hands dirty, and you simply can't compartmentalize a project like that. What it came down to, finally, was that we had to have a testbed in New Hampshire, whether Van Bush liked it or not."

It took Robert Goddard several weeks of lobbying to convince Vannevar Bush that some of the hands-on research had to be done by his people. Once Bush finally caved in, though, the next task was to locate an appropriate location for the construction of the new prototype. A giant rocket engine is difficult to conceal; it could not be constructed on a workbench in a former sportsmen's club.

One of the prime military contractors in Massachusetts was the Wyman-Gordon Company of Worcester, which was making aircraft forgings for the Army in its Madison Street factory. Upon meeting with Wyman-Gordon's president in Washington, D.C., Vannevar Bush managed to finagle the company into renting out a vacant warehouse on the factory grounds. Final assembly of Team 390's new prototype engine—referred to as "Big Bertha"—would be made in Warehouse Seven, from parts made across the country and secretly shipped to Wyman-Gordon. Big Bertha's aluminum outer casing was cast at Wyman-Gordon as well, although only a few select people at Wyman-Gordon knew exactly what it was.

Secrecy was paramount. Only a handful of Wyman-Gordon workers were involved in the construction of Big Bertha; all had survived extensive background checks by the FBI, and what they were told was on a strict "need to know" basis. The FBI put counterspies to work in the factory to guard against Nazi infiltrators, and work on Big Bertha was done only after midnight, when the least number of people were at the plant. When necessary, the Team 390 members were brought down from New Hampshire to the plant to supervise the engine's construction, making at least three transfers to different vehicles en route, with the final vehicle usually being a phony Coca-Cola delivery van owned by the FBI.

It was a little more difficult to find a suitable site for test-firing Big Bertha; Wyman-Gordon's plant was in the middle of a residential neighborhood. This time, though, the rocket team didn't leave it to the FBI; Henry Morse and Roy Cahill borrowed Esther Goddard's car and spent several days driving around southern New Hampshire trying to find a place for the test-firing. After only a few days, they finally located a dairy farm in nearby Jaffrey, New Hampshire.

Jaffrey had a freight line that ran straight up from Worcester, and the farm was only two miles from the siding. Its owner, Marion Hartnell, was a World War I veteran who just had lost his only son in the fighting in France. He had no love for the Nazis, and once he was approached by Goddard himself, he eagerly volunteered to let the team use his barn for the test-firing of Big Bertha. "We told Mr. Hartnell that there was a possibility that our rocket might blow up and take his barn with it," Cahill recalls. "The old duffer didn't bat an eyelash. 'So long as you can promise me you'll shoot that rocket of yours right up Hitler's wazoo,' that was his response. He even turned down our offer of rent."

On the night of November 24, 1943—Thanksgiving Eve, almost exactly six months before the launch of *Lucky Linda*—Big Bertha was loaded onto a flatcar at the Wyman-Gordon rail siding. A special freight train took it due north across the state line to Jaffrey, where after midnight on Thanksgiving Day the massive rocket engine was carefully off-loaded onto a flatbed truck, which in turn drove it to the Hartnell farm. An Army Corps of Engineers team from Fort Devens in Ashby, Massachusetts, spent the rest of the morning anchoring the prototype engine onto the concrete horizontal testbed that had been built in the barn. Shortly before noon, Goddard and his scientists began making preparations for the test while the townspeople of Jaffrey unwittingly enjoyed their Thanksgiving meals. Team 390 waited until exactly 10:00 P.M.; then

Robert Goddard threw the ignition switch on the control board outside the barn.

"I think everybody was standing a hundred feet away from the barn door when we lit the candle," Mander recalls. "When it went, I almost wet my pants. I thought we were going to blow up the whole damn farm."

Big Bertha didn't explode, though; the engine produced sixty tons of thrust for the requisite ninety seconds. "When it was over," Morse says, "Bob turned to us, let out his breath, and said, 'Gentlemen, we've got a success. Now let's go have that Thanksgiving dinner.' I swear, the old man was ready to cry."

The next night, Big Bertha was taken back to the Jaffrey railhead, loaded on another flatcar, and began its long journey across America to New Mexico. The first big hurdle of Blue Horizon had been jumped. Yet, despite the place he had earned in history, farmer Hartnell never told anyone about the Thanksgiving rocket test that had been made on his farm. He died in 1957 still maintaining secrecy, leaving the new owners of his farm puzzled at the strange concrete cradle that rested inside his barn.

The final months of Project Blue Horizon were a race against time. MI-6 and the OSS knew that the Nazis were in the final stages of building the *Amerika Bomber*, but the location of work was still unknown, and the Nazis' rate of progress was uncertain. "Silver" and "Gold" had long since been pulled out of Peenemünde, so the Allies were now blind as to what the Nazis were doing. Reconnaissance flights by the Allies over Germany had failed to locate the two-mile launch track that Sänger had specified in the Black Umbrella document. Unknown to MI-6, it had been built near Nordhausen by the Dora concentration camp prisoners and camouflaged with nets. The Luftwaffe's scientists were coming steadily closer to fulfilling their primary objective; within the secret caverns of Nordhausen, the sleek antipodal rocket plane was gradually taking shape and form.

Nonetheless, there was talk within the White House

and the Pentagon that the Black Umbrella report had been a red herring. There had already been one similar instance, earlier in the war, when the Nazis had been suspected of developing an atomic weapon. In response, the War Department had begun a crash program to develop its own atomic bomb. This program, based in rural Tennessee and code-named the Manhattan Project, had been unsuccessfully struggling to develop an atomic bomb when a Danish physicist, Niels Bohr, managed to escape to the West with the reliable news that the Nazis were nowhere close to attaining controlled nuclear fission, let along perfecting an atomic bomb.

Although minimal atomic research was secretly continued at the Brookhaven National Laboratory on Long Island, the Manhattan Project had been scrapped, mainly to fund Project Blue Horizon. Now, however, some people within the Pentagon were saying that Sänger's antipodal bomber was another chimera and that vital Americàn resources were being wasted. On their side in the White House was Vice President Harry S Truman, who had begun referring to the American rocket program as "Project Buck Rogers." Yet Vannevar Bush persisted; unlike the atomic bomb scare, there was no proof that the Nazis were *not* developing the *Amerika Bomber*. Roosevelt pragmatically followed his advice, and Project Blue Horizon was not canceled.

"Not knowing what the Germans were doing was the scary part," Roy Cahill recalls, "so all we could do was work like bastards. We stopped thinking about it in terms of the glory of putting the first American in space. Now we only wanted to get someone up there without killing him."

Through the early part of 1944, Team 390 rarely left its makeshift laboratory at the former sportsmen's club. The ten scientists were constantly in the lodge's dining room, pulling twenty-hour days in its efforts to design the rest of the X-1. The FBI bodyguards had taken to cooking their meals for them, and the long table in the middle of the room was buried beneath books, slide rules, and teetering mounds of paper. Big Bertha had only been one component that had to be designed from scratch; life-support, avionics, telemetry and guidance systems, even the pilot's vacuum suit still had to be developed. As the long New Hampshire winter set in, the days became shorter and the nights colder; tempers became frayed. More than once, members of the team went outside to settle their disputes with their fists. The only instance of relaxation any of the team's survivors remember was the December morning after a nor'easter dropped seven inches of snow on them; they dropped work and had a spontaneous snowball fight on Lake Monomonock's frozen surface.

"Bob was the one who really suffered," Henry Morse remembers. "His health had never been good, and the overwork, plus the hard winter we had that year, started ganging up on him. Esther used to come up from Worcester to make sure he didn't overexert himself, that he rested once a day, but he started ignoring her advice after a while. None of us was sleeping or eating well. We were frightened to death that the very next day we would hear that the *Amerika Bomber* had firebombed New York. It was that much of a race."

Piece by piece, the X-1 was assembled in New Mexico from the specifications laid down by Team 390. Unlike Big Bertha, some vital components such as the inertial guidance system were installed virtually without testing. There was simply not enough time to run everything through the wringer. The White Sands engineers knew that they were working from sheer faith. If Goddard's people were crucially wrong in any one of thousands of areas, the spacecraft they were building would become a death trap for its pilot.

"How in the hell did we get a man into space?" After many years, Morse shakes his head. "Because we were scared of what would happen if we failed."

In the end, it was a photo finish. Both the *Amerika Bomber* and the X-1 were finished and brought to their respective launch pads in the same week. Goddard and his team left New Hampshire for White Sands on May 15 to oversee the final launch, whenever it occurred. It was now a matter of waiting for the Germans to launch the *Amerika Bomber*.

The denouement is well recorded in the history books. The vigil at White Sands ended early on the morning of May 24, 1944, when high-altitude recon planes and ground-based radar spotted the *Amerika Bomber* over the Pacific Ocean. Within twenty minutes the X-1—christened the *Lucky Linda* by its pilot after his wife—was successfully launched. Skid Sloman piloted the X-1 through a harrowing ascent and intercepted the A-9 in space above the Gulf of Mexico—during its final ascent skip before the dive that would have taken it over New York. Sloman destroyed the *Amerika Bomber* with a solid-fuel missile launched from the X-1's port wing. He then successfully guided his ship through atmospheric reentry to touchdown in Lakehurst, New Jersey.

With the landing of the *Lucky Linda*, Project Blue Horizon was no longer top secret. Once the X-1's mission was announced to the American public by Edward R. Murrow on CBS Radio, it became one of the most celebrated events of World War II. The destruction of the *Amerika Bomber* was also one of the final nails in the Nazi coffin. So many resources had been poured into the project that the rest of the German war machine suffered. Sänger's squadron of antipodal bombers was never built, and within a year Germany surrendered to the Allies. The *Lucky Linda* flew again in August 1945, modified to drop a massive incendiary bomb on Hiroshima, Japan. Japan surrendered a few days later, and World War II ended with the dawn of the space age.

Yet the story doesn't end there.

Because the technology that had produced the *Lucky Linda* was considered vital to national security, the OSS clamped the lid on the history of the spaceplane's development. The story that was fed to the press was that the ship had been entirely designed and built in New Mexico. The OSS felt it was necessary to hide the role that Robert Goddard and Team 390 had played.

In the long run, the OSS was correct. When the Third Reich fell, the Russian White Army rolled into Germany and took Nordhausen, capturing many of the German rocket scientists. Josef Stalin was interested in the *Amerika Bomber* and sought the expertise that had produced the spaceplane. Unknown to either the Americans or the Germans, the Soviet Union's Gas Dynamics Laboratory had been secretly working on its own rockets under the leadership of Fridrikh Tsander and Sergei Korolov. The Soviet rocket program had stalled during Russia's long "patriotic war," however, and Stalin wanted to regain the lead in astronautics. But von Braun, Oberth, and other German rocket scientists escaped the Russians and surrendered to American forces; eventually they came to the United States under Operation Paperclip and became the core of the American space program.

The lead was short-lived; in March 1949 the USSR put its own manned spacecraft into orbit. Shortly thereafter, Brookhaven physicists announced the sustenance of nuclear fission, demonstrated by the explosion of an atomic bomb in the Nevada desert. This was followed, in less than a year, by the detonation of a Soviet atomic bomb in Siberia. The new Cold War between the two superpowers moved into the heavens; for the next twenty-five years, until the passage of the United Nations Space Treaty in 1974, which outlawed nukesats, no person on Earth could ever feel safe again.

Nobel laureate Richard Feynman accurately assayed the situation in his memoirs, *Get Serious, Mr. Feynman:* "It was bad enough that the United States and USSR shared the capability to launch satellites into orbit; now they both had atomic bombs to put in the satellites. In a more sane world, it would have been bombs without rockets, or rockets without bombs—but, God help us, not both at once!"

Because the United States was now competing with the Soviet Union for dominance in space, the American rocket team lived under oaths of secrecy for more than forty years, forbidden to discuss publicly what they had done in Worcester and Rindge. Robert Goddard himself died on August 10, 1945, the day after the firebombing of Hiroshima. Esther Goddard remained silent about her husband's involvement with Blue Horizon until her death in 1982.

Other members of Team 390 passed away over the years with their lips sealed, yet almost all remained involved in the American space program. J. Jackson Jackson became the presidential science adviser during Robert Kennedy's administration, and Hamilton Ballou was the chief administrator of NASA during the time of the first lunar landing. Ham and Jack Cube are both dead now, but each May 24, the seven remaining members of Team 390 make their way to Rindge. Sometimes they are accompanied by children or grandchildren; in the last forty-seven years, seldom have any of the former teammates missed this anniversary. The Monomonock Gun & Rod Club belongs to them now, a gift from their grateful country.

They spend the day getting the club in shape for the summer—or, rather, telling the kids what to do, now that the youngest founding member is in his midsixties. The old men sit together in rocking chairs on the front porch, drinking beer, kidding each other that FBI agents are watching them from the woods. When the chores are done, they and their families have dinner together, sitting alongside each other on benches at the long oak table in the lodge's dining room where they once scrawled notes and bickered. This is always a festive occasion, punctuated by laughter and dirty jokes. Another tradition is seeing who can get raunchiest, within certain unspoken limits. Their wives roll their eyes in disgust and the kids make faces, but none of the seven men give a rotten damn what they think.

After dinner, as the wives and young people tend to the cleanup, the old men retire to the lodge's main room; Henry and Roy and Mike, Lloyd and Harry, Gerry and Taylor settle into chairs around the fieldstone fireplace, cigars and drinks in hand, their feet warmed by the fire. After a while, they begin to talk. As the wives and children and grandchildren gradually filter into the room, while the sun sets beyond the lake and the crickets and bullfrogs strike up the nocturnal orchestra, seven friends once again tell their secret tale.

On occasion they look at the framed photo of Robert Goddard that hangs above the mantel. At other times, though, their eyes wander to another, smaller picture that hangs beside it, a shot familiar to nearly every person in the civilized world: the space-suited figure of Neil Armstrong, the first American to set foot on Mars during the joint U.S.-Soviet expedition in 1976, opening an urn and scattering Goddard's cremated ashes across the landing site at the Utopia Planitia.

(The author extends his appreciation to Dorothy Mosakowski, Michael Warshaw, and Joe Thompson for their assistance.)

Manassas, Again

GREGORY BENFORD

There were worse things than getting swept up in the first battle of the first war in a over a century, but Bradley could not right away think of any.

They had been out on a lark, really. Bradley got his buddy Paul to go along, flying low over the hills to watch the grand formations of men and machines. Bradley knew how to keep below the radar screens, sometimes skimming along so close to the treetops that branches snapped on their understruts. They had come in before dawn, using Bradley's dad's luxury, ultraquiet cruiser—over the broad fields, using the sunrise to blind the optical sensors below.

It had been enormously exciting. The gleaming columns, the acrid smoke of ruin, the distant muffled coughs of combat.

Then somebody shot them down.

Not a full, square hit, luckily. Bradley had gotten them over two ranges of hills, lurching through shot-racked air. Then they came down heavily, air bags saving the two boys.

They had no choice but to go along with the team that picked them out of their wreckage. Dexter, a big, swarthy man, seemed to be in charge. He said, "We got word a bunch of mechs are comin' along this road. You stick with us, you can help out."

Bradley said irritably, "Why should we? I want to—"

"Cause it's not safe round here, kid," Dexter said. "You joyriding rich kids, maybe you'll learn something about that today."

Dexter grinned, showing two missing teeth, and waved the rest of his company to keep moving into the slanting early-morning glow.

Nobody had any food and Bradley was pretty sure they would not have shared it out if they had. The fighting over the ridge to the west had disrupted whatever supply lines there were into this open, once agricultural land.

They reached the crossroads by midmorning and right away knocked out a servant mech by mistake. It saw them come hiking over the hill through the thick oaks and started chuffing away, moving as fast as it could. It was an R class, shiny and chromed.

A woman who carried one of the long rods over her shoulder whipped the rod down and sighted along it and a loud boom startled Bradley. The R mech went down. "First one of the day," the woman named Angel said.

"Musta been a scout," Dexter said.

"For what?" Bradley asked, shocked as they walked down the slope toward the mech in air still cool and moist from the dawn.

Paul said tentatively, "The mech withdrawal?"

Dexter nodded. "Mechs're on their way through here. Bet they're scared plenty."

They saw the R mech had a small hole punched through it right in the servo controls near the back. "Not bad shootin'," a man said to Angel.

"I *tole* you these'd work," Angel said proudly. "I sighted mine in fresh this mornin'. It helps."

Bradley realized suddenly that the various machined rods these dozen people carried were all weapons, fabrications turned out of factories exclusively human-run. *Killing tools*, he thought in blank surprise. *Like the old days. You see them in dramas and stuff, but they've been illegal for a century.*

"Maybe this mech was just plain scared," Bradley said. "It's got software for that."

"We sent out a beeper warning," Dexter said, slapping the pack on his back. "Goes out of this li'l rig here. Any mech wants no trouble, all they got to do is come up on us slow and then lie down so we can have a look at their programming cubes."

"Disable it?"

"Sure. How else we going to be sure?"

"This one ran clear as anything," Angel said, reloading her rifle.

"Maybe it didn't understand," Bradley said. The R models were deft, subtle, terrific at social graces.

"It knew, all right," Angel said, popping the mech's central port open and pulling out its ID cube. "Look, it's from Sanfran."

"What's it doing all the way out here, then, if it's not a rebel?" a black man named Nelson asked.

"Yeah," Dexter said. "Enter it as reb." He handed Bradley a wrist comm. "We're keepin' track careful now. You'll be busy just takin' down score today, kid."

"Rebel, uh, I see," Bradley said, tapping into the comm. It was reassuring to do something simple while he straightened out his feelings.

"You bet," Nelson said, excitement lacing his voice. "Look at it. Fancy mech, smarter than most of them, tryin' to save itself. It's been runnin' away from our people. They just broke up a big mech force west of here."

"I never could afford one of these chrome jobs," Angel said. "They knew that, too. I had one of these classy R numbers meanmouth me in the market, try to grab a can of soybean stew." She laughed sarcastically. "That was when there was a few scraps left on the shelves."

"Elegant thing, wasn't it?" Nelson kicked the mech, which rolled farther downhill.

"You messed it up pretty well," Bradley said.

Dexter said, "Roll it down into that hollow so nobody can see it from the road." He gestured at Paul. "You go with the other party. Hey, Mercer!"

A tall man ambled over from where he had been carefully trying to pick the spines off a prickly pear growing in a gully. Everybody was hungry. Dexter said to him, "Go down across the road and set up shot. Take this kid—Paul's your name, right?—he'll help with the gruntwork. We'll catch 'em in a crossfire here."

Mercer went off with Paul. Bradley helped get the dead mech going and with Angel rolled it into the gully. Its flailing arms dug fresh wet gouges in the spring grass. The exposed mud exhaled moist scents. They threw manzanita brush over the shiny carcass to be sure, and by that time Dexter had deployed his people.

They were setting up what looked like traps of some kind well away from the blacktop crossroads. Bradley saw that this was to keep the crossroads from looking damaged or clogged. They wanted the mechs to come in fast and keep going.

As he worked he heard rolling bass notes, like the mumbles of a giant, come from the horizon. He could see that both the roads leading to the crossroads could carry mechs away from the distant battles. Dexter was everywhere, barking orders, Bradley noted with respect.

The adults talked excitedly to each other about what the mechs would make of it, how easy they were to fool about real-world stuff, and even threw in some insider mech slang—codes and acronyms that meant very little to mechs, really, but had gotten into the pop culture as hip new stuff. Bradley smiled at this. It gave him a moment of feeling superior to cover his uneasiness.

It was a crisp spring morning now that the sun had beamed up over the far hill at their backs. The perfect time for fresh growth, but the fields beyond had no plowing or signs of cultivation. Mechs should be there, laying in crops. Instead they were off over the rumpled ridgeline, clashing with the main body of humans and, Bradley hoped secretly, getting their asses kicked. Though mechs had no asses, he reminded himself.

Dexter and Bradley laid down behind a hummock halfway up the hill. Dexter was talking into his hushmike headset, face jumping with anticipation and concern. Bradley savored the rich scents of the sweet new grass and thought idly about eating some of it.

Dexter looked out over the setup his team was building and said, "Y'know, maybe we're too close, but I figure you can't be in too close as long as you have the firepower. These weapons, we need close, real close. Easier to hit them when they're moving fast but then it's easier for them to hit you, too."

Bradley saw that the man was more edgy here than he had been with his team. Nobody had done anything like this within living memory. Not in the civilized world, anyway.

"Got to be sure we can back out of this if it gets too hot," Dexter went on.

Bradley liked Dexter's no-nonsense scowl. "How did you learn how to fight?"

Dexter looked surprised. "Hobby of mine. Studied the great Roman campaigns in Africa."

"They used ambushes a lot?"

"Sometimes. Of course, after Sygnius of Albion invented the steam-driven machine gun, well sir, then the Romans could dictate terms to any tribes that gave them trouble." Dexter squinted at him. "You study history, kid?"

"I'm Bradley, sir. My parents don't let me read about battles very much. They're always saying we've gotten beyond that."

"Yeah, that Universal Peace Church, right?"

"Yessir. They say—"

"That stuff's fine for people. Mechs, they're different."

"Different how?"

Dexter sucked on his teeth, peering down the road. "Not human. Fair game."

"Think they'll be hard to beat?"

Dexter grinned. "We're programmed for this by a couple million years of evolution. They been around half a century."

"Since 1800? I thought we'd always had mechs."

"Geez, kids never know any history."

"Well, sir, I know all the big things, like the dates of American secession from the Empire, and the Imperial ban on weapons like the ones you've got here, and how—"

"Dates aren't history, son. They're just numbers. What's it matter when we finally got out from under the Romans? Bunch of lilly-livers, they were. 'Peace Empire'—contradiction in terms, kid. Though the way the 3D pumps you kids full of crap, not even allowin' any war shows or anything, except for prettified pussy historicals, no wonder you don't know which end of a gun does the business."

This seemed unfair to Bradley but he could see Dexter wasn't the kind of man he had known, so he shut up. *Fair game?* What did that mean? A fair game was where everybody enjoyed it and had a chance to win.

Maybe the world wasn't as simple as he had thought. There was something funny and tingly about the air here, a crackling that made his skin jump, his nerves strum.

Angel came back and lay beside them, wheezing, lugging a heavy contraption with tripod legs they had just assembled.

Nelson was downslope, cradling his rifle. He arranged the tripod and lifted onto it a big array of cylinders and dark, brushed-steel sliding parts unlike anything Bradley had ever seen. Sweating, Nelson stuck a long, curved clip into all this freshly made metal and worked the clacking mechanism. Nelson smiled, looking pleased at the way the parts slid easily.

Bradley was trying to figure out what all the various weapons did when he heard something coming fast down the road. He looked back along the snaky black line that came around the far hills and saw a big shape flitting among the ash trees.

It was an open-topped hauler filled with copper-jacketed mechs. They looked like factory hands packed like gleaming eggs in a carton.

Dexter talked into his hushmike and pointed toward three chalk-white stones set up by the road as aiming markers. The hauler came racing through the crossroads and plunged up the straight section of the road in front of Bradley. The grade increased here so they would slow as they passed the stones.

Bradley realized they had no way of knowing what the mechs were doing there, not for sure, and then he forgot that as a pulse-quickening sensation coursed through him. Dexter beside him looked like a cat that knows he has a canary stashed somewhere and can go sink his teeth into it any time he likes.

When the hauler reached the marker stones Angel opened fire. The sound was louder than anything Bradley had ever heard and his first reaction was to bury his face in the grass. When he looked up the hauler was slewing across the road and then it hit the ditch and rolled.

The coppery mechs in the back flew out in slow motion. Most just smacked into the grass and lay still. The hauler thumped solidly and stopped rolling. A few of the factory mechs got up and tried to get behind the hauler, maybe thinking that the rifle fire was only from Angel, but then the party from across the road opened up and the mechs pitched forward into the ditch and did not move. Then there was quiet in the little valley. Bradley could hear the hauler's engine still humming with electric energy and then some internal override cut in and it whined into silence.

"I hit that hauler square in the command dome, you see that?" Angel said loudly.

Bradley hadn't seen it but he said, "Yes ma'am, right."

Dexter said, "Try for that every time. Saves ammo if we don't have to shoot every one of them."

Nelson called up the slope, "Those're factory mechs, they look like Es and Fs, they're pretty heavy-built."

Angel nodded, grinning. "Easier just to slam 'em into that ditch."

Dexter didn't hear this as he spoke into his hushmike next to Bradley. "Myron, you guys get them off the road. Use those power-override keys and make them walk themselves into that place where the gully runs down into the stream. Tell 'em to jump right in the water."

"What about the hauler?" Bradley asked, and then was surprised at his own boldness.

Dexter frowned a moment. "The next batch, they'll think we hit it from the air. There was plenty of that yesterday to the west."

"I didn't see any of our planes today," Bradley said.

"We lost some. Rest are grounded because some mechs started to catch on just about sunset. They knocked three of our guys right out of the sky. Mechs won't know that, though. They'll figure it's like yesterday and that hauler was just unlucky." Dexter smiled and checked his own rifle, which he had not fired.

"I'll go help them," Bradley said, starting to get up.

"No; we only got so many of those keys. The guys know how to use 'em. You watch the road."

"But I'd like to—"

"Shut up," Dexter said in a way that was casual and yet was not.

Bradley used his pocket binoculars to study the road. The morning heat sent ripples climbing up from the valley floor and he was not sure at first that he saw true movement several kilometers away and then he was. Dexter alerted the others and there was a mad scramble to get the mechs out of sight.

They were dead, really, but the humans could access their power reserves and make them roll down the road on their wheels and treads and then jounce down the gully and pitch into the stream. Bradley could hear laughter as the team across the road watched the mechs splash into the brown water. Some shorted out and started flailing their arms and rotors around, comic imitations of humans swimming. That lasted only a few seconds and then they sank like the rest.

Nelson came running back up the hill, carrying on his back a long tube. "Here's that launcher you wanted. Rensink, he didn't look too happy to let go of it."

Dexter stood and looked down the road with his own binoculars. "Leave it here. We got higher elevation than Rensink."

Dexter took the steel tube, which looked to Bradley exactly like the telescopes he and his friends used to study the sky. Tentatively Bradley said, "If you're not going to use that rifle, uh, sir, I'd..."

Dexter grinned. "You want in, right?"

"Well, yes, I thought that since you're—"

"Sure. Here. Clip goes like this," he demonstrated, "you hold it so, sight along that notch. I machined that so I know it's good. We had to learn a whole lot of old-timey craft to make these things."

Bradley felt the heft and import of the piece and tentatively practiced sighting down at the road. He touched the trigger with the caution of a virgin lover. If he simply pulled on the cool bit of metal a hole would—well, might—appear in the carapace of fleeing mech. A mech they would not have to deal with again in the chaos to come. It was a simple way to think about the whole complex issue. Something in Bradley liked that simplicity.

The mechs still had not arrived but Bradley could see them well enough through the binoculars now to know why. They were riding on self-powered inventions of their own, modified forms of the getarounds mechs sometimes used on streets. These were three-wheeled and made of shiny brass.

They were going slowly, probably running out of energy. As he watched one deployed a solar panel on its back to catch the rising sun and then the others did but this did not speed them up any. They did not look like the elegant social mechs he usually saw zipping on the bike paths, bound on some errand. They were just N- or P-class mechs who had rigged up some wheels.

They came pedaling into the crossroads, using their arms. The one in front saw the hauler on its side and knew something was wrong right away and started pumping hard. Nelson shot at him then even though Dexter had said nothing. He hit the lead mech and it went end over end, arms caught up in its own drive chain. Angel could not resist and she took out the next three with a burst. Then the others came in with a chorus of rattling shots and loud bangs, no weapon sounding like the other, and in the noise Bradley squeezed and felt the butt of the rifle kick him.

He had been aiming at one of the mechs at the rear of the little column and when he looked next the mech was down, sliding across the road with sparks jetting behind it, metal ripping across asphalt.

"Stop! Stop shooting!" Dexter called, and in the sudden silence Bradley could hear the mechs clattering to a halt, clanging and squealing and thumping into the ditch.

"Get them off the road—quick!" Dexter called. He waved Bradley down the hill and the boy ran to see the damage. As he dashed toward them the mechs seemed to be undamaged except for some dents but then up close each showed a few holes. He had time to glance at Paul, who was red-faced, breathing hard, his eyes veiled. There was no time to talk.

The men and women from across the road got most of the mechs started up again on override keys but one had suffered some sort of internal explosion and the back was blown off. Bradley helped three men tilt it up enough to roll off the gentle rounded asphalt, and once they got it going it rolled and slid into a copse of eucalyptus. They threw branches over it. Bradley looked for the one he had shot at but it was impossible to tell which that was now.

He felt a prickly anticipation, a thickening of the air. The fragrances of trees and grass cut into his nostrils, vivid and sharp. They ran back up the slope. Bradley found the rifle he now thought of as his and sprawled down with it in the grass, getting down behind a hummock near Dexter.

Bradley lay there just breathing and looking at the rifle, which seemed to be made of a lot of complicated parts. Dexter tossed him three clips and a box of copper-sheathed ammunition. The box promised that they were armor-piercing. Bradley fumbled a little learning how to load the clips but then moved quickly, sliding the rounds in with a secure click as he heard the distant growl of a tracked vehicle.

It was coming closer along the other road. The crossroads looked pretty clear, no obvious signs of the ambush.

The Mercer team had laid two mines in the road. They had a chameleon surface and within a minute were indistinguishable from the asphalt. Bradley could tell where they were because they were lined up with the white marker stones and from up here were smoother than the asphalt.

He wondered if the mechs could sense that. Their sensorium was better than human in some ways, worse in others. He realized that he had never thought very much about the interior life of a mech, any more than he could truly delve into the inner world of animals. But in principle mechs *were* knowable. Their entire perspective could be digitized and examined minutely.

The clatter and roar of the approach blotted this from his mind. "Activate!" Dexter shouted, his tight voice giving away some of his own excitement.

A big tracked vehicle came flitting through the trees

that lined the black road, flickering like a video-game target. There were mechs perched all over it, hitching rides, and many more of them packed its rear platform. When Bradley looked back at the road nearby the mines jumped out at him like a spider on a lace tablecloth. The entire valley vibrated and sparkled with intense, sensory light. Smells coiled up his nostrils, the cool sheen of the rifle spoke to him through his hands.

The mech driver would surely see the mines, stop, and back away, he thought. And the mechs aboard would jump off and some of them would attack the humans, rolling down the road and shooting the lasers they had adapted from industrial purposes. Bradley had heard about mechs that could override their safety commands and fight.

He tightened his grip on his rifle. He was dimly aware of Dexter sighting along his tube-shaped weapon and of Angel muttering to herself as she waited.

"If they were like us they'd stop, first sign of trouble they see," Dexter muttered, probably to himself, but Bradley could hear. "Then they'd deploy fighter mechs on both sides of the road and they'd sweep us, outflank."

"Think they will?" Bradley asked wonderingly.

"Naw. They don't have what we do."

"What . . . what's that?" Bradley knew the wide range of special abilities mechs possessed.

"Balls."

The mechs perched atop the tracked vehicle were looking forward down the road and holding on tight against the rough swerves as they rounded curves.

Then one of them saw the mines and jerked a servo arm toward them. Some mechs sitting near the front began sending warning wails, and the track car slammed on its brakes and slewed across the road. It stopped at the lip of the ditch and made a heavy, grinding noise and began backing up.

Three mechs jumped off its front. Bradley brought his sights down onto one of them and the air splintered with a huge rolling blast that made him flinch and forget about everything else.

The gunmetal hood of the transport seemed to dissolve

into a blue cloud. The tailgate of the tracker flew backward with a sharp *whap*.

The air became a fine array of tumbling dots as debris spewed up like a dark fountain and then showered down all across the hillside. Thunks and whacks told of big mech parts hitting nearby. Bradley tucked his head into the grass. He yelped as something nicked his knee and something else tumbled over him and was gone. Pebbles thumped his back.

When Bradley looked up he expected to see nothing but small scraps left on the road. His ears roared with the memory of the sound and he wondered if he would be deaf. But through the smoke he saw several mechs lurching away from the disemboweled transport. There were five of them bunched closely together.

He brought his rifle up and shot very swiftly at the lead mech. It went down and he shot the next object and the next, seeing only the moving forms and the swirling blur of action.

Angel was firing and Nelson too, sharp bangs so regular and fast Bradley thought of the clack of a stick held by a boy as he ran by a picket fence—and in a few seconds there were no more mechs standing on the road.

But there were two in the ditch. Gray smoke billowed everywhere.

Bradley saw a mech moving just as a quick rod of light leaped from it, cutting through the smoke. He heard Angel yelp and swear. She held up her hand and it was bloody.

Another instantaneous rod of light stood for a second in the air and missed her and then a third struck her weapon. It flew to pieces with a loud bang. Bradley aimed at the mech and kept firing until he saw it and the second one sprawl across the ditch and stop moving.

A compressed silence returned to the valley. The transport was burning but beyond its snaps and pops he could see nothing moving on the road.

Angel was moaning with her wound and Nelson took care of her, pulling out a first-aid kit as he ran over. When they saw that her wound was manageable, Dexter and

Bradley walked slowly down to the road. Dexter said, "Bet that's the last big party. We'll get strays now, no problems."

Bradley's legs felt like logs thudding into the earth as he walked. He waved to Paul, who was already on the road, but he did not feel like talking to anybody. The air was crisp and layered with so many scents, he felt them sliding in and out of his lungs like separate flavors in an ice cream sundae.

"Hey!" Mercer called from the transport cab. "They got food in here!"

Everyone riveted attention on the cab. Mercer pitched out cartons of dry food, some cans, a case of soft drinks.

"Somethin', huh?—mechs carryin' food," Angel said wonderingly. For several minutes they ate and drank and then Paul called, "There's a boy here."

They found Paul standing over a boy who was half-concealed by a fallen mech. Bradley saw that the group of mechs had been shielding this boy when they were cut down. "Still alive," Paul said, "barely."

"The food was for him," Mercer said.

Bradley bent down. Paul cradled the boy but it was clear from the drawn, white face and masses of blood down the front, some fresh red and most brown, drying, that there was not much hope. They had no way to get him to cryopreservation. Thin lips opened, trembled, and the boy said, "Bad . . . Mommy . . . hurt . . ."

Dexter said, "This ID says he's under mech care."

"How come?" Angel asked.

"Says he's mentally deficient. These're medical care mechs." Dexter pushed one of the mech carcasses and it rolled, showing H-caste insignia.

"Damn, how'd they get mixed in with these reb mechs?" Nelson asked irritably, the way people do when they are looking for something or someone to blame.

"Accident," Dexter said simply. "Confusion. Prob'ly thought they were doing the best thing, getting their charge away from the fighting."

"Damn," Nelson said again. Then his lips moved but nothing came out.

Bradley knelt down and brushed some flies away from

the boy's face. He gave the boy some water but the eyes were far away and the lips just spit the water out. Angel was trying to find the wound and stop the bleeding but she had a drawn, waxy look.

"Damn war," Nelson said. "Mechs, they're to blame for this."

Bradley took a self-heating cup of broth from Paul and gave a little to the boy. The face was no more than fifteen and the eyes gazed abstractedly up into a cloudless sky. Bradley watched a butterfly land on the boy's arm. It fluttered its wings in the slanting yellow-gold sunlight and tasted the drying brown blood. Bradley wondered distantly if butterflies ate blood. Then the boy choked and the butterfly flapped away on a breeze, and when Bradley looked back the boy was dead.

They stood for a long moment around the body. The road was a chaos of ripped mech carapaces and tangled innards and the wreck of the exploded transport. Nobody was going to run into an ambush here anymore today and nobody made a move to clear the road.

"Y'know, these med-care mechs, they're pretty smart," Paul said. "They just made the wrong decision."

"Smarter than the boy, probably," Bradley said. The boy was not much younger than Bradley, but in the eyes there had been just an emptiness. "He was human, though."

The grand opening elation he had felt all morning slowly began to seep out of Bradley. "Hell of a note, huh?" he said to no one in particular. Others were doing that, just saying things to the breeze as they slowly dispersed and started to make order out of the shambles.

The snap and sparkle of the air were still with him, though. He had never felt so alive in his life. Suddenly he saw the soft, encased, abstract world he had inhabited since birth as an enclave, a preserve—a trap. The whole of human society had been in a cocoon, a velvet wrapping tended by mechs.

They had found an alternative to war: wealth. And simple human kindness. *Human* kindness.

Maybe that was all gone now.

And it was no tragedy, either. Not if it gave them back

the world as it could be, a life of tangs and zests and the gritty rub of real things. He had dwelled in the crystal spaces of the mind while beneath such cool antiseptic entertainments his body yearned for the hot raw earth and its moist mysteries.

Nelson and Mercer were collecting mech insignia. "Want an AB? We found one over here. Musta got caught up and brought along by these worker mechs?" Nelson asked Bradley.

"I'll just take down the serial numbers," Bradley said automatically, not wanting to talk to Nelson more than necessary. Or to anyone. There had been so much talk.

He spent time getting the numbers logged into his comm and then with shoving mech carcasses off the road.

Dexter came over to him and said, "Sure you don't want one of these?" It was a laser one of the reb mechs had used. Black, ribbed, with a glossy sheen. "Angel's keeping one. She'll be telling the story of her wound and showing the laser that maybe did it, prob'ly for the rest of her life."

Bradley looked at the sleek, sensuous thing. It gleamed in the raw sunlight like a promise. "No."

"Sure?"

"Take the damned stuff away."

Dexter looked at him funny and walked off. Bradley stared at the mechs he was shoving off the road and tried to think how they were different from the boy, who probably was indeed less intelligent than they were, but it was all clouded over with the memory of how much he liked the rifle and the sweet grass and shooting at the targets when they came up to the crossfire point in the sharp sun. It was hard to think at all as the day got its full heat and after a while he did not try. It was easier that way.

The Number of the Sand

GEORGE ZEBROWSKI

There are those who believe not only in the infinity of
number but in actual infinity, and others who deny
it, yet claim that the number of the sand cannot be said
because it is too large.

—ARCHIMEDES

Hannibal dismounts and walks out into the center of the valley of Zama, followed only by his interpreter, a trusted veteran of the Italian campaign. Scipio also approaches with only an interpreter. At each general's back, unseen armies wait in the hot Tunisian afternoon. The two leaders stop half a dozen steps apart and regard each other in silence.

Hannibal is the taller and older figure, with a sunburned face half-covered with a cloth that hides his graying hair. He turns his head slightly to benefit his good eye.

Scipio seems tense as he stands bareheaded, holding his helmet, but his expression is that of a proud, handsome man. There is gold inlay on his breastplate, but no other mark of Roman military rank.

"Do you prefer Latin or Greek?" Hannibal asks in Greek. "I know of your interest in the Hellenes."

"It is one of your loves also," Scipio replies. "I've heard that you write in Greek."

Both men glance at their interpreters, then return their attention to each other.

"They will only witness our discussion," Scipio says. "Neither of us needs the delay of having our words repeated."

Hannibal nods at this sign of respect, then stands straighter and shifts his weight to his right leg. "Luck has been with you, Consul," he says, "but we both know that good fortune cannot continue unbroken."

Scipio draws a deep breath and says, "Fortune had little to do with the fact that you were compelled by obvious necessity, and your own honorable character, to leave Italy and come to the defense of your native city. All wars must aim at a truer peace."

Hannibal smiles. "Why be modest? The necessity was of your making, and might have been otherwise." He pauses and waits for a reply, but Scipio waits longer, and Hannibal at last says, "You and I seem to be the only ones who understand that war should be a way to a more lasting peace. Our peoples will only benefit if we end our conflict here and now."

"What do you offer?" Scipio asks.

"The islands," Hannibal says, "even the smaller ones, such as the Malta group, between Italy and Africa. Carthage will also give up Spain."

"But this is less," Scipio replies, "than the terms of the armistice already signed in Rome."

"Which you drafted," Hannibal says quickly, "whether signed by your government or not."

"You offer us our own terms," Scipio counters, "but without the surrender of war vessels or the return of deserters and fugitives in your ranks." The Roman general raises a hand. "I know that they make up the majority of the army with which you fled Italy, and I realize that you will not betray your veterans, but I cannot accept less than Rome's original terms."

Hannibal sighs and nods. "I knew there was no possibility of peace between us, but I wished to meet you, and I do not regret it. We will have to attempt to destroy each other's force. Neither of us can shirk that duty."

The two men gaze at each other for a long, frozen moment, then make gestures of salute and turn away. . . .

A sea of simmering noise swallowed the scene at Zama. The historian ended his first observation of the meeting between Scipio and Hannibal in North Africa, near Carthage, in the year 202 B.C., as the first step in his *New Study of History*. Any randomly selected coordinate of any linear history would have served as well.

As the Prolegomena to his study, he had sampled numerous studies of history, observing how oral narratives gave way to the art of writing down a connected chronicle from surviving documents. This crude form of history was constructed not from a continuous flow of events, but from available, discontinuous samples; from these moments, no one could reconstruct any one true past, and the result was always biased toward the concerns of the investigating present.

When the first linear history machines become operational, the interpretive art of the old historians collapsed, as the whole linear range of human time could now be observed at any desired speed. The old studies of history were replaced by a half-million-year literal record, which could be observed at any point along its meandering course.

After nearly a century, despite the efforts of interpretive observers, the past became the dead past, because nothing usable could be learned from it beyond curious fact. As the old problems of history were settled, the world rushed toward a future-event horizon of incomprehensibility, on the other side of which waited a culture so changed in its biology and goals that little of history would have any meaning for it.

Even when the cliometricon uncovered quantum history, access to the infinity of historical variants only continued to lessen the importance of history in human affairs. Everything had happened and was going to happen; no lesson that could be extracted from the past had any meaning to an accelerating history. All previously false histories of the past became true in some world. Lessons could be applied, imperfectly, to restricted sequences of human experience, in which the time of one generation and the next was essentially unchanged; but to be led by the past in a quickening time would shackle the future, if it could even be done. The universe was not a closed, self-consistent system; it was open, unfinished, and infinite in all directions, including time. Its true nature was mirrored in the incompleteness of both natural and mathematical languages, and in the failure of human law to keep up with emergent circumstances.

The cliometricon's ability to retrieve decaying, fading information from the cosmic background had extended the history machine's capabilities, but without any clear advantage for humanity beyond the satisfaction of scholarly curiosity. Meanwhile, the history machine's ability to show the past, even the immediate, fleeing past measured in seconds and minutes, made possible the emergence, after a stormy transition, of the first panoptic human culture. This transition included the so-called privacy wars, and led to the acceptance of peeping as the right of every human being. Since there was no way to blind the all-seeing eye, humankind had simply faced up to the fact of peeping with a new social stability based on informational nakedness, in which everyone was rewarded. The price of peeping was to be peeped. For the first time in its history, humankind revealed itself to itself in a systematic way, settling many questions of individuality and human nature. Past humanity had only glimpsed itself through its poetries, fictions, and visual dramas; but now all curiosities were satisfied, and the result was greater understanding and compassion for some, and boredom for others.

Cliometricians continued to pursue greater issues, even though they routinely used linear history machines to verify the priority of their colleagues' areas of interest, personal as well as professional, and avoided poaching on all staked claims. But the profession always avoided facing up to the question of its legitimacy, which seemed irresolvable.

There could be no complete history of histories. Events ran to infinity in all directions, diverging at every moment, at every fraction of a moment, at every point in each variant of space-time. Yet this process always meant something to the interiors that were intelligent entities; even when it seemed to make no sense, meaning was felt. The cliometrician watched the embarrassment of the old historians as they were confronted with the living past—and their denials as they drowned in the ocean of truth, claiming that it was all a simulation constructed from massed data by imaging programs. They could not accept that human history was one of the masks of chaos, behind which there was nothing.

• • •

In the first hour of horizon light, a sleepless Hannibal watches from a hillock as the elephants stir and begin to advance. Behind them are Mago's men—silent Ligurians, complaining Gauls, wild Moors, and a small group of Spaniards. Well drilled, heavily armed and battlewise, the men advance shoulder to shoulder. A second force of Carthaginian recruits, led by the aging Hanno, advances behind the elephants, followed by the third force, Hannibal's veterans, the army of Bruttium, which deliberately lags behind, and is all but invisible to the Romans in the gray morning light.

Only Hannibal and his waiting messengers know why this is not his usual long battle line. If all goes according to plan, three separate battles will be fought at Zama.

But despite the starlight start of his first force, Hannibal sees that the Roman force is already moving across the valley, its standards a slow moving fence, flanked by horsemen. Three ranks of machinelike infantry—front, spearmen, and supporting legions of *triarii*—come forward. There are puzzling breaks in the line, which are defended by only a few javelin-throwers.

As the armies collide in the same place where Scipio and Hannibal had met, the Roman horns and trumpets cry out, startling Hannibal's elephants. Many of the beasts panic and rush into the openings in the Roman lines, where they are greeted with swarms of missiles and herded through the lines to the rear. Confused, the remaining elephants turn and charge the Carthaginian cavalry. Scipio's mounted force scatters Hannibal's horsemen. They struggle to regroup and fight, but are too few for Laelius's and Masinissa's squadrons. The massed riders move off as a single storm, out of sight.

Hannibal watches as Mago's Gauls and Ligurians lock man to man with the first Roman line and bring it to a stop; but the *triarii* slip through the openings, and the Roman line surges forward again. The second wave, Carthaginian recruits from the city itself, fail to relieve Mago's force, because Hannibal has ordered his three forces to keep apart. The survivors of the first wave retreat and turn with rage on the Carthaginian recruits, who push them back as the Roman line drops its spears and javelins and advances with shields and swords, supported by second-rank spearmen.

Desperately, the Carthaginians hold back the legions, but by late morning the last of Hannibal's two forces breaks to the sides of the valley, leaving the ground strewn with the dead and dying.

On his hillock, Hannibal knows that he must now send in his third force, the ten thousand veterans of Italy, who stand waiting for the moment when Scipio can no longer retreat, while on either side the survivors of the first two waves regroup.

Trumpets command the Romans to remove their wounded, recover weapons, and clear away debris. The standards still fly as the men drink water and rest.

Then, in response to swift new orders from Scipio, the three lines reform. Spearmen move off to one flank of the front line; the *triarii* take the other. The Roman line lengthens far beyond Hannibal's, and closes it on the weak Carthaginian flanks. The armies are equally matched now, except that Hannibal's veterans are fresh, and they have never known defeat at the hands of the Romans.

Suddenly the Roman cavalry returns—and charges into the rear of Hannibal's veterans. There is no Carthaginian cavalry left to stop them. The army of Italy is caught between the infantry and horsemen. The Bruttians turn to defend their flanks and rear.

They fight and die across the afternoon, until nearly all are killed. Hannibal sends a message to Carthage, counseling acceptance of all surrender terms, and with a few survivors flees eastward.

The historian returned to the first meeting between Scipio and Hannibal, and listened again to their great-souled but hopeless words. Then he crossed the lines, watching the variations.

A servile Hannibal admitted his crimes against Rome to a pompous Scipio, mouthing the words of Livy's history, which was true here and a lie elsewhen. The Tunisian landscape seemed frozen. Grains of sand hung suspended in the air at Zama. Hannibal's headcloth disappeared. He wore a patch over one eye. He became stooped, then stood taller and lost an arm. Scipio appeared, now wearing his helmet. Insignias of rank appeared on his breastplate. The two leaders spoke only through their interpreters, who seemed changeless. The viewtank flashed as the historian paused. Scipio and Hannibal were conversing from horseback.

"They hate me back in Rome," Scipio says in Greek, "and that hate will only increase if I defeat you here. There are those who fear my success."

Hannibal smiles and says, "I too am disappointed with the city I left behind as a boy. The fat rich rule it for their sons and daughters. Honor is dead."

"You might restore it," Scipio answers, "if you became its just ruler."

Hannibal laughs. "Your Senate will not tolerate a Carthage with me at its head!"

"But it might not fear a Carthage without you," Scipio answers.

Hannibal considers, then says, "You and I will not fight, then. Will you give me your word that Carthage will not burn?"

Scipio nods. The two men clasp arms, then turn and ride away.

The historian cut across the variants and found Hannibal alone again, looking out across the empty valley of Zama, where there had been no battle. Was Hannibal thinking of how he could have won? Was this aging soldier still in love with the craft of battle as he rode away, hoping for peace?

But in this variant Rome betrays Scipio, replaces him as commander of its forces in Africa, and burns Carthage to the ground. Scipio commits suicide. In Bithynia, far to the east, Hannibal receives the double news with sorrow, and drinks poison in the garden of his house as Roman soldiers approach. A servant flees north with his memoirs, forgetting the last piece of parchment, which lies on the table before the dead Carthaginian. In this variant, the writing reads: "The anxiety of the Romans is at an end. I am the old man for whose death you have waited so long. There will be only one Rome, but it might have been Rome or Carthage..."

While at Zama, the three battles that became one defeat flare across infinity, and each of its three struggles is an infinity, changing through infinitesimal steps. The Roman horsemen do not return, having been ambushed by the sons of Syphax and their Numidian cavalry, leaving Hannibal to an honest test of his Bruttians against Scipio's weary infantry. A few variants earlier, the Roman cavalry had arrived, but too late to save Scipio; and before that only at half-strength; and before that...

The historian watched Carthage destroyed, then built up into a Roman city because the site was too good a center for commerce to be ignored. He watched Rome leveled and raised into a Carthaginian city, for the same reason. The variants ran through endless minor differences in these two outcomes, until he left these lines behind.

He could have of probability what he wanted—but what was it? An endless flickering structured out of nothing, differentiated into individual things by measurementlike interactions among components, copying itself endlessly, providing examples but no prescriptions. These could be studied definitively and forever, but to no end. There was no wall around past quantum-transitional time, so he could have of it what he wanted, even though he could not stand apart from its infinity and see it whole. Only the quantum future was forbidden, even to licensed historical observers, whose linear and quantum history machines were restricted by basic design. There had been a time when the study of history had called for a concern with the future, then with alternate futures, extending the study of the past toward the creation of desirable futures; but the quantum-transitional cliometricon had stifled that new history. Futurity's informational influx into the past was feared and prevented; and yet there had to be variants in which it was embraced, where cultures of past and future mingled informationally without fear, because they understood that the stuff of being was blossoming into 100^{100+N} directions, matter and living flesh metamorphosing toward distant, ever more tenuous and mysterious states, and that these conscious innards of time must huddle all their histories together . . . .

He imagined history whole—as a writhing, boiling cloud. Cliometricians hurled themselves through the enigma but could not stand away from it, which was what it would take to penetrate its mystery. Objectivity was ruinously relative, after all; no one could have history as a separate object of study, even though it seemed that way in the viewtank, without remaining part of it . . . .

In Spain, a year before crossing the Alps into Italy, Hannibal marries a princess of Castulo, a dark-tressed woman of the Olcades people, to help secure the frontier between the Silver Mountains, the Iberians, and Carpetanians, to strengthen the Carthaginian presence in Spain.

On their wedding night, Hannibal mounts Imilce from the rear, but after a few powerful strokes reveal her discomfort, he turns her over on her back. She receives him again and wraps her legs around his middle. Her long hair is at her sides down to her waist. Her lips and pale breasts swell as she nears completion. The dark-skinned Hannibal cries out, bringing joy to her face.

"Come with me!" she whispers as he relaxes and strokes her neck. "At Carthage we'll take passage to Greece, where you can take up the life of study that you have desired."

The Carthaginian shakes his head in denial. "War is coming. My city will perish without me."

"You flatter yourself," she says. "Others also understand what needs to be done. They will step into your place."

"But they don't love the craft of war as I do. They will never see what is possible, and fail."

"The Romans are not fools," she says, and closes her eyes.

A year later, high in a stone tower, Imilce gives birth to a son. Hannibal puts wife and child on a ship for Carthage and marches his army toward the Alps. All through the sixteen-year raid on the Roman peninsula, he carries with him his wife's parting gift—a small Greek statue of Hercules—and rejects the enjoyment of captive women . . . .

But across the variants, Imilce prevails. Word by word, their discussion in the bridal chamber changes through a thousand small steps, until finally Hannibal travels with her and his son to Greece, where he perfects his use of the language and writes a series of dialogues encompassing the experience of Mediterranean peoples. Carthage withdraws from Spain. Rome is not roused from its republican state. The two cities prosper and make treaties of friendship, delaying the Punic Wars and the rise of imperial Rome by a century . . . .

The historian asked himself, what could it all ever mean? The significance of these varying moments had peaked when they were happening. No one else could ever have them from the *inside* except the original players. All historians tacitly entered the minds of past figures and imagined direct knowledge of their thoughts and feelings. Cliometricians were the extreme of panoptic humankind, which observed itself endlessly, down to the smallest details of life, displaying itself to itself, but never able to become one . . . .

Perhaps there should be walls around time, he told himself, and greater ones around individuals. The long-lived should practice periodic amnesia, following the way of the past's short-lived generations, because history is only important while it is being made . . .

. . . but there is never an empty moment. History is being made all the time, so it is always important, even though he could not say how. *Being* was adding to itself endlessly, an infinite growing thing, branching, probing through a greater infinity of probability, springing from no soil and obeying no tropism . . . .

In the endless array of gossamer display tanks, each one an event horizon on quantum-transitional times that can be observed but not entered, the historian watches himself contemplating history from the center of an infinite web of information. Once in a while he glances over his shoulder at his unseen alternates, who see him turn his head; but he can only see into the regress of variants in front of him. Do all the cliometricians glance back simultaneously, as if the entire infinite set were one mind? He imagines that vast intelligence sitting at the privileged observer's point, where all regress stops, even though he knows there can be no such point. He could traverse billions of variants and still hope to reach the privileged point on the next try. Attempted passages across an infinity always generated the question: Is this an infinity, or only very large? Aristotle had denied infinity because it could only be defined, but never possessed.

The historian knows that he has lost his struggle with history. Infinities are tractable only when treated as wholes, but the mathematician's way could never encompass the complexities of human events. He sits in his cul-de-sac and yearns for the closure that would end the dismay of infinities, the final, firm place to stand, from which there is no one to glance back to, where all perspectives converge into the sleepless eternity of perfect knowing that would never belong to him. He would never awake from the dream of history in which he was embedded and see it whole.

In the twenty years of wandering exile after his defeat at Zama, Hannibal is told by a Greek oracle that he will be buried in African soil. Untroubled that he will die before returning home, he writes his brief study of history in the house given to him by the king of Bithynia.

Across a million variants he glances out the window and sees Roman soldiers closing their circle around the house. He hides his manuscript in the hollow doorstone, then swallows the poison in his ring. In the billionth variant he learns too late that there is a place in Bithynia called Africa, and that this house stands on it. He smiles as he sits back in his chair, perhaps at the cleverness of the Greek oracles, and his life slips away before the Romans reach the house. . . .

In the same year, across the sea, Scipio also dies, and is buried outside Roman territory, in compliance with his last wishes . . . .

The soldiers break into the house in Bithynia . . . at the thousandth variant they find the manuscript in the stone . . . in the trillionth the room is empty, but under the table there is an open door into a tunnel that runs through the hillside to the harbor. Quinctius Flamininus, the Roman commander, notices that there is a note on the table addressed to him. He picks it up and reads:

> You are hardly a worthy descendant of the men who warned Pyrrhus against the poison prepared for them.
> —HANNIBAL

He grimaces, peers into the hole under the table as if it were a tunnel out of history, then hurries outside to the cliff's edge and searches the sea. Hannibal's ship is halfway to the horizon, running with wind and tide to fulfill the Greek oracle's prophecy.

If Lee Had Not Won the Battle of Gettysburg

THE RIGHT HONOURABLE WINSTON S. CHURCHILL, M.P.

The quaint conceit of imagining what would have happened if some important or unimportant event had settled itself differently, has become so fashionable that I am encouraged to enter upon an absurd speculation. What would have happened if Lee had not won the Battle of Gettysburg? Once a great victory is won it dominates not only the future but the past. All the chains of consequence clink out as if they never could stop. The hopes that were shattered, the passions that were quelled, the sacrifices that were ineffectual are all swept out of the land of reality. Still it may amuse an idle hour, and perhaps serve as a corrective to undue complacency, if at this moment in the twentieth century—so rich in assurance and prosperity, so calm and buoyant—we meditate for a spell upon the debt we owe to those Confederate soldiers who by a deathless feat of arms broke the Union front at Gettysburg and laid open a fair future to the world.

It always amuses historians and philosophers to pick out the tiny things, the sharp agate points, on which the ponderous balance of destiny turns; and certainly the details of the famous Confederate victory of Gettysburg furnish a fertile theme. There can be at this date no conceivable doubt that Pickett's charge would have been defeated, if Stuart with his encircling cavalry had not arrived in the rear of the Union position at the supreme moment. Stuart might have been arrested in his decisive swoop if any one of twenty commonplace incidents had occurred. If, for instance, General Meade had organised his lines of communication with posts for defence against raids, or if he had used his cavalry to scout upon his flanks, he would have received a timely warning. If General Warren had only thought of sending a battalion to hold

Little Round Top, the rapid advance of the masses of Confederate cavalry must have been detected. If only President Davis's letter to General Lee, captured by Captain Dahlgren, revealing the Confederacy plans had reached Meade a few hours earlier, he might have escaped Lee's clutches.

Anything, we repeat, might have prevented Lee's magnificent combinations from synchronising, and if so Pickett's repulse was sure. Gettysburg would have been a great Northern victory. It might have well been a final victory. Lee might, indeed, have made a successful retreat from the field. The Confederacy with its skillful generals and fierce armies might have survived for another year, or even two, but once defeated decisively at Gettysburg, its doom was inevitable. The fall of Vicksburg, which happened only two days after Lee's immortal triumph, would in itself by opening the Mississippi to the river fleets of the Union, have cut the Secessionist States almost in half. Without wishing to dogmatise, we feel we are on solid ground in saying that the Southern States could not have survived the loss of a great battle in Pennsylvania, and the almost simultaneous bursting open of the Mississippi.

However, all went well. Once again by the narrowest of margins the compulsive pinch of military genius and soldierly valour produced a perfect result. The panic which engulfed the whole left of Meade's massive army has never been made a reproach against the Yankee troops. Every one knows they were stout fellows. But defeat is defeat, and rout is ruin. Three days only were required after the cannon at Gettysburg had ceased to thunder before General Lee fixed his headquarters in Washington. We need not here dwell upon the ludicrous features of the hurried flight to New York of all the politicians, place hunters, contractors, sentimentalists and their retinues, which was so successfully accomplished. It is more agreeable to remember how Lincoln, "greatly falling with a falling State," preserved the poise and dignity of a nation. Never did his rugged yet sublime common sense render a finer service to his countrymen. He was never greater than in the hour of fatal defeat.

But, of course, there is no doubt whatever that the mere military victory which Lee gained at Gettysburg would not by itself have altered the history of the world. The loss of Washington would not have affected the immense numerical preponderance of the Union States. The advanced situation of their capital and its fall would have exposed them to a grave injury, would no doubt have considerably prolonged the war; but standing by itself this military episode, dazzling though it may be, could not have prevented the ultimate victory of the North. It is in the political sphere that we have to look to find the explanation of the triumphs begun upon the battlefield.

Curiously enough, Lee furnishes an almost unique example of a regular and professional soldier who achieved the highest excellence both as a general and as a statesman. His ascendancy throughout the Confederate States on the morrow of his Gettysburg victory threw Jefferson Davis and his civil government irresistibly, indeed almost unconsciously, into the shade. The beloved and victorious commander, arriving in the capital of his mighty antagonists, found there the title deeds which enabled him to pronounce the grand decrees of peace. Thus it happened that the guns of Gettysburg fired virtually the last shots in the American Civil War.

The movement of events then shifted to the other side of the Atlantic Ocean. England—the name by which the British Empire was then commonly described—had been riven morally in twain by the drama of the American struggle. We have always admired the steadfastness with which the Lancashire cotton operatives, though starved of cotton by the Northern blockade—our most prosperous county reduced to penury, almost become dependent upon the charity of the rest of England—nevertheless adhered to the Northern cause. The British working classes on the whole judged the quarrel through the eyes of Disraeli and rested solidly upon the side of the abolition of slavery. Indeed, all Mr. Gladstone's democratic flair and noble eloquence would have failed, even upon the then restricted franchise, to carry England into the Confederate camp as a measure of policy. If Lee after his triumphal entry into

Washington had merely been the soldier, his achievements would have ended on the battlefield. It was his august declaration that the victorious Confederacy would pursue no policy towards the African negroes, which was not in harmony with the moral conceptions of Western Europe, that opened the high roads along which we are now marching so prosperously.

But even this famous gesture might have failed if it had not been caught up and implemented by the practical genius and trained parliamentary aptitudes of Gladstone. There is practically no doubt at this stage that the basic principle upon which the colour question in the Southern States of America has been so happily settled, owed its origin mainly to Gladstonian ingenuity, and to the long statecraft of Britain in dealing with alien and more primitive populations. There was not only the need to declare the new fundamental relationship between master and servant, but the creation for the liberated slaves of institutions suited to their own cultural development and capable of affording them a different, yet honourable status in a commonwealth, destined eventually to become almost world-wide.

Let us only think what would have happened supposing the liberation of the slaves had been followed by some idiotic assertion of racial equality, and even by attempts to graft white democratic institutions upon the simple, docile, gifted African race belonging to a much earlier chapter in human history. We might have seen the whole of the Southern States invaded by gangs of carpet-bagging politicians exploiting the ignorant and untutored coloured vote against the white inhabitants and bringing the time-honoured forms of parliamentary government into unmerited disrepute. We might have seen the sorry face of black legislatures attempting to govern their former masters. Upon the rebound from this there must inevitably have been a strong reassertion of local white supremacy. By one device or another the franchises accorded to the negroes would have been taken from them. The constitutional principles of the Republic would have been proclaimed, only to be evaded or subverted; and many a warm-hearted philanthropist would have found his sojourn in the South no better than "A Fool's Errand."

But we must return to our main theme and to the procession of tremendous events which followed the Northern defeat at Gettysburg and the surrender of Washington. Lee's declaration abolishing slavery, coupled as it was with the inflexible resolve to secede from the American Union, opened the way for British intervention.

Within a month the formal treaty of alliance between the British Empire and the Confederacy had been signed. The terms of this alliance being both offensive and defensive, revolutionised the military and naval situation. The Northern blockade could not be maintained even for a day in the face of the immense naval power of Britain. The opening of the Southern ports released the pent-up cotton, restored the finances and replenished the arsenals of the Confederacy. The Northern forces at New Orleans were themselves immediately cut off and forced to capitulate. There could be no doubt of the power of the new allies to clear the Mississippi of Northern vessels throughout the whole of its course through the Confederate States. The prospect of a considerable British army embarking for Canada threatened the Union with a new military front.

But none of these formidable events in the sphere of arms and material force would have daunted the resolution of President Lincoln, or weakened the fidelity of the Northern States and armies. It was Lee's declaration abolishing slavery which by a single master stroke gained the Confederacy an all-powerful ally, and spread a moral paralysis far and wide through the ranks of their enemies. The North were waging war against Secession, but as the struggle had proceeded, the moral issue of slavery had first sustained and then dominated the political quarrel. Now that the moral issue was withdrawn, now that the noble cause which inspired the Union armies and the Governments behind them was gained, there was nothing left but a war of reconquest to be waged under circumstances infinitely more difficult and anxious than those which had already led to so much disappointment and defeat. Here was the South victorious, reinvigorated, reinforced, offering of her own free will to make a more complete abolition of the servile status on the American continent than even Lincoln had himself seen fit to demand. Was the war to continue against what soon must be heavy odds merely to assert the domination of one set of English-speaking people over another; was blood to flow indefinitely in an ever-broadening stream to gratify national pride or martial revenge?

It was this deprivation of the moral issue which undermined the obduracy of the Northern States. Lincoln no longer rejected the Southern appeal for independence. "If," he declared in his famous speech in Madison Square Gardens in New York, "our brothers in the South are willing faithfully to cleanse this continent of negro slavery, and if they will dwell beside us in neighbourly goodwill as an independent but friendly nation, it would not be right to prolong the slaughter on the question of sovereignty alone."

Thus peace came more swiftly than war had come. The Treaty of Harper's Ferry which was signed between the Union and Confederate States on the 6th September 1863 embodied the two fundamental propositions, that the South was independent, and the slaves were free. If the spirit of old John Brown had revisited the battle-scarred township which had been the scene of his life and death, it would have seen his cause victorious; but at a cost to the United States terrible indeed. Apart from the loss of blood and treasure, the American Union was riven in twain. Henceforth there would be two Americas in the same northern continent. One of them would have renewed in a modern and embattled form its old ties of kinship and affiliation with the Mother Country across the ocean. It was evident though peace might be signed and soldiers furl their flags, profound antagonisms, social, economic and military, underlay the life of the English-speaking world. Still slavery was abolished. As John Bright said, "At last after the smoke of the battlefield has cleared away, the horrid shape which had cast its shadow over the whole continent, had vanished and was gone for ever."

• • •

At this date when all seems as simple and clear, one has hardly the patience to chronicle the bitter and lamentable developments which occupied the two succeeding generations.

But we may turn aside in our speculation to note how strangely the careers of Mr. Gladstone and Mr. Disraeli would have been altered if Lee had not won the Battle of Gettysburg. Mr. Gladstone's threatened resignation from Lord Palmerston's Cabinet on the morrow of General Lee's pronouncement in favour of abolition, induced a political crisis in England of the most intense character. Old friendships were severed, old rancours died, and new connections and resentments took their place. Lord Palmerston found himself at the parting of the ways. Having to choose between Mr. Gladstone and Lord John Russell, he did not hesitate. A Coalition Government was formed in which Lord Robert Cecil (afterwards the great Lord Salisbury) became Foreign Secretary, but of which Mr. Gladstone was henceforward the driving force. We remember how he had said at Newcastle on 7th October 1862, "We know quite well that the people of the Northern States have not yet drunk of the cup—they will try hard to hold it far from their lips—which all the rest of the world see they nevertheless must drink. We may have our own ideas about slavery; we may be for or against the South; but there is no doubt that Jefferson Davis and the other soldiers of the South have made an army; they are making, it appears, a navy; *and they have made what is more than either, they have made a nation.*" Now the slavery obstacle was out of the way and under the aegis of his aged chief, Lord Palmerston, who in Mr. Gladstone's words "desired the severance (of North and South) as the diminution of a dangerous power," and aided by the tempered incisiveness of Lord Robert Cecil, Mr. Gladstone achieved not merely the recognition but an abiding alliance between Great Britain and the Southern States. But this carried him far. In the main the friends of the Confederacy in England belonged to the aristocratic well-to-do and Tory classes of the nation; the democracy, as yet almost entirely unenfranchised and most of the Liberal elements, sympathised with the North. Lord Palmerston's new Government formed in September 1863, although nominally Coalition, almost entirely embodied the elements of Tory strength and inspiration. No one can say that Gladstone's reunion with the Tories would have been achieved apart from Gettysburg and Lee's declaration at Washington.

However, it was achieved, and henceforward the union of Mr. Gladstone and Lord Robert Cecil on all questions of Church, State, and Empire, became an accomplished and fruitful fact. Once again the "rising hope of the stern and unbending Tories" had come back to his old friends, and the combination, armed as it was with prodigious executive success, reigned for a decade irresistible.

It is strange, musing on Mr. Gladstone's career, how easily he might have drifted into radical and democratic courses. How easily he might have persuaded himself that he, a Tory and authoritarian to his finger-tips, was fitted to be the popular and even populist, leader of the working classes. There might in this event have stood to his credit nothing but sentimental pap, pusillanimous surrenders of British interests, and the· easy and relaxing cosmopolitanism which would in practice have made him the friend of every country but his own. But the sabres of Jeb Stuart's cavalry and the bayonets of Pickett's division had, on the slopes of Gettysburg, embodied him forever in a revivified Tory party. His career thus became a harmony instead of a discord; and he holds his place in the series of great builders to whom the largest synthesis of the world is due.

Precisely the reverse effect operated upon Mr. Disraeli. What had he to do with the Tory aristocracy? In his early days he was prejudiced in their eyes as a Jew by race. He had, indeed, only been saved from the stigma of exclusion from public life before the repeal of the Jewish disabilities by the fact of his having been baptized in infancy. He had stood originally for Parliament as a Radical. His natural place was with the left-out millions, with the dissenters, with the merchants of the North, with the voteless proletariat. He might never have found his place, if Lee had not won the Battle of Gettysburg. But for that he might have continued leading the Conservative Party, educating them against their will, dragging them into all sorts of social policies which they resented, making them serve as agents for extensions of the franchise. Always indispensable, always distrusted, but for Lee and Gettysburg he might well have ended his life in the House of Lords with the exclamation, "Power has come to me too late!"

But once he was united by the astonishing events of 1863 with the democratic and Radical forces of the nation, the real power of the man became apparent. He was in his native element. He had always espoused the cause of the North; and what he was pleased to describe as "the selfish and flagitious intrigue (of the Palmerston-Gladstone Government) to split the American Union and to rebuild out of the miseries of a valiant nation the vanished empire of George III," aroused passions in England strong enough to cast him once and for all from Tory circles. He went where his instinct and nature led him, to the Radical masses which were yearly gathering strength. It is to this we owe his immense contribution to our social services. If Disraeli had not been drawn out of the Conservative Party, the whole of those great schemes of social and industrial insurance which are forever associated with his name, which followed so logically upon his speeches—"Health and the laws of health," "sanitas sanitatum omnia sanitas" —might never have been passed into law in the nineteenth century. They might no doubt well have come about in the twentieth. It might have been left to some sprout of the new democracy or some upstart from Scotland, Ireland, or even Wales, to give to England what her latest Socialist Prime Minister has described as "our incomparable social services." But "Dizzy," "The people's Dizzy," would never have set these merciful triumphs in his record.

We must return to the main theme. We may, however, note, by the way, that if Lee had not won the Battle of Gettysburg, Gladstone would not have become the greatest of Conservative Empire and Commonwealth builders, nor would Disraeli have been the idol of the toiling masses. Such is Fate.

But we cannot occupy ourselves too long upon the fortunes of individuals. During the whole of the rest of the nineteenth century the United States of America, as the truncated Union continued to style itself, grew in wealth and population. An iron determination seemed to have taken hold of the entire people. By the 'eighties they were already cleared of their war debt, and indeed all traces of the war, except in the hearts of men, were entirely eradicated. But the hearts of men are strange things, and the hearts of nations are still stranger. Never could the American Union endure the ghastly amputation which had been forced upon it. Just as France after 1870 nursed for more than forty years her dream of *revanche*, so did the multiplying peoples of the American Union concentrate their thoughts upon another trial of arms.

And to tell the truth, the behaviour of the independent Confederacy helped but little in mitigating the ceaselessly fermenting wrath. The former Confederate States saw themselves possessed of a veteran army successful against numerous odds, and commanded by generals to whose military aptitude history has borne unquestioned tribute. To keep this army intact and—still more important— employed, became a high problem of state. To the south of the Confederacy lay Mexico, in perennial alternation between anarchy and dictatorship. Lee's early experiences in the former Mexican War familiarised him with the military aspects of the country and its problems, and we must admit that it was natural that he should wish to turn the bayonets of the army of northern Virginia upon this sporadically defended Eldorado. In spite of the pious protests of Mr. Disraeli's Liberal and pacifist Government of 1884, the Confederate States after three years' sanguinary guerrilla fighting conquered, subdued and reorganised the vast territories of Mexico. These proceedings involved a continuous accretion of Southern military forces. At the close of the Mexican War seven hundred thousand trained and well-tried soldiers were marshalled under what the

North still called "the rebel flag." In the face of these potentially menacing armaments who can blame the Northern States for the precautions they took? Who can accuse them of provocation because they adopted the principle of compulsory military service? And when this was retorted by similar measures south of the Harper's Ferry Treaty line, can we be surprised that they increased the period of compulsory service from one year to two, and thereby turned their multitudinous militia into the cadres of an army "second to none." The Southern States, relying on their alliance with the supreme naval power of Britain, did not expend their money upon a salt-water navy. Their powerful ironclad fleet was designed solely for the Mississippi. Nevertheless, on land and water the process of armament and counter-armament proceeded ceaselessly over the whole expanse of the North American continent. Immense fortresses guarded the frontiers on either side and sought to canalise the lines of reciprocal invasion. The wealth of the Union States enabled them at enormous sacrifice at once to fortify their southern front and to maintain a strong fleet and heavy military garrison in the fortified harbours of the great lakes of the Canadian frontier. By the 'nineties North America bristled with armaments of every kind, and what with the ceaseless growth of the Confederate army—in which the reconciled negro population now formed a most important element—and the very large forces which England and Canada maintained in the North, it was computed that not less than two million armed men with trained reserves of six millions were required to preserve the uneasy peace of the North American continent. Such a process could not go on without a climax of tragedy or remedy.

The climax which came in 1905 was perhaps induced by the agitation of war excitement arising from the Russo-Japanese conflict. The roar of Asiatic cannon reverberated around the globe, and everywhere found immense military organisations in an actively receptive state. Never has the atmosphere of the world been so loaded with explosive forces. Europe and North America were armed camps, and a war of first magnitude was actually raging in Manchuria.

At any moment, as the Dogger Bank incident had shown, the British Empire might be involved in war with Russia. Indeed, we had been within the ace on that occasion. And apart from such accidents the British Treaty obligations towards Japan might automatically have drawn us in. The President of the United States had been formally advised by the powerful and highly competent American General Staff that the entry of Great Britain into such a war would offer in every way a favourable opportunity for settling once and for all with the Southern Republic. This fact was also obvious to most people. Thus at the same time throughout Europe and America precautionary measures of all kinds by land and sea were actively taken; and everywhere fleets and armies were assembled and arsenals clanged and flared by night and day.

Now that these awful perils have been finally warded off it seems to us almost incomprehensible that they could have existed. Nevertheless, it is horrible even to reflect that scarcely a quarter of a century ago English-speaking people ranged on opposite sides, watched each other with ceaseless vigilance and drawn weapons. By the end of 1905 the tension was such that nothing could long avert a fratricidal struggle on a gigantic scale, except some great melting of hearts, some wave of inspiration which should lift the dull, deadly antagonisms of the hour to a level so high that—even as a mathematical quantity passing through infinity changes its sign—they would become actual unities.

We must not underrate the strength of the forces which on both sides of the Atlantic Ocean and on both sides of the American continental frontiers were labouring faithfully and dauntlessly to avert the hideous doom which kindred races seemed resolved to prepare for themselves. But these deep currents of sanity and goodwill would not have been effective unless the decisive moment had found simultaneously in England and the United States leaders great enough to dominate events and marvelously placed upon the summits of national power. In President Roosevelt and Mr. Arthur Balfour, the British Prime Minister, were present two diverse personalities which together embodied all the qualities necessary alike for profound negotiation and for supreme decision.

After all, when it happened it proved to be the easiest thing in the world. In fact, it seemed as if it could not help happening, and we who look back upon it take it so much for granted that we cannot understand how easily the most beneficent Covenant of which human records are witness might have been replaced by the most horrible conflict and world tragedy.

The Balfour-Roosevelt negotiations had advanced some distance before President Wilson, the enlightened Virginian chief of the Southern Republic, was involved in them. It must be remembered that whatever may be thought of Mr. Gladstone's cold-blooded *coup* in 1863, the policy of successive British Governments had always been to assuage the antagonism between North and South. At every stage the British had sought to promote goodwill and close association between her southern ally and the mighty northern power with whom she had so much in common. For instance, we should remember how in the Spanish-American War of 1895 the influence of Great Britain was used to the utmost and grave risks were run in order to limit the quarrel and to free the United States from any foreign menace. The restraining counsels of England on this occasion had led the Southern Republic to adopt a neutrality not only benevolent, but actively helpful. Indeed, in this war several veteran generals of the Confederate army had actually served as volunteers with the Union forces. So that one must understand that side by side with the piling up of armaments and the old antagonisms, there was an immense under-tide of mutual liking and respect. It is the glory of Balfour, Roosevelt and Wilson—this august triumvirate—that they were able so to direct these tides that every opposing circumstance or element was swept before them.

On Christmas Day 1905 was signed the Covenant of the English-speaking Association. The essence of this extraordinary measure was crystal clear. The doctrine of common citizenship for all the peoples involved in the agreement was proclaimed. There was not the slightest interference with the existing arrangements of any member. All that happened was that henceforward the peoples of the British Empire and of what were happily called in the language of the line "The Re-United States," deemed themselves to be members of one body and inheritors of one estate. The flexibility of the plan which invaded no national privacy, which left all particularisms entirely unchallenged, which altered no institutions and required no elaborate machinery, was its salvation. It was, in fact, a moral and psychological rather than political reaction. Hundreds of millions of people suddenly adopted a new point of view. Without prejudice to their existing loyalties and sentiments, they gave birth in themselves to a new higher loyalty and a wider sentiment. The autumn of 1905 had seen the English-speaking world on the verge of catastrophe. The year did not die before they were associated by indissoluble ties for the maintenance of peace between themselves, for the prevention of war among outside Powers and for the economic development of their measureless resources and possessions.

The Association had not been in existence for a decade before it was called upon to face an emergency not less grave than that which had called it into being. Every one remembers the European crisis of August 1914. The murder of the Archduke at Sarejevo, the disruption or decay of the Austrian and Turkish Empires, the old quarrel between Germany and France, and the increasing armaments of Russia—all taken together produced the most dangerous conjunction which Europe has ever known. Once the orders for Russian, Austrian, German, and French mobilisation had been given and twelve million soldiers were gathering upon the frontiers of their respective countries, it seemed that nothing could avert a war which might well have become Armageddon itself.

What the course and consequences of such a war would have been are matters upon which we can only speculate. M. Bloch in his thoughtful book published in 1909, indicated that such a war if fought with modern weapons would not be a short one. He predicted that field operations would quickly degenerate into long lines of fortifications, and that a devastating stalemate with siege warfare, or trench warfare, lasting for years, might well ensue. We know his opinions are not accepted by the leading military experts of most countries. But, at any rate, we cannot doubt that a war in which four or five of the greatest European Powers were engaged might well have led to the loss of many millions of lives, and to the destruction of capital that twenty years of toil, thrift, and privation could not have replaced. It is no exaggeration to say that had the crisis of general mobilisation of August 1914 been followed by war, we might to-day in this island see income tax at four or five shillings in the pound, and have two and a half million unemployed workmen on our hands. Even the United States far across the ocean, might against all its traditions have been dragged into a purely European quarrel.

But in the nick of time friendly though resolute hands intervened to save Europe from what might well have been her ruin. It was inherent in the Covenant of the English-speaking Association that the ideal of mutual disarmament to the lowest point compatible with their joint safety should be adopted by the signatory members. It was also settled that every third year a Conference of the whole Association should be held in such places as might be found convenient. It happened that the third disarmament conference of the English-speaking Association—the E.S.A. as it is called for short—was actually in session in July 1914. The Association had found itself hampered in its policy of disarmament by the immense military and naval establishments maintained in Europe. Their plenipotentiaries were actually assembled to consider this problem when the infinitely graver issue burst upon them. They acted as men accustomed to deal with the greatest events. They felt so sure of themsélves that they were able to run risks for others. On the 1st August when the German armies were already approaching the frontiers of Belgium, when the Austrian armies had actually begun the bombardment of Belgrade, and when all along the Russian and French frontiers desultory picket firing had broken out, the E.S.A. tendered its friendly offices to all the mobilised

Powers, counselling them to halt their armies within ten miles of their own frontiers, and to seek a solution of their differences by peaceful discussion. The memorable document added "that failing a peaceful outcome the Association must deem itself *ipso facto* at war with any Power in either combination whose troops invaded the territory of its neighbour."

Although this suave yet menacing communication was received with indignation in many quarters, it in fact secured for Europe the breathing space which was so desperately required. The French had already forbidden their troops to approach within ten miles of the German frontier, and they replied in this sense. The Czar eagerly embraced the opportunity offered to him. The secret wishes of the Kaiser and his emotions at this juncture have necessarily been much disputed. There are those who allege that carried away by the excitement of mobilisation and the clang and clatter of moving armies, he was not disposed to halt his troops already on the threshold of the Duchy of Luxembourg. Others avow that he received the message with a scream of joy and fell exhausted into a chair, exclaiming, "Saved! Saved! Saved!" Whatever may have been the nature of the Imperial convulsion, all we know is that the acceptance of Germany was the last to reach the Association. With its arrival, although there yet remained many weeks of anxious negotiation, the danger of a European war may be said to have passed away.

Most of us have been so much absorbed by the immense increases of prosperity and wealth, or by the commercial activity and scientific and territorial development and exploitation which have been the history of the English-speaking world since 1905, that we have been inclined to allow European affairs to fall into a twilight of interest. Once the perils of 1914 had been successfully averted and the disarmament of Europe had been brought into harmony with that already effected by the E.S.A., the idea of "An United States of Europe" was bound to occur continually. The glittering spectacle of the great English-speaking combination, its assured safety, its boundless power, the rapidity with which wealth was created and widely distributed within its bounds, the sense of buoyancy and hope which seemed to pervade the entire population; all this pointed to European eyes a moral which none but the dullest could ignore. Whether the Emperor Wilhelm II will be successful in carrying the project of European unity forward by another important stage at the forthcoming Pan-European Conference at Berlin in 1932, is still a matter of prophecy. Should he achieve his purpose he will have raised himself to a dazzling pinnacle of fame and honour, and no one will be more pleased than the members of the E.S.A. to witness the gradual formation of another great area of tranquillity and co-operation like that in which we ourselves have learned to dwell. If this prize should fall to his Imperial Majesty, he may perhaps reflect how easily his career might have been wrecked in 1914 by the outbreak of a war which might have cost him his throne, and have laid his country in the dust. If to-day he occupies in his old age the most splendid situation in Europe, let him not forget that he might well have found himself eating the bitter bread of exile, a dethroned sovereign and a broken man loaded with unutterable reproach. And this, we repeat, might well have been his fate, if Lee had not won the Battle of Gettysburg.

Over There

MIKE RESNICK

I respectfully ask permission immediately to raise two divisions for immediate service at the front under the bill which has just become law, and hold myself ready to raise four divisions, if you so direct. I respectfully refer for details to my last letters to the Secretary of War.

—Theodore Roosevelt
telegram to President Woodrow Wilson, May 18, 1917

I very much regret that I cannot comply with the request in your telegram of yesterday. The reasons I have stated in a public statement made this morning, and I need not assure you that my conclusions were based upon imperative considerations of public policy and not upon personal or private choice.

—Woodrow Wilson,
telegram to Theodore Roosevelt, May 19, 1917

The date was May 22, 1917.

Woodrow Wilson looked up at the burly man standing impatiently before his desk.

"This will necessarily have to be an extremely brief meeting, Mr. Roosevelt," he said wearily. "I have consented to it only out of respect for the fact that you formerly held the office that I am now privileged to hold."

"I appreciate that, Mr. President," said Theodore Roosevelt, shifting his weight anxiously from one leg to the other.

"Well, then?" said Wilson.

"You know why I'm here," said Roosevelt bluntly. "I want your permission to reassemble my Rough Riders and take them over to Europe."

"As I keep telling you, Mr. Roosevelt—that's out of the question."

"You haven't told *me* anything!" snapped Roosevelt. "And I have no interest in what you tell the press."

"Then I'm telling you now," said Wilson firmly. "I can't just let any man who wants to gather up a regiment go fight in the war. We have procedures, and chains of command, and—"

"I'm not just *any* man," said Roosevelt. "And I have every intention of honoring our procedures and chain of command." He glared at the president. "I created many of those procedures myself."

Wilson stared at his visitor for a long moment. "Why are you so anxious to go to war, Mr. Roosevelt? Does violence hold so much fascination for you?"

"I abhor violence and bloodshed," answered Roosevelt. "I believe that war should never be resorted to when it is honorably possible to avoid it. But once war has begun, then the only thing to do is win it as swiftly and decisively as possible. I believe that I can help to accomplish that end."

"Mr. Roosevelt, may I point out that you are fifty-eight years old, and according to my reports you have been in poor health ever since returning from Brazil three years ago?"

"Nonsense!" said Roosevelt defensively. "I feel as fit as a bull moose!"

"A one-eyed bull moose," replied Wilson dryly. Roosevelt seemed about to protest, but Wilson raised a hand to silence him. "Yes, Mr. Roosevelt, I know that you lost the vision in your left eye during a boxing match while you were president." He couldn't quite keep the distaste for such juvenile and adventurous escapades out of his voice.

"I'm not here to discuss my health," answered Roosevelt gruffly, "but the reactivation of my commission as a colonel in the United States Army."

Wilson shook his head. "You have my answer. You've told me nothing that might change my mind."

"I'm about to."

"Oh?"

"Let's be perfectly honest, Mr. President. The Republican nomination is mine for the asking, and however the war turns out, the Democrats will be sitting ducks. Half the people hate you for entering the war so late, and the other half hate you for entering it at all." Roosevelt paused. "If you will return me to active duty and allow me to organize my Rough Riders, I will give you my personal pledge that I will neither seek nor accept the Republican nomination in 1920."

"It means that much to you?" asked Wilson, arching a thin eyebrow.

"It does, sir."

"I'm impressed by your passion, and I don't doubt your sincerity, Mr. Roosevelt," said Wilson. "But my answer must still be no. I am serving my second term. I have no intention of running again in 1920, I do not need your political support, and I will not be a party to such a deal."

"Then you are a fool, Mr. President," said Roosevelt. "Because I am going anyway, and you have thrown away your only opportunity, slim as it may be, to keep the Republicans out of the White House."

"I will not reactivate your commission, Mr. Roosevelt."

Roosevelt pulled two neatly folded letters out of his lapel pocket and placed them on the president's desk.

"What are these?" asked Wilson, staring at them as if they might bite him at any moment.

"Letters from the British and the French, offering me commissions in *their* armies." Roosevelt paused. "I am first, foremost, and always an American, Mr. President, and I had entertained no higher hopes than leading my men into battle under the Stars and Stripes—but I am going to participate in this war, and you are not going to stop me." And now, for the first time, he displayed the famed Roosevelt grin. "I have some thirty reporters waiting for me on the lawn of the White House. Shall I tell them that I am fighting for the country that I love, or shall I tell them that our European allies are more concerned with winning this damnable war than our own president?"

"This is blackmail, Mr. Roosevelt!" said Wilson, outraged.

"I believe that is the word for it," said Roosevelt, still grinning. "I would like you to direct Captain Frank McCoy to leave his current unit and report to me. I'll handle the rest of the details myself." He paused again. "The press is waiting, Mr. President. What shall I tell them?"

"Tell them anything you want," muttered Wilson furiously. "Only get out of this office."

"Thank you, sir," said Roosevelt, turning on his heel and marching out with an energetic bounce to his stride.

Wilson waited a moment, then spoke aloud. "You can come in now, Joseph."

Joseph Tummulty, his personal secretary, entered the Oval Office.

"Were you listening?" asked Wilson.

"Yes, sir."

"Is there any way out of it?"

"Not without getting a black eye in the press."

"That's what I was afraid of," said Wilson.

"He's got you over a barrel, Mr. President."

"I wonder what he's really after?" mused Wilson thoughtfully. "He's been a governor, an explorer, a war hero, a police commissioner, an author, a big-game hunter, and a president." He paused, mystified. "What more can he want from life?"

"Personally, sir," said Tummulty, making no attempt to hide the contempt in his voice, "I think that damned cowboy is looking to charge up one more San Juan Hill."

Roosevelt stood before his troops, as motley an assortment of warriors as had been assembled since the last incarnation of the Rough Riders. There were military men and cowboys, professional athletes and adventurers, hunters and ranchers, barroom brawlers and Indians, tennis players and wrestlers, even a trio of Maasai *elmoran* he had met on safari in Africa.

"Some of 'em look a little long in the tooth, Colonel," remarked Frank McCoy, his second-in-command.

"Some of *us* are a little long in the tooth, too, Frank," said Roosevelt with a smile.

"And some of 'em haven't started shaving yet," continued McCoy wryly.

"Well, there's nothing like a war to grow them up in a hurry."

Roosevelt turned away from McCoy and faced his men, waiting briefly until he had their attention. He paused for a moment to make sure that the journalists who were traveling with the regiment had their pencils and notebooks out, and then spoke.

"Gentlemen," he said, "we are about to embark upon a great adventure. We are privileged to be present at a crucial point in the history of the world. In the terrible whirlwind of war, all the great nations of the world are facing the supreme test of their courage and dedication. All the alluring but futile theories of the pacifists have vanished at the first sound of gunfire."

Roosevelt paused to clear his throat, then continued in his surprisingly high-pitched voice. "This war is the greatest the world has ever seen. The vast size of the armies, the tremendous slaughter, the loftiness of the heroism shown and the hideous horror of the brutalities committed, the valor of the fighting men and the extraordinary ingenuity of those who have designed and built the fighting machines, the burning patriotism of the peoples who defend their homelands and the far-reaching complexity of the plans of the leaders—all are on a scale so huge that nothing in history can compare with them.

"The issues at stake are fundamental. The free peoples of the world have banded together against tyrannous militarism, and it is not too much to say that the outcome will largely determine, for those of us who love liberty above all else, whether or not life remains worth living."

He paused again, and stared up and down the ranks of his men.

"Against such a vast and complex array of forces, it may seem to you that we will just be another cog in the military machine of the allies, that one regiment cannot possibly make a difference." Roosevelt's chin jutted forward pugnaciously. "I say to you that this is rubbish! We represent a society dedicated to the proposition that every free man makes a difference. And I give you my solemn pledge that the Rough Riders will make a difference in the fighting to come!"

It was possible that his speech wasn't finished, that he still had more to say. . . but if he did, it was drowned out beneath the wild and raucous cheering of his men.

One hour later they boarded the ship to Europe.

Roosevelt summoned a corporal and handed him a handwritten letter. The man saluted and left, and Roosevelt returned to his chair in front of his tent. He was about to pick up a book when McCoy approached him.

"Your daily dispatch to General Pershing?" he asked dryly.

"Yes," answered Roosevelt. "I can't understand what is wrong with the man. Here we are, primed and ready to fight, and he's kept us well behind the front for the better part of two months!"

"I know, Colonel."

"It just doesn't make any sense! Doesn't he know what the Rough Riders did at San Juan Hill?"

"That was a long time ago, sir," said McCoy.

"I tell you, Frank, these men are the elite—the cream of the crop! They weren't drafted by lottery. Every one of them volunteered, and every one was approved personally by you or by me. Why are we being wasted here? There's a war to be won!"

"Pershing's got a lot to consider, Colonel," said McCoy. "He's got half a million American troops to disperse, he's got to act in concert with the French and the British, he's got to consider his lines of supply, he's—"

"Don't patronize me, Frank!" snapped Roosevelt. "We've assembled a brilliant fighting machine here, and he's ignoring us. There *has* to be a reason. I want to know what it is!"

McCoy shrugged helplessly. "I have no answer, sir."

"Well, I'd better get one soon from Pershing!" muttered Roosevelt. "We didn't come all this way to help in some mopping-up operation after the battle's been won." He stared at the horizon. "There's a glorious crusade being fought in the name of liberty, and I plan to be a part of it."

He continued staring off into the distance long after McCoy had left him.

A private approached Roosevelt as the former president was eating lunch with his officers.

"Dispatch from General Pershing, sir," said the private, handing him an envelope with a snappy salute.

"Thank you," said Roosevelt. He opened the envelope, read the message, and frowned.

"Bad news, Colonel?" asked McCoy.

"He says to be patient," replied Roosevelt. "Patient?" he repeated furiously. "By God, I've been patient long enough! Jake—saddle my horse!"

"What are you going to do, Colonel?" asked one of his lieutenants.

"I'm going to go meet face-to-face with Pershing," said Roosevelt, getting to his feet. "This is intolerable!"

"We don't even know where he is, sir."

"I'll find him," replied Roosevelt confidently.

"You're more likely to get lost or shot," said McCoy, the only man who dared to speak to him so bluntly.

"Runs With Deer! Matupu!" shouted Roosevelt. "Saddle your horses!"

A burly Indian and a tall Maasai immediately got to their feet and went to the stable area.

Roosevelt turned back to McCoy. "I'm taking the two best trackers in the regiment. Does that satisfy you, Mr. McCoy?"

"It does not," said McCoy. "I'm coming along, too."

Roosevelt shook his head. "You're in command of the regiment in my absence. You're staying here."

"But—"

"That's an order," said Roosevelt firmly.

"Will you at least take along a squad of sharpshooters, Colonel?" persisted McCoy.

"Frank, we're forty miles behind the front, and I'm just going to talk to Pershing, not shoot him."

"We don't even know where the front *is*," said McCoy.

"It's where we're *not*," said Roosevelt grimly. "And that's what I'm going to change."

He left the mess tent without another word.

The first four French villages they passed were deserted, and consisted of nothing but the burned skeletons of of houses and shops. The fifth had two buildings still standing—a manor house and a church—and they had been turned into Allied hospitals. Soldiers with missing limbs, soldiers with faces swatched in filthy bandages, soldiers with gaping holes in their bodies lay on cots and floors, shivering in the cold damp air, while an under-manned and harassed medical team did their best to keep them alive.

Roosevelt stopped long enough to determine General Pershing's whereabouts, then walked among the wounded to offer words of encouragement while trying to ignore the unmistakable stench of gangrene and the stinging scent of disinfectant. Finally he remounted his horse and joined his two trackers.

They passed a number of corpses on their way to the front. Most had been plundered of their weapons, and one, lying upon its back, displayed a gruesome, toothless smile.

"Shameful!" muttered Roosevelt as he looked down at the grinning body.

"Why?" asked Runs With Deer.

"It's obvious that the man had gold teeth, and they have been removed."

"It is honorable to take trophies of the enemy," asserted the Indian.

"The Germans have never advanced this far south," said Roosevelt. "This man's teeth were taken by his companions." He shook his head. "Shameful!"

Matupu the Maasai merely shrugged. "Perhaps this is not an honorable war."

"We are fighting for an honorable principle," stated Roosevelt. "That makes it an honorable war."

"Then it is an honorable war being waged by dishonorable men," said Matupu.

"Do the Maasai not take trophies?" asked Runs With Deer.

"We take cows and goats and women," answered Matupu. "We do not plunder the dead." He paused. "We do not take scalps."

"There was a time when *we* did not, either," said Runs With Deer. "We were taught to, by the French."

"And we are in France now," said Matupu with some satisfaction, as if everything now made sense to him.

They dismounted after two more hours and walked their horses for the rest of the day, then spent the night in a bombed-out farmhouse. The next morning they were mounted and riding again, and they came to General Pershing's field headquarters just before noon. There were thousands of soldiers bustling about, couriers bringing in hourly reports from the trenches, weapons and tanks being dispatched, convoys of trucks filled with food and water slowly working their way into supply lines.

Roosevelt was stopped a few yards into the camp by a young lieutenant.

"May I ask your business here, sir?"

"I'm here to see General Pershing," answered Roosevelt.

"Just like that?" said the soldier with a smile.

"Son," said Roosevelt, taking off his hat and leaning over the lieutenant, "take a good look at my face." He paused for a moment. "Now go tell General Pershing that Teddy Roosevelt is here to see him."

The lieutenant's eyes widened. "By God, you *are* Teddy Roosevelt!" he exclaimed. Suddenly he reached his hand out. "May I shake your hand first, Mr. President? I just want to be able to tell my parents I did it."

Roosevelt grinned and took the young man's hand in his own, then waited astride his horse while the lieutenant went off to Pershing's quarters. He gazed around the camp: There were ramshackle buildings and ramshackle soldiers, each of which had seen too much action and too little glory. The men's faces were haggard, their eyes haunted, their bodies stooped with exhaustion. The main paths through the camp had turned to mud, and the constant drizzle brought rust, rot, and disease with an equal lack of cosmic concern.

The lieutenant approached Roosevelt, his feet sinking inches into the mud with each step.

"If you'll follow me, Mr. President, he'll see you immediately."

"Thank you," said Roosevelt.

"Watch yourself, Mr. President," said the lieutenant as Roosevelt dismounted. "I have a feeling he's not happy about meeting with you."

"He'll be a damned sight less happy when I'm through with him," said Roosevelt firmly. He turned to his companions. "See to the needs of the horses."

"Yes, sir," said Runs With Deer. "We'll be waiting for you right here."

"How is the battle going?" Roosevelt asked as he and the lieutenant began walking through the mud toward Pershing's quarters. "My Rough Riders have been practically incommunicado since we arrived."

The lieutenant shrugged. "Who knows? All we hear are rumors. The enemy is retreating, the enemy is advancing, we've killed thousands of them, they've killed thousands of us. Maybe the general will tell you; he certainly hasn't seen fit to tell *us*."

They reached the entrance to Pershing's quarters.

"I'll wait here for you, sir," said the lieutenant.

"You're sure you don't mind?" asked Roosevelt. "You can find some orderly to escort me back if it will be a problem."

"No, sir," said the young man earnestly. "It'll be an honor, Mr. President."

"Well, thank you, son," said Roosevelt. He shook the lieutenant's hand again, then walked through the doorway and found himself facing General John J. Pershing.

"Good afternoon, Jack," said Roosevelt, extending his hand.

Pershing looked at Roosevelt's outstretched hand for a moment, then took it.

"Have a seat, Mr. President," he said, indicating a chair.

"Thank you," said Roosevelt, pulling up a chair as Pershing seated himself behind a desk that was covered with maps.

"I mean no disrespect, Mr. President," said Pershing, "but exactly who gave you permission to leave your troops and come here?"

"No one," answered Roosevelt.

"Then why did you do it?" asked Pershing. "I'm told you were accompanied only by a red Indian and a black savage. That's hardly a safe way to travel in a war zone."

"I came here to find out why you have consistently refused my requests to have my Rough Riders moved to the front."

Pershing lit a cigar and offered one to Roosevelt, who refused it.

"There are proper channels for such a request," said the general at last. "You yourself helped create them."

"And I have been using them for almost two months, to no avail."

Pershing sighed. "I *have* been a little busy conducting this damned war."

"I'm sure you have," said Roosevelt. "And I have assembled a regiment of the finest fighting men to be found in America, which I am placing at your disposal."

"For which I thank you, Mr. President."

"I don't want you to thank me!" snapped Roosevelt. "I want you to unleash me!"

"When the time is right, your Rough Riders will be brought into the conflict," said Pershing.

"When the time is right?" repeated Roosevelt. "Your men are dying like flies! Every village I've passed has become a bombed-out ghost town! You needed us two months ago, Jack!"

"Mr. President, I've got half a million men to maneuver. I'll decide when and where I need your regiment."

"When?" persisted Roosevelt.

"You'll be the first to know."

"That's not good enough!"

"It will have to be."

"You listen to me, Jack Pershing!" said Roosevelt heatedly. "I *made* you a general! I think the very least you owe me is an answer. When will my men be brought into the conflict?"

Pershing stared at him from beneath shaggy black eyebrows for a long moment. "What the hell did you have to come here for, anyway?" he said at last.

"I told you: to get an answer."

"I don't mean to my headquarters," said Pershing. "I mean, what is a fifty-eight-year-old man with a blind eye and a game leg doing in the middle of a war?"

"This is the greatest conflict in history, and it's being fought over principles that every free man holds dear. How could I not take part in it?"

"You could have just stayed home and made speeches and raised funds."

"And you could have retired after Mexico and spent the rest of your life playing golf," Roosevelt shot back. "But you didn't, and I didn't, because neither of us is that kind of man. Damn it, Jack—I've assembled a regiment the likes of which hasn't been seen in almost twenty years, and if you've any sense at all, you'll make use of us. Our horses and our training give us an enormous advantage on this terrain. We can mobilize and strike at the enemy as easily as this fellow Lawrence seems to be doing in the Arabian desert."

Pershing stared at him for a long moment, then sighed deeply.

"I can't do it, Mr. President," said Pershing.

"Why not?" demanded Roosevelt.

"The truth? Because of you, sir."

"What are you talking about?"

"You've made my position damnably awkward," said Pershing bitterly. "You are an authentic American hero, possibly the first since Abraham Lincoln. You are as close to being worshiped as a man can be." He paused. "You're a goddamned icon, Mr. Roosevelt."

"What has *that* got to do with anything?"

"I am under direct orders not to allow you to participate in any action that might result in your death." He glared at Roosevelt across the desk. "*Now* do you understand? If I move you to the front, I'll have to surround you with at least three divisions to make sure nothing happens to you—and I'm in no position to spare that many men."

"Who issued that order, Jack?"

"My commander-in-chief."

"Woodrow Wilson?"

"That's right. And I'd no more disobey him than I would disobey you if you still held that office." He paused, then spoke again more gently. "You're an old man, sir. Not old by your standards, but too damned old to be leading charges against the Germans. You should be home writing your memoirs and giving speeches and rallying the people to our cause, Mr. President."

"I'm not ready to retire to Sagamore Hill and have my

face carved on Mount Rushmore yet," said Roosevelt. "There are battles to be fought and a war to be won."

"Not by you, Mr. President," answered Pershing. "When the enemy is beaten and on the run, I'll bring your regiment up. The press can go crazy photographing you chasing the few German stragglers back to Berlin. But I cannot and will not disobey a direct order from my commander-in-chief. Until I can guarantee your safety, you'll stay where you are."

"I see," said Roosevelt after a moment's silence. "And what if I relinquish my command? Will you utilize my Rough Riders then?"

Pershing shook his head. "I have no use for a bunch of tennis players and college professors who think they can storm across the trenches on their polo ponies," he said firmly. "The only men you have with battle experience are as old as you are." He paused. "Your regiment might be effective if the Apaches ever leave the reservation, but they are ill-prepared for a modern, mechanized war. I hate to be so blunt, but it's the truth, sir."

"You're making a huge mistake, Jack."

"You're the one who made the mistake, sir, by coming here. It's my job to see that you don't die because of it."

"Damn it, Jack, we could make a difference!"

Pershing paused and stared, not without sympathy, at Roosevelt. "War has changed, Mr. President," he said at last. "No one regiment can make a difference any longer. It's been a long time since Achilles fought Hector outside the walls of Troy."

An orderly entered with a dispatch, and Pershing immediately read and initialed it.

"I don't mean to rush you, sir," he said, getting to his feet, "but I have an urgent meeting to attend."

Roosevelt stood up. "I'm sorry to have bothered you, General."

"I'm still Jack to you, Mr. President," said Pershing. "And it's as your friend Jack that I want to give you one final word of advice."

"Yes?"

"Please, for your own sake and the sake of your men, don't do anything rash."

"Why would I do something rash?" asked Roosevelt innocently.

"Because you wouldn't be Teddy Roosevelt if the thought of ignoring your orders hadn't already crossed your mind," said Pershing.

Roosevelt fought back a grin, shook Pershing's hand, and left without saying another word. The young lieutenant was just outside the door, and escorted him back to where Runs with Deer and Matupu were waiting with the horses.

"Bad news?" asked Runs With Deer as he studied Roosevelt's face.

"No worse than I had expected."

"Where do we go now?" asked the Indian.

"Back to camp," said Roosevelt firmly. "There's a war to be won, and no college professor from New Jersey is going to keep me from helping to win it!"

"Well, that's the story," said Roosevelt to his assembled officers after he had laid out the situation to them in the large tent he had reserved for strategy sessions. "Even if I resign my commission and return to America, there is no way that General Pershing will allow you to see any action."

"I knew Black Jack Pershing when he was just a captain," growled Buck O'Neill, one of the original Rough Riders. "Just who the hell does he think he is?"

"He's the supreme commander of the American forces," answered Roosevelt wryly.

"What are we going to do, sir?" asked McCoy. "Surely you don't plan just to sit back here and then let Pershing move us up when all the fighting's done with?"

"No, I don't," said Roosevelt.

"Let's hear what you got to say, Teddy," said O'Neill.

"The issues at stake in this war haven't changed since I went to see the general," answered Roosevelt. "I plan to harass and harry the enemy to the best of our ability. If need be we will live off the land while utilizing our superior mobility in a number of tactical strikes, and we will do our valiant best to bring this conflict to a successful conclusion."

He paused and looked around at his officers. "I realize that in doing this I am violating my orders, but there are greater principles at stake here. I am flattered that the president thinks I am indispensable to the American public, but our nation is based on the principle that no one man deserves any rights or privileges not offered to all men." He took a deep breath and cleared his throat. However, since I *am* contravening a direct order, I believe that not only each one of you, but every one of the men as well, should be given the opportunity to withdraw from the Rough Riders. I will force no man to ride against his conscience and his beliefs. I would like you to go out now and put the question to the men; I will wait here for your answer."

To nobody's great surprise, the regiment voted unanimously to ride to glory with Teddy Roosevelt.

3 August, 1917
My Dearest Edith:

As strange as this may seem to you (and it seems surpassingly strange to me), I will soon be a fugitive from justice, opposed not only by the German army but quite possibly by the U.S. military as well.

My Rough Riders have embarked upon a bold adventure, contrary to both the wishes and the direct orders of the president of the United States. When I think back to the day he finally approved my request to reassemble the regiment, I cringe with chagrin at my innocence and naiveté; he sent us here only so that I would not have access to the press and he would no longer have to listen to my demands. Far from being permitted to play a leading role in this noblest of battles, my men have been held far behind the front, and Jack Pershing was under orders from Wilson himself not to allow any harm to come to us.

When I learned of this, I put a proposition to my men, and I am extremely proud of their response. To a one, they voted to break camp and ride to the front so as to strike at the heart of the German military machine. By dong so, I am disobeying the orders of my commander-in-chief, and because of this somewhat peculiar situation, I doubt that I shall be able to send too many more letters to you until I have helped to end this war. At that time, I shall turn myself over to Pershing, or whoever is in charge, and argue my case before whatever tribunal is deemed proper.

However, before that moment occurs, we shall finally see action, bearing the glorious banner of the Stars and Stripes. My men are a finely-tuned fighting machine, and I daresay that they will give a splendid account of themselves before the conflict is over. We have not made contact with the enemy yet, nor can I guess where we shall finally meet, but we are primed and eager for our first taste of battle. Our spirit is high, and many of the old-timers spend their hours singing the old battle songs from Cuba. We are all looking forward to a bully battle, and we plan to teach the Hun a lesson he won't soon forget.

Give my love to the children, and when you write to Kermit and Quentin, tell them that their father has every intention of reaching Berlin before they do!

All my love,
Theodore

Roosevelt, who had been busily writing an article on ornithology, looked up from his desk as McCoy entered his tent.

"Well?"

"We think we've found what we've been looking for, Mr. President," said McCoy.

"Excellent!" said Roosevelt, carefully closing his notebook. "Tell me about it."

McCoy spread a map out on the desk.

"Well, the front lines, as you know, are *here*, about fifteen miles to the north of us. The Germans are entrenched *here*, and we haven't been able to move them for almost three weeks." McCoy paused. "The word I get from my old outfit is that the Americans are planning a major push on the German left, right about *here*."

"When?" demanded Roosevelt.

"At sunrise tomorrow morning."

"Bully!" said Roosevelt. He studied the map for a moment, then looked up. "Where is Jack Pershing?"

"Almost ten miles west and eight miles north of us," answered McCoy. "He's dug in, and from what I hear, he came under pretty heavy mortar fire today. He'll have his hands full without worrying about where an extra regiment of American troops came from."

"Better and better," said Roosevelt. "We not only get to fight, but we may even pull Jack's chestnuts out of the fire." He turned his attention back to the map. "All right," he said, "the Americans will advance along this line. What would you say will be their major obstacle?"

"You mean besides the mud and the Germans and the mustard gas?" asked McCoy wryly.

"You know what I mean, Frank."

"Well," said McCoy, "there's a small rise here—I'd hardly call it a hill, certainly not like the one we took in Cuba—but it's manned by four machine guns, and it gives the Germans an excellent view of the territory the Americans have got to cross."

"Then that's our objective," said Roosevelt decisively. "If we can capture that hill and knock out the machine guns, we'll have made a positive contribution to the battle that even that Woodrow Wilson will be forced to acknowledge." The famed Roosevelt grin spread across his face. "We'll show him that the dodo may be dead, but the Rough Riders are very much alive." He paused. "Gather the men, Frank. I want to speak to them before we leave."

McCoy did as he was told, and Roosevelt emerged from his tent some ten minutes later to address the assembled Rough Riders.

"Gentlemen," he said, "tomorrow morning we will meet the enemy on the battlefield."

A cheer arose from the ranks.

"It has been suggested that modern warfare deals only in masses and logistics, that there is no room left for heroism, that the only glory remaining to men of action is upon the sporting fields. I tell you that this is a lie. *We matter!* Honor and courage are not outmoded virtues, but are the very ideals that make us great as individuals and as a nation. Tomorrow we will prove it in terms that our detractors and our enemies will both understand." He paused, then saluted them. "Saddle up—and may God be with us!"

They reached the outskirts of the battlefield, moving silently with hooves and harnesses muffled, just before sunrise. Even McCoy, who had seen action in Mexico, was unprepared for the sight that awaited them.

The mud was littered with corpses as far as the eye could see in the dim light of the false dawn. The odor of death and decay permeated the moist, cold morning air. Thousands of bodies lay there in the pouring rain, many of them grotesquely swollen. Here and there they had virtually exploded, either when punctured by bullets or when the walls of the abdominal cavities collapsed. Attempts had been made during the previous month to drag them back off the battlefield, but there was simply no place left to put them. There was almost total silence as the men in both trenches began preparing for another day of bloodletting.

Roosevelt reined his horse to a halt and surveyed the carnage. Still more corpses were hung up on barbed wire, and more than a handful of bodies attached to the wire still moved feebly. The rain pelted down, turning the plain between the enemy trenches into a brown, gooey slop.

"My God, Frank!" murmured Roosevelt.

"It's pretty awful," agreed McCoy.

"This is not what civilized men do to each other," said Roosevelt, stunned by the sight before his eyes. "This isn't war, Frank—it's butchery!"

"It's what war has become."

"How long have these two lines been facing each other?"

"More than a month, sir."

Roosevelt stared, transfixed, at the sea of mud.

"A month to cross a quarter mile of *this*?"

"That's correct, sir."

"How many lives have been lost trying to cross this strip of land?"

McCoy shrugged. "I don't know. Maybe eighty thousand, maybe a little more."

Roosevelt shook his head. "Why, in God's name? Who cares about it? What purpose does it serve?"

McCoy had no answer, and the two men sat in silence for another moment, surveying the battlefield.

"This is madness!" said Roosevelt at last. "Why doesn't Pershing simply march around it?"

"That's a question for a general to answer, Mr. President," said McCoy. "Me, I'm just a captain."

"We can't continue to lose American boys for *this*!" said Roosevelt furiously. "Where is that machine-gun encampment, Frank?"

McCoy pointed to a small rise about three hundred yards distant.

"And the main German lines?"

"Their first row of trenches are in line with the hill."

"Have we tried to take the hill before?"

"I can't imagine that we haven't, sir," said McCoy. "As long as they control it, they'll mow our men down like sitting ducks in a shooting gallery." He paused. "The problem is the mud. The average infantryman can't reach the hill in less than two minutes, probably closer to three—and until you've seen them in action, you can't believe the damage these guns can do in that amount of time."

"So as long as the hill remains in German hands, this is a war of attrition."

McCoy sighed. "It's been a war of attrition for three years, sir."

Roosevelt sat and stared at the hill for another few minutes, then turned back to McCoy.

"What are our chances, Frank?"

McCoy shrugged. "If it was dry, I'd say we had a chance to take them out—"

"But it's not."

"No, it's not," echoed McCoy.

"Can we do it?"

"I don't know, sir. Certainly not without heavy casualties."

"How heavy?"

"*Very* heavy."

"I need a number," said Roosevelt.

McCoy looked him in the eye. "Ninety percent—if we're lucky."

Roosevelt stared at the hill again. "They predicted fifty percent casualties at San Juan Hill," he said. "We had to charge up a much steeper slope in the face of enemy machine-gun fire. Nobody thought we had a chance—but I did it, Frank, and I did it alone. I charged up that hill and knocked out the machine-gun nest myself, and then the rest of my men followed me."

"The circumstances were different then, Mr. President," said McCoy. "The terrain offered cover and solid footing, and you were facing Cuban peasants who had been conscripted into service, not battle-hardened professional German soldiers."

"I know, I know," said Roosevelt. "But if we knock those machine guns out, how many American lives can we save today?"

"I don't know," admitted McCoy. "Maybe ten thousand, maybe none. It's possible that the Germans are dug in so securely that they can beat back any American charge even without the use of those machine guns."

"But at least it would prolong some American lives," persisted Roosevelt.

"By a couple of minutes."

"It would give them a *chance* to reach the German bunkers."

"I don't know."

"More of a chance than if they had to face machine-gun fire from the hill."

"What do you want me to say, Mr. President?" asked McCoy. "That if we throw away our lives charging the hill that we'll have done something glorious and affected the outcome of the battle? I just don't know!"

"We came here to help win a war, Frank. Before I send my men into battle, I have to know that it will make a difference."

"I can't give you any guarantees, sir. We came to fight a war, all right. But look around you, Mr. President—*this* isn't the war we came to fight. They've changed the rules on us."

"There are hundreds of thousands of American boys in the trenches who didn't come to fight this kind of war," answered Roosevelt. "In less than an hour, most of them are going to charge across the sea of mud into a barrage of machine-gun fire. If we can't shorten the war, then perhaps we can at least lengthen their lives."

"At the cost of our own."

"We are idealists and adventurers, Frank—perhaps the last this world will ever see. We knew what we were coming here to do." He paused. "Those boys are here because of speeches and decisions that politicians have made, myself included. Left to their own devices, they'd go home to be with their families. Left to ours, we'd find another cause to fight for."

"This isn't a cause, Mr. President," said McCoy. "It's a slaughter."

"Then maybe this is where men who want to prevent further slaughter belong," said Roosevelt. He looked up at the sky. "They'll be mobilizing in another half hour, Frank."

"I know, Mr. President."

"If we leave now, if we don't try to take that hill, then Wilson and Pershing were right and I was wrong. The time for heroes is past, and I *am* an anachronism who should be sitting at home in a rocking chair, writing memoirs and exhorting younger men to go to war." He paused, staring at the hill once more. "If we don't do what's required of us this day, we are agreeing with them that we don't matter, that men of courage and ideals can't make a difference. If that's true, there's no sense waiting for a more equitable battle, Frank—we might as well ride south and catch the first boat home."

"That's your decision, Mr. President?" asked McCoy.

"Was there really ever any other option?" replied Roosevelt wryly.

"No, sir," said McCoy. "Not for men like us."

"Thank you for your support, Frank," said Roosevelt, reaching out and laying a heavy hand on McCoy's shoulder. "Prepare the men."

"Yes, sir," said McCoy, saluting and riding back to the main body of the Rough Riders.

"Madness!" muttered Roosevelt, looking out at the bloated corpses. "Utter madness!"

McCoy returned a moment later.

"The men are awaiting your signal, sir," he said.

"Tell them to follow me," said Roosevelt.

"Sir . . ." said McCoy.

"Yes?"

"We would prefer you not lead the charge. The first ranks will face the heaviest bombardment, not only from the hill but also from the cannons behind the bunkers."

"I can't ask my men to do what I myself won't do," said Roosevelt.

"You are too valuable to lose, sir. We plan to attack in three waves. You belong at the back of the third wave, Mr. President."

Roosevelt shook his head. "There's nothing up ahead except bullets, Hank, and I've faced bullets before—in the Dakota Bad Lands, in Cuba, in Milwaukee. But if I hang back, if I send my men to do a job I was afraid to do, then I've have to face myself—and as any Democrat will tell you, I'm a lot tougher than any bullet ever made."

"You won't reconsider?" asked McCoy.

"Would you have left your unit and joined the Rough Riders if you thought I might?" asked Roosevelt with a smile.

"No, sir," admitted McCoy. "No, sir, I probably wouldn't have."

Roosevelt shook his hand. "You're a good man, Frank."

"Thank you, Mr. President."

"Are the men ready?"

"Yes, sir."

"Then," said Roosevelt, turning his horse toward the small rise, "let's do what must be done."

He pulled his rifle out, unlatched the safety catch, and dug his heels into his horse's sides.

Suddenly he was surrounded by the first wave of his own men, all screaming their various war cries in the face of the enemy.

For just a moment there was no response. Then the machine guns began their sweeping fire across the muddy plain. Buck O'Neill was the first to fall, his body riddled with bullets. An instant later Runs With Deer screamed in agony as his arm was blown away. Horses had their legs shot from under them, men were blown out of their saddles, limbs flew crazily through the wet morning air, and still the charge continued.

Roosevelt had crossed half the distance when Matupu fell directly in front of him, his head smashed to a pulp. He heard McCoy groan as half a dozen bullets thudded home in his chest, but looked neither right nor left as his horse leaped over the fallen Maasai's bloody body.

Bullets and cannonballs flew to the right and left of him, in front and behind, and yet miraculously he was unscathed as he reached the final hundred yards. He dared a quick glance around and saw that he was the sole survivor from the first wave, then heard the screams of the second wave as the machine guns turned on them.

Now he was seventy yards away, now fifty. He yelled a challenge to the Germans, and as he looked into the blinking eye of a machine gun, for one brief, final, glorious instant it was San Juan Hill all over again.

18 September 1917
Dispatch from General John J. Pershing to Commander-in-Chief, President Woodrow Wilson

Sir:
I regret to inform you that Theodore Roosevelt died last Tuesday of wounds received in battle. He had disobeyed his orders, and led his men in a futile charge against an entrenched German position. His entire regiment, the so-called Rough Riders, was lost.

His death was almost certainly instantaneous, although it was two days before his body could be retrieved from the battlefield.

I shall keep the news of Mr. Roosevelt's death from the press until receiving instructions from you. It is true that he was an anachronism, that he belonged more to the nineteenth century than the twentieth, and yet it is entirely possible that he was the last authentic hero our country shall ever produce. The charge he led was ill-conceived and foolhardy in the extreme, nor did it diminish the length of the conflict by a single day, yet I cannot help but believe that if I had fifty thousand men with his courage and spirit, I could bring this war to a swift and satisfactory conclusion by the end of the year.

That Theodore Roosevelt died the death of a fool is beyond question, but I am certain in my heart that with his dying breath he felt he was dying the death of a hero. I await your instructions, and will release whatever version of his death you choose upon hearing from you.

— General John J. Pershing

22 September 1917
Dispatch from President Woodrow Wilson to General John J. Pershing, Commander of American Forces in Europe.

John:
That man continues to harass me from the grave.
Still, we have had more than enough fools in our history. Therefore, he died a hero.
Just between you and me, the time for heroes is past. I hope with all my heart that he was our last.
—Woodrow Wilson

And he was.